Beatrice by H. Rider Haggard

Sir Henry Rider Haggard, KBE was born on June 22nd, 1856 at Bradenham in Norfolk, England.

After his education he was pushed towards an Army career but failed the entrance exam. Next Haggard was positioned to work for the British Foreign Office but he seems not to have sat that exam. Using family connections, he was sent to Southern Africa by his father in search of a further opportunity of a career.

Haggard spent six years there before a return to England and marriage. He had begun to write and publish some non-fiction in Africa but it was only after studying Law in the hope it might prove to be the proper career his father wanted for him that Haggard began to write fiction, using his African experiences as the basis.

His first fiction was published in 1885 and the following year King Solomon's Mines was published. It was a phenomenal success. His career was set.

Haggard wrote well and wrote often. He managed to sympathise with the local populations even though they were exploited and manipulated by Europeans intent on amassing fortunes in money, people and resources. His writing career covered the great sprint to Empire of several European powers and both reflects and criticizes these events through his well-loved characters including Allan Quatermain and Ayesha.

In his later years Haggard pursued much in the way social reform as well as standing for Parliament and writing a great many letters to The Times.

Henry Rider Haggard died on May 14th, 1925 at the age of 68. His ashes were buried at Ditchingham Church.

Index of Contents

CHAPTER I

A MIST WRAITH

The autumn afternoon was fading into evening. It had been cloudy weather, but the clouds had softened and broken up. Now they were lost in slowly darkening blue. The sea was perfectly and utterly still. It seemed to sleep, but in its sleep it still waxed with the rising tide. The eye could not mark its slow increase, but Beatrice, standing upon the farthest point of the Dog Rocks, idly noted that the long brown weeds which clung about their sides began to lift as the water took their weight, till at last the delicate pattern floated out and lay like a woman's hair upon the green depth of sea. Meanwhile a mist was growing dense and soft upon the quiet waters. It was not blown up from the west, it simply grew like the twilight, making the silence yet more silent and blotting away the outlines of the land. Beatrice gave up studying the seaweed and watched the gathering of these fleecy hosts.

"What a curious evening," she said aloud to herself, speaking in a low full voice. "I have not seen one like it since mother died, and that is seven years ago. I've grown since then, grown every way," and she laughed somewhat sadly, and looked at her own reflection in the quiet water.

She could not have looked at anything more charming, for it would have been hard to find a girl of nobler mien than Beatrice Granger as on this her twenty-second birthday, she stood and gazed into that misty sea.

Of rather more than middle height, and modelled like a statue, strength and health seemed to radiate from her form. But it was her face with the stamp of intellect and power shadowing its woman's loveliness that must have made her remarkable among women even more beautiful than herself. There are many girls who have rich brown hair, like some autumn leaf here and there just yellowing into gold, girls whose deep grey eyes can grow tender as a dove's, or flash like the stirred waters of a northern sea, and whose bloom can bear comparison with the wilding rose. But few can show a face like that which upon this day first dawned on Geoffrey Bingham to his sorrow and his hope. It was strong and pure and sweet as the keen sea breath, and looking on it one must know that beneath this fair cloak lay a wit as fair. And yet it was all womanly; here was not the hard sexless stamp of the "cultured" female. She who owned it was capable of many things. She could love and she could suffer, and if need be, she could dare or die. It was to be read upon that lovely brow and face, and in the depths of those grey eyes—that is, by those to whom the book of character is open, and who wish to study it.

But Beatrice was not thinking of her loveliness as she gazed into the water. She knew that she was beautiful of course; her beauty was too obvious to be overlooked, and besides it had been brought home to her in several more or less disagreeable ways.

"Seven years," she was thinking, "since the night of the 'death fog;' that was what old Edward called it, and so it was. I was only so high then," and following her thoughts she touched herself upon the breast. "And I was happy too in my own way. Why can't one always be fifteen, and believe everything one is told?" and she sighed. "Seven years and nothing done yet. Work, work, and nothing coming out of the work, and everything fading away. I think that life is very dreary when one has lost everything, and found nothing, and loves nobody. I wonder what it will be like in another seven years."

She covered her eyes with her hands, and then taking them away, once more looked at the water. Such light as struggled through the fog was behind her, and the mist was thickening. At first she had some difficulty in tracing her own likeness upon the glassy surface, but gradually she marked its outline. It stretched away from her, and its appearance was as though she herself were lying on her back in the water wrapped about with the fleecy mist. "How curious it seems," she thought; "what is it that reflection reminds me of with the white all round it?"

Next instant she gave a little cry and turned sharply away. She knew now. It recalled her mother as she had last seen her seven years ago.

CHAPTER II

AT THE BELL ROCK

A mile or more away from where Beatrice stood and saw visions, and further up the coast-line, a second group of rocks, known from their colour as the Red Rocks, or sometimes, for another reason, as the Bell Rocks, juts out between half and three-quarters of a mile into the waters of the Welsh Bay that lies behind Rumball Point. At low tide these rocks are bare, so that a man may walk or wade to their extremity, but when the flood is full only one or two of the very largest can from time to time be seen projecting their weed-wreathed heads through the wash of the shore-bound waves. In certain sets of the wind and tide this is a terrible and most dangerous spot in rough weather, as more than one vessel have learnt to their cost. So long ago as 1780 a three-decker man-of-war went ashore there in a furious winter gale, and, with one exception, every living soul on board of her, to the number of seven hundred, was drowned. The one exception was a man in irons, who came safely and serenely ashore seated upon a piece of wreckage. Nobody ever knew how the shipwreck happened, least of all the survivor in irons, but the tradition of the terror of the scene yet lives in the district, and the spot where the bones of the drowned men still peep grimly through the sand is not unnaturally supposed to be haunted. Ever since this catastrophe a large bell (it was originally the bell of the ill-fated vessel itself, and still bears her name, "H.M.S. Thunder," stamped upon its metal) has been fixed upon the highest rock, and in times of storm and at high tide sends its solemn note of warning booming across the deep.

But the bell was quiet now, and just beneath it, in the shadow of the rock whereon it was placed, a man half hidden in seaweed, with which he appeared to have purposely covered himself, was seated upon a piece of wreck. In appearance he was a very fine man, big-shouldered and broad limbed, and his age might have been thirty-five or a little more. Of his frame, however, what between the mist and the unpleasantly damp seaweed with which he was wreathed, not much was to be seen. But such light as there was fell upon his face as he peered eagerly over and round the rock, and glinted down the barrels of the double ten-bore gun which he held across his knee. It was a striking countenance, with its brownish eyes, dark peaked beard and strong features, very powerful and very able. And yet there was a certain softness in the face, which hovered round the region of the mouth like light at the edge of a dark cloud, hinting at gentle sunshine. But little of this was visible now. Geoffrey Bingham, barrister-at-law of the Inner Temple, M.A., was engaged with a very serious occupation. He was trying to shoot curlew as they passed over his hiding-place on their way to the mud banks where they feed further along the coast.

Now if there is a thing in the world which calls for the exercise of man's every faculty it is curlew shooting in a mist. Perhaps he may wait for an hour or even two hours and see nothing, not even an oyster-catcher. Then at last from miles away comes the faint wild call of curlew on the wing. He strains his eyes, the call comes nearer, but nothing can he see. At last, seventy yards or more to the right, he catches sight of the flicker of beating wings, and, like a flash, they are gone. Again a call—the curlew are flighting. He looks and looks, in his excitement struggling to his feet and raising his head incautiously far above the sheltering rock. There they come, a great flock of thirty or more, bearing straight down on him, a hundred yards off—eighty—sixty—now. Up goes the gun, but alas and alas! they catch a glimpse of the light glinting on the barrels, and perhaps of the head behind them, and in another second they have broken and scattered this way and that way, twisting off like a wisp of gigantic snipe, to vanish with melancholy cries into the depth of mist.

This is bad, but the ardent sportsman sits down with a groan and waits, listening to the soft lap of the tide. And then at last virtue is rewarded. First of all two wild duck come over, cleaving the air like arrows. The mallard is missed, but the left barrel reaches the duck, and down it comes with a full and satisfying thud. Hardly have the cartridges been replaced when the wild cry of the curlew is once more heard—quite close this time. There they are, looming large against the fog. Bang! down goes the first and lies flapping among the rocks. Like a flash the second is away to the left. Bang! after him, and caught him too! Hark to the splash as he falls into the deep water fifty yards away. And then the mist closes in so densely that shooting is done with for the day. Well, that right and left has been worth three hours' wait in the wet seaweed and the violent cold that may follow—that is, to any man who has a soul for true sport.

Just such an experience as this had befallen Geoffrey Bingham. He had bagged his wild duck and his brace of curlew—that is, he had bagged one of them, for the other was floating in the sea—when a sudden increase in the density of the mist put a stop to further operations. He shook the wet seaweed off his rough clothes, and, having lit a short briar pipe, set to work to hunt for the duck and the first curfew. He found them easily enough, and then, walking to the edge of the rocks, up the sides of which the tide was gradually creeping, peered into the mist to see if he could find the other. Presently the fog lifted a little, and he discovered the bird floating on the oily water about fifty yards away. A little to the left the rocks ran out in a peak, and he knew from experience that the tide setting towards the shore would carry the curlew past this peak. So he went to its extremity, sat down upon a big stone and waited. All this while the tide was rising fast, though, intent as he was upon bringing the curlew to bag, he did not pay much heed to it, forgetting that it was cutting him off from the land. At last, after more than half-an-hour of waiting, he caught sight of the curlew again, but, as bad luck would have it, it was still twenty yards or more from him and in deep water. He was determined, however, to get the bird if he could, for Geoffrey hated leaving his game, so he pulled up his trousers and set to work to wade towards it. For the first few steps all went well, but the fourth or fifth landed him in a hole that wet his right leg nearly up to the thigh and gave his ankle a severe twist. Reflecting that it would be very awkward if he sprained his ankle in such a lonely place, he beat a retreat, and bethought him, unless the curlew was to become food for the dog-fish, that he had better strip bodily and swim for it. This—for Geoffrey was a man of determined mind—he decided to do, and had already taken off his coat and waistcoat to that end, when suddenly some sort of a boat—he judged it to be a canoe from the slightness of its shape—loomed up in the mist before him. An idea struck him: the canoe or its occupant, if anybody could be insane enough to come out canoeing in such water, might fetch the curlew and save him a swim.

"Hi!" he shouted in stentorian tones. "Hullo there!"

"Yes," answered a woman's gentle voice across the waters.

"Oh," he replied, struggling to get into his waistcoat again, for the voice told him that he was dealing with some befogged lady, "I'm sure I beg your pardon, but would you do me a favour? There is a dead curlew floating about, not ten yards from your boat. If you wouldn't mind—"

A white hand was put forward, and the canoe glided on towards the bird. Presently the hand plunged downwards into the misty waters and the curlew was bagged. Then, while Geoffrey was still struggling with his waistcoat, the canoe sped towards him like a dream boat, and in another moment it was beneath his rock, and a sweet dim face was looking up into his own.

Now let us go back a little (alas! that the privilege should be peculiar to the recorder of things done), and see how it came about that Beatrice Granger was present to retrieve Geoffrey Bingham's dead curlew.

Immediately after the unpleasant idea recorded in the last, or, to be more accurate, in the first chapter of this comedy, had impressed itself upon Beatrice's mind, she came to the conclusion that she had seen enough of the Dog Rocks for one afternoon. Thereon, like a sensible person, she set herself to quit them in the same way that she had reached them, namely by means of a canoe. She got into her canoe safely enough, and paddled a little way out to sea, with a view of returning to the place whence she came. But the further she went out, and it was necessary that she should go some way on account of the rocks and the currents, the denser grew the fog. Sounds came through it indeed, but she could not clearly distinguish whence they came, till at last, well as she knew the coast, she grew confused as to whither she was heading. In this dilemma, while she rested on her paddle staring into the dense surrounding mist and keeping her grey eyes as wide open as nature would allow, and that was very wide, she heard the report of a gun behind her to the right. Arguing to herself that some wild-fowler on the water must have fired it who would be able to direct her, she turned the canoe round and paddled swiftly in the direction whence the sound came. Presently she heard the gun again; both barrels were fired, in there to the right, but some way off. She paddled on vigorously, but now no more shots came to guide her, therefore for a while her search was fruitless. At last, however, she saw something looming through the mist ahead; it was the Red Rocks, though she did not know it, and she drew near with caution till Geoffrey's shout broke upon her ears.

She picked up the dead bird and paddled towards the dim figure who was evidently wrestling with something, she could not see what.

"Here is the curlew, sir," she said.

"Oh, thank you," answered the figure on the rock. "I am infinitely obliged to you. I was just going to swim for it, I can't bear losing my game. It seems so cruel to shoot birds for nothing."

"I dare say that you will not make much use of it now that you have got it," said the gentle voice in the canoe. "Curlew are not very good eating."

"That is scarcely the point," replied the Crusoe on the rock. "The point is to bring them home. Après cela—"

"The birdstuffer?" said the voice.

"No," answered Crusoe, "the cook—"

A laugh came back from the canoe—and then a question.

"Pray, Mr. Bingham, can you tell me where I am? I have quite lost my reckoning in the mist."

He started. How did this mysterious young lady in a boat know his name?

"You are at the Red Rocks; there is the bell, that grey thing, Miss—Miss—"

"Beatrice Granger," she put in hastily. "My father is the clergyman of Bryngelly. I saw you when you and Lady Honoria Bingham looked into the school yesterday. I teach in the school." She did not tell him, however, that his face had interested her so much that she had asked his name.

Again he started. He had heard of this young lady. Somebody had told him that she was the prettiest girl in Wales, and the cleverest, but that her father was not a gentleman.

"Oh," he said, taking off his hat in the direction of the canoe. "Isn't it a little risky, Miss Granger, for you to be canoeing alone in this mist?"

"Yes," she answered frankly, "but I am used to it; I go out canoeing in all possible weathers. It is my amusement, and after all the risk does not matter much," she added, more to herself than to him.

While he was wondering what she meant by that dark saying, she went on quickly:

"Do you know, Mr. Bingham, I think that you are in more danger than I am. It must be getting near seven o'clock, and the tide is high at a quarter to eight. Unless I am mistaken there is by now nearly half a mile of deep water between you and the shore."

"My word!" he said. "I forgot all about the tide. What between the shooting and looking for that curlew, and the mist, it never occurred to me that it was getting late. I suppose I must swim for it, that is all."

"No, no," she answered earnestly, "it is very dangerous swimming here; the place is full of sharp rocks, and there is a tremendous current."

"Well, then, what is to be done? Will your canoe carry two? If so, perhaps you would kindly put me ashore?"

"Yes," she said, "it is a double canoe. But I dare not take you ashore here; there are too many rocks, and it is impossible to see the ripple on them in this mist. We should sink the canoe. No, you must get in and I must paddle you home to Bryngelly, that's all. Now that I know where I am I think that I can find the way."

"Really," he said, "you are very good."

"Not at all," she answered, "you see I must go myself anyhow, so I shall be glad of your help. It is nearly five miles by water, you know, and not a pleasant night."

There was truth in this. Geoffrey was perfectly prepared to risk a swim to the shore on his own account, but he did not at all like the idea of leaving this young lady to find her own way back to Bryngelly through the mist and gathering darkness, and in that frail canoe. He would not have liked it if she had been a man, for he knew that there was great risk in such a voyage. So after making one more fruitless suggestion that they should try and reach the shore, taking the chance of rocks, sunken or otherwise, and then walk home, to which Beatrice would not consent, he accepted her offer.

"At the least you will allow me to paddle," he said, as she skilfully brought the canoe right under his rock, which the tide was now high enough to allow her to do.

"If you like," she answered doubtfully. "My hands are a little sore, and, of course," with a glance at his broad shoulders, "you are much stronger. But if you are not used to it I dare say that I should get on as well as you."

"Nonsense," he said sharply. "I will not allow you to paddle me for five miles."

She yielded without another word, and very gingerly shifted her seat so that her back was towards the bow of the canoe, leaving him to occupy the paddling place opposite to her.

Then he handed her his gun, which, together with the dead birds, she carefully stowed in the bottom of the frail craft. Next, with great caution, he slid down the rock till his feet rested in the canoe.

"Be careful or you will upset us," she said, leaning forward and stretching out her hand for him to support himself by.

Then it was, as he took it, that he for the first time really saw her face, with the mist drops hanging to the bent eyelashes, and knew how beautiful it was.

CHAPTER III

A CONFESSION OF FAITH

"Are you ready?" he said, recovering himself from the pleasing shock of this serge-draped vision of the mist.

"Yes," said Beatrice. "You must head straight out to sea for a little—not too far, for if we get beyond the shelter of Rumball Point we might founder in the rollers—there are always rollers there—then steer to the left. I will tell you when. And, Mr. Bingham, please be careful of the paddle; it has been spliced, and won't bear rough usage."

"All right," he answered, and they started gaily enough, the light canoe gliding swiftly forward beneath his sturdy strokes.

Beatrice was leaning back with her head bent a little forward, so that he could only see her chin and the sweet curve of the lips above it. But she could see all his face as it swayed towards her with each motion of the paddle, and she watched it with interest. It was a new type of face to her, so strong and manly, and yet so gentle about the mouth—almost too gentle she thought. What made him marry Lady Honoria? Beatrice wondered; she did not look particularly gentle, though she was such a graceful woman.

And thus they went on for some time, each wondering about the other and at heart admiring the other, which was not strange, for they were a very proper pair, but saying no word till at last, after about a quarter of an hour's hard paddling, Geoffrey paused to rest.

"Do you do much of this kind of thing, Miss Granger?" he said with a gasp, "because it is rather hard work."

She laughed. "Ah," she said, "I thought you would scarcely go on paddling at that rate. Yes, I canoe a great deal in the summer time. It is my way of taking exercise, and I can swim well, so I am not afraid of an upset. At least it has been my way for the last two years since a lady who was staying here gave me the canoe when she went away. Before that I used to row in a boat—that is, before I went to college."

"College? What college? Girton?"

"Oh, no, nothing half so grand. It was a college where you get certificates that you are qualified to be a mistress in a Board school. I wish it had been Girton."

"Do you?"—you are too good for that, he was going to add, but changed it to—"I think you were as well away. I don't care about the Girton stamp; those of them whom I have known are so hard."

"So much the better for them," she answered. "I should like to be hard as a stone; a stone cannot feel. Don't you think that women ought to learn, then?"

"Do you?" he asked.

"Yes, certainly."

"Have you learnt anything?"

"I have taught myself a little and picked up something at the college. But I have no real knowledge, only a smattering of things."

"What do you know—French and German?"

"Yes."

"Latin?"

"Yes, I know something of it."

"Greek?"

"I can read it fairly, but I am not a Greek scholar."

"Mathematics?"

"No, I gave them up. There is no human nature about mathematics. They work everything to a fixed conclusion that must result. Life is not like that; what ought to be a square comes out a right angle, and x always equals an unknown quantity, which is never ascertained till you are dead."

"Good gracious!" thought Geoffrey to himself between the strokes of the paddle, "what an extraordinary girl. A flesh-and-blood blue-stocking, and a lovely one into the bargain. At any rate I will bowl her out this time."

"Perhaps you have read law too?" he said with suppressed sarcasm.

"I have read some," she answered calmly. "I like law, especially Equity law; it is so subtle, and there is such a mass of it built upon such a small foundation. It is like an overgrown mushroom, and the top will fall off one day, however hard the lawyers try to prop it up. Perhaps you can tell me—"

"No, I'm sure I cannot," he answered. "I'm not a Chancery man. I am Common law, and I don't take all knowledge for my province. You positively alarm me, Miss Granger. I wonder that the canoe does not sink beneath so much learning."

"Do I?" she answered sweetly. "I am glad that I have lived to frighten somebody. I meant that I like Equity to study; but if I were a barrister, I would be Common law, because there is so much more life and struggle about it. Existence is not worth having unless one is struggling with something and trying to overcome it."

"Dear me, what a reposeful prospect," said Geoffrey, aghast. He had certainly never met such a woman as this before.

"Repose is only good when it is earned," went on the fair philosopher, "and in order to fit one to earn some more, otherwise it becomes idleness, and that is misery. Fancy being idle when one has such a little time to live. The only thing to do is to work and stifle thought. I suppose that you have a large practice, Mr. Bingham?"

"You should not ask a barrister that question," he answered, laughing; "it is like looking at the pictures which an artist has turned to the wall. No, to be frank, I have not. I have only taken to practising in earnest during the last two years. Before I was a barrister in name, and that is all."

"Then why did you suddenly begin to work?"

"Because I lost my prospects, Miss Granger—from necessity, in short."

"Oh, I beg your pardon!" she said, with a blush, which of course he could not see. "I did not mean to be rude. But it is very lucky for you, is it not?"

"Indeed! Some people don't think so. Why is it lucky?"

"Because you will now rise and become a great man, and that is more than being a rich man."

"And why do you think that I shall become a great man?" he asked, stopping paddling in his astonishment and looking at the dim form before him.

"Oh! because it is written on your face," she answered simply.

Her words rang true; there was no flattery or artifice in them. Geoffrey felt that the girl was saying just what she thought.

"So you study physiognomy as well," he said. "Well, Miss Granger, it is rather odd, considering all things, but I will say to you what I have never said to any one before. I believe that you are right. I shall rise. If I live I feel that I have it in me."

At this point it possibly occurred to Beatrice that, considering the exceeding brevity of their acquaintance, they were drifting into somewhat confidential conversation. At any rate, she quickly changed the topic.

"I am afraid you are growing tired," she said; "but we must be getting on. It will soon be quite dark and we have still a long way to go. Look there," and she pointed seaward.

He looked. The whole bank of mist was breaking up and bearing down on them in enormous billows of vapour. Presently, these were rolling over them, so darkening the heavy air that, though the pair were within four feet of each other, they could scarcely see one another's faces. As yet they felt no wind. The dense weight of mist choked the keen, impelling air.

"I think the weather is breaking; we are going to have a storm," said Beatrice, a little anxiously.

Scarcely were the words out of her mouth when the mist passed away from them, and from all the seaward expanse of ocean. Not a wrack of it was left, and in its place the strong sea-breath beat upon their faces. Far in the west the angry disc of the sun was sinking into the foam. A great red ray shot from its bent edge and lay upon the awakened waters, like a path of fire. The ominous light fell full upon the little boat and full upon Beatrice's lips. Then it passed on and lost itself in the deep mists which still swathed the coast.

"Oh, how beautiful it is!" she cried, raising herself and pointing to the glory of the dying sun.

"It is beautiful indeed!" he answered, but he looked, not at the sunset, but at the woman's face before him, glowing like a saint's in its golden aureole. For this also was most beautiful—so beautiful that it stirred him strangely.

"It is like—" she began, and broke off suddenly.

"What is it like?" he asked.

"It is like finding truth at last," she answered, speaking as much to herself as to him. "Why, one might make an allegory out of it. We wander in mist and darkness shaping a vague course for home. And then suddenly the mists are blown away, glory fills the air, and there is no more doubt, only before us is a splendour making all things clear and lighting us over a deathless sea. It sounds rather too grand," she added, with a charming little laugh; "but there is something in it somewhere, if only I could express myself. Oh, look!"

As she spoke a heavy storm-cloud rolled over the vanishing rim of the sun. For a moment the light struggled with the eclipsing cloud, turning its dull edge to the hue of copper, but the cloud was too strong and the light vanished, leaving the sea in darkness.

"Well," he said, "your allegory would have a dismal end if you worked it out. It is getting as dark as pitch, and there's a good deal in that, if only I could express myself."

Beatrice dropped poetry, and came down to facts in a way that was very commendable.

"There is a squall coming up, Mr. Bingham," she said; "you must paddle as hard as you can. I do not think we are more than two miles from Bryngelly, and if we are lucky we may get there before the weather breaks."

"Yes, if we are lucky," he said grimly, as he bent himself to the work. "But the question is where to paddle to—it's so dark. Had not we better run for the shore?"

"We are in the middle of the bay now," she answered, "and almost as far from the nearest land as we are from Bryngelly, besides it is all rocks. No, you must go straight on. You will see the Poise light beyond Coed presently. You know Coed is four miles on the other side of Bryngelly, so when you see it head to the left."

He obeyed her, and they neither of them spoke any more for some time. Indeed the rising wind made conversation difficult, and so far as Geoffrey was concerned he had little breath left to spare for words. He was a strong man, but the unaccustomed labour was beginning to tell on him, and his hands were blistering. For ten minutes or so he paddled on through a darkness which was now almost total, wondering where on earth he was wending, for it was quite impossible to see. For all he knew to the contrary, he might be circling round and round. He had only one thing to direct him, the sweep of the continually rising wind and the wash of the gathering waves. So long as these struck the canoe, which now began to roll ominously, on the starboard side, he must, he thought, be keeping a right course. But in the turmoil of the rising gale and the confusion of the night, this was no very satisfactory guide. At length, however, a broad and brilliant flash sprung out across the sea, almost straight ahead of him. It was the Poise light.

He altered his course a little and paddled steadily on. And now the squall was breaking. Fortunately, it was not a very heavy one, or their frail craft must have sunk and they with it. But it was quite serious enough to put them in great danger. The canoe rose to the waves like a feather, but she was broadside on, and rise as she would they began to ship a little water. And they had not seen the worst of it. The weather was still thickening.

Still he held on, though his heart sank within him, while Beatrice said nothing. Presently a big wave came; he could just see its white crest gleaming through the gloom, then it was on them. The canoe rose to it gallantly; it seemed to curl right over her, making the craft roll till Geoffrey thought that the end had come. But she rode it out, not, however, without shipping more than a bucket of water. Without saying a word, Beatrice took the cloth cap from her head and, leaning forward, began to bale as best she could, and that was not very well.

"This will not do," he called. "I must keep her head to the sea or we shall be swamped."

"Yes," she answered, "keep her head up. We are in great danger."

He glanced to his right; another white sea was heaving down on him; he could just see its glittering crest. With all his force he dug the paddle into the water; the canoe answered to it; she came round just in time to ride out the wave with safety, but the paddle snapped. It was already sprung, and the weight he put upon it was more than it could bear. Right in two it broke, some nine inches above that blade which at the moment was buried in the water. He felt it go, and despair took hold of him.

"Great heavens!" he cried, "the paddle is broken."

Beatrice gasped.

"You must use the other blade," she said; "paddle first one side and then on the other, and keep her head on."

"Till we sink," he answered.

"No, till we are saved—never talk of sinking."

The girl's courage shamed him, and he obeyed her instructions as best he could. By dint of continually shifting what remained of the paddle from one side of the canoe to the other, he did manage to keep her head on to the waves that were now rolling in apace. But in their hearts they both wondered how long this would last.

"Have you got any cartridges?" she asked presently.

"Yes, in my coat pocket," he answered.

"Give me two, if you can manage it," she said.

In an interval between the coming of two seas he contrived to slip his hand into a pocket and transfer the cartridges. Apparently she knew something of the working of a gun, for presently there was a flash and a report, quickly followed by another.

"Give me some more cartridges," she cried. He did so, but nothing followed.

"It is no use," she said at length, "the cartridges are wet. I cannot get the empty cases out. But perhaps they may have seen or heard them. Old Edward is sure to be watching for me. You had better throw the rest into the sea if you can manage it," she added by way of an afterthought; "we may have to swim presently."

To Geoffrey this seemed very probable, and whenever he got a chance he acted on the hint till at length he was rid of all his cartridges. Just then it began to rain in torrents. Though it was not warm the perspiration was streaming from him at every pore, and the rain beating on his face refreshed him somewhat; also with the rain the wind dropped a little.

But he was becoming tired out and he knew it. Soon he would no longer be able to keep the canoe straight, and then they must be swamped, and in all human probability drowned. So this was to be the end of his life and its ambitions. Before another hour had run its course, he would be rolling to and fro in the arms of that angry sea. What would his wife Honoria say when she heard the news, he wondered? Perhaps it would shock her into some show of feeling. And Effie, his dear little six-year-old daughter? Well, thank God, she was too young to feel his loss for long. By the time that she was a woman she would almost have forgotten that she ever had a father. But how would she get on without him to guide her? Her mother did not love children, and a growing girl would continually remind her of her growing years. He could not tell; he could only hope for the best.

And for himself! What would become of him after the short sharp struggle for life? Should he find endless sleep, or what? He was a Christian, and his life had not been worse than that of other men. Indeed, though he would have been the last to think it, he had some redeeming virtues. But now at the end the spiritual horizon was as dark as it had been at the beginning. There before him were the Gates of Death, but not yet would they roll aside and show the traveller what lay beyond their frowning face. How could he tell? Perhaps they would not open at all. Perhaps he now bade his last farewell to consciousness, to earth and sky and sea and love and all lovely things. Well, that might be better than some prospects. At that moment Geoffrey Bingham, in the last agony of doubt, would gladly have exchanged his hopes of life beyond for a certainty of eternal sleep. That faith which enables some of us to tread this awful way with an utter confidence is not a wide prerogative, and, as yet, at any rate, it was not his, though the time might come when he would attain it. There are not very many, even among those without reproach, who can lay them down in the arms of Death, knowing most certainly that when the veil is rent away the countenance that they shall see will be that of the blessed Guardian of Mankind. Alas! he could not be altogether sure, and where doubt exists, hope is but a pin-pricked bladder. He sighed heavily, murmured a little formula of prayer that had been on his lips most nights during thirty years—he had learnt it as a child at his mother's knee—and then, while the tempest roared around him, gathered up his strength to meet the end which seemed inevitable. At any rate he would die like a man.

Then came a reaction. His vital forces rose again. He no longer felt fearful, he only wondered with a strange impersonal wonder, as a man wonders about the vital affairs of another. Then from wondering about himself he began to wonder about the girl who sat opposite to him. With the rain came a little lightning, and by the first flash he saw her clearly. Her beautiful face was set, and as she bent forward searching the darkness with her wide eyes, it wore, he thought, an almost defiant air.

The canoe twisted round somewhat. He dug his broken paddle into the water and once more brought her head on to the sea. Then he spoke.

"Are you afraid?" he asked of Beatrice.

"No," she answered, "I am not afraid."

"Do you know that we shall probably be drowned?"

"Yes, I know it. They say the death is easy. I brought you here. Forgive me that. I should have tried to row you ashore as you said."

"Never mind me; a man must meet his fate some day. Do not think of me. But I can't keep her head on much longer. You had better say your prayers."

Beatrice bent forward till her head was quite near his own. The wind had blown some of her hair loose, and though he did not seem to notice it at the time, he remembered afterwards that a lock of it struck him on the face.

"I cannot pray," she said; "I have nothing to pray to. I am not a Christian."

The words struck him like a blow. It seemed so awful to think of this proud and brilliant woman, now balanced on the verge of what she believed to be utter annihilation. Even the courage that induced her at such a moment to confess her hopeless state seemed awful.

"Try," he said with a gasp.

"No," she answered, "I do not fear to die. Death cannot be worse than life is for most of us. I have not prayed for years, not since—well, never mind. I am not a coward. It would be cowardly to pray now because I may be wrong. If there is a God who knows all, He will understand that."

Geoffrey said no more, but laboured at the broken paddle gallantly and with an ever-failing strength. The lightning had passed away and the darkness was very great, for the hurrying clouds hid the starlight. Presently a sound arose above the turmoil of the storm, a crashing thunderous sound towards which the send of the sea gradually bore them. The sound came from the waves that beat upon the Bryngelly reef.

"Where are we drifting to?" he cried.

"Into the breakers, where we shall be lost," she answered calmly. "Give up paddling, it is of no use, and try to take off your coat. I have loosened my skirt. Perhaps we can swim ashore."

He thought to himself that in the dark and breakers such an event was not probable, but he said nothing, and addressed himself to the task of getting rid of his coat and waistcoat—no easy one in that confined space. Meanwhile the canoe was whirling round and round like a walnut shell upon a flooded gutter. For some distance before the waves broke upon the reef and rocks they swept in towards them with a steady foamless swell. On reaching the shallows, however, they pushed their white shoulders high into the air, curved up and fell in thunder on the reef.

The canoe rode towards the breakers, sucked upon its course by a swelling sea.

"Good-bye," called Geoffrey to Beatrice, as stretching out his wet hand he found her own and took it, for companionship makes death a little easier.

"Good-bye," she cried, clinging to his hand. "Oh, why did I bring you into this?"

For in their last extremity this woman thought rather of her companion in peril than of herself.

One more turn, then suddenly the canoe beneath them was lifted like a straw and tossed high into the air. A mighty mass of water boiled up beneath it and around it. Then the foam rushed in, and vaguely Geoffrey knew that they were wrapped in the curve of a billow.

A swift and mighty rush of water. Crash!—and his senses left him.

CHAPTER IV

THE WATCHER AT THE DOOR

This was what had happened. Just about the centre of the reef is a large flat-topped rock—it may be twenty feet in the square—known to the Bryngelly fishermen as Table Rock. In ordinary weather, even at high tide, the waters scarcely cover this rock, but when there is any sea they wash over it with great violence. On to this rock Geoffrey and Beatrice had been hurled by the breaker. Fortunately for them it was thickly overgrown with seaweed, which to some slight extent broke the violence of their fall. As it chanced, Geoffrey was knocked senseless by the shock; but Beatrice, whose hand he still held, fell on to him and, with the exception of a few bruises and a shake, escaped unhurt.

She struggled to her knees, gasping. The water had run off the rock, and her companion lay quiet at her side. She put down her face and called into his ear, but no answer came, and then she knew that he was either dead or senseless.

At this second Beatrice caught a glimpse of something white gleaming in the darkness. Instinctively she flung herself upon her face, gripping the long tough seaweed with one hand. The other she passed round the body of the helpless man beside her, straining him with all her strength against her side.

Then came a wild long rush of foam. The water lifted her from the rock, but the seaweed held, and when at length the sea had gone boiling by, Beatrice found herself and the senseless form of Geoffrey once more lying side by side. She was half choked. Desperately she struggled up and round, looking shoreward through the darkness. Heavens! there, not a hundred yards away, a light shone upon the waters. It was a boat's light, for it moved up and down. She filled her lungs with air and sent one long cry for help ringing across the sea. A moment passed and she thought that she heard an answer, but because of the wind and the roar of the breakers she could not be sure. Then she turned and glanced seaward. Again the foaming terror was rushing down upon them; again she flung herself upon the rock and grasping the slippery seaweed twined her left arm about the helpless Geoffrey.

It was on them.

Oh, horror! Even in the turmoil of the boiling waters Beatrice felt the seaweed give. Now they were being swept along with the rushing wave, and Death drew very near. But still she clung to Geoffrey. Once more the air touched her face. She had risen to the surface and was floating on the stormy water. The wave had passed. Loosing her hold of Geoffrey she slipped her hand upwards, and as he began to sink clutched him by the hair. Then treading water with her feet, for happily for them both she was as good a swimmer as could be found upon that coast, she managed to open her eyes. There, not sixty yards away, was the boat's light. Oh, if only she could reach it. She spat the salt water from her mouth and once more cried aloud. The light seemed to move on.

Then another wave rolled forward and once more she was pushed down into the cruel depths, for with that dead weight hanging to her she could not keep above them. It flashed into her mind that if she let him go she might even now save herself, but even in that last terror this Beatrice would not do. If he went, she would go with him.

It would have been better if she had let him go.

Down she went—down, down! "I will hold him," Beatrice said in her heart; "I will hold him till I die." Then came waves of light and a sound as of wind whispering through the trees, and—all grew dark.

"I tell yer it ain't no good, Eddard," shouted a man in the boat to an old sailor who was leaning forward in the bows peering into the darkness. "We shall be right on to the Table Rocks in a minute and all drown together. Put about, mate—put about."

"Damn yer," screamed the old man, turning so that the light from the lantern fell on his furrowed, fiercely anxious face and long white hair streaming in the wind. "Damn yer, ye cowards. I tells yer I heard her voice—I heard it twice screaming for help. If you put the boat about, by Goad when I get ashore I'll kill yer, ye lubbers—old man as I am I'll kill yer, if I swing for it!"

This determined sentiment produced a marked effect upon the boat's crew; there were eight of them altogether. They did not put the boat about, they only lay upon their oars and kept her head to the seas.

The old man in the bow peered out into the gloom. He was shaking, not with cold but with agitation.

Presently he turned his head with a yell.

"Give way—give way! there's something on the wave."

The men obeyed with a will.

"Back," he roared again—"back water!"

They backed, and the boat answered, but nothing was to be seen.

"She's gone! Oh, Goad, she's gone!" groaned the old man. "You may put about now, lads, and the Lord's will be done."

The light from the lantern fell in a little ring upon the seething water. Suddenly something white appeared in the centre of this illuminated ring. Edward stared at it. It was floating upwards. It vanished—it appeared again. It was a woman's face. With a yell he plunged his arms into the sea.

"I have her—lend an hand, lads."

Another man scrambled forward and together they clutched the object in the water.

"Look out, don't pull so hard, you fool. Blow me if there ain't another and she's got him by the hair. So, steady, steady!"

A long heave from strong arms and the senseless form of Beatrice was on the gunwale. Then they pulled up Geoffrey beside her, for they could not loose her desperate grip of his dark hair, and together rolled them into the boat.

"They're dead, I doubt," said the second man.

"Help turn 'em on their faces over the seat, so—let the water drain from their innards. It's the only chance. Now give me that sail to cover them—so. You'll live yet, Miss Beatrice, you ain't dead, I swear. Old Eddard has saved you, Old Eddard and the good Goad together!"

Meanwhile the boat had been got round, and the men were rowing for Bryngelly as warm-hearted sailors will when life is at stake. They all knew Beatrice and loved her, and they remembered it as they rowed. The gloom was little hindrance to them for they could almost have navigated the coast blindfold. Besides here they were sheltered by the reef and shore.

In five minutes they were round a little headland, and the lights of Bryngelly were close before them. On the beach people were moving about with lanterns.

Presently they were there, hanging on their oars for a favourable wave to beach with. At last it came, and they gave way together, running the large boat half out of the surf. A dozen men plunged into the water and dragged her on. They were safe ashore.

"Have you got Miss Beatrice?" shouted a voice.

"Ay, we've got her and another too, but I doubt they're gone. Where's doctor?"

"Here, here!" answered a voice. "Bring the stretchers."

A stout thick-set man, who had been listening, wrapped up in a dark cloak, turned his face away and uttered a groan. Then he followed the others as they went to work, not offering to help, but merely following.

The stretchers were brought and the two bodies laid upon them, face downwards and covered over.

"Where to?" said the bearers as they seized the poles.

"The Vicarage," answered the doctor. "I told them to get things ready there in case they should find her. Run forward one of you and say that we are coming."

The men started at a trot and the crowd ran after them.

"Who is the other?" somebody asked.

"Mr. Bingham—the tall lawyer who came down from London the other day. Tell policeman—run to his wife. She's at Mrs. Jones's, and thinks he has lost his way in the fog coming home from Bell Rock."

The policeman departed on his melancholy errand and the procession moved swiftly across the sandy beach and up the stone-paved way by which boats were dragged down the cliff to the sea. The village of Bryngelly lay to the right. It had grown away from the church, which stood dangerously near the edge of the cliff. On the further side of the church, and a little behind it, partly sheltered from the sea gales by a group of stunted firs, was the Vicarage, a low single-storied stone-roofed building, tenanted for twenty-five years past and more by Beatrice's father, the Rev. Joseph Granger. The best approach to it from the Bryngelly side was by the churchyard, through which the men with the stretchers were now winding, followed by the crowd of sightseers.

"Might as well leave them here at once," said one of the bearers to the other in Welsh. "I doubt they are both dead enough."

The person addressed assented, and the thick-set man wrapped in a dark cloak, who was striding along by Beatrice's stretcher, groaned again. Clearly, he understood the Welsh tongue. A few seconds more and they were passing through the stunted firs up to the Vicarage door. In the doorway stood a group of people. The light from a lamp in the hall struck upon them, throwing them into strong relief. Foremost, holding a lantern in his hand, was a man of about sixty, with snow-white hair which fell in confusion over his rugged forehead. He was of middle height and carried himself with something of a stoop. The eyes were small and shifting, and the mouth hard. He wore short whiskers which, together with the eyebrows, were still tinged with yellow. The face was ruddy and healthy looking, indeed, had it not been for the dirty white tie and shabby black coat, one would have taken him to be what he was in heart, a farmer of the harder sort, somewhat weather-beaten and anxious about the times—a man who would take advantage of every drop in the rate of wages. In fact he was Beatrice's father, and a clergyman.

By his side, and leaning over him, was Elizabeth, her elder sister. There was five years between them. She was a poor copy of Beatrice, or, to be more accurate, Beatrice was a grand development of Elizabeth. They both had brown hair, but Elizabeth's was straighter and faint-coloured, not rich and ruddying into gold. Elizabeth's eyes were also grey, but it was a cold washed-out grey like that of a February sky. And so with feature after feature, and with the expression also. Beatrice's was noble and open, if at times defiant. Looking at her you knew that she might be a mistaken woman, or a headstrong woman, or both, but she could never be a mean woman. Whichever of the ten commandments she might choose to break, it would not be that which forbids us to bear false witness against our neighbour. Anybody might read it in her eyes. But in her sister's, he might discern her father's shifty hardness watered by woman's weaker will into something like cunning. For the rest Elizabeth had a very fair figure, but lacked her sister's rounded loveliness, though the two were so curiously alike that at a distance you might well mistake the one for the other. One might almost fancy that nature had experimented upon Elizabeth before she made up her mind to produce Beatrice, just to get the lines and distances. The elder sister was to the other what the pale unfinished model of clay is to the polished statue in ivory and gold.

"Oh, my God! my God!" groaned the old man; "look, they have got them on the stretchers. They are both dead. Oh, Beatrice! Beatrice! and only this morning I spoke harshly to her."

"Don't be so foolish, father," said Elizabeth sharply. "They may only be insensible."

"Ah, ah," he answered; "it does not matter to you, you don't care about your sister. You are jealous of her. But I love her, though we do not understand each other. Here they come. Don't stand staring there. Go and see that the blankets and things are hot. Stop, doctor, tell me, is she dead?"

"How can I tell till I have seen her?" the doctor answered, roughly shaking him off, and passing through the door.

Bryngelly Vicarage was a very simply constructed house. On entering the visitor found himself in a passage with doors to the right and left. That to the right led to the sitting-room, that to the left to the dining-room, both of them long, low and narrow chambers. Following the passage down for some seven paces, it terminated in another which ran at right angles to it for the entire length of the house. On the further side of this passage were several bedroom doors and a room at each end. That at the end to the right was occupied by Beatrice and her sister, the next was empty, the third was Mr. Granger's, and the fourth the spare room. This, with the exception of the kitchens and servants' sleeping place, which were beyond the dining-room, made up the house.

Fires had been lit in both of the principal rooms. Geoffrey was taken into the dining-room and attended by the doctor's assistant, and Beatrice into the sitting-room, and attended by the doctor himself. In a few seconds the place had been cleared of all except the helpers, and the work began. The doctor looked at Beatrice's cold shrunken form, and at the foam upon her lips. He lifted the eyelid, and held a light before the contracted pupil. Then he shook his head and set to work with a will. We need not follow him through the course of his dreadful labours, with which most people will have some acquaintance. Hopeless as they seemed, he continued them for hour after hour.

Meanwhile the assistant and some helpers were doing the same service for Geoffrey Bingham, the doctor himself, a thin clever-looking man, occasionally stepping across the passage to direct them and see how things were getting on. Now, although Geoffrey had been in the water the longer, his was by far the better case, for when he was immersed he was already insensible, and a person in this condition is very hard to drown. It is your struggling, fighting, breathing creature who is soonest made an end of in deep waters. Therefore it came to pass that when the scrubbing with hot cloths and the artificial respiration had gone on for somewhere about twenty minutes, Geoffrey suddenly crooked a finger. The doctor's assistant, a buoyant youth fresh from the hospitals, gave a yell of exultation, and scrubbed and pushed away with ever-increasing energy. Presently the subject coughed, and a minute later, as the agony of returning life made itself felt, he swore most heartily.

"He's all right now!" called the assistant to his employer. "He's swearing beautifully."

Dr. Chambers, pursuing his melancholy and unpromising task in the other room, smiled sadly, and called to the assistant to continue the treatment, which he did with much vigour.

Presently Geoffrey came partially to life, still suffering torments. The first thing he grew aware of was that a tall elegant woman was standing over him, looking at him with a half puzzled and half horrified air. Vaguely he wondered who it might be. The tall form and cold handsome face were so familiar to him, and yet he could not recall the name. It was not till she spoke that his numbed brain realized that he was looking on his own wife.

"Well, dear," she said, "I am so glad that you are better. You frightened me out of my wits. I thought you were drowned."

"Thank you, Honoria," he said faintly, and then groaned as a fresh attack of tingling pain shook him through and through.

"I hope nobody said anything to Effie," Geoffrey said presently.

"Yes, the child would not go to bed because you were not back, and when the policeman came she heard him tell Mrs. Jones that you were drowned, and she has been almost in a fit ever since. They had to hold her to prevent her from running here."

Geoffrey's white face assumed an air of the deepest distress. "How could you frighten the child so?" he murmured. "Please go and tell her that I am all right."

"It was not my fault," said Lady Honoria with a shrug of her shapely shoulders. "Besides, I can do nothing with Effie. She goes on like a wild thing about you."

"Please go and tell her, Honoria," said her husband.

"Oh, yes, I'll go," she answered. "Really I shall not be sorry to get out of this; I begin to feel as though I had been drowned myself;" and she looked at the steaming cloths and shuddered. "Good-bye, Geoffrey. It is an immense relief to find you all right. The policeman made me feel quite queer. I can't get down to give you a kiss or I would. Well, good-bye for the present, my dear."

"Good-bye, Honoria," said her husband with a faint smile.

The medical assistant looked a little surprised. He had never, it is true, happened to be present at a meeting between husband and wife, when one of the pair had just been rescued by a hair's-breadth from a violent and sudden death, and therefore wanted experience to go on. But it struck him that there was something missing. The lady did not seem to him quite to fill the part of the Heaven-thanking spouse. It puzzled him very much. Perhaps he showed this in his face. At any rate, Lady Honoria, who was quick enough, read something there.

"He is safe now, is he not?" she asked. "It will not matter if I go away."

"No, my lady," answered the assistant, "he is out of danger, I think; it will not matter at all."

Lady Honoria hesitated a little; she was standing in the passage. Then she glanced through the door into the opposite room, and caught a glimpse of Beatrice's rigid form and of the doctor bending over it. Her head was thrown back and the beautiful brown hair, which was now almost dry again, streamed in masses to the ground, while on her face was stamped the terrifying seal of Death.

Lady Honoria shuddered. She could not bear such sights. "Will it be necessary for me to come back to-night?" she said.

"I do not think so," he answered, "unless you care to hear whether Miss Granger recovers?"

"I shall hear that in the morning," she said. "Poor thing, I cannot help her."

"No, Lady Honoria, you cannot help her. She saved your husband's life, they say."

"She must be a brave girl. Will she recover?"

The assistant shook his head. "She may, possibly. It is not likely now."

"Poor thing, and so young and beautiful! What a lovely face, and what an arm! It is very awful for her," and Lady Honoria shuddered again and went.

Outside the door a small knot of sympathisers was still gathered, notwithstanding the late hour and the badness of the weather.

"That's his wife," said one, and they opened to let her pass.

"Then why don't she stop with him?" asked a woman audibly. "If it had been my husband I'd have sat and hugged him for an hour."

"Ay, you'd have killed him with your hugging, you would," somebody answered.

Lady Honoria passed on. Suddenly a thick-set man emerged from the shadow of the pines. She could not see his face, but he was wrapped in a large cloak.

"Forgive me," he said in the hoarse voice of one struggling with emotions which he was unable to conceal, "but you can tell me. Does she still live?"

"Do you mean Miss Granger?" she asked.

"Yes, of course. Beatrice—Miss Granger?"

"They do not know, but they think—"

"Yes, yes—they think—"

"That she is dead."

The man said never a word. He dropped his head upon his breast and, turning, vanished again into the shadow of the pines.

"How very odd," thought Lady Honoria as she walked rapidly along the cliff towards her lodging. "I suppose that man must be in love with her. Well, I do not wonder at it. I never saw such a face and arm. What a picture that scene in the room would make! She saved Geoffrey and now she's dead. If he had saved her I should not have wondered. It is like a scene in a novel."

From all of which it will be seen that Lady Honoria was not wanting in certain romantic and artistical perceptions.

CHAPTER V

ELIZABETH IS THANKFUL

Geoffrey, lying before the fire, newly hatched from death, had caught some of the conversation between his wife and the assistant who had recovered him to life. So she was gone, that brave, beautiful atheist girl—gone to test the truth. And she had saved his life!

For some minutes the assistant did not enter. He was helping in another room. At last he came.

"What did you say to Lady Honoria?" Geoffrey asked feebly. "Did you say that Miss Granger had saved me?"

"Yes, Mr. Bingham; at least they tell me so. At any rate, when they pulled her out of the water they pulled you after her. She had hold of your hair."

"Great heavens!" he groaned, "and my weight must have dragged her down. Is she dead, then?"

"We cannot quite say yet, not for certain. We think that she is."

"Pray God she is not dead," he said more to himself than to the other. Then aloud—"Leave me; I am all right. Go and help with her. But stop, come and tell me sometimes how it goes with her."

"Very well. I will send a woman to watch you," and he went.

Meanwhile in the other room the treatment of the drowned went slowly on. Two hours had passed, and as yet Beatrice showed no signs of recovery. The heart did not beat, no pulse stirred; but, as the doctor knew, life might still linger in the tissues. Slowly, very slowly, the body was turned to and fro, the head swaying, and the long hair falling now this way and now that, but still no sign. Every resource known to medical skill, such as hot air, rubbing, artificial respiration, electricity, was applied and applied in vain, but still no sign!

Elizabeth, pale and pinched, stood by handing what might be required. She did not greatly love her sister, they were antagonistic and their interests clashed, or she thought they did, but this sudden death was awful. In a corner, pitiful to see, offering groans and ejaculated prayers to heaven, sat the old clergymen, their father, his white hair about his eyes. He was a weak, coarse-grained man, but in his own way his clever and beautiful girl was dear to him, and this sight wrung his soul as it had not been wrung for years.

"She's gone," he said continually, "she's gone; the Lord's will be done. There must be another mistress at the school now. Seventy pounds a year she will cost—seventy pounds a year!"

"Do be quiet, father," said Elizabeth sharply.

"Ay, ay, it is very well for you to tell me to be quiet. You are quiet because you don't care. You never loved your sister. But I have loved her since she was a little fair-haired child, and so did your poor mother. 'Beatrice' was the last word she spoke."

"Be quiet, father!" said Elizabeth, still more sharply. The old man, making no reply, sank back into a semi-torpor, rocking himself to and fro upon his chair.

Meanwhile without intermission the work went on.

"It is no use," said the assistant at last, as he straightened his weary frame and wiped the perspiration from his brow. "She must be dead; we have been at it nearly three hours now."

"Patience," said the doctor. "If necessary I shall go on for four—or till I drop," he added.

Ten minutes more passed. Everybody knew that the task was hopeless, but still they hoped.

"Great Heavens!" said the assistant presently, starting back from the body and pointing at its face. "Did you see that?"

Elizabeth and Mr. Granger sprang to their feet, crying, "What, what?"

"Sit still, sir," said the doctor, waving them back. Then addressing his helper, and speaking in a constrained voice: "I thought I saw the right eyelid quiver, Williams. Pass the battery."

"So did I," answered Williams as he obeyed.

"Full power," said the doctor again. "It is kill or cure now."

The shock was applied for some seconds without result. Then suddenly a long shudder ran up the limbs, and a hand stirred. Next moment the eyes were opened, and with pain and agony Beatrice drew a first breath of returning life. Ten minutes more and she had passed through the gates of Death back to this warm and living world.

"Let me die," she gasped faintly. "I cannot bear it. Oh, let me die!"

"Hush," said the doctor; "you will be better presently."

Ten minutes more passed, when the doctor saw by her eyes that Beatrice wished to say something. He bent his head till it nearly touched her lips.

"Dr. Chambers," she whispered, "was he drowned?"

"No, he is safe; he has been brought round."

She sighed—a long-drawn sigh, half of pain, half of relief. Then she spoke again.

"Was he washed ashore?"

"No, no. You saved his life. You had hold of him when they pulled you out. Now drink this and go to sleep."

Beatrice smiled sweetly, but said nothing. Then she drank as much of the draught as she could, and shortly afterwards obeyed the last injunction also, and went to sleep.

Meanwhile a rumour of this wonderful recovery had escaped to without the house—passing from one watcher to the other till at length it reached the ears of the solitary man crouched in the shadow of the pines. He heard, and starting as though he had been shot, strode to the door of the Vicarage. Here his courage seemed to desert him, for he hesitated.

"Knock, squire, knock, and ask if it is true," said a woman, the same who had declared that she would have hugged her husband back to life.

This remark seemed to encourage the man, at any rate he did knock. Presently the door was opened by Elizabeth.

"Go away," she said in her sharp voice; "the house must be kept quiet."

"I beg your pardon, Miss Granger," said the visitor, in a tone of deep humiliation. "I only wanted to know if it was true that Miss Beatrice lives."

"Why," said Elizabeth with a start, "is it you, Mr. Davies? I am sure I had no idea. Step into the passage and I will shut the door. There! How long have you been outside?"

"Oh, since they brought them up. But is it true?"

"Yes, yes, it is true. She will recover now. And you have stood all this time in the wet night. I am sure that Beatrice ought to be flattered."

"Not at all. It seemed so awful, and—I—I take such an interest—" and he broke off.

"Such an interest in Beatrice," said Elizabeth drily, supplying the hiatus. "Yes, so it seems," and suddenly, as though by chance, she moved the candle which she held, in such fashion that the light fell full upon Owen Davies' face. It was a slow heavy countenance, but not without comeliness. The skin was fresh as a child's, the eyes were large, blue, and mild, and the brown hair grew in waves that many a woman might have envied. Indeed had it not been for a short but strongly growing beard, it would have been easy to believe that the countenance was that of a boy of nineteen rather than of a man over thirty. Neither time nor care had drawn a single line upon it; it told of perfect and robust health and yet bore the bloom of childhood. It was the face of a man who might live to a hundred and still look young, nor did the form belie it.

Mr. Davies blushed up to his eyes, blushed like a girl beneath Elizabeth's scrutiny. "Naturally I take an interest in a neighbour's fate," he said, in his slow deliberate way. "She is quite safe, then?"

"I believe so," answered Elizabeth.

"Thank God!" he said, or rather it seemed to break from him in a sigh of relief. "How did the gentleman, Mr. Bingham, come to be found with her?"

"How should I know?" she answered with a shrug. "Beatrice saved his life somehow, clung fast to him even after she was insensible."

"It is very wonderful. I never heard of such a thing. What is he like?"

"He is one of the finest-looking men I ever saw," answered Elizabeth, always watching him.

"Ah. But he is married, I think, Miss Granger?"

"Oh, yes, he is married to the daughter of a peer, very much married—and very little, I should say."

"I do not quite understand, Miss Granger."

"Don't you, Mr. Davies? then use your eyes when you see them together."

"I should not see anything. I am not quick like you," he added.

"How do you mean to get back to the Castle to-night, Mr. Davies? You cannot row back in this wind, and the seas will be breaking over the causeway."

"Oh, I shall manage. I am wet already. An extra ducking won't hurt me, and I have had a chain put up to prevent anybody from being washed away. And now I must be going. Good-night."

"Good-night, Mr. Davies."

He hesitated a moment and then added: "Would you—would you mind telling your sister—of course I mean when she is stronger—that I came to inquire after her?"

"I think that you can do that for yourself, Mr. Davies," Elizabeth said almost roughly. "I mean it will be more appreciated," and she turned upon her heel.

Owen Davies ventured no further remarks. He felt that Elizabeth's manner was a little crushing, and he was afraid of her as well. "I suppose that she does not think I am good enough to pay attention to her sister," he thought to himself as he plunged into the night and rain. "Well, she is quite right—I am not fit to black her boots. Oh, God, I thank Thee that Thou hast saved her life. I thank Thee—I thank Thee!" he went on, speaking aloud to the wild winds as he made his way along the cliff. "If she had been dead, I think that I must have died too. Oh, God, I thank Thee—I thank Thee!"

The idea that Owen Davies, Esq., J.P., D.L., of Bryngelly Castle, absolute owner of that rising little watering-place, and of one of the largest and most prosperous slate quarries in Wales, worth in all somewhere between seven and ten thousand a year, was unfit to black her beautiful sister's boots, was not an idea that had struck Elizabeth Granger. Had it struck her, indeed, it would have moved her to laughter, for Elizabeth had a practical mind.

What did strike her, as she turned and watched the rich squire's sturdy form vanish through the doorway into the dark beyond, was a certain sense of wonder. Supposing she had never seen that shiver of returning life run up those white limbs, supposing that they had grown colder and colder, till at length it was evident that death was so firmly citadelled within the silent heart, that no human skill could beat his empire back? What then? Owen Davies loved her sister; this she knew and had known for years. But would he not have got over it in time? Would he not in time have been overpowered by the sense of his own utter loneliness and given his hand, if not his heart, to some other woman? And could not she who held his hand learn to reach his heart? And to whom would that hand have been given, the hand and all that went with it? What woman would this shy Welsh hermit, without friends or relations, have ever been thrown in with except herself—Elizabeth—who loved him as much as she could love anybody, which, perhaps, was not very much; who, at any rate, desired sorely to be his wife. Would not all this have come about if she had never seen that eyelid tremble, and that slight quiver run up her sister's limbs? It would—she knew it would.

Elizabeth thought of it as for a moment she stood in the passage, and a cold hungry light came into her neutral tinted eyes and shone upon her pale face. But she choked back the thought; she was scarcely wicked enough to wish that her sister had not been brought back to life. She only speculated on what might have happened if this had come about, just as one works out a game of chess from a given hypothetical situation of the pieces.

Perhaps, too, the same end might be gained in some other way. Perhaps Mr. Davies might still be weaned from his infatuation. The wall was difficult, but it would have to be very difficult if she could not find a way to climb it. It never occurred to Elizabeth that there might be an open gate. She could not conceive it possible that a woman might positively reject Owen Davies and his seven or ten thousand a year, and that woman a person in an unsatisfactory and uncongenial, almost in a menial position. Reject Bryngelly Castle with all its luxury and opportunities of wealth and leisure? No, the sun would set in the east before such a thing happened. The plan was to prevent the occasion from arising. The hungry light died on Elizabeth's face, and she turned to enter the sick room when suddenly she met her father coming out.

"Who was that at the front?" he asked, carefully closing the door.

"Mr. Davies of Bryngelly Castle, father."

"And what did Mr. Davies want at this time of night? To know about Beatrice?"

"Yes," she answered slowly, "he came to ask after Beatrice, or to be more correct he has been waiting outside for three hours in the rain to learn if she recovered."

"Waiting outside for three hours in the rain," said the clergyman astonished—"Squire Davies standing outside the house! What for?"

"Because he was so anxious about Beatrice and did not like to come in, I suppose."

"So anxious about Beatrice—ah, so anxious about Beatrice! Do you think, Elizabeth—um—you know there is no doubt Beatrice is very well favoured—very handsome they say—"

"I do not think anything about it, father," she answered, "and as for Beatrice's looks they are a matter of opinion. I have mine. And now don't you think we had better go to bed? The doctors and Betty are going to stop up all night with Mr. Bingham and Beatrice."

"Yes, Elizabeth, I suppose that we had better go. I am sure we have much to be thankful for to-night. What a merciful deliverance! And if poor Beatrice had gone the parish must have found another schoolmistress, and it would have meant that we lost the salary. We have a great deal to be thankful for, Elizabeth."

"Yes," said Elizabeth, very deliberately, "we have."

CHAPTER VI

OWEN DAVIES AT HOME

Owen Davies tramped along the cliff with a light heart. The wild lashing of the rain and the roaring of the wind did not disturb him in the least. They were disagreeable, but he accepted them as he accepted existence and all its vanities, without remark or mental comment. There is a class of mind of which this is the prevailing attitude. Very early in their span of life, those endowed with such a mind come to the conclusion that the world is too much for them. They cannot understand it, so they abandon the attempt, and, as a consequence, in their own torpid way they are among the happiest and most contented of men. Problems, on which persons of keener intelligence and more aspiring soul fret and foam their lives away as rushing water round a rock, do not even break the placid surface of their days. Such men slip past them. They look out upon the stars and read of the mystery of the universe speeding on for ever through the limitless wastes of space, and are not astonished. In their childhood they were taught that God made the sun and the stars to give light on the earth; that is enough for them. And so it is with everything. Poverty and suffering; war, pestilence, and the inequalities of fate; madness, life and death, and the spiritual wonders that hedge in our being, are things not to be inquired into but accepted. So they accept them as they do their dinner or a tradesman's circular.

In some cases this mental state has its root in deep and simple religious convictions, and in some it springs from a preponderance of healthful animal instincts over the higher but more troublesome spiritual parts. The ox chewing the cud in the fresh meadow does not muse upon the past and future, and the gull blown like a foam-flake out against the sunset, does not know the splendour of the sky and sea. Even the savage is not much troubled about the scheme of things. In the beginning he was "torn out of the reeds," and in the end he melts into the Unknown, and for the rest, there are beef and wives, and foes to conquer. But then oxen and gulls are not, so far as we know, troubled with any spiritual parts at all, and in the noble savage such things are not cultivated. They come with civilization.

But perhaps in the majority this condition, so necessary to the more placid forms of happiness, is born of a conjunction of physical and religious developments. So it was, at least, with the rich and fortunate man whom we have seen trudging along the wind-swept cliff. By nature and education he was of a strongly and simply religious mind, as he was in body powerful, placid, and healthy to an exasperating degree. It may be said that it is easy to be religious and placid on ten thousand a year, but Owen Davies had not always enjoyed ten thousand a year and one of the most romantic and beautiful seats in Wales. From the time he was seventeen, when his mother's death left him an orphan, till he reached the age of thirty, some six years from the date of the opening of this history, he led about as hard a life as fate could find for any man. Some people may have heard of sugar drogers, or sailing brigs, which trade between this country and the West Indies, carrying coal outwards and sugar home.

On board one of these, Owen Davies worked in various capacities for thirteen long years. He did his drudgery well; but he made no friends, and always remained the same shy, silent, and pious man. Then suddenly a relation died without a will, and he found himself heir-in-law to Bryngelly Castle and all its revenues. Owen expressed no surprise, and to all appearance felt none. He had never seen his relation, and never dreamed of this romantic devolution of great estates upon himself. But he accepted the good fortune as he had accepted the ill, and said nothing. The only people who knew him were his shipmates, and they could scarcely be held to know him. They were acquainted with his appearance and the sound of his voice, and his method of doing his duty. Also, they were aware, although he never spoke of religion, that he read a chapter of the Bible every evening, and went to church whenever they touched at a port. But of his internal self they were in total ignorance. This did not, however, prevent them from prophesying that Davies was a "deep one," who, now that he had got the cash, would "blue it" in a way which would astonish them.

But Davies did not "excel in azure feats." The news of his good fortune reached him just as the brig, on which he was going to sail as first-mate, was taking in her cargo for the West Indies. He had signed his contract for the voyage, and, to the utter astonishment of the lawyer who managed the estates, he announced that he should carry it out. In vain did the man of affairs point out to his client that with the help of a cheque of £100 he could arrange the matter for him in ten minutes. Mr. Davies merely replied that the property could wait, he should go the voyage and retire afterwards. The lawyer held up his hands, and then suddenly remembered that there are women in the West Indies as in other parts of the world. Doubtless his queer client had an object in this voyage. As a matter of fact, he was totally wrong. Owen Davies had never interchanged a tender word with a woman in his life; he was a creature of routine, and it was part of his routine to carry out his agreements to the letter. That was all.

As a last resource, the lawyer suggested that Mr. Davies should make a will.

"I do not think it necessary," was the slow and measured answer. "The property has come to me by chance. If I die, it may as well go to somebody else in the same way."

The lawyer stared. "Very well," he said; "it is against my advice, but you must please yourself. Do you want any money?"

Owen thought for a moment. "Yes," he said, "I think I should like to have ten pounds. They are building a theatre there, and I want to subscribe to it."

The lawyer gave him the ten pounds without a word; he was struck speechless, and in this condition he remained for some minutes after the door had closed behind his client. Then he sprung up with a single ejaculation, "Mad, mad! like his great uncle!"

But Owen Davies was not in the least mad, at any rate not then; he was only a creature of habit. In due course, his agreement fulfilled, he sailed his brig home from the West Indies (for the captain was drowned in a gale). Then he took a second-class ticket to Bryngelly, where he had never been in his life before, and asked his way to the Castle. He was told to go to the beach, and he would see it. He did so, leaving his sea-chest behind him, and there, about two hundred paces from the land, and built upon a solitary mountain of rock, measuring half a mile or so round the base, he perceived a vast mediæval pile of fortified buildings, with turrets towering three hundred feet into the air, and edged with fire by the setting sun. He gazed on it with perplexity. Could it be that this enormous island fortress belonged to him, and, if so, how on earth did one get to it? For some little time he walked up and down, wondering, too shy to go to the village for information. Meanwhile, though he did not notice her, a well-grown girl of about fifteen, remarkable for her great grey eyes and the promise of her beauty, was watching his evident perplexity from a seat beneath a rock, not without amusement. At last she rose, and, with the confidence of bold fifteen, walked straight up to him.

"Do you want to get the Castle, sir?" she asked in a low sweet voice, the echoes of which Owen Davies never forgot.

"Yes—oh, I beg your pardon," for now for the first time he saw that he was talking to a young lady.

"Then I am afraid that you are too late—Mrs. Thomas will not show people over after four o'clock. She is the housekeeper, you know."

"Ah, well, the fact is I did not come to see over the place. I came to live there. I am Owen Davies, and the place was left to me."

Beatrice, for of course it was she, stared at him in amazement. So this was the mysterious sailor about whom there had been so much talk in Bryngelly.

"Oh!" she said, with embarrassing frankness. "What an odd way to come home. Well, it is high tide, and you will have to take a boat. I will show you where you can get one. Old Edward will row you across for sixpence," and she led the way round a corner of the beach to where old Edward sat, from early morn to dewy eve, upon the thwarts of his biggest boat, seeking those whom he might row.

"Edward," said the young lady, "here is the new squire, Mr. Owen Davies, who wants to be rowed across to the Castle." Edward, a gnarled and twisted specimen of the sailor tribe, with small eyes and a face that reminded the observer of one of those quaint countenances on the handle of a walking stick, stared at her in astonishment, and then cast a look of suspicion on the visitor.

"Have he got papers of identification about him, miss?" he asked in a stage whisper.

"I don't know," she answered laughing. "He says that he is Mr. Owen Davies."

"Well, praps he is and praps he ain't; anyway, it isn't my affair, and sixpence is sixpence."

All of this the unfortunate Mr. Davies overheard, and it did not add to his equanimity.

"Now, sir, if you please," said Edward sternly, as he pulled the little boat up to the edge of the breakwater. A vision of Mrs. Thomas shot into Owen's mind. If the boatman did not believe in him, what chance had he with the housekeeper? He wished he had brought the lawyer down with him, and then he wished that he was back in the sugar brig.

"Now, sir," said Edward still more sternly, putting down his hesitation to an impostor's consciousness of guilt.

"Um!" said Owen to the young lady, "I beg your pardon. I don't even know your name, and I am sure I have no right to ask it, but would you mind rowing across with me? It would be so kind of you; you might introduce me to the housekeeper."

Again Beatrice laughed the merry laugh of girlhood; she was too young to be conscious of any impropriety in the situation, and indeed there was none. But her sense of humour told her that it was funny, and she became possessed with a not unnatural curiosity to see the thing out.

"Oh, very well," she said, "I will come."

The boat was pushed off and very soon they reached the stone quay that bordered the harbour of the Castle, about which a little village of retainers had grown up. Seeing the boat arrive, some of these people sauntered out of the cottages, and then, thinking that a visitor had come, under the guidance of Miss Beatrice, to look at the antiquities of the Castle, which was the show place of the neighbourhood, sauntered back again. Then the pair began the zigzag ascent of the rock mountain, till at last they stood beneath the mighty mass of building, which, although it was hoary with antiquity, was by no means lacking in the comforts of modern civilization, the water, for instance, being brought in pipes laid beneath the sea from a mountain top two miles away on the mainland.

"Isn't there a view here?" said Beatrice, pointing to the vast stretch of land and sea. "I think, Mr. Davies, that you have the most beautiful house in the whole world. Your great-uncle, who died a year ago, spent more than fifty thousand pounds on repairing and refurbishing it, they say. He built the big drawing-room there, where the stone is a little lighter; it is fifty-five feet long. Just think, fifty thousand pounds!"

"It is a large sum," said Owen, in an unimaginative sort of way, while in his heart he wondered what on earth he should do with this white elephant of a mediæval castle, and its drawing room fifty-five feet long.

"He does not seem much impressed," thought Beatrice to herself, as she tugged away at the postern bell; "I think he must be stupid. He looks stupid."

Presently the door was opened by an active-looking little old woman with a high voice.

"Mrs. Thomas," thought Owen to himself; "she is even worse than I expected."

"Now you must please to go away," began the formidable housekeeper in her shrillest key; "it is too late to show visitors over. Why, bless us, it's you, Miss Beatrice, with a strange man! What do you want?"

Beatrice looked at her companion as a hint that he should explain himself, but he said nothing.

"This is your new squire," she said, not without a certain pride. "I found him wandering about the beach. He did not know how to get here, so I brought him over."

"Lord, Miss Beatrice, and how do you know it's him?" said Mrs. Thomas. "How do you know it ain't a housebreaker?"

"Oh, I'm sure he cannot be," answered Beatrice aside, "because he isn't clever enough."

Then followed a long discussion. Mrs. Thomas stoutly refused to admit the stranger without evidence of identity, and Beatrice, embracing his cause, as stoutly pressed his claims. As for the lawful owner, he made occasional feeble attempts to prove that he was himself, but Mrs. Thomas was not to be imposed upon in this way. At last they came to a dead lock.

"Y'd better go back to the inn, sir," said Mrs. Thomas with scathing sarcasm, "and come up to-morrow with proofs and your luggage."

"Haven't you got any letters with you?" suggested Beatrice as a last resource.

As it happened Owen had a letter, one from the lawyer to himself about the property, and mentioning Mrs. Thomas's name as being in charge of the Castle. He had forgotten all about it, but at this interesting juncture it was produced and read aloud by Beatrice. Mrs. Thomas took it, and having examined it carefully through her horn-rimmed spectacles, was constrained to admit its authenticity.

"I'm sure I apologise, sir," she said with a half-doubtful courtesy and much tact, "but one can't be too careful with all these trampseses about; I never should have thought from the look of you, sir, how as you was the new squire."

This might be candid, but it was not flattering, and it caused Beatrice to snigger behind her handkerchief in true school-girl fashion. However, they entered, and were led by Mrs. Thomas with solemn pomp through the great and little halls, the stone parlour and the oak parlour, the library and the huge drawing-room, in which the white heads of marble statues protruded from the bags of brown holland wherewith they were wrapped about in a manner ghastly to behold. At length they reached a small octagon-shaped room that, facing south, commanded a most glorious view of sea and land. It was called the Lady's Boudoir, and joined another of about the same size, which in its former owner's time had been used as a smoking-room.

"If you don't mind, madam," said the lord of all this magnificence, "I should like to stop here, I am getting tired of walking." And there he stopped for many years. The rest of the Castle was shut up; he scarcely ever visited it except occasionally to see that the rooms were properly aired, for he was a methodical man.

As for Beatrice, she went home, still chuckling, to receive a severe reproof from Elizabeth for her "forwardness." But Owen Davies never forgot the debt of gratitude he owed her. In his heart he felt convinced that had it not been for her, he would have fled before Mrs. Thomas and her horn-rimmed eyeglasses, to return no more. The truth of the matter was, however, that young as was Beatrice, he fell in love with her then and there, only to fall deeper and deeper into that drear abyss as years went on.

He never said anything about it, he scarcely even gave a hint of his hopeless condition, though of course Beatrice divined something of it as soon as she came to years of discretion. But there grew up in Owen's silent, lonely breast a great and overmastering desire to make this grey-eyed girl his wife. He measured time by the intervals that elapsed between his visions of her. No period in his life was so wretched and utterly purposeless as those two years which passed while she was at her Training College. He was a very passive lover, as yet his gathering passion did not urge him to extremes, and he could never make up his mind to declare it. The box was in his hand, but he feared to throw the dice.

But he drew as near to her as he dared. Once he gave Beatrice a flower, it was when she was seventeen, and awkwardly expressed a hope that she would wear it for his sake. The words were not much and the flower was not much, but there was a look about the man's eyes, and a suppressed passion and energy in his voice, which told their tale to the keen-witted girl. After this he found that she avoided him, and bitterly regretted his boldness. For Beatrice did not like him in that way. To a girl of her curious stamp his wealth was nothing. She did not covet wealth, she coveted independence, and had the sense to know that marriage with such a man would not bring it. A cage is a cage, whether the bars are of iron or gold. He bored her, she despised him for his want of intelligence and enterprise. That a man with all this wealth and endless opportunity should waste his life in such fashion was to her a thing intolerable. She knew if she had half his chance, that she would make her name ring from one end of Europe to the other. In short, Beatrice held Owen as deeply in contempt as her sister Elizabeth, studying him from another point of view, held him in reverence. And putting aside any human predilections, Beatrice would never have married a man whom she despised. She respected herself too much.

Owen Davies saw all this as through a glass darkly, and in his own slow way cast about for a means of drawing near. He discovered that Beatrice was passionately fond of learning, and also that she had no means to obtain the necessary books. So he threw open his library to her; it was one of the best in Wales. He did more; he gave orders to a London bookseller to forward him every new book of importance that appeared in certain classes of literature, and all of these he placed at her disposal, having first carefully cut the leaves with his own hand. This was a bait Beatrice could not resist. She might dread or even detest Mr. Davies, but she loved his books, and if she quarrelled with him her well of knowledge would simply run dry, for there were no circulating libraries at Bryngelly, and if there had been she could not have afforded to subscribe to them. So she remained on good terms with him, and even smiled at his futile attempts to keep pace with her studies. Poor man, reading did not come naturally to him; he was much better at cutting leaves. He studied the Times and certain religious works, that was all. But he wrestled manfully with many a detested tome, in order to be able to say something to Beatrice about it, and the worst of it was that Beatrice always saw through it, and showed him that she did. It was not kind, perhaps, but youth is cruel.

And so the years wore on, till at length Beatrice knew that a crisis was at hand. Even the tardiest and most retiring lover must come to the point at last, if he is in earnest, and Owen Davies was very much in earnest. Of late, to her dismay, he had so far come out of his shell as to allow himself to be nominated a member of the school council. Of course she knew that this was only to give him more opportunities of seeing her. As a member of the council, he could visit the school of which she was mistress as often as he chose, and indeed he soon learned to take a lively interest in village education. About twice a week he would come in just as the school was breaking up and offer to walk home with her, seeking for a favourable opportunity to propose. Hitherto she had always warded off this last event, but she knew that it must happen. Not that she was actually afraid of the man himself; he was too much afraid of her for that. What she did fear was the outburst of wrath from her father and sister when they learned that she had refused Owen Davies. It never occurred to her that Elizabeth might be playing a hand of her own in the matter.

From all of which it will be clear, if indeed it has not become so already, that Beatrice Granger was a somewhat ill-regulated young woman, born to bring trouble on herself and all connected with her. Had she been otherwise, she would have taken her good fortune and married Owen Davies, in which case her history need never have been written.

CHAPTER VII

A MATRIMONIAL TALE

Before Geoffrey Bingham dropped off into a troubled sleep on that eventful night of storm, he learned that the girl who had saved his life at the risk and almost at the cost of her own was out of danger, and in his own and more reticent way he thanked Providence as heartily as did Owen Davies. Then he went to sleep.

When he woke, feeling very sick and so stiff and sore that he could scarcely move, the broad daylight was streaming through the blinds. The place was perfectly quiet, for the doctor's assistant who had brought him back to life, and who lay upon a couch at the further end of the room, slept the sleep of youth and complete exhaustion. Only an eight-day clock on the mantelpiece ticked in that solemn and aggressive way which clocks affect in the stillness. Geoffrey strained his eyes to make out the time, and finally discovered that it wanted a few minutes to six o'clock. Then he fell to wondering how Miss Granger was, and to repeating in his own mind every scene of their adventure, till the last, when they were whirled out of the canoe in the embrace of that white-crested billow.

He remembered nothing after that, nothing but a rushing sound and a vision of foam. He shuddered a little as he thought of it, for his nerves were shaken; it is not pleasant to have been so very near the End and the Beginning; and then his heart went out with renewed gratitude towards the girl who had restored him to life and light and hope. Just at this moment he thought that he heard a sound of sobbing outside the window. He listened; the sound went on. He tried to rise, only to find that he was too stiff to manage it. So, as a last resource, he called the doctor.

"What is the matter?" answered that young gentleman, jumping up with the alacrity of one accustomed to be suddenly awakened. "Do you feel queer?"

"Yes, I do rather," answered Geoffrey, "but it isn't that. There is somebody crying outside here."

The doctor put on his coat, and, going to the window, drew the blind.

"Why, so there is," he said. "It's a little girl with yellow hair and without a hat."

"A little girl," answered Geoffrey. "Why, it must be Effie, my daughter. Please let her in."

"All right. Cover yourself up, and I can do that through the window; it isn't five feet from the ground." Accordingly he opened the window, and addressing the little girl, asked her what her name was.

"Effie," she sobbed in answer, "Effie Bingham. I've come to look for daddie."

"All right, my dear, don't cry so; your daddie is here. Come and let me lift you in."

Another moment and there appeared through the open window the very sweetest little face and form that ever a girl of six was blessed with. For the face was pink and white, and in it were set two beautiful dark eyes, which, contrasting with the golden hair, made the child a sight to see. But alas! just now the cheeks were stained with tears, and round the large dark eyes were rings almost as dark. Nor was this all. The little dress was hooked awry, on one tiny foot all drenched with dew there was no boot, and on the yellow curls no hat.

"Oh! daddie, daddie," cried the child, catching sight of him and struggling to reach her father's arms, "you isn't dead, is you, daddie?"

"No, my love, no," answered her father, kissing her. "Why should you think that I was dead? Didn't your mother tell you that I was safe?"

"Oh! daddie," she answered, "they came and said that you was drownded, and I cried and wished that I was drownded too. Then mother came home at last and said that you were better, and was cross with me because I went on crying and wanted to come to you. But I did go on crying. I cried nearly all night, and when it got light I did dress myself, all but one shoe and my hat, which I could not find, and I got out of the house to look for you."

"And how did you find me, my poor little dear?"

"Oh, I heard mother say you was at the Vicarage, so I waited till I saw a man, and asked him which way to go, and he did tell me to walk along the cliff till I saw a long white house, and then when he saw that I had no shoe he wanted to take me home, but I ran away till I got here. But the blinds were down, so I did think that you were dead, daddie dear, and I cried till that gentleman opened the window."

After that Geoffrey began to scold her for running away, but she did not seem to mind it much, for she sat upon the edge of the couch, her little face resting against his own, a very pretty sight to see.

"You must go back to Mrs. Jones, Effie, and tell your mother where you have been."

"I can't, daddie, I've only got one shoe," she answered, pouting.

"But you came with only one shoe."

"Yes, daddie, but I wanted to come and I don't want to go back. Tell me how you was drownded."

He laughed at her logic and gave way to her, for this little daughter was very near to his heart, nearer than anything else in the world. So he told her how he was "drownded" and how a lady had saved his life.

Effie listened with wide set eyes, and then said that she wanted to see the lady, which she presently did. At that moment there came a knock at the door, and Mr. Granger entered, accompanied by Dr. Chambers.

"How do you do, sir?" said the former. "I must introduce myself, seeing that you are not likely to remember me. When last I saw you, you looked as dead as a beached dog-fish. My name's Granger, the Reverend J. Granger, Vicar of Bryngelly, one of the very worst livings on this coast, and that's saying a great deal."

"I am sure, Mr. Granger, I'm under a deep debt of gratitude to you for your hospitality, and under a still deeper one to your daughter, but I hope to thank her personally for that."

"Never speak of it," said the clergyman. "Hot water and blankets don't cost much, and you will have to pay for the brandy and the doctor. How is he, doctor?"

"He is getting on very well indeed, Mr. Granger. But I daresay you find yourself rather stiff, Mr. Bingham. I see your head is pretty badly bruised."

"Yes," he answered, laughing, "and so is my body. Shall I be able to go home to-day?"

"I think so," said the doctor, "but not before this evening. You had better keep quiet till then. You will be glad to hear that Miss Beatrice is getting on very well. Hers was a wonderful recovery, the most wonderful I ever saw. I had quite given her up, though I should have kept on the treatment for another hour. You ought to be grateful to Miss Beatrice, Mr. Bingham. But for her you would not have been here."

"I am most grateful," he answered earnestly. "Shall I be able to see her to-day?"

"Yes, I think so, some time this afternoon, say at three o'clock. Is that your little daughter? What a lovely child she is. Well, I will look in again about twelve. All that you require to do now is to keep quiet and rub in some arnica."

About an hour afterwards the servant girl brought Geoffrey some breakfast of tea and toast. He felt quite hungry, but when it came to the pinch he could not eat much. Effie, who was starving, made up for this deficiency, however; she ate all the toast and a couple of slices of bread and butter after it. Scarcely had they finished, when her father observed a shade of anxiety come upon his little daughter's face.

"What is it, Effie?" he asked.

"I think," replied Effie in evident trepidation, "I think that I hear mother outside and Anne too."

"Well, dear, they have come to see me."

"Yes, and to scold me because I ran away," and the child drew nearer to her father in a fashion which would have made it clear to any observer that the relations between her and her mother were somewhat strained.

Effie was right. Presently there was a knock at the door and Lady Honoria entered, calm and pale and elegant as ever. She was followed by a dark-eyed somewhat impertinent-looking French bonne, who held up her hands and ejaculated, "Mon Dieu!" as she appeared.

"I thought so," said Lady Honoria, speaking in French to the bonne. "There she is," and she pointed at the runaway Effie with her parasol.

"Mon Dieu!" said the woman again. "Vous voilà enfin, et moi, qui suis accablée de peur, et votre chère mère aussi; oh, mais que c'est méchant; et regardez donc, avec un soulier seulement. Mais c'est affreux!"

"Hold your tongue," said Geoffrey sharply, "and leave Miss Effie alone. She came to see me."

Anne ejaculated, "Mon Dieu!" once more and collapsed.

"Really, Geoffrey," said his wife, "the way you spoil that child is something shocking. She is wilful as can be, and you make her worse. It is very naughty of her to run away like that and give us such a hunt. How are we to get her home, I wonder, with only one shoe."

Her husband bit his lip, and his forehead contracted itself above the dark eyes. It was not the first time that he and Lady Honoria had come to words about the child, with whom his wife was not in sympathy. Indeed she had never forgiven Effie for appearing in this world at all. Lady Honoria did not belong to that class of women who think maternity is a joy.

"Anne," he said, "take Miss Effie and carry her till you can find a donkey. She can ride back to the lodgings." The nurse murmured something in French about the child being as heavy as lead.

"Do as I bid you," he said sharply, in the same language. "Effie, my love, give me a kiss and go home. Thank you for coming to see me."

The child obeyed and went. Lady Honoria stood and watched her go, tapping her little foot upon the floor, and with a look upon her cold, handsome face that was not altogether agreeable to see.

It had sometimes happened that, in the course of his married life, Geoffrey returned home with a little of that added fondness which absence is fabled to beget. On these occasions he was commonly so unfortunate as to find that Lady Honoria belied the saying, that she greeted him with arrears of grievances and was, if possible, more frigid than ever.

Was this to be repeated now that he had come back from what was so near to being the longest absence of all? It looked like it. He noted symptoms of the rising storm, symptoms with which he was but too well acquainted, and both for his own sake and for hers—for above all things Geoffrey dreaded these bitter matrimonial bickerings—tried to think of something kind to say. It must be owned that he did not show much tact in the subject he selected, though it was one which might have stirred the sympathies of some women. It is so difficult to remember that one is dealing with a Lady Honoria.

"If ever we have another child—" he began gently.

"Excuse me interrupting you," said the lady, with a suavity which did not however convey any idea of the speaker's inward peace, "but it is a kindness to prevent you from going on in that line. One darling is ample for me."

"Well," said the miserable Geoffrey, with an effort, "even if you don't care much about the child yourself, it is a little unreasonable to object because she cares for me and was sorry when she thought that I was dead. Really, Honoria, sometimes I wonder if you have any heart at all. Why should you be put out because Effie got up early to come and see me?—an example which I must admit you did not set her. And as to her shoe—" he added smiling.

"You may laugh about her shoe, Geoffrey," she interrupted, "but you forget that even little things like that are no laughing matter now to us. The child's shoes keep me awake at night sometimes. Defoy has not been paid for I don't know how long. I have a mind to get her sabots—and as to heart—"

"Well," broke in Geoffrey, reflecting that bad as was the emotional side of the question, it was better than the commercial—"as to 'heart?'"

"You are scarcely the person to talk of it, that is all. I wonder how much of yours you gave me?"

"Really, Honoria," he answered, not without eagerness, and his mind filled with wonder. Was it possible that his wife had experienced some kind of "call," and was about to concern herself with his heart one way or the other? If so it was strange, for she had never shown the slightest interest in it before.

"Yes," she went on rapidly and with gathering vehemence, "you speak about your heart"—which he had not done—"and yet you know as well as I do that if I had been a girl of no position you would never have offered me the organ on which you pretend to set so high a value. Or did your heart run wildly away with you, and drag us into love and a cottage—a flat, I mean? If so, I should prefer a little less heart and a little more common sense."

Geoffrey winced, twice indeed, feeling that her ladyship had hit him as it were with both barrels. For, as a matter of fact, he had not begun with any passionate devotion, and again Lady Honoria and he were now just as poor as though they had really married for love.

"It is hardly fair to go back on bygones and talk like this," he said, "even if your position had something to do with it; only at first of course, you must remember that when we married mine was not without attractions. Two thousand a year to start on and a baronetcy and eight thousand a year in the near future were not—but I hate talking about that kind of thing. Why do you force me to it? Nobody could know that my uncle, who was so anxious that I should marry you, would marry himself at his age, and have a son and heir. It was not my fault, Honoria. Perhaps you would not have married me if you could have foreseen it."

"Very probably not," she answered calmly, "and it is not my fault that I have not yet learned to live with peace of mind and comfort on seven hundred a year. It was hard enough to exist on two thousand till your uncle died, and now—"

"Well, and now, Honoria, if you will only have patience and put up with things for a while, you shall be rich enough; I will make money for you, as much money as you want. I have many friends. I have not done so badly at the Bar this year."

"Two hundred pounds, nineteen shillings and sevenpence, minus ninety-seven pounds rent of chambers and clerk," said Lady Honoria, with a disparaging accent on the sevenpence.

"I shall double it next year, and double that again the next, and so on. I work from morning till night to get on, that you may have—what you live for," he said bitterly.

"Ah, I shall be sixty before that happy day comes, and want nothing but scandal and a bath chair. I know the Bar and its moaning," she added, with acid wit. "You dream, you imagine what you would like to come true, but you are deceiving me and yourself. It will be like the story of Sir Robert Bingham's property once again. We shall be beggars all our days. I tell you, Geoffrey, that you had no right to marry me."

Then at length he lost his temper. This was not the first of these scenes—they had grown frequent of late, and this bitter water was constantly dropping.

"Right?" he said, "and may I ask what right you had to marry me when you don't even pretend you ever cared one straw for me, but just accepted me as you would have accepted any other man who was a tolerably good match? I grant that I first thought of proposing to you because my uncle wished it, but if I did not love you I meant to be a good husband to you, and I should have loved you if you would let me. But you are cold and selfish; you looked upon a husband merely as a stepping-stone to luxury; you have never loved anybody except yourself. If I had died last night I believe that you would have cared more about having to go into mourning than for the fact of my disappearance from your life. You showed no more feeling for me when you came in than you would have if I had been a stranger—not so much as some women might have for a stranger. I wonder sometimes if you have any feeling left in you at all. I should think that you treat me as you do because you do not care for me and do care for some other person did I not know you to be utterly incapable of caring for anybody. Do you want to make me hate you, Honoria?"

Geoffrey's low concentrated voice and earnest manner told his wife, who was watching him with something like a smile upon her clear-cut lips, how deeply he was moved. He had lost his self-control, and exposed his heart to her—a thing he rarely did, and that in itself was a triumph which she did not wish to pursue at the moment. Geoffrey was not a man to push too far.

"If you have quite finished, Geoffrey, there is something I should like to say—"

"Oh, curse it all!" he broke in.

"Yes?" she said calmly and interrogatively, and made a pause, but as he did not specially apply his remark to anybody or anything, she continued: "If these flowers of rhetoric are over, what I have to say is this: I do not intend to stay in this horrid place any longer. I am going to-morrow to my brother Garsington. They asked us both, you may remember, but for reasons best known to yourself, you would not go."

"You know my reasons very well, Honoria."

"I beg your pardon. I have not the slightest idea what they were," said Lady Honoria with conviction. "May I hear them?"

"Well, if you wish to know, I will not go to the house of a man who has—well, left my club as Garsington left it, and who, had it not been for my efforts, would have left it in an even more unpleasant and conspicuous fashion. And his wife is worse than he is—"

"I think you are mistaken," Lady Honoria said coldly, and with the air of a person who shuts the door of a room into which she does not wish to look. "And, any way, it all happened years ago and has blown over. But I do not see the necessity of discussing the subject further. I suppose that we shall meet at dinner to-night. I shall take the early train to-morrow."

"Do what suits you, Honoria. Perhaps you would prefer not returning at all."

"Thank you, no. I will not lay myself open to imputations. I shall join you in London, and will make the best of a bad business. Thank Heaven, I have learned how to bear my misfortunes," and with this Parthian shot she left the room.

For a minute or two her husband felt as though he almost hated her. Then he thrust his face into the pillow and groaned.

"She is right," he said to himself; "we must make the best of a bad business. But, somehow, I seem to have made a mess of my life. And yet I loved her once—for a month or two."

This was not an agreeable scene, and it may be said that Lady Honoria was a vulgar person. But not even the advantage of having been brought up "on the knees of marchionesses" is a specific against vulgarity, if a lady happens, unfortunately, to set her heart, what there is of it, meanly on mean things.

CHAPTER VIII

EXPLANATORY

About two o'clock Geoffrey rose, and with some slight assistance from his reverend host, struggled into his clothes. Then he lunched, and while he did so Mr. Granger poured his troubles into his sympathetic ear.

"My father was a Herefordshire farmer, Mr. Bingham," he said, "and I was bred up to that line of life myself. He did well, my father did, as in those days a careful man might. What is more, he made some money by cattle-dealing, and I think that turned his head a little; anyway, he was minded to make 'a gentleman of me,' as he called it. So when I was eighteen I was packed off to be made a parson of, whether I liked it or no. Well, I became a parson, and for four years I had a curacy at a town called Kingston, in Herefordshire, not a bad sort of little town—perhaps you happen to know it. While I was there, my father, who was getting beyond himself, took to speculating. He built a row of villas at Leominster, or at least he lent a lawyer the money to build them, and when they were built nobody would hire them. It broke my father; he was ruined over those villas. I have always hated the sight of a villa ever since, Mr. Bingham. And shortly afterwards he died, as near bankruptcy as a man's nose is to his mouth.

"After that I was offered this living, £150 a year it was at the best, and like a fool I took it. The old parson who was here before me left an only daughter behind him. The living had ruined him, as it ruins me, and, as I say, he left his daughter, my wife that was, behind him, and a pretty good bill for dilapidations I had against the estate. But there wasn't any estate, so I made the best of a bad business and married the daughter, and a sweet pretty woman she was, poor dear, very like my Beatrice, only without the brains. I can't make out where Beatrice's brains come from indeed, for I am sure I don't set up for having any. She was well born, too, my wife was, of an old Cornish family, but she had nowhere to go to, and I think she married me because she didn't know what else to do, and was fond of the old place. She took me on with it, as it were. Well, it turned out pretty well, till some eleven years ago, when our boy was born, though I don't think we ever quite understood each other. She never got her health back after that, and seven years ago she died. I remember it was on a night wonderfully like last night—mist first, then storm. The boy died a few years afterwards. I thought it would have broken Beatrice's heart; she has never been the same girl since, but always full of queer ideas I don't pretend to follow.

"And as for the life I've had of it here, Mr. Bingham, you wouldn't believe it if I was to tell you. The living is small enough, but the place is as full of dissent as a mackerel-boat of fish, and as for getting the tithes—well, I cannot, that's all. If it wasn't for a bit of farming that I do, not but what the prices are down to nothing, and for what the visitors give in the season, and for the help of Beatrice's salary as certificated mistress, I should have been in the poor-house long ago, and shall be yet, I often think. I have had to take in a border before now to make both ends meet, and shall again, I expect.

"And now I must be off up to my bit of a farm; the old sow is due to litter, and I want to see how she is getting on. Please God she'll have thirteen again and do well. I'll order the fly to be here at five, though I shall be back before then—that is, I told Elizabeth to do so. She has gone out to do some visiting for me, and to see if she can't get in two pounds five of tithe that has been due for three months. If anybody can get it it's Elizabeth. Well, good-bye; if you are dull and want to talk to Beatrice, she is up and in there. I daresay you will suit one another. She's a very queer girl, Beatrice, quite beyond me with her ideas, and it was a funny thing her holding you so tight, but I suppose Providence arranged that. Good-bye for the present, Mr. Bingham," and this curious specimen of a clergyman vanished, leaving Geoffrey quite breathless.

It was half-past two o'clock, and the doctor had told him that he could see Miss Granger at three. He wished that it was three, for he was tired of his own thoughts and company, and naturally anxious to renew his acquaintance with the strange girl who had begun by impressing him so deeply and ended by saving his life. There was complete quiet in the house; Betty, the maid-of-all-work, was employed in the kitchen, both the doctors had gone, and Elizabeth and her father were out. To-day there was no wind, it had blown itself away during the night, and the sight of the sunbeams streaming through the windows made Geoffrey long to be in the open air. He had no book at hand to read, and whenever he tried to think his mind flew back to that hateful matrimonial quarrel.

It was hard on him, Geoffrey thought, that he should be called upon to endure such scenes. He could no longer disguise the truth from himself—he had buried his happiness on his wedding-day. Looking back across the years, he well remembered how different a life he had imagined for himself. In those days he was tired of knocking about and of youthful escapades; even that kind of social success which must attend a young man who was handsome, clever, a good fellow, and blessed with large expectations, had, at the age of six-and-twenty, entirely lost its attractiveness. Therefore he had turned no deaf ear to his uncle, Sir Robert Bingham, who was then going on for seventy, when he suggested that it might be well of Geoffrey settled down, and introduced him to Lady Honoria.

Lady Honoria was eighteen then, and a beauty of the rather thin but statuesque type, which attracts men up to five or six and twenty and then frequently bores, if it does not repel them. Moreover, she was clever and well read, and pretended to be intellectually and poetically inclined, as ladies not specially favoured by Apollo sometimes do—before they marry. Cold she always was; nobody ever heard of Lady Honoria stretching the bounds of propriety; but Geoffrey put this down to a sweet and becoming modesty, which would vanish or be transmuted in its season. Also she affected a charming innocence of all vulgar business matters, which both deceived and enchanted him. Never but once did she allude to ways and means before marriage, and then it was to say that she was glad that they should be so poor till dear Sir Robert died (he had promised to allow them fifteen hundred a year, and they had seven more between them), as this would enable them to see so much more of each other.

At last came the happy day, and this white virgin soul passed into Geoffrey's keeping. For a week or so things went fairly well, and then disenchantment began. He learned by slow but sure degrees that his wife was vain, selfish and extravagant, and, worst of all, that she cared very little about him. The first shock was when he accidentally discovered, four or five days after marriage, that Honoria was intimately acquainted with every detail of Sir Robert Bingham's property, and, young as she was, had already formed a scheme to make it more productive after the old man's death.

They went to live in London, and there he found that Lady Honoria, although by far too cold and prudent a woman to do anything that could bring a breath of scandal upon her name, was as fond of admiration as she was heartless. It seemed to Geoffrey that he could never be free from the collection of young men who hung about her skirts. Some of them were very good fellows whom he liked exceedingly; still, on the whole he would have preferred to remain unmarried and associate with them at the club. Also the continual round of society and going out brought heavier expenses on him that he could well support. And thus, little by little, poor Geoffrey's dream of matrimonial bliss faded into thin air. But, fortunately for himself, he possessed a certain share of logic and sweet reasonableness. In time he learnt to see that the fault was not altogether with his wife, who was by no means a bad sort of woman in her degree. But her degree differed from his degree. She had married for freedom and wealth and to gain a larger scope wherein to exercise those tastes which inherited disposition and education had given to her, as she believed that he had married her because she was the daughter of a peer.

Lady Honoria, like many another woman of her stamp, was the overbred, or sometimes the underbred, product of a too civilized age and class. Those primitive passions and virtues on which her husband had relied to make the happiness of their married life simply did not exist for her. The passions had been bred and educated out of her; for many generations they have been found inconvenient and disquieting attributes in woman. As for the old virtues, such as love of children and the ordinary round of domestic duty, they simply bored her. On the whole, though sharp of tongue, she rarely lost her temper, for her vices, like her virtues, were of a somewhat negative order; but the fury which seized her when she learned for certain that she was to become a mother was a thing that her unfortunate husband never forgot and never wished to see again. At length the child was born, a fact for which Geoffrey, at least, was very thankful.

"Take it away. I do not want to see it!" said Lady Honoria to the scandalised nurse when the little creature was brought to her, wrapped in its long robes.

"Give it to me, nurse—I do," said her husband.

From that moment Geoffrey gave all the pent-up affection of his bruised soul to this little daughter, and as the years went on they grew very dear to each other. But an active-minded, strong-hearted, able-bodied man cannot take a babe as the sole companion of his existence. Probably Geoffrey would have found this out in time, and might have drifted into some mode of life more or less undesirable, had not an accident occurred to prevent it. In his dotage, Geoffrey's old uncle Sir Robert Bingham fell a victim to the wiles of an adventuress and married her. Then he promptly died, and eight months afterwards a posthumous son was born.

To Geoffrey this meant ruin. His allowance stopped and his expectations vanished at one fell swoop. He pulled himself together, however, as a brave-hearted man does under such a shock, and going to his wife he explained to her that he must now work for his living, begging her to break down the barrier that was between them and give him her sympathy and help. She met him with tears and reproaches. The one thing that touched her keenly, the one thing which she feared and hated was poverty, and all that poverty means to women of her rank and nature. But there was no help for it; the charming house in Bolton Street had to be given up, and purgatory must be faced, in a flat, near the Edgware Road. Lady Honoria was miserable, indeed had it not been that fortunately for herself she possessed plenty of relations more or less grand, whom she might continually visit for weeks and even for months at a stretch, she could scarcely have endured her altered life.

But strangely enough Geoffrey soon found that he was happier than he had been since his marriage. To begin with, he set to work like a man, and work is a great source of happiness to all vigorous-minded folk. It is not, in truth, a particularly cheerful occupation to pass endless days in hanging about law-courts amongst a crowd of unbriefed Juniors, and many nights in reading up the law one has forgotten and threading the many intricacies of the Judicature Act. But it happened that his father, a younger brother of Sir Robert's, had been a solicitor, and though he was dead, and all direct interest with the firm was severed, yet another uncle remained in it, and the partners did not forget Geoffrey in his difficulties.

They sent him what work they could without offending their standing counsel, and he did it well. Then by degrees he built up quite a large general practice of the kind known as deviling. Now there are few things more unsatisfactory than doing another man's work for nothing, but every case fought means knowledge gained, and what is more it is advertisement. So it came to pass that within less than two years from the date of his money misfortunes, Geoffrey Bingham's dark handsome face and square strong form became very well known in the Courts.

"What is that man's name?" said one well-known Q.C. to another still more well known, as they sat waiting for their chops in the Bar Grill Room, and saw Geoffrey, his wig pushed back from his forehead, striding through the doorway on the last day of the sitting which preceded the commencement of this history.

"Bingham," answered the other. "He's only begun to practise lately, but he'll be at the top of the tree before he has done. He married very well, you know, old Garsington's daughter, a charming woman, and handsome too."

"He looks like it," grunted the first, and as a matter of fact such was the general opinion.

For, as Beatrice had said, Geoffrey Bingham was a man who had success written on his forehead. It would have been almost impossible for him to fail in whatever he undertook.

CHAPTER IX

WHAT BEATRICE DREAMED

Geoffrey lay upon his back, watching the still patch of sunshine and listening to the ticking of the clock, as he passed all these and many other events in solemn review, till the series culminated in his vivid recollection of the scene of that very morning.

"I am sick of it," he said at last aloud, "sick and tired. She makes my life wretched. If it wasn't for Effie upon my word I'd . . . By Jove, it is three o'clock; I will go and see Miss Granger. She's a woman, not a female ghost at any rate, though she is a freethinker—which," he added as he slowly struggled off the couch, "is a very foolish thing to be."

Very shakily, for he was sadly knocked about, Geoffrey hobbled down the long narrow room and through the door, which was ajar. The opposite door was also set half open. He knocked softly, and getting no answer pushed it wide and looked in, thinking that he had, perhaps, made some mistake as to the room. On a sofa placed about two-thirds down its length, lay Beatrice asleep. She was wrapped in a kind of dressing-gown of some simple blue stuff, and all about her breast and shoulders streamed her lovely curling hair. Her sweet face was towards him, its pallor relieved only by the long shadow of the dark lashes and the bent bow of the lips. One white wrist and hand hung down almost to the floor, and beneath the spread curtain of the sunlit hair her bosom heaved softly in her sleep. She looked so wondrously beautiful in her rest that he stopped almost awed, and gazed, and gazed again, feeling as though a present sense and power were stilling his heart to silence. It is dangerous to look upon such quiet loveliness, and very dangerous to feel that pressure at the heart. A truly wise man feeling it would have fled, knowing that seeds sown in such silences may live to bloom upon a bitter day, and shed their fruit into the waters of desolation. But Geoffrey was not wise—who would have been? He still stood and gazed till the sight stamped itself so deeply on the tablets of his heart that through all the years to come no heats of passion, no frosts of doubt, and no sense of loss could ever dull its memory.

The silent sun shone on, the silent woman slept, and in silence the watcher gazed. And as he looked a great fear, a prescience of evil that should come, entered into Geoffrey and took possession of him. A cloud without crossed the ray of sunlight and turned it. It wavered, for a second it rested on his breast, flashed back to hers, then went out; and as it flashed and died, he seemed to know that henceforth, for life till death, ay! and beyond, his fate and that sleeping woman's were one fate. It was but a momentary knowledge; the fear shook him, and was gone almost before he understood its foolishness. But it had been with him, and in after days he remembered it.

Just then Beatrice woke, opening her grey eyes. Their dreamy glance fell upon him, looking through him and beyond him, rather than at him. Then she raised herself a little and stretching out both her arms towards him, spoke aloud.

"So have you have come back to me at last," she said. "I knew that you would come and I have waited."

He made no answer, he did not know what to say; indeed he began to think that he also must be dreaming. For a little while Beatrice still looked at him in the same absent manner, then suddenly started up, the red blood streaming to her brow.

"Why, Mr. Bingham," she said, "is it really you? What was it that I said? Oh, pray forgive me, whatever it was. I have been asleep dreaming such a curious dream, and talking in my sleep."

"Do not alarm yourself, Miss Granger," he answered, recovering himself with a jerk; "you did not say anything dreadful, only that you were glad to see me. What were you dreaming about?"

Beatrice looked at him doubtfully; perhaps his words did not ring quite true.

"I think that I had better tell you as I have said so much," she answered. "Besides, it was a very curious dream, and if I believed in dreams it would rather frighten me, only fortunately I do not. Sit down and I will tell it to you before I forget it. It is not very long."

He took the chair to which she pointed, and she began, speaking in the voice of one yet laden with the memories of sleep.

"I dreamed that I stood in space. Far to my right was a great globe of light, and to my left was another globe, and I knew that the globes were named Life and Death. From the globe on the right to the globe on the left, and back again, a golden shuttle, in which two flaming eyes were set, was shot continually, and I knew also that this was the shuttle of Destiny, weaving the web of Fate. Presently the shuttle flew, leaving behind it a long silver thread, and the eyes in the shuttle were such as your eyes. Again the shuttle sped through space, and this time its eyes were like my eyes, and the thread it left behind it was twisted from a woman's hair. Half way between the globes of Life and Death my thread was broken, but the shuttle flew on and vanished. For a moment the thread hung in air, then a wind rose and blew it, so that it floated away like a spider's web, till it struck upon your silver thread of life and began to twist round and round it. As it twisted it grew larger and heavier, till at last it was thick as a great tress of hair, and the silver line bent beneath the weight so that I saw it soon must break. Then while I wondered what would happen, a white hand holding a knife slid slowly down the silver line, and with the knife severed the wrappings of woman's hair, which fell and floated slowly away, like a little cloud touched with sunlight, till they were lost in darkness. But the thread of silver that was your line of life, sprang up quivering and making a sound like sighs, till at last it sighed itself to silence.

"Then I seemed to sleep, and when I woke I was floating upon such a misty sea as we saw last night. I had lost all sight of land, and I could not remember what the stars were like, nor how I had been taught to steer, nor understand where I must go. I called to the sea, and asked it of the stars, and the sea answered me thus:

"'Hope has rent her raiment, and the stars are set.'

"I called again, and asked of the land where I should go, and the land did not answer, but the sea answered me a second time:

"'Child of the mist, wander in the mist, and in darkness seek for light.'

"Then I wept because Hope had rent her starry garment and in darkness I must seek for light. And while I still wept, you rose out of the sea and sat before me in the boat. I had never seen you before, and still I felt that I had known you always. You did not speak, and I did not speak, but you looked into my heart and saw its trouble. Then I looked into your heart, and read what was written. And this was written:

"'Woman whom I knew before the Past began, and whom I shall know when the Future is ended, why do you weep?'

"And my heart answered, 'I weep because I am lost upon the waters of the earth, because Hope has rent her starry robes, and in everlasting darkness I must seek for light that is not.' Then your heart said, 'I will show you light,' and bending forward you touched me on the breast.

"And suddenly an agony shook me like the agonies of birth and death, and the sky was full of great-winged angels who rolled up the mist as a cloth, and drew the veils from the eyes of Night, and there, her feet upon the globe, and her star-set head piercing the firmament of heaven, stood Hope breathing peace and beauty. She looked north and south and east and west, then she looked upwards through the arching vaults of heaven, and wherever she set her eyes, bright with holy tears, the darkness shrivelled and sorrow ceased, and from corruption arose the Incorruptible. I gazed and worshipped, and as I did so, again the sea spoke unquestioned:

"'In darkness thou hast found light, in Death seek for wisdom.'

"Then once more Hope rent her starry robes, and the angels drew down a veil over the eyes of Night, and the sea swallowed me, and I sank till I reached the deep foundations of mortal death. And there in the Halls of Death I sat for ages upon ages, till at last I saw you come, and on your lips was the word of wisdom that makes all things clear, but what it was I cannot remember. Then I stretched out my hand to greet you, and woke, and that is all my dream."

Beatrice ceased, her grey eyes set wide, as though they still strove to trace their spiritual vision upon the air of earth, her breast heaving, and her lips apart.

"Great heaven!" he said, "what an imagination you must have to dream such a dream as that."

"Imagination," she answered, returning to her natural manner. "I have none, Mr. Bingham. I used to have, but I lost it when I lost—everything else. Can you interpret my dream? Of course you cannot; it is nothing but nonsense—such stuff as dreams are made of, that is all."

"It may be nonsense, I daresay it is, but it is beautiful nonsense," he answered. "I wish ladies had more of such stuff to give the world."

"Ah, well, dreams may be wiser than wakings, and nonsense than learned talk, for all we know. But there's an end of it. I do not know why I repeated it to you. I am sorry that I did repeat it, but it seemed so real it shook me out of myself. This is what comes of breaking in upon the routine of life by being three parts drowned. One finds queer things at the bottom of the sea, you know. By the way I hope that you are recovering. I do not think that you will care to go canoeing again with me, Mr. Bingham."

There was an opening for a compliment here, but Geoffrey felt that it would be too much in earnest if spoken, so he resisted the temptation.

"What, Miss Granger," he said, "should a man say to a lady who but last night saved his life, at the risk, indeed almost at the cost, of her own?"

"It was nothing," she answered, colouring; "I clung to you, that was all, more by instinct than from any motive. I think I had a vague idea that you might float and support me."

"Miss Granger, the occasion is too serious for polite fibs. I know how you saved my life. I do not know how to thank you for it."

"Then don't thank me at all, Mr. Bingham. Why should you thank me? I only did what I was bound to do. I would far rather die than desert a companion in distress, of any sort; we all must die, but it would be dreadful to die ashamed. You know what they say, that if you save a person from drowning you will do them an injury afterwards. That is how they put it here; in some parts the saying is the other way about, but I am not likely ever to do you an injury, so it does not make me unhappy. It was an awful experience: you were senseless, so you cannot know how strange it felt lying upon the slippery rock, and seeing those great white waves rush upon us through the gloom, with nothing but the night above, and the sea around, and death between the two. I have been lonely for many years, but I do not think that I ever quite understood what loneliness really meant before. You see," she added by way of an afterthought, "I thought that you were dead, and there is not much company in a corpse."

"Well," he said, "one thing is, it would have been lonelier if we had gone."

"Do you think so?" she answered, looking at him inquiringly. "I don't quite see how you make that out. If you believe in what we have been taught, as I think you do, wherever it was you found yourself there would be plenty of company, and if, like me, you do not believe in anything, why, then, you would have slept, and sleep asks for nothing."

"Did you believe in nothing when you lay upon the rock waiting to be drowned, Miss Granger?"

"Nothing!" she answered; "only weak people find revelation in the extremities of fear. If revelation comes at all, surely it must be born in the heart and not in the senses. I believed in nothing, and I dreaded nothing, except the agony of death. Why should I be afraid? Supposing that I am mistaken, and there is something beyond, is it my fault that I cannot believe? What have I done that I should be afraid? I have never harmed anybody that I know of, and if I could believe I would. I wish I had died," she went on, passionately; "it would be all over now. I am tired of the world, tired of work and helplessness, and all the little worries which wear one out. I am not wanted here, I have nothing to live for, and I wish that I had died!"

"Some day you will think differently, Miss Granger. There are many things that a woman like yourself can live for—at the least, there is your work."

She laughed drearily. "My work! If you only knew what it is like you would not talk to me about it. Every day I roll my stone up the hill, and every night it seems to roll down again. But you have never taught in a village school. How can you know? I work all day, and in the evening perhaps I have to mend the tablecloths, or—what do you think?—write my father's sermons. It sounds curious, does it not, that I should write sermons? But I do. I wrote the one he is going to preach next Sunday. It makes very little difference to him what it is so long as he can read it, and, of course, I never say anything which can offend anybody, and I do not think that they listen much. Very few people go to church in Bryngelly."

"Don't you ever get any time to yourself, then?"

"Oh, yes, sometimes I do, and then I go out in my canoe, or read, and am almost happy. After all, Mr. Bingham, it is very wrong and ungrateful of me to speak like this. I have more advantages than nine-tenths of the world, and I ought to make the best of them. I don't know why I have been speaking as I have, and to you, whom I never saw till yesterday. I never did it before to any living soul, I assure you. It is just like the story of the man who came here last year with the divining rod. There is a cottage down on the cliff—it belongs to Mr. Davies, who lives in the Castle. Well, they have no drinking water near, and the new tenant made a great fuss about it. So Mr. Davies hired men, and they dug and dug and spent no end of money, but could not come to water. At last the tenant fetched an old man from some parish a long way off, who said that he could find springs with a divining rod. He was a curious old man with a crutch, and he came with his rod, and hobbled about till at last the rod twitched just at the tenant's back door—at least the diviner said it did. At any rate, they dug there, and in ten minutes struck a spring of water, which bubbled up so strongly that it rushed into the house and flooded it. And what do you think? After all, the water was brackish. You are the man with the divining rod, Mr. Bingham, and you have made me talk a great deal too much, and, after all, you see it is not nice talk. You must think me a very disagreeable and wicked young woman, and I daresay I am. But somehow it is a relief to open one's mind. I do hope, Mr. Bingham, that you will see—in short, that you will not misunderstand me."

"Miss Granger," he answered, "there is between us that which will always entitle us to mutual respect and confidence—the link of life and death. Had it not been for you, I should not sit here to listen to your confidence to-day. You may tell me that a mere natural impulse prompted you to do what you did. I know better. It was your will that triumphed over your natural impulse towards self-preservation. Well, I will say no more about it, except this: If ever a man was bound to a woman by ties of gratitude and respect, I am bound to you. You need not fear that I shall take advantage of or misinterpret your confidence." Here he rose and stood before her, his dark handsome face bowed in proud humility. "Miss Granger, I look upon it as an honour done to me by one whom henceforth I must reverence among all women. The life you gave back to me, and the intelligence which directs it, are in duty bound to you, and I shall not forget the debt."

Beatrice listened to his words, spoken in that deep and earnest voice, which in after years became so familiar to Her Majesty's judges and to Parliament—listened with a new sense of pleasure rising in her heart. She was this man's equal; what he could dare, she could dare; where he could climb, she could follow—ay, and if need be, show the path, and she felt that he acknowledged it. In his sight she was something more than a handsome girl to be admired and deferred to for her beauty's sake. He had placed her on another level—one, perhaps, that few women would have wished to occupy. But Beatrice was thankful to him. It was the first taste of supremacy that she had ever known.

It is something to stir the proud heart of such a woman as Beatrice, in that moment when for the first time she feels herself a conqueror, victorious, not through the vulgar advantage of her sex, not by the submission of man's coarser sense, but rather by the overbalancing weight of mind.

"Do you know," she said, suddenly looking up, "you make me very proud," and she stretched out her hand to him.

He took it, and, bending, touched it with his lips. There was no possibility of misinterpreting the action, and though she coloured a little—for, till then, no man had even kissed the tip of her finger—she did not misinterpret it. It was an act of homage, and that was all.

And so they sealed the compact of their perfect friendship for ever and a day.

Then came a moment's silence. It was Geoffrey who broke it.

"Miss Granger," he said, "will you allow me to preach you a lecture, a very short one?"

"Go on," she said.

"Very well. Do not blame me if you don't like it, and do not set me down as a prig, though I am going to tell you your faults as I read them in your own words. You are proud and ambitious, and the cramped lines in which you are forced to live seem to strangle you. You have suffered, and have not learned the lesson of suffering—humility. You have set yourself up against Fate, and Fate sweeps you along like spray upon the gale, yet you go unwilling. In your impatience you have flown to learning for refuge, and it has completed your overthrow, for it has induced you to reject as non-existent all that you cannot understand. Because your finite mind cannot search infinity, because no answer has come to all your prayers, because you see misery and cannot read its purpose, because you suffer and have not found rest, you have said there is naught but chance, and become an atheist, as many have done before you. Is it not true?"

"Go on," she answered, bowing her head to her breast so that the long rippling hair almost hid her face.

"It seems a little odd," Geoffrey said with a short laugh, "that I, with all my imperfections heaped upon me, should presume to preach to you—but you will know best how near or how far I am from the truth. So I want to say something. I have lived for thirty-five years, and seen a good deal and tried to learn from it, and I know this. In the long run, unless we of our own act put away the opportunity, the world gives us our due, which generally is not much. So much for things temporal. If you are fit to rule, in time you will rule; if you do not, then be content and acknowledge your own incapacity. And as for things spiritual, I am sure of this—though of course one does not like to talk much of these matters—if you only seek for them long enough in some shape you will find them, though the shape may not be that which is generally recognised by any particular religion. But to build a wall deliberately between oneself and the unseen, and then complain that the way is barred, is simply childish."

"And what if one's wall is built, Mr. Bingham?"

"Most of us have done something in that line at different times," he answered, "and found a way round it."

"And if it stretches from horizon to horizon, and is higher than the clouds, what then?"

"Then you must find wings and fly over it."

"And where can any earthly woman find those spiritual wings?" she asked, and then sank her head still deeper on her breast to cover her confusion. For she remembered that she had heard of wanderers in the dusky groves of human passion, yes, even Mænad wanderers, who had suddenly come face to face with their own soul; and that the cruel paths of earthly love may yet lead the feet which tread them to the ivory gates of heaven.

And remembering these beautiful myths, though she had no experience of love, and knew little of its ways, Beatrice grew suddenly silent. Nor did Geoffrey give her an answer, though he need scarcely have feared to do so.

For were they not discussing a purely abstract question?

CHAPTER X

LADY HONORIA MAKES ARRANGEMENTS

In another moment somebody entered the room; it was Elizabeth. She had returned from her tithe collecting expedition—with the tithe. The door of the sitting-room was still ajar, and Geoffrey had his back towards it. So it happened that nobody heard Elizabeth's rather cat-like step, and for some seconds she stood in the doorway without being perceived. She stood quite still, taking in the whole scene at a glance. She noticed that her sister held her head down, so that her hair shadowed her, and guessed that she did so for some reason—probably because she did not wish her face to be seen. Or was it to show off her lovely hair? She noticed also the half shy, half amused, and altogether interested expression upon Geoffrey's countenance—she could see that in the little gilt-edged looking-glass which hung over the fire-place, nor did she overlook the general air of embarrassment that pervaded them both.

When she came in, Elizabeth had been thinking of Owen Davies, and of what might have happened had she never seen the tide of life flow back into her sister's veins. She had dreamed of it all night and had thought of it all day; even in the excitement of extracting the back tithe from the recalcitrant and rather coarse-minded Welsh farmer, with strong views on the subject of tithe, it had not been entirely forgotten. The farmer was a tenant of Owen Davies, and when he called her a "parson in petticoats, and wus," and went on, in delicate reference to her powers of extracting cash, to liken her to a "two-legged corkscrew only screwier," she perhaps not unnaturally reflected, that if ever—pace Beatrice—certain things should come about, she would remember that farmer. For Elizabeth was blessed with a very long memory, as some people had learnt to their cost, and generally, sooner or later, she paid her debts in full, not forgetting the overdue interest.

And now, as she stood in the doorway unseen and noted these matters, something occurred to her in connection with this dominating idea, which, like ideas in general, had many side issues. At any rate a look of quick intelligence shone for a moment in her light eyes, like a sickly sunbeam on a faint December mist; then she moved forward, and when she was close behind Geoffrey, spoke suddenly.

"What are you both thinking about?" she said in her clear thin voice; "you seem to have exhausted your conversation."

Geoffrey made an exclamation and fairly jumped from his chair, a feat which in his bruised condition really hurt him very much. Beatrice too started violently; she recovered herself almost instantly, however.

"How quietly you move, Elizabeth," she said.

"Not more quietly than you sit, Beatrice. I have been wondering when anybody was going to say anything, or if you were both asleep."

For her part Beatrice speculated how long her sister had been in the room. Their conversation had been innocent enough, but it was not one that she would wish Elizabeth to have overheard. And somehow Elizabeth had a knack of overhearing things.

"You see, Miss Granger," said Geoffrey coming to the rescue, "both our brains are still rather waterlogged, and that does not tend to a flow of ideas."

"Quite so," said Elizabeth. "My dear Beatrice, why don't you tie up your hair? You look like a crazy Jane. Not but what you have very nice hair," she added critically. "Do you admire good hair, Mr. Bingham."

"Of course I do," he answered gallantly, "but it is not common."

Only Beatrice bit her lip with vexation. "I had almost forgotten about my hair," she said; "I must apologise for appearing in such a state. I would have done it up after dinner only I was too stiff, and while I was waiting for Betty, I went to sleep."

"I think there is a bit of ribbon in that drawer. I saw you put it there yesterday," answered the precise Elizabeth. "Yes, here it is. If you like, and Mr. Bingham will excuse it, I can tie it back for you," and without waiting for an answer she passed behind Beatrice, and gathering up the dense masses of her sister's locks, tied them round in such fashion that they could not fall forward, though they still rolled down her back.

Just then Mr. Granger came back from his visit to the farm. He was in high good humour. The pig had even surpassed her former efforts, and increased in a surprising manner, to the number of fifteen indeed. Elizabeth thereon produced the two pounds odd shillings which she had "corkscrewed" out of the recalcitrant dissenting farmer, and the sight added to Mr. Granger's satisfaction.

"Would you believe it, Mr. Bingham," he said, "in this miserably paid parish I have nearly a hundred pounds owing to me, a hundred pounds in tithe. There is old Jones who lives out towards the Bell Rock, he owes three years' tithe—thirty-four pounds eleven and fourpence. He can pay and he won't pay— says he's a Baptist and is not going to pay parson's dues—though for the matter of that he is nothing but an old beer tub of a heathen."

"Why don't you proceed against him, then, Mr. Granger?"

"Proceed, I have proceeded. I've got judgment, and I mean to issue execution in a few days. I won't stand it any longer," he went on, working himself up and shaking his head as he spoke till his thin white hair fell about his eyes. "I will have the law of him and the others too. You are a lawyer and you can help me. I tell you there's a spirit abroad which just comes to just—no man isn't to pay his lawful debts, except of course the parson and the squire. They must pay or go to the court. But there is law left, and I'll have it, before they play the Irish game on us here." And he brought down his fist with a bang upon the table.

Geoffrey listened with some amusement. So this was the weak old man's sore point—money. He was clearly very strong about that—as strong as Lady Honoria indeed, but with more excuse. Elizabeth also listened with evident approval, but Beatrice looked pained.

"Don't get angry, father," she said; "perhaps he will pay after all. It is bad to take the law if you can manage any other way—it breeds so much ill blood."

"Nonsense, Beatrice," said her sister sharply. "Father is quite right. There's only one way to deal with them, and that is to seize their goods. I believe you are socialist about property, as you are about everything else. You want to pull everything down, from the Queen to the laws of marriage, all for the good of humanity, and I tell you that your ideas will be your ruin. Defy custom and it will crush you. You are running your head against a brick wall, and one day you will find which is the harder."

Beatrice flushed, but answered her sister's attack, which was all the sharper because it had a certain spice of truth in it.

"I never expressed any such views, Elizabeth, so I do not see why you should attribute them to me. I only said that legal proceedings breed bad blood in a parish, and that is true."

"I did not say you expressed them," went on the vigorous Elizabeth; "you look them—they ooze out of your words like water from a peat bog. Everybody knows you are a radical and a freethinker and everything else that is bad and mad, and contrary to that state of life in which it has pleased God to call you. The end of it will be that you will lose the mistressship of the school—and I think it is very hard on father and me that you should bring disgrace on us with your strange ways and immoral views, and now you can make what you like of it."

"I wish that all radicals were like Miss Beatrice," said Geoffrey, who was feeling exceedingly uncomfortable, with a feeble attempt at polite jocosity. But nobody seemed to hear him. Elizabeth, who was now fairly in a rage, a faint flush upon her pale cheeks, her light eyes all ashine, and her thin fingers clasped, stood fronting her beautiful sister, and breathing spite at every pore. But it was easy for Geoffrey who was watching her to see that it was not her sister's views she was attacking; it was her sister. It was that soft strong loveliness and the glory of that face; it was the deep gentle mind, erring from its very greatness, and the bright intellect which lit it like a lamp; it was the learning and the power that, give them play, would set a world aflame, as easily as they did the heart of the slow-witted hermit squire, whom Elizabeth coveted—these were the things that Elizabeth hated, and bitterly assailed.

Accustomed to observe, Geoffrey saw this instantly, and then glanced at the father. The old man was frightened; clearly he was afraid of Elizabeth, and dreaded a scene. He stood fidgeting his feet about, and trying to find something to say, as he glanced apprehensively at his elder daughter, through his thin hanging hair.

Lastly, Geoffrey looked at Beatrice, who was indeed well worth looking at. Her face was quite pale and the clear grey eyes shone out beneath their dark lashes. She had risen, drawing herself to her full height, which her exquisite proportions seemed to increase, and was looking at her sister. Presently she said one word and one only, but it was enough.

"Elizabeth."

Her sister opened her lips to speak again, but hesitated, and changed her mind. There was something in Beatrice's manner that checked her.

"Well," she said at length, "you should not irritate me so, Beatrice."

Beatrice made no reply. She only turned towards Geoffrey, and with a graceful little bow, said:

"Mr. Bingham, I am sure that you will forgive this scene. The fact is, we all slept badly last night, and it has not improved our tempers."

There was a pause, of which Mr. Granger took a hurried and rather undignified advantage.

"Um, ah," he said. "By the way, Beatrice, what was it I wanted to say? Ah, I know—have you written, I mean written out, that sermon for next Sunday? My daughter," he added, addressing Geoffrey in explanation—"um, copies my sermons for me. She writes a very good hand—"

Remembering Beatrice's confidence as to her sermon manufacturing functions, Geoffrey felt amused at her father's naïve way of describing them, and Beatrice also smiled faintly as she answered that the sermon was ready. Just then the roll of wheels was heard without, and the only fly that Bryngelly could boast pulled up in front of the door.

"Here is the fly come for you, Mr. Bingham," said Mr. Granger—"and as I live, her ladyship with it. Elizabeth, see if there isn't some tea ready," and the old gentleman, who had all the traditional love of the lower middle-class Englishman for a title, trotted off to welcome "her ladyship."

Presently Lady Honoria entered the room, a sweet, if rather a set smile upon her handsome face, and with a graceful mien, that became her tall figure exceedingly well. For to do Lady Honoria justice, she was one of the most ladylike women in the country, and so far as her personal appearance went, a very perfect type of the class to which she belonged.

Geoffrey looked at her, saying to himself that she had clearly recovered her temper, and that he was thankful for it. This was not wonderful, for it is observable that the more aristocratic a lady's manners are, the more disagreeable she is apt to be when she is crossed.

"Well, Geoffrey dear," she said, "you see I have come to fetch you. I was determined that you should not get yourself drowned a second time on your way home. How are you now?—but I need not ask, you look quite well again."

"It is very kind of you, Honoria," said her husband simply, but it was doubtful if she heard him, for at the moment she was engaged in searching out the soul of Beatrice, with one of the most penetrating and comprehensive glances that young lady had ever enjoyed the honour of receiving. There was nothing rude about the look, it was too quick, but Beatrice felt that quick as it might be it embraced her altogether. Nor was she wrong.

"There is no doubt about it," Lady Honoria thought to herself, "she is lovely—lovely everywhere. It was clever of her to leave her hair down; it shows the shape of her head so well, and she is tall enough to stand it. That blue wrapper suits her too. Very few women could show such a figure as hers—like a

Greek statue. I don't like her; she is different from most of us; just the sort of girl men go wild about and women hate."

All this passed through her mind in a flash. For a moment Lady Honoria's blue eyes met Beatrice's grey ones, and she knew that Beatrice liked her no better than she did Beatrice. Those eyes were a trifle too honest, and, like the deep clear water they resembled, apt to throw up shadows of the passing thoughts above.

"False and cold and heartless," thought Beatrice. "I wonder how a man like that could marry her; and how much he loves her."

Thus the two women took each other's measure at a glance, each finding the other wanting by her standard. Nor did they ever change that hastily formed judgment.

It was all done in a few seconds—in that hesitating moment before the words we summon answer on our lips. The next, Lady Honoria was sweeping towards her with outstretched hand, and her most gracious smile.

"Miss Granger," she said, "I owe you a debt I never can repay—my dear husband's life. I have heard all about how you saved him; it is the most wonderful thing—Grace Darling born again. I can't think how you could do it. I wish I were half as brave and strong."

"Please don't, Lady Honoria," said Beatrice. "I am so tired of being thanked for doing nothing, except what it was my duty to do. If I had let Mr. Bingham go while I had the strength to hold on to him I should have felt like a murderess to-day. I beg you to say no more about it."

"One does not often find such modesty united to so much courage, and, if you will allow me to say it, so much beauty," answered Lady Honoria graciously. "Well, I will do as you wish, but I warn you your fame will find you out. I hear they have an account of the whole adventure in to-day's papers, headed, 'A Welsh Heroine.'"

"How did you hear that, Honoria?" asked her husband.

"Oh, I had a telegram from Garsington, and he mentions it," she answered carelessly.

"Telegram from Garsington! Hence these smiles," thought he. "I suppose that she is going to-morrow."

"I have some other news for you, Miss Granger," went on Lady Honoria. "Your canoe has been washed ashore, very little injured. The old boatman—Edward, I think they call him—has found it; and your gun in it too, Geoffrey. It had stuck under the seat or somewhere. But I fancy that you must both have had enough canoeing for the present."

"I don't know, Lady Honoria," answered Beatrice. "One does not often get such weather as last night's, and canoeing is very pleasant. Every sweet has its salt, you know; or, in other words, one may always be upset."

At that moment, Betty, the awkward Welsh serving lass, with a fore-arm about as shapely as the hind leg of an elephant, and a most unpleasing habit of snorting audibly as she moved, shuffled in with the tea-tray. In her wake came the slim Elizabeth, to whom Lady Honoria was introduced.

After this, conversation flagged for a while, till Lady Honoria, feeling that things were getting a little dull, set the ball rolling again.

"What a pretty view you have of the sea from these windows," she said in her well-trained and monotonously modulated voice. "I am so glad to have seen it, for, you know, I am going away to-morrow."

Beatrice looked up quickly.

"My husband is not going," she went on, as though in answer to an unspoken question. "I am playing the part of the undutiful wife and running away from him, for exactly three weeks. It is very wicked of me, isn't it? but I have an engagement that I must keep. It is most tiresome."

Geoffrey, sipping his tea, smiled grimly behind the shelter of his cup. "She does it uncommonly well," he thought to himself.

"Does your little girl go with you, Lady Honoria?" asked Elizabeth.

"Well, no, I think not. I can't bear parting with her—you know how hard it is when one has only one child. But I think she would be so bored where I am going to stay, for there are no other children there; and besides, she positively adores the sea. So I shall have to leave her to her father's tender mercies, poor dear."

"I hope Effie will survive it, I am sure," said Geoffrey laughing.

"I suppose that your husband is going to stay on at Mrs. Jones's," said the clergyman.

"Really, I don't know. What are you going to do, Geoffrey? Mrs. Jones's rooms are rather expensive for people in our impoverished condition. Besides, I am sure that she cannot look after Effie. Just think, she has eight children of her own, poor old dear. And I must take Anne with me; she is Effie's French nurse, you know, a perfect treasure. I am going to stay in a big house, and my experience of those big houses is, that one never gets waited on at all unless one takes a maid. You see, what is everybody's business is nobody's business. I'm sure I don't know how you will get on with the child, Geoffrey; she takes such a lot of looking after."

"Oh, don't trouble about that, Honoria," he answered. "I daresay that Effie and I will manage somehow."

Here one of those peculiar gleams of intelligence which marked the advent of a new idea passed across Elizabeth's face. She was sitting next her father, and bending, whispered to him. Beatrice saw it and made a motion as though to interpose, but before she could do so Mr. Granger spoke.

"Look here, Mr. Bingham," he said, "if you want to move, would you like a room here? Terms strictly moderate, but can't afford to put you up for nothing you know, and living rough and ready. You'd have to take us as you find us; but there is a dressing-room next to my room, where your little girl could sleep, and my daughters would look after her between them, and be glad of the job."

Again Beatrice opened her lips as though to speak, but closed them without speaking. Thus do our opportunities pass before we realise that they are at hand.

Instinctively Geoffrey had glanced towards Beatrice. He did not know if this idea was agreeable to her. He knew that her work was hard, and he did not wish to put extra trouble upon her, for he guessed that the burden of looking after Effie would ultimately fall upon her shoulders. But her face told him nothing: it was quite passive and apparently indifferent.

"You are very kind, Mr. Granger," he said, hesitating. "I don't want to go away from Bryngelly just at present, and it would be a good plan in some ways, that is if the trouble to your daughters would not be too much."

"I am sure that it is an excellent plan," broke in Lady Honoria, who feared lest difficulties should arise as to her appropriation of Anne's services; "how lucky that I happened to mention it. There will be no trouble about our giving up the rooms at Mrs. Jones's, because I know she has another application for them."

"Very well," said Geoffrey, not liking to raise objections to a scheme thus publicly advocated, although he would have preferred to take time to consider. Something warned him that Bryngelly Vicarage would prove a fateful abode for him. Then Elizabeth rose and asked Lady Honoria if she would like to see the rooms her husband and Effie would occupy.

She said she should be delighted and went off, followed by Mr. Granger fussing in the rear.

"Don't you think that you will be a little dull here, Mr. Bingham?" said Beatrice.

"On the contrary," he answered. "Why should I be dull? I cannot be so dull as I should be by myself."

Beatrice hesitated, and then spoke again. "We are a curious family, Mr. Bingham; you may have seen as much this afternoon. Had you not better think it over?"

"If you mean that you do not want me to come, I won't," he said rather bluntly, and next second felt that he had made a mistake.

"I!" Beatrice answered, opening her eyes. "I have no wishes in the matter. The fact is that we are poor, and let lodgings—that is what it comes to. If you think they will suit you, you are quite right to take them."

Geoffrey coloured. He was a man who could not bear to lay himself open to the smallest rebuff from a woman, and he had brought this on himself. Beatrice saw it and relented.

"Of course, Mr. Bingham, so far as I am concerned, I shall be the gainer if you do come. I do not meet so many people with whom I care to associate, and from whom I can learn, that I wish to throw a chance away."

"I think you misunderstand me a little," he said; "I only meant that perhaps you would not wish to be bothered with Effie, Miss Granger."

She laughed. "Why, I love children. It will be a great pleasure to me to look after her so far as I have time."

Just then the others returned, and their conversation came to an end.

"It's quite delightful, Geoffrey—such funny old-fashioned rooms. I really envy you." (If there was one thing in the world that Lady Honoria hated, it was an old-fashioned room.) "Well, and now we must be going. Oh! you poor creature, I forgot that you were so knocked about. I am sure Mr. Granger will give you his arm."

Mr. Granger ambled forward, and Geoffrey having made his adieus, and borrowed a clerical hat (Mr. Granger's concession to custom, for in most other respects he dressed like an ordinary farmer), was safely conveyed to the fly.

And so ended Geoffrey's first day at Bryngelly Vicarage.

CHAPTER XI

BEATRICE MAKES AN APPOINTMENT

Lady Honoria leaned back in the cab, and sighed a sigh of satisfaction.

"That is a capital idea," she said. "I was wondering what arrangements you could make for the next three weeks. It is ridiculous to pay three guineas a week for rooms just for you and Effie. The old gentleman only wants that for board and lodging together, for I asked him."

"I daresay it will do," said Geoffrey. "When are we to shift?"

"To-morrow, in time for dinner, or rather supper: these barbarians eat supper, you know. I go by the morning train, you see, so as to reach Garsington by tea-time. I daresay you will find it rather dull, but you like being dull. The old clergyman is a low stamp of man, and a bore, and as for the eldest daughter, Elizabeth, she's too awful—she reminds me of a rat. But Beatrice is handsome enough, though I think her horrid too. You'll have to console yourself with her, and I daresay you will suit each other."

"Why do you think her horrid, Honoria?"

"Oh, I don't know; she is clever and odd, and I hate odd women. Why can't they be like other people? Think of her being strong enough to save your life like that too. She must have the muscle of an Amazon—it's downright unwomanly. But there is no doubt about her beauty. She is as nearly perfect as any girl I ever saw, though too independent looking. If only one had a daughter like that, how one might marry her. I would not look at anything under twenty thousand a year. She is too good for that lumbering Welsh squire she's engaged too—the man who lives in the Castle—though they say that he is fairly rich."

"Engaged," said Geoffrey, "how do you know that she is engaged?"

"Oh, I don't know it at all, but I suppose she is. If she isn't, she soon will be, for a girl in that position is not likely to throw such a chance away. At any rate, he's head over ears in love with her. I saw that last night. He was hanging about for hours in the rain, outside the door, with a face like a ghost, till he knew whether she was dead or alive, and he has been there twice to inquire this morning. Mr. Granger told me. But she is too good for him from a business point of view. She might marry anybody, if only she were put in the way of it."

Somehow, Geoffrey's lively interest in Beatrice sensibly declined on the receipt of this intelligence. Of course it was nothing to him; indeed he was glad to hear that she was in the way of such a comfortable settlement, but it is unfortunately a fact that one cannot be quite as much interested in a young and lovely lady who is the potential property of a "lumbering Welsh squire," as in one who belongs to herself.

The old Adam still survives in most men, however right-thinking they may be, and this is one of its methods of self-assertion.

"Well," he said, "I am glad to hear she is in such a good way; she deserves it. I think the Welsh squire is in luck; Miss Granger is a remarkable woman."

"Too remarkable by half," said Lady Honoria drily. "Here we are, and there is Effie, skipping about like a wild thing as usual. I think that child is demented."

On the following morning—it was Friday—Lady Honoria, accompanied by Anne, departed in the very best of tempers. For the next three weeks, at any rate, she would be free from the galling associations of straightened means—free to enjoy the luxury and refined comfort to which she had been accustomed, and for which her soul yearned with a fierce longing that would be incomprehensible to folk of a simpler mind. Everybody has his or her ideal Heaven, if only one could fathom it. Some would choose a sublimated intellectual leisure, made happy by the best literature of all the planets; some a model state (with themselves as presidents), in which (through their beneficent efforts) the latest radical notions could actually be persuaded to work to everybody's satisfaction; others a happy hunting ground, where the game enjoyed the fun as much as they did; and so on, ad infinitum.

Lady Honoria was even more modest. Give her a well appointed town and country house, a few powdered footmen, plenty of carriages, and other needful things, including of course the entrée to the upper celestial ten, and she would ask no more from age to age. Let us hope that she will get it one day. It would hurt nobody, and she is sure to find plenty of people of her own way of thinking—that is, if this world supplies the raw material.

She embraced Effie with enthusiasm, and her husband with a chastened warmth, and went, a pious prayer on her lips that she might never again set eyes upon Bryngelly.

It will not be necessary for us to follow Lady Honoria in her travels. That afternoon Effie and her father had great fun. They packed up. Geoffrey, who was rapidly recovering from his stiffness, pushed the things into the portmanteaus and Effie jumped on them. Those which would not go in they bundled loose into the fly, till that vehicle looked like an old clothes ship. Then, as there was no room left for them inside, they walked down to the Vicarage by the beach, a distance of about three-quarters of a mile, stopping on their way to admire the beautiful castle, in one corner of which Owen Davies lived and moved.

"Oh, daddy," said the child, "I wish you would buy a house like that for you and me to live in. Why don't you, daddy?"

"Haven't got the money, dear," he answered.

"Will you ever have the money, daddy?"

"I don't know, dear, perhaps one day—when I am too old to enjoy it," he added to himself.

"It would take a great many pennies to buy a house like that, wouldn't it, daddy?" said Effie sagely.

"Yes, dear, more than you could count," he answered, and the conversation dropped.

Presently they came to a boat-shed, placed opposite the village and close to high-water mark. Here a man, it was old Edward, was engaged in mending a canoe. Geoffrey glanced at it and saw that it was the identical canoe out of which he had so nearly been drowned.

"Look, Effie," said he, "that is the boat out of which I was upset." Effie opened her wide eyes, and stared at the frail craft.

"It is a horrid boat," she said; "I don't want to look at it."

"You're quite right, little miss," said old Edward, touching his cap. "It ain't safe, and somebody will be drowned out of it one of these days. I wish it had gone to the bottom, I do; but Miss Beatrice, she is that foolhardy there ain't no doing nothing with her."

"I fancy that she has learnt a lesson," said Geoffrey.

"May be, may be," grumbled the old man, "but women folk are hard to teach; they never learn nothing till it's too late, they don't, and then when they've been and done it they're sorry, but what's the good o' that?"

Meanwhile another conversation was in progress not more than a quarter of a mile away. On the brow of the cliff stood the village of Bryngelly, and at the back of the village was a school, a plain white-washed building, roofed with stone, which, though amply sufficient and suitable to the wants of the place, was little short of an abomination in the eyes of Her Majesty's school inspectors, who from time to time descended upon Bryngelly for purposes of examination and fault-finding. They yearned to see a stately red-brick edifice, with all the latest improvements, erected at the expense of the rate-payers, but as yet they yearned in vain. The school was supported by voluntary contributions, and thanks to Beatrice's energy and good teaching, the dreaded Board, with its fads and extravagance, had not yet clutched it.

Beatrice had returned to her duties that afternoon, for a night's rest brought back its vigour to her strong young frame. She had been greeted with enthusiasm by the children, who loved her, as well they might, for she was very gentle and sweet with them, though few dared to disobey her. Besides, her beauty impressed them, though they did not know it. Beauty of a certain sort has perhaps more effect on children than on any other class, heedless and selfish as they often seem to be. They feel its power; it is an outward expression of the thoughts and dreams that bud in their unknowing hearts, and is somehow mixed up with their ideas of God and Heaven. Thus there was in Bryngelly a little girl of ten, a very clever and highly excitable child, Jane Llewellyn by name, born of parents of strict Calvinistic views. As it chanced, some months before the opening of this story, a tub thumper, of high renown and considerable rude oratorical force, visited the place, and treated his hearers to a lively discourse on the horrors of Hell.

In the very front row, her eyes wide with fear, sat this poor little child between her parents, who listened to the Minister with much satisfaction, and a little way back sat Beatrice, who had come out of curiosity.

Presently the preacher, having dealt sufficiently in terrifying generalities, went on to practical illustrations, for, after the manner of his class, he was delivering an extempory oration. "Look at that child," he said, pointing to the little girl; "she looks innocent, does she not? but if she does not find salvation, my brethren, I tell you that she is damned. If she dies to-night, not having found salvation, she will go to Hell. Her delicate little body will be tormented for ever and ever—"

Here the unfortunate child fell forward with a shriek.

"You ought to be ashamed of yourself, sir," said Beatrice aloud.

She had been listening to all this ill-judged rant with growing indignation, and now, in her excitement, entirely forgot that she was in a place of worship. Then she ran forward to the child, who had swooned. Poor little unfortunate, she never recovered the shock. When she came to herself, it was found that her finely strung mind had given way, and she lapsed into a condition of imbecility. But her imbecility was not always passive. Occasionally fits of passionate terror would seize upon her. She would cry out that the fiends were coming to drag her down to torment, and dash herself against the wall, in fear hideous to behold. Then it was found that there was but one way to calm her: it was to send for Beatrice. Beatrice would come and take the poor thin hands in hers and gaze with her calm deep eyes upon the wasted horror-stricken face till the child grew quiet again and, shivering, sobbed herself to sleep upon her breast.

And so it was with all the children; her power over them was almost absolute. They loved her, and she loved them all.

And now the schooling was almost done for the day. It was Beatrice's custom to make the children sing some simple song before they broke up. She stood in front of them and gave the time while they sung, and a pretty sight it was to see her do it. On this particular afternoon, just as the first verse was finished, the door of the room opened, and Owen Davies entered, bearing some books under his arm. Beatrice glanced round and saw him, then, with a quick stamp of her foot, went on giving the time.

The children sung lustily, and in front of them stood Beatrice, dressed in simple white, her graceful form swaying as she marked the music's time. Nearer and nearer drew Owen Davies, till at length he stood quite close, his lips slightly apart, his eyes fixed upon her like the eyes of one who dreams, and his slow heavy face faintly lit with the glow of strong emotion.

The song ended, the children at a word from their mistress filed past her, headed by the pupil teachers, and then with a shout, seizing their caps, ran forth this way and that, welcoming the free air. When they were all gone, and not till then, Beatrice turned suddenly round.

"How do you do, Mr. Davies?" she said.

He started visibly. "I did not know that you had seen me," he answered.

"Oh, yes, I saw you, Mr. Davies, only I could not stop the song to say how do you do. By the way, I have to thank you for coming to inquire after me."

"Not at all, Miss Beatrice, not at all; it was a most dreadful accident. I cannot tell you how thankful I am—I can't, indeed."

"It is very good of you to take so much interest in me," said Beatrice.

"Not at all, Miss Beatrice, not at all. Who—who could help taking interest in you? I have brought you some books—the Life of Darwin—it is in two volumes. I think that I have heard you say that Darwin interests you?"

"Yes, thank you very much. Have you read it?"

"No, but I have cut it. Darwin doesn't interest me, you know. I think that he was a rather misguided person. May I carry the books home for you?"

"Thank you, but I am not going straight home; I am going to old Edward's shed to see my canoe."

As a matter of fact this was true, but the idea was only that moment born in her mind. Beatrice had been going home, as she wanted to see that all things were duly prepared for Geoffrey and his little daughter. But to reach the Vicarage she must pass along the cliff, where there were few people, and this she did not wish to do. To be frank, she feared lest Mr. Davies should take the opportunity to make that offer of his hand and heart which hung over her like a nightmare. Now the way to Edward's shed lay through the village and down the cliff, and she knew that he would never propose in the village.

It was very foolish of her, no doubt, thus to seek to postpone the evil day, but the strongest-minded women have their weak points, and this was one of Beatrice's. She hated the idea of this scene. She knew that when it did come there would be a scene. Not that her resolution to refuse the man had ever faltered. But it would be painful, and in the end it must reach the ears of her father and Elizabeth that she had actually rejected Mr. Owen Davies, and then what would her life be worth? She had never suspected it, it had never entered into her mind to suspect, that, though her father might be vexed enough, nothing on this earth would more delight the heart of Elizabeth.

Presently, having fetched her hat, Beatrice, accompanied by her admirer, bearing the Life of Darwin under his arm, started to walk down to the beach. They went in silence, Beatrice just a little ahead. She ventured some remark about the weather, but Owen Davies made no reply; he was thinking, he wanted to say something, but he did not know how to say it. They were at the head of the cliff now, and if he wished to speak he must do so quickly.

"Miss Beatrice," he said in a somewhat constrained voice.

"Yes, Mr. Davies—oh, look at that seagull; it nearly knocked my hat off."

But he was not to be put off with the seagull. "Miss Beatrice," he said again, "are you going out walking next Sunday afternoon?"

"How can I tell, Mr. Davies? It may rain."

"But if it does not rain—please tell me. You generally do walk on the beach on Sunday. Miss Beatrice, I want to speak to you. I hope you will allow me, I do indeed."

Then suddenly she came to a decision. This kind of thing was unendurable; it would be better to get it over. Turning round so suddenly that Owen started, she said:

"If you wish to speak to me, Mr. Davies, I shall be in the Amphitheatre opposite the Red Rocks, at four o'clock on Sunday afternoon, but I had much rather that you did not come. I can say no more."

"I shall come," he answered doggedly, and they went down the steps to the boat-shed.

"Oh, look, daddy," said Effie, "here comes the lady who was drownded with you and a gentleman," and to Beatrice's great relief the child ran forward and met them.

"Ah!" thought Geoffrey to himself, "that is the man Honoria said she was engaged to. Well, I don't think very much of her taste."

In another minute they had arrived. Geoffrey shook hands with Beatrice, and was introduced to Owen Davies, who murmured something in reply, and promptly took his departure.

They examined the canoe together, and then walked slowly up to the Vicarage, Beatrice holding Effie by the hand. Opposite the reef they halted for a minute.

"There is the Table Rock on which we were thrown, Mr. Bingham," said Beatrice, "and here is where they carried us ashore. The sea does not look as though it would drown any one to-night, does it? See!"—and she threw a stone into it—"the ripples run as evenly as they do on a pond."

She spoke idly and Geoffrey answered her idly, for they were not thinking of their words. Rather were they thinking of the strange chance that had brought them together in an hour of deadly peril and now left them together in an hour of peace. Perhaps, too, they were wondering to what end this had come about. For, agnostics, atheists or believers, are we not, most of us, fatalists at heart?

CHAPTER XII

THE WRITING ON THE SAND

Geoffrey found himself very comfortable at the Vicarage, and as for Effie, she positively revelled in it. Beatrice looked after her, taking her to bed at night and helping her to dress in the morning, and Beatrice was a great improvement upon Anne. When Geoffrey became aware of this he remonstrated, saying that he had never expected her to act as nurse to the child, but she replied that it was a pleasure to her to do so, which was the truth. In other ways, too, the place was all that he desired. He did not like Elizabeth, but then he did not see very much of her, and the old farmer clergyman was amusing in his way, with his endless talk of tithes and crops, and the iniquities of the rebellious Jones, on whom he was going to distrain.

For the first day or two Geoffrey had no more conversations with Beatrice. Most of the time she was away at the school, and on the Saturday afternoon, when she was free, he went out to the Red Rocks curlew shooting. At first he thought of asking her to come too, but then it occurred to him that she might wish to go out with Mr. Davies, to whom he still supposed she was engaged. It was no affair of his, yet he was glad when he came back to find that she had been out with Effie, and not with Mr. Davies.

On Sunday morning they all went to church, including Beatrice. It was a bare little church, and the congregation was small. Mr. Granger went through the service with about as much liveliness as a horse driving a machine. He ground it out, prayers, psalms, litany, lessons, all in the same depressing way, till Geoffrey felt inclined to go to sleep, and then took to watching Beatrice's sweet face instead. He wondered what made her look so sad. Hers was always a sad face when in repose, that he knew, but to-day it was particularly so, and what was more, she looked worried as well as sad. Once or twice he saw her glance at Mr. Davies, who was sitting opposite, the solitary occupant of an enormous pew, and he thought that there was apprehension in her look. But Mr. Davies did not return the glance. To judge from his appearance nothing was troubling his mind.

Indeed, Geoffrey studying him in the same way that he instinctively studied everybody whom he met, thought that he had never before seen a man who looked quite so ox-like and absolutely comfortable. And yet he never was more completely at fault. The man seemed stolid and cold indeed, but it was the coldness of a volcano. His heart was a-fire. All the human forces in him, all the energies of his sturdy life, had concentrated themselves in a single passion for the woman who was so near and yet so far from him. He had never drawn upon the store, had never frittered his heart away. This woman, strange and unusual as it may seem, was absolutely the first whose glance or voice had ever stirred his blood. His passion for her had grown slowly; for years it had been growing, ever since the grey-eyed girl on the brink of womanhood had conducted him to his castle home. It was no fancy, no light desire to pass with the year which brought it. Owen had little imagination, that soil from which loves spring with the rank swiftness of a tropic bloom to fade at the first chill breath of change. His passion was an unalterable fact. It was rooted like an oak on our stiff English soil, its fibres wrapped his heart and shot his being through, and if so strong a gale should rise that it must fall, then he too would be overthrown.

For years now he had thought of little else than Beatrice. To win her he would have given all his wealth, ay, thrice over, if that were possible. To win her, to know her his by right and his alone, ah, that would be heaven! His blood quivered and his mind grew dim when he thought of it. What would it be to see her standing by him as she stood now, and know that she was his wife! There is no form of passion more terrible than this. Its very earthiness makes it awful.

The service went on. At last Mr. Granger mounted the pulpit and began to read his sermon, of which the text was, "But the greatest of these is charity." Geoffrey noticed that he bungled over some of the words, then suddenly remembered Beatrice had told him that she had written the sermon, and was all attention. He was not disappointed. Notwithstanding Mr. Granger's infamous reading, and his habit of dropping his voice at the end of a sentence, instead of raising it, the beauty of the thoughts and diction was very evident. It was indeed a discourse that might equally well have been delivered in a Mahomedan or a Buddhist place of worship; there was nothing distinctively Christian about it, it merely appealed to the good in human nature. But of this neither the preacher nor his audience seemed to be aware, indeed, few of the latter were listening at all. The sermon was short and ended with a passage of real power and beauty—or rather it did not end, for, closing the MS. sheets, Mr. Granger followed on with a few impromptu remarks of his own.

"And now, brethren," he said, "I have been preaching to you about charity, but I wish to add one remark, Charity begins at home. There is about a hundred pounds of tithe owing to me, and some of it has been owing for two years and more. If that tithe is not paid I shall have to put distraint on some of you, and I thought that I had better take this opportunity to tell you so."

Then he gave the Benediction.

The contrast between this business-like speech, and the beautiful periods which had gone before, was so ridiculous that Geoffrey very nearly burst out laughing, and Beatrice smiled. So did the rest of the congregation, excepting one or two who owed tithe, and Owen Davies, who was thinking of other things.

As they went through the churchyard, Geoffrey noticed something. Beatrice was a few paces ahead holding Effie's hand. Presently Mr. Davies passed him, apparently without seeing him, and greeted Beatrice, who bowed slightly in acknowledgment. He walked a little way without speaking, then Geoffrey, just as they reached the church gate, heard him say, "At four this afternoon, then." Again she bowed her head, and he turned and went. As for Geoffrey, he wondered what it all meant: was she engaged to him, or was she not?

Dinner was a somewhat silent meal. Mr. Granger was thinking about his tithe, also about a sick cow. Elizabeth's thoughts pursued some dark and devious course of their own, not an altogether agreeable one to judge from her face. Beatrice looked pale and worried; even Effie's sallies did not do more than make her smile. As for Geoffrey himself, he was engaged in wondering in an idle sort of way what was going to happen at four o'clock.

"You is all very dull," said Effie at last, with a charming disregard of grammar.

"People ought to be dull on Sunday, Effie," answered Beatrice, with an effort. "At least, I suppose so," she added.

Elizabeth, who was aggressively religious, frowned at this remark. She knew her sister did not mean it.

"What are you going to do this afternoon, Beatrice?" she asked suddenly. She had seen Owen Davies go up and speak to her sister, and though she had not been near enough to catch the words, scented an assignation from afar.

Beatrice coloured slightly, a fact that escaped neither her sister nor Geoffrey.

"I am going to see Jane Llewellyn," she answered. Jane Llewellyn was the crazy little girl whose tale has been told. Up to that moment Beatrice had no idea of going to see her, but she knew that Elizabeth would not follow her there, because the child could not endure Elizabeth.

"Oh, I thought that perhaps you were going out walking."

"I may walk afterwards," answered Beatrice shortly.

"So there is an assignation," thought Elizabeth, and a cold gleam of intelligence passed across her face.

Shortly after dinner, Beatrice put on her bonnet and went out. Ten minutes passed, and Elizabeth did the same. Then Mr. Granger announced that he was going up to the farm (there was no service till six) to see about the sick cow, and asked Geoffrey if he would like to accompany him. He said that he might as well, if Effie could come, and, having lit his pipe, they started.

Meanwhile Beatrice went to see the crazy child. She was not violent to-day, and scarcely knew her. Before she had been in the house ten minutes, the situation developed itself.

The cottage stood about two-thirds of the way down a straggling street, which was quite empty, for Bryngelly slept after dinner on Sunday. At the top of this street appeared Elizabeth, a Bible in her hand, as though on district visiting intent. She looked down the street, and seeing nobody, went for a little walk, then, returning, once more looked down the street. This time she was rewarded. The door of the Llewellyns' cottage opened, and Beatrice appeared. Instantly Elizabeth withdrew to such a position that she could see without being seen, and, standing as though irresolute, awaited events. Beatrice turned and took the road that led to the beach.

Then Elizabeth's irresolution disappeared. She also turned and took the road to the cliff, walking very fast. Passing behind the Vicarage, she gained a point where the beach narrowed to a width of not more than fifty yards, and sat down. Presently she saw a man coming along the sand beneath her, walking quickly. It was Owen Davies. She waited and watched. Seven or eight minutes passed, and a woman in a white dress passed. It was Beatrice, walking slowly.

"Ah!" said Elizabeth, setting her teeth, "as I thought." Rising, she pursued her path along the cliff, keeping three or four hundred yards ahead, which she could easily do by taking short cuts. It was a long walk, and Elizabeth, who was not fond of walking, got very tired of it. But she was a woman with a purpose, and as such, hard to beat. So she kept on steadily for nearly an hour, till, at length, she came to the spot known as the Amphitheatre. This Amphitheatre, situated almost opposite the Red Rocks, was a half-ring of cliff, the sides of which ran in a semicircle almost down to the water's edge, that is, at high tide. In the centre of the segment thus formed was a large flat stone, so placed that anybody in certain positions on the cliff above could command a view of it, though it was screened by the projecting walls of rock from observation from the beach. Elizabeth clambered a little way down the sloping side of the cliff and looked; on the stone, his back towards her, sat Owen Davies. Slipping from stratum to stratum of the broken cliff, Elizabeth drew slowly nearer, till at length she was within fifty paces of the seated man. Here, ensconcing herself behind a cleft rock, she also sat down; it was not safe to go closer; but in case she should by any chance be observed from above, she opened the Bible on her knee, as though she had sought this quiet spot to study its pages.

Three or four minutes passed, and Beatrice appeared round the projecting angle of the Amphitheatre, and walked slowly across the level sand. Owen Davies rose and stretched out his hand to welcome her, but she did not take it, she only bowed, and then seated herself upon the large flat stone. Owen also seated himself on it, but some three or four feet away. Elizabeth thrust her white face forward till it was almost level with the lips of the cleft rock and strained her ears to listen. Alas! she could not hear a single word.

"You asked me to come here, Mr. Davies," said Beatrice, breaking the painful silence. "I have come."

"Yes," he answered; "I asked you to come because I wanted to speak to you."

"Yes?" said Beatrice, looking up from her occupation of digging little holes in the sand with the point of her parasol. Her face was calm enough, but her heart beat fast beneath her breast.

"I want to ask you," he said, speaking slowly and thickly, "if you will be my wife?"

Beatrice opened her lips to speak, then, seeing that he had only paused because his inward emotion checked his words, shut them again, and went on digging little holes. She wished to rely on the whole case, as a lawyer would say.

"I want to ask you," he repeated, "to be my wife. I have wished to do so for some years, but I have never been able to bring myself to it. It is a great step to take, and my happiness depends on it. Do not answer me yet," he went on, his words gathering force as he spoke. "Listen to what I have to tell you. I have been a lonely man all my life. At sea I was lonely, and since I have come into this fortune I have been lonelier still. I never loved anybody or anything till I began to love you. And then I loved you more and more and more; till now I have only one thought in all my life, and that thought is of you. While I am awake I think of you, and when I am asleep I dream of you. Listen, Beatrice, listen!—I have never loved any other woman, I have scarcely spoken to one—only you, Beatrice. I can give you a great deal; and everything I have shall be yours, only I should be jealous of you—yes, very jealous!"

Here she glanced at his face. It was outwardly calm but white as death, and in the blue eyes, generally so placid, shone a fire that by contrast looked almost unholy.

"I think that you have said enough, Mr. Davies," Beatrice answered. "I am very much obliged to you. I am much honoured, for in some ways I am not your equal, but I do not love you, and I cannot marry you, and I think it best to tell you so plainly, once and for all," and unconsciously she went on digging the holes.

"Oh, do not say that," he answered, almost in a moan. "For God's sake don't say that! It will kill me to lose you. I think I should go mad. Marry me and you will learn to love me."

Beatrice glanced at him again, and a pang of pity pierced her heart. She did not know it was so bad a case as this. It struck her too that she was doing a foolish thing, from a worldly point of view. The man loved her and was very eligible. He only asked of her what most women are willing enough to give under circumstances so favourable to their well-being—herself. But she never liked him, he had always repelled her, and she was not a woman to marry a man whom she did not like. Also, during the last week this dislike and repulsion had hardened and strengthened. Vaguely, as he pleaded with her, Beatrice wondered why, and as she did so her eye fell upon the pattern she was automatically pricking in the sand. It had taken the form of letters, and the letters were G E O F F R E—Great heaven! Could that be the answer? She flushed crimson with shame at the thought, and passed her foot across the tell-tale letters, as she believed, obliterating them.

Owen saw the softening of her eyes and saw the blush, and misinterpreted them. Thinking that she was relenting, by instinct, rather than from any teaching of experience, he attempted to take her hand. With a turn of the arm, so quick that even Elizabeth watching with all her eyes saw nothing of the movement, Beatrice twisted herself free.

"Don't touch me," she said sharply, "you have no right to touch me. I have answered you, Mr. Davies."

Owen withdrew his hand abashed, and for a moment sat still, his chin resting on his breast, a very picture of despair. Nothing indeed could break the stolid calm of his features, but the violence of his emotion was evident in the quick shivering of his limbs and his short deep breaths.

"Can you give me no hope?" he said at last in a slow heavy voice. "For God's sake think before you answer—you don't know what it means to me. It is nothing to you—you cannot feel. I feel, and your words cut like a knife. I know that I am heavy and stupid, but I feel as though you had killed me. You are heartless, quite heartless."

Again Beatrice softened a little. She was touched and flattered. Where is the woman who would not have been?

"What can I say to you, Mr. Davies?" she answered in a kinder voice. "I cannot marry you. How I can I marry you when I do not love you?"

"Plenty of women marry men whom they do not love."

"Then they are bad women," answered Beatrice with energy.

"The world does not think so," he said again; "the world calls those women bad who love where they cannot marry, and the world is always right. Marriage sanctifies everything."

Beatrice laughed bitterly. "Do you think so?" she said. "I do not. I think that marriage without love is the most unholy of our institutions, and that is saying a good deal. Supposing I should say yes to you, supposing that I married you, not loving you, what would it be for? For your money and your position, and to be called a married woman, and what do you suppose I should think of myself in my heart then? No, no, I may be bad, but I have not fallen so low as that. Find another wife, Mr. Davies; the world is wide and there are plenty of women in it who will love you for your own sake, or who at any rate will not be so particular. Forget me, and leave me to go my own way—it is not your way."

"Leave you to go your own way," he answered almost with passion—"that is, leave you to some other man. Oh! I cannot bear to think of it. I am jealous of every man who comes near you. Do you know how beautiful you are? You are too beautiful—every man must love you as I do. Oh, if you took anybody else I think that I should kill him."

"Do not speak like that, Mr. Davies, or I shall go."

He stopped at once. "Don't go," he said imploringly. "Listen. You said that you would not marry me because you did not love me. Supposing that you learned to love me, say in a year's time, Beatrice, would you marry me then?"

"I would marry any man whom I loved," she answered.

"Then if you learn to love me you will marry me?"

"Oh, this is ridiculous," she said. "It is not probable, it is hardly possible, that such a thing should happen. If it had been going to happen it would have happened before."

"It might come about," he answered; "your heart might soften towards me. Oh, say yes to this. It is a small request, it costs you nothing, and it gives me hope, without which I cannot live. Say that I may ask you once more, and that then if you love me you will marry me."

Beatrice thought for a moment. Such a promise could do her no harm, and in the course of six months or a year he might get used to the idea of living without her. Also it would prevent a scene. It was weak of her, but she dreaded the idea of her having refused Owen Davies coming to her father's ears.

"If you wish it, Mr. Davies," she said, "so be it. Only I ask you to understand this, I am in no way tied to you. I give you no hope that my answer, should you renew this offer a year hence or at any other time, will differ from that I give you to-day. I do not think there is the slightest probability of such a thing. Also, it must be understood that you are not to speak to my father about this matter, or to trouble me in any way. Do you consent?"

"Yes," he answered, "I consent. You have me at your mercy."

"Very well. And now, Mr. Davies, good-bye. No, do not walk back with me. I had rather go by myself. But I want to say this: I am very sorry for what has happened. I have not wished it to happen. I have never encouraged it, and my hands are clean of it. But I am sorry, sorry beyond measure, and I repeat what I said before—seek out some other woman and marry her."

"That is the cruellest thing of all the cruel things which you have said," he answered.

"I did not mean it to be cruel, Mr. Davies, but I suppose that the truth often is. And now good-bye," and Beatrice stretched out her hand.

He touched it, and she turned and went. But Owen did not go. He sat upon the rock, his head bowed in misery. He had staked all his hopes upon this woman. She was the one desirable thing to him, the one star in his somewhat leaden sky, and now that star was eclipsed. Her words were unequivocal, they gave but little hope. Beatrice was scarcely a woman to turn round in six months or a year. On the contrary, there was a fixity about her which frightened him. What could be the cause of it? How came it that she should be so ready to reject him, and all he had to offer her? After all, she was a girl in a small position. She could not be looking forward to a better match. Nor would the prospect move her one way or another. There must be a reason for it. Perhaps he had a rival, surely that must be the cause. Some enemy had done this thing. But who?

At this moment a woman's shadow fell athwart him.

"Oh, have you come back?" he cried, springing to his feet.

"If you mean Beatrice," answered a voice—it was Elizabeth's—"she went down to the beach ten minutes ago. I happened to be on the cliff, and I saw her."

"Oh, I beg your pardon, Miss Granger," he said faintly. "I did not see who it was."

Elizabeth sat down upon the rock where her sister had sat, and, seeing the little holes in the breach, began indolently to clear them of the sand which Beatrice had swept over them with her foot. This was no difficult matter, for the holes were deeply dug, and it was easy to trace their position. Presently they were nearly all clear—that is, the letters were legible.

"You have had a talk with Beatrice, Mr. Davies?"

"Yes," he answered apathetically.

Elizabeth paused. Then she took her bull by the horns.

"Are you going to marry Beatrice, Mr. Davies?" she asked.

"I don't know," he answered slowly and without surprise. It seemed natural to him that his own central thought should be present in her mind. "I love her dearly, and want to marry her."

"She refused you, then?"

"Yes."

Elizabeth breathed more freely.

"But I can ask her again."

Elizabeth frowned. What could this mean? It was not an absolute refusal. Beatrice was playing some game of her own.

"Why did she put you off so, Mr. Davies? Do not think me inquisitive. I only ask because I may be able to help you."

"I know; you are very kind. Help me and I shall always be grateful to you. I do not know—I almost think that there must be somebody else, only I don't know who it can be."

"Ah!" said Elizabeth, who had been gazing intently at the little holes in the beach which she had now cleared of the sand. "Of course that is possible. She is a curious girl, Beatrice is. What are those letters, Mr. Davies?"

He looked at them idly. "Something your sister was writing while I talked to her. I remember seeing her do it."

"G E O F F R E—why, it must be meant for Geoffrey. Yes, of course it is possible that there is somebody else, Mr. Davies. Geoffrey!—how curious!"

"Why is it curious, Miss Granger? Who is Geoffrey?"

Elizabeth laughed a disagreeable little laugh that somehow attracted Owen's attention more than her words.

"How should I know? It must be some friend of Beatrice's, and one of whom she is thinking a great deal, or she would not write his name unconsciously. The only Geoffrey that I know is Mr. Geoffrey Bingham, the barrister, who is staying at the Vicarage, and whose life Beatrice saved." She paused to watch her companion's face, and saw a new idea creep across its stolidity. "But of course," she went on, "it cannot be Mr. Bingham that she was thinking of, because you see he is married."

"Married?" he said, "yes, but he's a man for all that, and a very handsome one."

"Yes, I should call him handsome—a fine man," Elizabeth answered critically; "but, as Beatrice said the other day, the great charm about him is his talk and power of mind. He is a very remarkable man, and the world will hear of him before he has done. But, however, all this is neither here nor there. Beatrice is a curious woman, and has strange ideas, but I am sure that she would never carry on with a married man."

"But he might carry on with her, Miss Elizabeth."

She laughed. "Do you really think that a man like Mr. Bingham would try to flirt with girls without encouragement? Men like that are as proud as women, and prouder; the lady must always be a step ahead. But what is the good of talking about such a thing? It is all nonsense. Beatrice must have been thinking of some other Geoffrey—or it was an accident of something. Why, Mr. Davies, if you for one moment really believed that dear Beatrice could be guilty of such a shameless thing as to carry on a flirtation with a married man, would you have asked her to marry you? Would you still think of asking such a woman as she must be to become your wife?"

"I don't know; I suppose not," he said doubtfully.

"You suppose not. I know you better than you know yourself. You would rather never marry at all than take such a woman as she would be proved to be. But it is no good talking such stuff. If you have a rival you may be sure it is some unmarried man."

Owen reflected in his heart that on the whole he would rather it was a married one, since a married man, at any rate, could not legally take possession of Beatrice. But Elizabeth's rigid morality alarmed him, and he did not say so.

"Do you know I feel a little upset, Miss Elizabeth," he answered. "I think I will be going. By the way, I promised to say nothing of this to your father. I hope that you will not do so, either."

"Most certainly not," said Elizabeth, and indeed it would be the last thing she would wish to do. "Well, good-bye, Mr. Davies. Do not be downhearted; it will all come right in the end. You will always have me to help you, remember."

"Thank you, thank you," he said earnestly, and went.

Elizabeth watched him round the wall of rock with a cold and ugly smile set upon her face.

"You fool," she thought, "you fool! To tell me that you 'love her dearly and want to marry her;' you want to get that sweet face of hers, do you? You never shall; I'd spoil it first! Dear Beatrice, she is not capable of carrying on a love affair with a married man—oh, certainly not! Why, she's in love with him already, and he is more than half in love with her. If she hadn't been, would she have put Owen off? Not she. Give them time, and we shall see. They will ruin each other—they must ruin each other; it won't be child's play when two people like that fall in love. They will not stop at sighs, there is too much human nature about them. It was a good idea to get him into the house. And to see her go on with that child Effie, just as though she was its mother—it makes me laugh. Ah, Beatrice, with all your wits you are a silly woman! And one day, my dear girl, I shall have the pleasure of exposing you to Owen; the idol will be unveiled, and there will be an end of your chances with him, for he can't marry you after that. Then my turn will come. It is a question of time—only a question of time!"

So brooded Elizabeth in her heart, madded with malicious envy and passionate jealousy. She loved this man, Owen Davies, as much as she could love anybody; at the least, she dearly loved the wealth and station of which he was the visible centre, and she hated the sister whom he desired. If she could only discredit that sister and show her to be guilty of woman's worst crime, misplaced, unlegalised affection, surely, she thought, Owen would reject her.

She was wrong. She did not know how entirely he desired to make Beatrice his wife, or realise how forgiving a man can be who has such an end to gain. It is of the women who already weary them and of their infidelity that men are so ready to make examples, not of those who do not belong to them, and whom they long for night and day. To these they can be very merciful.

CHAPTER XIII

GEOFFREY LECTURES

Meanwhile Beatrice was walking homewards with an uneasy mind. The trouble was upon her. She had, it is true, succeeded in postponing it a little, but she knew very well that it was only a postponement. Owen Davies was not a man to be easily shaken off. She almost wished now that she had crushed the idea once and for all. But then he would have gone to her father, and there must have been a scene, and she was weak enough to shrink from that, especially while Mr. Bingham was in the house. She could well imagine the dismay, not to say the fury, of her money-loving old father if he were to hear that she had refused—actually refused—Owen Davies of Bryngelly Castle, and all his wealth.

Then there was Elizabeth to be reckoned with. Elizabeth would assuredly make her life a burden to her. Beatrice little guessed that nothing would suit her sister's book better. Oh, if only she could shake the dust of Bryngelly off her feet! But that, too, was impossible. She was quite without money. She might, it was true, succeed in getting another place as mistress to a school in some distant part of England, were it not for an insurmountable obstacle. Here she received a salary of seventy-five pounds a year; of this she kept fifteen pounds, out of which slender sum she contrived to dress herself; the rest she gave to her father. Now, as she well knew, he could not keep his head above water without this assistance, which, small as it was, made all the difference to their household between poverty and actual want. If she went away, supposing even that she found an equally well-paid post, she would require every farthing of the money to support herself, there would be nothing left to send home. It was a pitiable position; here was she, who had just refused a man worth thousands a year, quite unable to get out of the way of his importunity for the want of seventy-five pounds, paid quarterly. Well, the only thing to do was to face it out and take her chance. On one point she was, however, quite clear; she would not marry Owen Davies. She might be a fool for her pains, but she would not do it. She respected herself too much to marry a man she did not love; a man whom she positively disliked. "No, never!" she exclaimed aloud, stamping her foot upon the shingle.

"Never what?" said a voice, within two yards of her.

She started violently, and looked round. There, his back resting against a rock, a pipe in his mouth, an open letter on his knee, and his hat drawn down almost over his eyes, sat Geoffrey. He had left Effie to go home with Mr. Granger, and climbing down a sloping place in the cliff, had strolled along the beach. The letter on his knee was one from his wife. It was short, and there was nothing particular in it. Effie's name was not even mentioned. It was to see if he had not overlooked it that he was reading the note through again. No, it merely related to Lady Honoria's safe arrival, gave a list of the people staying at the Hall—a fast lot, Geoffrey noticed, a certain Mr. Dunstan, whom he particularly disliked, among them—and the number of brace of partridges which had been killed on the previous day. Then came an assurance that Honoria was enjoying herself immensely, and that the new French cook was "simply perfect;" the letter ending "with love."

"Never what, Miss Granger?" he said again, as he lazily folded up the sheet.

"Never mind, of course," she answered, recovering herself. "How you startled me, Mr. Bingham! I had no idea there was anybody on the beach."

"It is quite free, is it not?" he answered, getting up. "I thought you were going to trample me into the pebbles. It's almost alarming when one is thinking about a Sunday nap to see a young lady striding along, then suddenly stop, stamp her foot, and say, 'No, never!' Luckily I knew that you were about or I should really have been frightened."

"How did you know that I was about?" Beatrice asked a little defiantly. It was no business of his to observe her movements.

"In two ways. Look!" he said, pointing to a patch of white sand. "That, I think, is your footprint."

"Well, what of it?" said Beatrice, with a little laugh.

"Nothing in particular, except that it is your footprint," he answered. "Then I happened to meet old Edward, who was loafing along, and he informed me that you and Mr. Davies had gone up the beach; there is his footprint—Mr. Davies's, I mean—but you don't seem to have been very sociable, because here is yours right in the middle of it. Therefore you must have been walking in Indian file, and a little way back in parallel lines, with quite thirty yards between you."

"Why do you take the trouble to observe things so closely?" she asked in a half amused and half angry tone.

"I don't know—a habit of the legal mind, I suppose. One might make quite a romance out of those footprints on the sand, and the little subsequent events. But you have not heard all my thrilling tale. Old Edward also informed me that he saw your sister, Miss Elizabeth, going along the cliff almost level with you, from which he concluded that you had argued as to the shortest way to the Red Rocks and were putting the matter to the proof."

"Elizabeth," said Beatrice, turning a shade paler; "what can she have been doing, I wonder."

"Taking exercise, probably, like yourself. Well, I seat myself with my pipe in the shadow of that rock, when suddenly I see Mr. Davies coming along towards Bryngelly as though he were walking for a wager, his hat fixed upon the back of his head. Literally he walked over my legs and never saw me. Then you follow and ejaculate, 'No, never!'—and that is the end of my story. Have I your permission to walk with you, or shall I interfere with the development of the plot?"

"There is no plot, and as you said just now the beach is free," Beatrice answered petulantly.

They walked on a few yards and then he spoke in another tone—the meaning of the assignation he had overheard in the churchyard grew clear to him now.

"I believe that I have to congratulate you, Miss Granger," he said, "and I do so very heartily. It is not everybody who is so fortunate as to—"

Beatrice stopped, and half turning faced him.

"What do you mean, Mr. Bingham?" she said. "I do not understand your dark sayings."

"Mean! oh, nothing particular, except that I wished to congratulate you on your engagement."

"My engagement! what engagement?"

"It seems that there is some mistake," he said, and struggle as he might to suppress it his tone was one of relief. "I understood that you had become engaged to be married to Mr. Owen Davies. If I am wrong I am sure I apologise."

"You are quite wrong, Mr. Bingham; I don't know who put such a notion into your head, but there is no truth in it."

"Then allow me to congratulate you on there being no truth in it. You see that is the beauty of nine affairs matrimonial out of ten—there are two or more sides of them. If they come off the amiable and disinterested observer can look at the bright side—as in this case, lots of money, romantic castle by the sea, gentleman of unexceptional antecedents, &c., &c, &c. If, on the other hand, they don't, cause can still be found for thankfulness—lady might do better after all, castle by the sea rather draughty and cold in spring, gentlemen most estimable but perhaps a little dull, and so on, you see."

There was a note of mockery about his talk which irritated Beatrice exceedingly. It was not like Mr. Bingham to speak so. It was not even the way that a gentleman out of his teens should speak to a lady on such a subject. He knew this as well as she did and was secretly ashamed of himself. But the truth must out: though Geoffrey did not admit it even to himself he was bitterly and profoundly jealous, and jealous people have no manners. Beatrice could not, however, be expected to know this, and naturally grew angry.

"I do not quite understand what you are talking about, Mr. Bingham," she said, putting on her most dignified air, and Beatrice could look rather alarming. "You have picked up a piece of unfounded gossip and now you take advantage of it to laugh at me, and to say rude things of Mr. Davies. It is not kind."

"Oh, no; it was the footsteps, Miss Granger, and the gossip, and the appointment you made in the churchyard, that I unwillingly overheard, not the gossip alone which led me into my mistake. Of course I have now to apologise."

Again Beatrice stamped her foot. She saw that he was still mocking her, and felt that he did not believe her.

"There," he went on, stung into unkindness by his biting but unacknowledged jealousy, for she was right—on reflection he did not quite believe what she said as to her not being engaged. "How unfortunate I am—I have said something to make you angry again. Why did you not walk with Mr. Davies? I should then have remained guiltless of offence, and you would have had a more agreeable companion. You want to quarrel with me; what shall we quarrel about? There are many things on which we are diametrically opposed; let us start one."

It was too much, for though his words were nothing the tone in which he spoke gave them a sting. Beatrice, already disturbed in mind by the scene through which she had passed, her breast already throbbing with a vague trouble of which she did not know the meaning, for once in her life lost control of herself and grew hysterical. Her grey eyes filled with tears, the corners of her sweet mouth dropped, and she looked very much as though she were going to burst out weeping.

"It is most unkind of you," she said, with a half sob. "If you knew how much I have to put up with, you would not speak to me like that. I know that you do not believe me; very well, I will tell you the truth. Yes, though I have no business to do it, and you have no right—none at all—to make me do it, I will tell you the truth, because I cannot bear that you should not believe me. Mr. Davies did want me to marry him and I refused him. I put him off for a while; I did this because I knew that if I did not he would go to my father. It was cowardly, but my father would make my life wretched—" and again she gave a half-choked sob.

Much has been said and written about the effect produced upon men by the sight of a lady in, or on the border line of tears, and there is no doubt that this effect is considerable. Man being in his right mind is deeply moved by such a spectacle, also he is frightened because he dreads a scene. Now most people would rather walk ten miles in their dress shoes than have to deal with a young lady in hysterics, however modified. Putting the peculiar circumstances of the case aside, Geoffrey was no exception to this rule. It was all very well to cross spears with Beatrice, who had quite an equal wit, and was very capable of retaliation, but to see her surrender at discretion was altogether another thing. Indeed he felt much ashamed of himself.

"Please don't—don't—be put out," he said. He did not like to use the word "cry." "I was only laughing at you, but I ought not to have spoken as I did. I did not wish to force your confidence, indeed I did not. I never thought of such a thing. I am so sorry."

His remorse was evidently genuine, and Beatrice felt somewhat appeased. Perhaps it did not altogether grieve her to learn that she could make him feel sorry.

"You did not force my confidence," she said defiantly, quite forgetting that a moment before she had reproached him for making her speak. "I told you because I did not choose that you should think I was not speaking the truth—and now let us change the subject." She imposed no reserve on him as to what she had revealed; she knew that there was no necessity to do so. The secret would be between them— another dangerous link.

Beatrice recovered her composure and they walked slowly on.

"Tell me, Mr. Bingham," she said presently, "how can a woman earn her living—I mean a girl like myself without any special qualifications? Some of them get on."

"Well," he answered, "that depends upon the girl. What sort of a living do you mean? You are earning a living now, of a kind."

"Yes, but sometimes, if only I could manage it, I think that I should like to get away from here, and take another line, something bigger. I do not suppose that I ever shall, but I like to think of it sometimes."

"I only know of two things which a woman can turn to," he said, "the stage and literature. Of course," he added hastily, "the first is out of the question in your case."

"And so is the other, I am afraid," she answered shaking her head, "that is if by literature you mean imaginative writing, and I suppose that is the only way to get into notice. As I told you I lost my imagination—well, to be frank, when I lost my faith. At one time I used to have plenty, as I used to have plenty of faith, but the one went with the other, I do not understand why."

"Don't you? I think I do. A mind without religious sentiment is like a star without atmosphere, brighter than other stars but not so soft to see. Religion, poetry, music, imagination, and even some of the more exalted forms of passion, flourish in the same soil, and are, I sometimes think, different manifestations of the same thing. Do you know it is ridiculous to hear you talk of having lost your faith, because I don't believe it. At the worst it has gone to sleep, and will wake up again one day. Possibly you may not accept some particular form of faith, but I tell you frankly that to reject all religion simply because you cannot understand it, is nothing but a form of atrocious spiritual vanity. Your mind is too big for you, Miss Granger: it has run away with you, but you know it is tied by a string—it cannot go far. And now perhaps you will be angry again."

"No, indeed, why should I be angry? I daresay that you are quite right, and I only hope that I may be able to believe again. I will tell you how I lost belief. I had a little brother whom I loved more than anything else in the world, indeed after my mother died he was the only thing I really had to love, for I think that my father cares more for Elizabeth than he does for me, she is so much the better at business matters, and Elizabeth and I never quite got on. I daresay that the fault is mine, but the fact remains—we are sisters but we are not intimate. Well, my brother fell ill of a fever, and for a long time he lay between life and death, and I prayed for him as I never prayed for anybody or anything before—yes, I prayed that I might die instead of him. Then he passed through the crisis and got better, and I thanked God, thinking that my prayers had been answered; oh, how happy I was for those ten days! And then this happened:— My brother got a chill, a relapse followed, and in three days he was dead. The last words that he spoke to me were, 'Oh, don't let me die, Bee!'—he used to call me Bee—'Please don't let me die, dear Bee!' But he died, died in my arms, and when it was over I rose from his side feeling as though my heart was dead also. I prayed no more after that. It seemed to me as though my prayers had been mocked at, as though he had been given back to me for a little while in order that the blow might be more crushing when it fell."

"Don't you think that you were a little foolish in taking such a view?" said Geoffrey. "Have you not been amused, sometimes, to read about the early Christians?—how the lead would not boil the martyr, or the lion would not eat him, or the rain from a blue sky put out the fire, and how the pagan king at once was converted and accepted a great many difficult doctrines without further delay. The Athanasian Creed was not necessarily true because the fire would not light or the sword would not cut, nor, excuse me, were all your old beliefs wrong because your prayer was unanswered. It is an ancient story, that we cannot tell whether the answering of our petitions will be good or ill for us. Of course I do not know anything about such things, but it seems to me rash to suppose that Providence is going to alter the working of its eternal laws merely to suit the passing wishes of individuals—wishes, too, that in many cases would bring unforeseen sorrows if fulfilled. Besides I daresay that the poor child is happier dead than he would have been had he lived. It is not an altogether pleasant world for most of us."

"Yes, Mr. Bingham, I know, and I daresay that I should have got over the shock in time, only after that I began to read. I read the histories of the religions and compared them, and I read the works of those writers who have risen up to attack them. I found, or I thought that I found, the same springs of superstition in them all—superstitions arising from elementary natural causes, and handed on with variations from race to race, and time to time. In some I found the same story, only with a slightly altered face, and I learned, moreover, that each faith denied the other, and claimed truth for itself alone.

"After that, too, I went to the college and there I fell in with a lady, one of the mistresses, who was the cleverest woman that I ever knew, and in her way a good woman, but one who believed that religion was the curse of the world, and who spent all her spare time in attacking it in some form or other. Poor thing, she is dead now. And so, you see, what between these causes and the continual spectacle of human misery which to my mind negatives the idea of a merciful and watching Power, at last it came to pass that the only altar left in my temple is an altar to the 'Unknown God.'"

Geoffrey, like most men who have had to think on these matters, did not care to talk about them much, especially to women. For one thing, he was conscious of a tendency to speech less reverent than his thought. But he had not entered Beatrice's church of Darkness, indeed he had turned his back on it for ever, though, like most people, he had at different periods of his past life tarried an hour in its porch. So he ventured on an objection.

"I am no theologian," he said, "and I am not fond of discussion on such matters. But there are just one or two things I should like to say. It is no argument, to my mind at least, to point to the existence of evil and unhappiness among men as a proof of the absence of a superior Mercy; for what are men that such things should not be with them? Man, too, must own some master. If he has doubts let him look up at the marshalling of the starry heaven, and they will vanish."

"No," said Beatrice, "I fear not. Kant said so, but before that Molière had put the argument in the mouth of a fool. The starry heavens no more prove anything than does the running of the raindrops down the window-pane. It is not a question of size and quantity."

"I might accept the illustration," answered Geoffrey; "one example of law is as good as another for my purpose. I see in it all the working of a living Will, but of course that is only my way of looking at it, not yours."

"No; I am afraid," said Beatrice, "all this reasoning drawn from material things does not touch me. That is how the Pagans made their religions, and it is how Paley strives to prove his. They argued from the Out to the In, from the material to the spiritual. It cannot be; if Christianity is true it must stand upon spiritual feet and speak with a spiritual voice, to be heard, not in the thunderstorm, but only in the hearts of men. The existence of Creative Force does not demonstrate the existence of a Redeemer; if anything, it tends to negative it, for the power that creates is also the power which destroys. What does touch me, however, is the thought of the multitude of the Dead. That is what we care for, not for an Eternal Force, ever creating and destroying. Think of them all—all the souls of unheard-of races, almost animal, who passed away so long ago. Can ours endure more than theirs, and do you think that the spirit of an Ethiopian who died in the time of Moses is anywhere now?"

"There was room for them all on earth," answered Geoffrey. "The universe is wide. It does not dismay me. There are mysteries in our nature, the nature we think we know—shall there be none in that which we know not? Worlds die, to live again when, after millions of ages, the conditions become once more favourable to life, and why should not a man? We are creatures of the world, we reflect its every light and shadow, we rejoice in its rejoicing, its every feature has a tiny parallel in us. Why should not our fate be as its fate, and its fate is so far as we know eternal. It may change from gas to chaos, from chaos to active life, from active life to seeming death. Then it may once more pass into its elements, and from those elements back again to concrete being, and so on for ever, always changing, but always the same. So much for nature's allegory. It is not a perfect analogy, for Man is a thing apart from all things else; it may be only a hint or a type, but it is something.

"Now to come to the question of our religion. I confess I draw quite a different conclusion from your facts. You say that you trace the same superstitions in all religions, and that the same spiritual myths are in some shape present in almost all. Well, does not this suggest that the same great truth underlies them all, taking from time to time the shape which is best suited to the spiritual development of those professing each. Every great new religion is better than the last. You cannot compare Osirianism with Buddhism, or Buddhism with Christianity, or Mahomedanism with the Arabian idol worship. Take the old illustration—take a cut crystal and hold it in the sun, and you will see many different coloured rays come from its facets. They look different, but they are all born of the same great light; they are all the same light. May it not be so with religion? Let your altar be to the 'Unknown God,' if you like—for who can give an unaltering likeness to the Power above us?—but do not knock your altar down.

"Depend upon it, Miss Granger, all indications to the contrary notwithstanding, there is a watching Providence without the will of which we cannot live, and if we deliberately reject that Providence, setting up our intelligence in its place, sorrow will come of it, even here; for it is wiser than we. I wish that you would try and look at the question from another point of view—from a higher point of view. I think you will find that it will bear a great deal of examination, and that you will come to the conclusion that the dictum of the wise-acre who says there is nothing because he can see nothing, is not necessarily a true one. There, that is all I have to say, and I wish that I could say it better."

"Thank you," said Beatrice, "I will. Why here we are at home; I must go and put Effie to bed."

And here it may be stated that Geoffrey's advice was not altogether thrown away. Beatrice did try looking at the question again, and if Faith did not altogether come back to her at least Hope did, and "the greatest of these, which is Charity," had never deserted her. Hope came slowly back, not by argument probably, but rather by example. In the sea of Doubt she saw another buoyed up, if it were but on broken pieces of the ship. This encouraged her. Geoffrey believed, and she—believed in Geoffrey. Indeed, is not this the secret of woman's philosophy—even, to some extent, of that of such a woman as Beatrice? "Let the faith or unfaith of This, That, or the other Rabbi answer for me," she says— it is her last argument. She believes in This, or That, or some other philosopher: that is her creed. And Geoffrey was the person in whom Beatrice began to believe, all the more wholly because she had never believed in any one before. Whatever else she was to lose, this at least she won when she saved his life.

CHAPTER XIV

DRIFTING

On the day following their religious discussion an accident happened which resulted in Geoffrey and Beatrice being more than ever thrown in the company of each other. During the previous week two cases of scarlatina had been reported among the school children, and now it was found that the complaint had spread so much that it was necessary to close the school. This meant, of course, that Beatrice had all her time upon her hands. And so had Geoffrey. It was his custom to bathe before breakfast, after which he had nothing to do for the rest of the day. Beatrice with little Effie also bathed before breakfast from the ladies' bathing-place, a quarter of a mile off, and sometimes he would meet her as she returned, glowing with health and beauty like Venus new risen from the Cyprian sea, her half-dried hair hanging in heavy masses down her back. Then after breakfast they would take Effie down to the beach, and her "auntie," as the child learned to call Beatrice, would teach her lessons and poetry till she was tired, and ran away to paddle in the sea or look for prawns among the rocks.

Meanwhile the child's father and Beatrice would talk—not about religion, they spoke no more on that subject, nor about Owen Davies, but of everything else on earth. Beatrice was a merry woman when she was happy, and they never lacked subjects of conversation, for their minds were very much in tune. In book-learning Beatrice had the advantage of Geoffrey, for she had not only read enormously, she also remembered what she read and could apply it. Her critical faculty, too, was very keen. He, on the other hand, had more knowledge of the world, and in his rich days had travelled a good deal, and so it came to pass that each could always find something to tell the other. Never for one second were they dull, not even when they sat for an hour or so in silence, for it was the silence of complete companionship.

So the long morning would wear away all too quickly, and they would go in to dinner, to be greeted with a cold smile by Elizabeth and heartily enough by the old gentleman, who never thought of anything out of his own circle of affairs. After dinner it was the same story. Either they went walking to look for ferns and flowers, or perhaps Geoffrey took his gun and hid behind the rocks for curlew, sending Beatrice, who knew the coast by heart, a mile round or more to some headland in order to put them on the wing. Then she would come back, springing towards him from rock to rock, and crouch down beneath a neighbouring seaweed-covered boulder, and they would talk together in whispers, or perhaps they would not talk at all, for fear lest they should frighten the flighting birds. And Geoffrey would first search the heavens for curlew or duck, and, seeing none, would let his eyes fall upon the pure beauty of Beatrice's face, showing so clearly against the tender sky, and wonder what she was thinking about; till, suddenly feeling his gaze, she would turn with a smile as sweet as the first rosy blush of dawn upon the waters, and ask him what he was thinking about. And he would laugh and answer "You," whereon she would smile again and perhaps blush a little, feeling glad at heart, she knew not why.

Then came tea-time and the quiet, when they sat at the open window, and Geoffrey smoked and listened to the soft surging of the sea and the harmonious whisper of the night air in the pines. In the corner Mr. Granger slept in his armchair, or perhaps he had gone to bed altogether, for he liked to go to bed at half-past eight, as the old Herefordshire farmer, his father, had done before him; and at the far end of the room sat Elizabeth, doing her accounts by the light of a solitary candle, or, if they failed her, reading some book of a devotional and inspired character. But over the edge of the book, or from the page of crabbed accounts, her eyes would glance continually towards the handsome pair in the window-place, and she would smile as she saw that it went well. Only they never saw the glances or noted the smile. When Geoffrey looked that way, which was not often, for Elizabeth—old Elizabeth, as he always called her to himself—did not attract him, all he saw was her sharp but capable-looking form bending over her work, and the light of the candle gleaming on her straw-coloured hair and falling in gleaming white patches on her hard knuckles.

And so the happy day would pass and bed-time come, and with it unbidden dreams.

Geoffrey thought no ill of all this, as of course he ought to have thought. He was not the ravening lion of fiction—so rarely, if ever, to be met with in real life—going about seeking whom he might devour. He had absolutely no designs on Beatrice's affections, any more than she had on his, and he had forgotten that first fell prescience of evil to come. Once or twice, it is true, qualms of doubt did cross his mind in the earlier days of their intimacy. But he put them by as absurd. He was no believer in the tender helplessness of full-grown women, his experience having been that they are amply capable—and, for the most part, more than capable—of looking after themselves. It seemed to him a thing ridiculous that such a person as Beatrice, who was competent to form opinions and a judgment upon all the important questions of life, should be treated as a child, and that he should remove himself from Bryngelly lest her young affections should become entangled. He felt sure that they would never be entrapped in any direction whatsoever without her full consent.

Then he ceased to think about the matter at all. Indeed, the mere idea of such a thing involved a supposition that would only have been acceptable to a conceited man—namely, that there was a possibility of this young lady's falling in love with him. What right had he to suppose anything of the sort? It was an impertinence. That there was another sort of possibility—namely, of his becoming more attached to her than was altogether desirable—did, however, occur to him once or twice. But he shrugged his shoulders and put it by. After all, it was his look out, and he did not much care. It would do her no harm at the worst. But very soon all these shadowy forebodings of dawning trouble vanished quite. They were lost in the broad, sweet lights of friendship. By-and-by, when friendship's day was done, they might arise again, called by other names and wearing a sterner face.

It was ridiculous—of course it was ridiculous; he was not going to fall in love like a boy at his time of life; all he felt was gratitude and interest—all she felt was amusement in his society. As for the intimacy—felt rather than expressed—the intimacy that could already almost enable the one to divine the other's thought, that could shape her mood to his and his to hers, that could cause the same thing of beauty to be a common joy, and discover unity of mind in opinions the most opposite—why, it was only natural between people who had together passed a peril terrible to think of. So they took the goods the gods provided, and drifted softly on—whither they did not stop to inquire.

One day, however, a little incident happened that ought to have opened the eyes of both. They had arranged, or rather there was a tacit understanding, that they should go out together in the afternoon. Geoffrey was to take his gun and Beatrice a book, but it chanced that, just before dinner, as she walked back from the village, where she had gone to buy some thread to mend Effie's clothes, Beatrice came face to face with Mr. Davies. It was their first meeting without witnesses since the Sunday of which the events have been described, and, naturally, therefore, rather an awkward one. Owen stopped short so that she could not pass him with a bow, and then turned and walked beside her. After a remark or two about the weather, the springs of conversation ran dry.

"You remember that you are coming up to the Castle this afternoon?" he said, at length.

"To the Castle!" she answered. "No, I have heard nothing of it."

"Did not your sister tell you she made an engagement for herself and you a week or more ago? You are to bring the little girl; she wants to see the view from the top of the tower."

Then Beatrice remembered. Elizabeth had told her, and she had thought it best to accept the situation. The whole thing had gone out of her mind.

"Oh, I beg your pardon! I do remember now, but I have made another plan—how stupid of me!"

"You had forgotten," he said in his heavy voice; "it is easy for you to forget what I have been looking forward to for a whole week. What is your plan—to go out walking with Mr. Bingham, I suppose?"

"Yes," answered Beatrice, "to go out with Mr. Bingham."

"Ah! you go out with Mr. Bingham every day now."

"And what if I do?" said Beatrice quickly; "surely, Mr. Davies, I have a right to go out with whom I like?"

"Yes, of course; but the engagement to come to the Castle was made first; are you not going to keep it?"

"Of course I am going to keep it; I always keep my engagements when I have any."

"Very well, then; I shall expect you at three o'clock."

Beatrice went on home in a curiously irritated condition of mind. She did not, naturally, want to go to the Castle, and she did want to go out with Geoffrey. However, there was no help for it.

When she came in to dinner she found that Geoffrey was not there. He had, it seemed, gone to lunch with Dr. Chambers, whom he had met on the beach. Before he returned they were all three starting for the Castle, Beatrice leaving a message to this effect with Betty.

About a quarter of an hour afterwards, Geoffrey came back to fetch his gun and Beatrice, but Beatrice was gone, and all that he could extract from Betty was that she had gone to see Mr. Davies.

He was perfectly furious, though all the while he knew how unreasonable was his anger. He had been looking forward to the expedition, and this sudden change of plan was too much for his temper. Off he started, however, to pass a thoroughly miserable afternoon. He seemed to miss Beatrice more each step and gradually to grow more and more angry at what he called her "rudeness." Of course it never occurred to him that what he was really angry at was her going to see Mr. Davies, or that, in truth, her society had become so delightful to him that to be deprived of it even for an afternoon was to be wretched. To top everything, he only got three good shots that afternoon, and he missed them all, which made him crosser than ever.

As for Beatrice, she enjoyed herself just as little at the Castle as Geoffrey did on the beach. Owen Davies took them through the great unused rooms and showed them the pictures, but she had seen them before, and though some of them were very fine, did not care to look at them again—at any rate, not that afternoon. But Elizabeth gazed at them with eager eyes and mentally appraised their value, wondering if they would ever be hers.

"What is this picture?" she asked, pointing to a beautiful portrait of a Dutch Burgomaster by Rembrandt.

"That," answered Davies heavily, for he knew nothing of painting and cared less, "that is a Velasquez, valued for probate at £3,000—no," referring to the catalogue and reading, "I beg your pardon, the next is the Velasquez; that is a Rembrandt in the master's best style, showing all his wonderful mastery over light and shade. It was valued for probate at £4,000 guineas."

"Four thousand guineas!" said Elizabeth, "fancy having a thing worth four thousand guineas hanging on a wall!"

And so they went on, Elizabeth asking questions and Owen answering them by the help of the catalogue, till, to Beatrice's relief, they came at length to the end of the pictures. Then they took some tea in the little sitting room of the master of all this magnificence. Owen, to her great annoyance, sat opposite to Beatrice, staring at her with all his eyes while she drank her tea, with Effie sitting in her lap, and Elizabeth, observing it, bit her lip in jealousy. She had thought it well to bring her sister here; it would not do to let Mr. Davies think she was keeping Beatrice out of his way, but his mute idol worship was trying to her feelings. After tea they went to the top of the tower, and Effie rejoiced exceedingly in the view, which was very beautiful. Here Owen got a word with Elizabeth.

"Your sister seems to be put out about something," he said.

"I daresay," she answered carelessly; "Beatrice has an uncertain temper. I think she wanted to go out shooting with Mr. Bingham this afternoon."

Had Owen been a less religious person he might have sworn; as it was, he only said, "Mr. Bingham—it is always Mr. Bingham from morning to night! When is he going away?"

"In another week, I believe. Beatrice will be sorry, I think; she makes a great companion of him. And now I think that we must be getting home," and she went, leaving this poisoned shaft to rankle in his breast.

After they had returned to the vicarage and Beatrice had heard Effie her prayers and tucked her up in her small white bed, she went down to the gate to be quiet for a little while before supper. Geoffrey had not yet come in.

It was a lovely autumn evening; the sea seemed to sleep, and the little clouds, from which the sunset fires had paled, lay like wreaths of smoke upon the infinite blue sky. Why had not Mr. Bingham come back, she wondered; he would scarcely have time to dress. Supposing that an accident had happened to him. Nonsense! what accident could happen? He was so big and strong he seemed to defy accidents; and yet had it not been for her there would be little enough left of his strength to-day. Ah! she was glad that she had lived to be able to save him from death. There he came, looming like a giant in the evening mist.

There was a small hand-gate beside the large one on which she leant. Geoffrey stalked straight up to it as though he did not see her; he saw her well enough, but he was cross with her.

She allowed him to pass through the gate, which he shut slowly, perhaps to give her an opportunity of speaking, if she wished to do so; then thinking that he did not see her she spoke in her soft, musical voice.

"Did you have good sport, Mr. Bingham?"

"No," he answered shortly; "I saw very little, and I missed all I saw."

"I am so sorry, except for the birds. I hate the birds to be killed. Did you not see me in this white dress? I saw you fifty yards away."

"Yes, Miss Granger," he answered, "I saw you."

"And you were going by without speaking to me; it was very rude of you—what is the matter?"

"Not so rude as it was of you to arrange to walk out with me and then to go and see Mr. Davies instead."

"I could not help it, Mr. Bingham; it was an old engagement, which I had forgotten."

"Quite so, ladies generally have an excuse for doing what they want to do."

"It is not an excuse, Mr. Bingham," Beatrice answered, with dignity; "there is no need for me to make excuses to you about my movements."

"Of course not, Miss Granger; but it would be more polite to tell me when you change your mind—next time, you know. However, I have no doubt that the Castle has attractions for you."

She flashed one look at him and turned to go, and as she did so his heart relented; he grew ashamed.

"Miss Granger, don't go; forgive me. I do not know what has become of my manners, I spoke as I should not. The fact is, I was put out at your not coming. To tell you the honest truth, I missed you dreadfully."

"You missed me. That is very nice of you; one likes to be missed. But, if you missed me for one afternoon, how will you get on a week hence when you go away and miss me altogether?"

Beatrice spoke in a bantering tone, and laughed as she spoke, but the laugh ended in something like a sigh. He looked at her for a moment, looked till she dropped her eyes.

"Heaven only knows!" he answered sadly.

"Let us go in," said Beatrice, in a constrained voice; "how chill the air has turned."

CHAPTER XV

ONLY GOOD-NIGHT

Five more days passed, all too quickly, and once more Monday came round. It was the 22nd of October, and the Michaelmas Sittings began on the 24th. On the morrow, Tuesday, Geoffrey was to return to London, there to meet Lady Honoria and get to work at Chambers. That very morning, indeed, a brief, the biggest he had yet received—it was marked thirty guineas—had been forwarded to him from his chambers, with a note from his clerk to the effect that the case was expected to be in the special jury list on the first day of the sittings, and that the clerk had made an appointment for him with the solicitors for 5.15 on the Tuesday. The brief was sent to him by his uncle's firm, and marked, "With you the Attorney-General, and Mr. Candleton, Q.C.," the well-known leader of the Probate and Divorce Court Bar. Never before had Geoffrey found himself in such honourable company, that is on the back of a brief, and not a little was he elated thereby.

But when he came to look into the case his joy abated somewhat, for it was one of the most perplexing that he had ever known. The will contested, which was that of a Yorkshire money-lender, disposed of property to the value of over £80,000, and was propounded by a niece of the testator who, when he died, if not actually weak in his mind, was in his dotage, and superstitious to the verge of insanity. The niece to whom all the property was left—to the exclusion of the son and daughter of the deceased, both married, and living away from home—stayed with the testator and looked after him. Shortly before his death, however, he and this niece had violently quarrelled on account of an intimacy which the latter had formed with a married man of bad repute, who was a discharged lawyer's clerk. So serious had been the quarrel that only three days before his death the testator had sent for a lawyer and formally, by means of a codicil, deprived the niece of a sum of £2,000 which he had left her, all the rest of his property being divided between his son and daughter. Three days afterwards, however, he duly executed a fresh will, in the presence of two servants, by which he left all his property to the niece, to the entire exclusion of his own children. This will, though very short, was in proper form and was written by nobody knew whom. The servants stated that the testator before signing it was perfectly acquainted with its contents, for the niece had made him repeat them in their presence. They also declared, however, that he seemed in a terrible fright, and said twice, "It's behind me; it's behind me!"

Within an hour of the signing of the will the testator was found dead, apparently from the effects of fear, but the niece was not in the room at the time of death. The only other remarkable circumstance in the case was that the disreputable lover of the niece had been seen hanging about the house at dusk, the testator having died at ten o'clock at night. There was also a further fact. The son, on receiving a message from the niece that his father was seriously worse, had hurried with extraordinary speed to the house, passing some one or something—he could not tell what—that seemed to be running, apparently from the window of the sick man's room, which was on the ground floor, and beneath which footmarks were afterwards found. Of these footmarks two casts had been taken, of which photographs were forwarded with the brief. They had been made by naked feet of small size, and in each case the little joint of the third toe of the right foot seemed to be missing. But all attempts to find the feet that made them had hitherto failed. The will was contested by the next of kin, for whom Geoffrey was one of the counsel, upon the usual grounds of undue influence and fraud; but as it seemed at present with small prospect of success, for, though the circumstances were superstitious enough, there was not the slightest evidence of either. This curious case, of which the outlines are here written, is briefly set out, because it proved to be the foundation of Geoffrey's enormous practice and reputation at the Bar.

He read the brief through twice, thought it over well, and could make little of it. It was perfectly obvious to him that there had been foul play somewhere, but he found himself quite unable to form a workable hypothesis. Was the person who had been seen running away concerned in the matter?—if it was a person. If so, was he the author of the footprints? Of course the ex-lawyer's clerk had something to do with it, but what? In vain did Geoffrey cudgel his brains; every idea that occurred to him broke down somewhere or other.

"We shall lose this," he said aloud in despair; "suspicious circumstances are not enough to upset a will," and then, addressing Beatrice, who was sitting at the table, working:

"Here, Miss Granger, you have a smattering of law, see if you can make anything of this," and he pushed the heavy brief towards her.

Beatrice took it with a laugh, and for the next three-quarters of an hour her fair brow was puckered up in a way quaint to see. At last she finished and shut the brief up. "Let me look at the photographs," she said.

Geoffrey handed them to her. She very carefully examined first one and then the other, and as she did so a light of intelligence broke out upon her face.

"Well, Portia, have you got it?" he asked.

"I have got something," she answered. "I do not know if it is right. Don't you see, the old man was superstitious; they frightened him first of all by a ghostly voice or some such thing into signing the will, and then to death after he had signed it. The lawyer's clerk prepared the will—he would know how to do it. Then he was smuggled into the room under the bed, or somewhere, dressed up as a ghost perhaps. The sending for the son by the niece was a blind. The thing that was seen running away was a boy—those footprints were made by a boy. I have seen so many thousands on the sands here that I could swear to it. He was attracted to the house from the road, which was quite near, by catching sight of something unusual through the blind; the brief says there were no curtains or shutters. Now look at the photographs of the footprints. See in No. 1, found outside the window, the toes are pressed down deeply into the mud. The owner of the feet was standing on tip-toe to get a better view. But in No. 2, which was found near where the son thought he saw a person running, the toes are spread out quite wide. That is the footprint of some one who was in a great hurry. Now it is not probable that a boy had anything to do with the testator's death. Why, then, was the boy running so hard? I will tell you: because he was frightened at something he had seen through the blind. So frightened was he, that he will not come forward, or answer the advertisements and inquiries. Find a boy in that town who has a joint missing on the third toe of the right foot, and you will soon know all about it."

"By Jove," said Geoffrey, "what a criminal lawyer you would make! I believe that you have got it. But how are we to find this boy with the missing toe-joint? Every possible inquiry has already been made and failed. Nobody has seen such a boy, whose deficiency would probably be known by his parents, or schoolfellows."

"Yes," said Beatrice, "it has failed because the boy has taken to wearing shoes, which indeed he would always have to do at school. His parents, if he has any, would perhaps not speak of his disfigurement, and no one else might know of it, especially if he were a new-comer in the neighbourhood. It is quite possible that he took off his boots in order to creep up to the window. And now I will tell you how I should set to work to find him. I should have every bathing-place in the river running through the town—there is a river—carefully watched by detectives. In this weather" (the autumn was an unusually warm one) "boys of that class often paddle and sometimes bathe. If they watch close enough, they will probably find a boy with a missing toe joint among the number."

"What a good idea," said Geoffrey. "I will telegraph to the lawyers at once. I certainly believe that you have got the clue."

And as it turned out afterwards Beatrice had got it; her suppositions were right in almost every particular. The boy, who proved to be the son of a pedlar who had recently come into the town, was found wading, and by a clever trick, which need not be detailed, frightened into telling the truth, as he had previously frightened himself into holding his tongue. He had even, as Beatrice conjectured, taken off his boots to creep up to the window, and as he ran away in his fright, had dropped them into a ditch full of water. There they were found, and went far to convince the jury of the truth of his story. Thus it was that Beatrice's quick wit laid the foundations of Geoffrey's great success.

This particular Monday was a field day at the Vicarage. Jones had proved obdurate; no power on earth could induce him to pay the £34 11s. 4d. due on account of tithe. Therefore Mr. Granger, fortified by a judgment duly obtained, had announced his intention of distraining upon Jones's hay and cattle. Jones had replied with insolent defiance. If any bailiff, or auctioneer, or such people came to sell his hay he would kill him, or them.

So said Jones, and summoned his supporters, many of whom owed tithe, and none of whom wished to pay it, to do battle in his cause. For his part, Mr. Granger retained an auctioneer of undoubted courage who was to arrive on this very afternoon, supported by six policemen, and carry out the sale. Beatrice felt nervous about the whole thing, but Elizabeth was very determined, and the old clergyman was now bombastic and now despondent. The auctioneer arrived duly by the one o'clock train. He was a tall able-bodied man, not unlike Geoffrey in appearance, indeed at twenty yards distance it would have been difficult to tell them apart. The sale was fixed for half-past two, and Mr. Johnson—that was the auctioneer's name—went to the inn to get his dinner before proceeding to business. He was informed of the hostile demonstration which awaited him, and that an English member of Parliament had been sent down especially to head the mob, but being a man of mettle pooh-poohed the whole affair.

"All bark, sir," he said to Geoffrey, "all bark and no bite; I'm not afraid of these people. Why, if they won't bid for the stuff, I will buy it in myself."

"All right," said Geoffrey, "but I advise you to look out. I fancy that the old man is a rough customer."

Then Geoffrey went back to his dinner.

As they sat at the meal, through a gap in the fir trees they saw that the great majority of the population of Bryngelly was streaming up towards the scene of the sale, some to agitate, and some to see the fun.

"It is pretty well time to be off," said Geoffrey. "Are you coming, Mr. Granger?"

"Well," answered the old gentleman, "I wished to do so, but Elizabeth thinks that I had better keep away. And after all, you know," he added airily, "perhaps it is as well for a clergyman not to mix himself up too much in these temporal matters. No, I want to go and see about some pigs at the other end of the parish, and I think that I shall take this opportunity."

"You are not going, Mr. Bingham, are you?" asked Beatrice in a voice which betrayed her anxiety.

"Oh, yes," he answered, "of course I am. I would not miss the chance for worlds. Why, Beecham Bones is going to be there, the member of Parliament who has just done his four months for inciting to outrage. We are old friends; I was at school with him. Poor fellow, he was mad even in those days, and I want to chaff him."

"I think that you had far better not go, Mr. Bingham," said Beatrice; "they are a very rough set."

"Everybody is not so cowardly as you are," put in Elizabeth. "I am going at any rate."

"That's right, Miss Elizabeth," said Geoffrey; "we will protect each other from the revolutionary fury of the mob. Come, it is time to start."

And so they went, leaving Beatrice a prey to melancholy forebodings.

She waited in the house for the best part of an hour, making pretence to play with Effie. Then her anxiety got the better of her; she put on her hat and started, leaving Effie in charge of the servant Betty.

Beatrice walked quickly along the cliff till she came in sight of Jones's farm. From where she stood she could make out a great crowd of men, and even, when the wind turned towards her, catch the noise of shouting. Presently she heard a sound like the report of a gun, saw the crowd break up in violent confusion, and then cluster together again in a dense mass.

"What could it mean?" Beatrice wondered.

As the thought crossed her mind, she perceived two men running towards her with all their speed, followed by a woman. Three minutes more and she saw that the woman was Elizabeth.

The men were passing her now.

"What is it?" she cried.

"Murder!" they answered with one voice, and sped on towards Bryngelly.

Another moment and Elizabeth was at hand, horror written on her pale face.

Beatrice clutched at her. "Who is it?" she cried.

"Mr. Bingham," gasped her sister. "Go and help; he's shot dead!" And she too was gone.

Beatrice's knees loosened, her tongue clave to the roof of her mouth; the solid earth spun round and round. "Geoffrey killed! Geoffrey killed!" she cried in her heart; but though her ears seemed to hear the sound of them, no words came from her lips. "Oh, what should she do? Where should she hide herself in her grief?"

A few yards from the path grew a stunted tree with a large flat stone at its root. Thither Beatrice staggered and sank upon the stone, while still the solid earth spun round and round.

Presently her mind cleared a little, and a keener pang of pain shot through her soul. She had been stunned at first, now she felt.

"Perhaps it was not true; perhaps Elizabeth had been mistaken or had only said it to torment her." She rose. She flung herself upon her knees, there by the stone, and prayed, this first time for many years—she prayed with all her soul. "Oh, God, if Thou art, spare him his life and me this agony." In her dreadful pangs of grief her faith was thus re-born, and, as all human beings must in their hour of mortal agony, Beatrice realised her dependence on the Unseen. She rose, and weak with emotion sank back on to the stone. The people were streaming past her now, talking excitedly. Somebody came up to her and stood over her.

Oh, Heaven, it was Geoffrey!

"Is it you?" she gasped. "Elizabeth said that you were murdered."

"No, no. It was not I; it is that poor fellow Johnson, the auctioneer. Jones shot him. I was standing next him. I suppose your sister thought that I fell. He was not unlike me, poor fellow."

Beatrice looked at him, went red, went white, then burst into a flood of tears.

A strange pang seized upon his heart. It thrilled through him, shaking him to the core. Why was this woman so deeply moved? Could it be—? Nonsense; he stifled the thought before it was born.

"Don't cry," Geoffrey said, "the people will see you, Beatrice" (for the first time he called her by her christian name); "pray do not cry. It distresses me. You are upset, and no wonder. That fellow Beecham Bones ought to be hanged, and I told him so. It is his work, though he never meant it to go so far. He's frightened enough now, I can tell you."

Beatrice controlled herself with an effort.

"What happened," he said, "I will tell you as we walk along. No, don't go up to the farm. He is not a pleasant sight, poor fellow. When I got up there, Beecham Bones was spouting away to the mob—his long hair flying about his back—exciting them to resist laws made by brutal thieving landlords, and all that kind of gibberish; telling them that they would be supported by a great party in Parliament, &c., &c. The people, however, took it all good-naturedly enough. They had a beautiful effigy of your father swinging on a pole, with a placard on his breast, on which was written, 'The robber of the widow and the orphan,' and they were singing Welsh songs. Only I saw Jones, who was more than half drunk, cursing and swearing in Welsh and English. When the auctioneer began to sell, Jones went into the house and Bones went with him. After enough had been sold to pay the debt, and while the mob was still laughing and shouting, suddenly the back door of the house opened and out rushed Jones, now quite drunk, a gun in his hand and Bones hanging on to his coat-tails. I was talking to the auctioneer at the moment, and my belief is that the brute thought that I was Johnson. At any rate, before anything could be done he lifted the gun and fired, at me, as I think. The charge, however, passed my head and hit poor Johnson full in the face, killing him dead. That is all the story."

"And quite enough, too," said Beatrice with a shudder. "What times we live in! I feel quite sick."

Supper that night was a very melancholy affair. Old Mr. Granger was altogether thrown off his balance; and even Elizabeth's iron nerves were shaken.

"It could not be worse, it could not be worse," moaned the old man, rising from the table and walking up and down the room.

"Nonsense, father," said Elizabeth the practical. "He might have been shot before he had sold the hay, and then you would not have got your tithe."

Geoffrey could not help smiling at this way of looking at things, from which, however, Mr. Granger seemed to draw a little comfort. From constantly thinking about it, and the daily pressure of necessity, money had come to be more to the old man than anything else in the world.

Hardly was the meal done when three reporters arrived and took down Geoffrey's statement of what had occurred, for publication in various papers, while Beatrice went away to see about packing Effie's things. They were to start by a train leaving for London at half-past eight on the following morning. When Beatrice came back it was half-past ten, and in his irritation of mind Mr. Granger insisted upon everybody going to bed. Elizabeth shook hands with Geoffrey, congratulating him on his escape as she did so, and went at once; but Beatrice lingered a little. At last she came forward and held out her hand.

"Good-night, Mr. Bingham," she said.

"Good-night. I hope that this is not good-bye also," he added with some anxiety.

"Of course not," broke in Mr. Granger. "Beatrice will go and see you off. I can't; I have to go and meet the coroner about the inquest, and Elizabeth is always busy in the house. Luckily they won't want you; there were so many witnesses."

"Then it is only good-night," said Beatrice.

She went to her room. Elizabeth, who shared it, was already asleep, or pretending to be asleep. Then Beatrice undressed and got into bed, but rest she could not. It was "only good-night," a last good-night. He was going away—back to his wife, back to the great rushing world, and to the life in which she had no share. Very soon he would forget her. Other interests would arise, other women would become his friends, and he would forget the Welsh girl who had attracted him for a while, or remember her only as the companion of a rough adventure. What did it mean? Why was her heart so sore? Why had she felt as though she should die when they told her that he was dead?

Then the answer rose in her breast. She loved him; it was useless to deny the truth—she loved him body, and heart and soul, with all her mind and all her strength. She was his, and his alone—to-day, to-morrow, and for ever. He might go from her sight, she might never, never see him more, but love him she always must. And he was married!

Well, it was her misfortune; it could not affect the solemn truth. What should she do now, how should she endure her life when her eyes no longer saw his eyes, and her ears never heard his voice? She saw the future stretch itself before her as a vision. She saw herself forgotten by this man whom she loved, or from time to time remembered only with a faint regret. She saw herself growing slowly old, her beauty fading yearly from her face and form, companioned only by the love that grows not old. Oh, it was bitter, bitter! and yet she would not have it otherwise. Even in her pain she felt it better to have found this deep and ruinous joy, to have wrestled with the Angel and been worsted, than never to have looked upon his face. If she could only know that what she gave was given back again, that he loved her as she loved him, she would be content. She was innocent, she had never tried to draw him to her; she had used no touch or look, no woman's arts or lures such as her beauty placed at her command. There had been no word spoken, scarcely a meaning glance had passed between them, nothing but frank and free companionship as of man with man. She knew he did not love his wife and that his wife did not love him—this she could see. But she had never tried to win him from her, and though she sinned in thought, though her heart was guilty—oh, her hands were clean!

Her restlessness overcame her. She could no longer lie in bed. Elizabeth, watching through her veil of sleep, saw Beatrice rise, put on a wrapper, and, going to the window, throw it wide. At first she thought of interfering, for Elizabeth was a prudent person and did not like draughts; but her sister's movements excited her curiosity, and she refrained. Beatrice sat down on the foot of her bed, and leaning her arm upon the window-sill looked out upon the lovely quiet night. How dark the pine trees massed against the sky; how soft was the whisper of the sea, and how vast the heaven through which the stars sailed on.

What was it, then, this love of hers? Was it mere earthly passion? No, it was more. It was something grander, purer, deeper, and quite undying. Whence came it, then? If she was, as she had thought, only a child of earth, whence came this deep desire which was not of the earth? Had she been wrong, had she a soul—something that could love with the body and through the body and beyond the body—something of which the body with its yearnings was but the envelope, the hand or instrument? Oh, now it seemed to Beatrice that this was so, and that called into being by her love she and her soul stood face to face acknowledging their unity. Once she had held that it was phantasy: that such spiritual hopes were but exhalations from a heart unsatisfied; that when love escapes us on the earth, in our despair, we swear it is immortal, and that we shall find it in the heavens. Now Beatrice believed this no more. Love had kissed her on the eyes, and at his kiss her sleeping spirit was awakened, and she saw a vision of the truth.

Yes, she loved him, and must always love him! But she could never know on earth that he was hers, and if she had a spirit to be freed after some few years, would not his spirit have forgotten hers in that far hereafter of their meeting?

She dropped her brow upon her arm and softly sobbed. What was there left for her to do except to sob—till her heart broke?

Elizabeth, lying with wide-open ears, heard the sobs. Elizabeth, peering through the moonlight, saw her sister's form tremble in the convulsion of her sorrow, and smiled a smile of malice.

"The thing is done," she thought; "she cries because the man is going. Don't cry, Beatrice, don't cry! We will get your plaything back for you. Oh, with such a bait it will be easy. He is as sweet on you as you on him."

There was something evil, something almost devilish, in this scene of the one watching woman holding a clue to and enjoying the secret tortures of the other, plotting the while to turn them to her innocent rival's destruction and her own advantage. Elizabeth's jealousy was indeed bitter as the grave.

Suddenly Beatrice ceased sobbing. She lifted her head, and by a sudden impulse threw out the passion of her heart with all her concentrated strength of mind towards the man she loved, murmuring as she did so some passionate, despairing words which she knew.

At this moment Geoffrey, sleeping soundly, dreamed that he saw Beatrice seated by her window and looking at him with eyes which no earthly obstacle could blind. She was speaking; her lips moved, but though he could hear no voice the words she spoke floated into his mind—

"Be a god and hold me With a charm! Be a man and fold me With thine arm.

Teach me, only teach, Love! As I ought I will speak thy speech, Love, Think thy thought—

Meet, if thou require it, Both demands, Laying flesh and spirit In thy hands.

That shall be to-morrow Not to-night: I must bury sorrow Out of sight.

Must a little weep, Love, (Foolish me!) And so fall asleep, Love, Loved by thee."

Geoffrey heard them in his heart. Then they were gone, the vision of Beatrice was gone, and suddenly he awoke.

Oh, what was this flood of inarticulate, passion-laden thought that beat upon his brain telling of Beatrice? Wave after wave it came, utterly overwhelming him, like the heavy breath of flowers stirred by a night wind—like a message from another world. It was real; it was no dream, no fancy; she was present with him though she was not there; her thought mingled with his thought, her being beat upon his own. His heart throbbed, his limbs trembled, he strove to understand and could not. But in the mystery of that dread communion, the passion he had trodden down and refused acknowledgment took life and form within him; it grew like the Indian's magic tree, from seed to blade, from blade to bud, and from bud to bloom. In that moment it became clear to him: he knew he loved her, and knowing what such a love must mean, for him if not for her, Geoffrey sank back and groaned.

And Beatrice? Of a sudden she ceased speaking to herself; she felt her thought flung back to her weighted with another's thought. She had broken through the barriers of earth; the quick electric message of her heart had found a path to him she loved and come back answered. But in what tongue was that answer writ? Alas! she could not read it, any more than he could read the message. At first she doubted; surely it was imagination. Then she remembered it was absolutely proved that people dying could send a vision of themselves to others far away; and if that could be, why not this? No, it was truth, a solemn truth; she knew he felt her thought, she knew that his life beat upon her life. Oh, here was mystery, and here was hope, for if this could be, and it was, what might not be? If her blind strength of human love could so overstep the boundaries of human power, and, by the sheer might of its volition, mock the physical barriers that hemmed her in, what had she to fear from distance, from separation, ay, from death itself? She had grasped a clue which might one day, before the seeming end or after—what did it matter?—lay strange secrets open to her gaze. She had heard a whisper in an unknown tongue that could still be learned, answering Life's agonizing cry with a song of glory. If only he loved her, some day all would be well. Some day the barriers would fall. Crumbling with the flesh, they would fall and set her naked spirit free to seek its other self. And then, having found her love, what more was there to seek? What other answer did she desire to all the problems of her life than this of Unity attained at last—Unity attained in Death!

And if he did not love her, how could he answer her? Surely that message could not pass except along the golden chord of love, which ever makes its sweetest music when Pain strikes it with a hand of fear.

The troubled glory passed—it throbbed itself away; the spiritual gusts of thought grew continually fainter, till, like the echoes of a dying harp, like the breath of a falling gale, they slowly sank to nothingness. Then wearied with an extreme of wild emotion Beatrice sought her bed again and presently was lost in sleep.

When Geoffrey woke on the next morning, after a little reflection, he came to the decision that he had experienced a very curious and moving dream, consequent on the exciting events of the previous day, or on the pain of his impending departure. He rose, packed his bag—everything else was ready—and went in to breakfast. Beatrice did not appear till it was half over. She looked very pale, and said that she had been packing Effie's things. Geoffrey noticed that she barely touched his fingers when he rose to shake hands with her, and that she studiously avoided his glance. Then he began to wonder if she also had strangely dreamed.

Next came the bustle of departure. Effie was despatched in the fly with the luggage and Betty, the fat Welsh servant, to look after her. Beatrice and Geoffrey were to walk to the station.

"Time for you to be going, Mr. Bingham," said Mr. Granger. "There, good-bye, good-bye! God bless you! Never had such charming lodgers before. Hope you will come back again, I'm sure. By the way, they are certain to summon you as a witness at the trial of that villain Jones."

"Good-bye, Mr. Granger," Geoffrey answered; "you must come and see me in town. A change will do you good."

"Well, perhaps I may. I have not had a change for twenty-five years. Never could afford it. Aren't you going to say good-bye to Elizabeth?"

"Good-bye, Miss Granger," said Geoffrey politely. "Many thanks for all your kindness. I hope we shall meet again."

"Do you?" answered Elizabeth; "so do I. I am sure that we shall meet again, and I am sure that I shall be glad to see you when we do, Mr. Bingham," she added darkly.

In another minute he had left the Vicarage and, with Beatrice at his side, was walking smartly towards the station.

"This is very melancholy," he said, after a few moments' silence.

"Going away generally is," she answered—"either for those who go or those who stay behind," she added.

"Or for both," he said.

Then came another pause; he broke it.

"Miss Beatrice, may I write to you?"

"Certainly, if you like."

"And will you answer my letters?"

"Yes, I will answer them."

"If I had my way, then, you should spend a good deal of your time in writing," he said. "You don't know," he added earnestly, "what a delight it has been to me to learn to know you. I have had no greater pleasure in my life."

"I am glad," Beatrice answered shortly.

"By the way," Geoffrey said presently, "there is something I want to ask you. You are as good as a reference book for quotations, you know. Some lines have been haunting me for the last twelve hours, and I cannot remember where they come from."

"What are they?" she asked, looking up, and Geoffrey saw, or thought he saw, a strange fear shining in her eyes.

"Here are four of them," he answered unconcernedly; "we have no time for long quotations:

"'That shall be to-morrow, Not to-night: I must bury sorrow Out of sight.'"

Beatrice heard—heard the very lines which had been upon her lips in the wild midnight that had gone. Her heart seemed to stop; she became white as the dead, stumbled, and nearly fell. With a supreme effort she recovered herself.

"I think that you must know the lines, Mr. Bingham," she said in a low voice. "They come from a poem of Browning's, called 'A Woman's Last Word.'"

Geoffrey made no answer; what was he to say? For a while they walked on in silence. They were getting close to the station now. Separation, perhaps for ever, was very near. An overmastering desire to know the truth took hold of him.

"Miss Beatrice," he said again, "you look pale. Did you sleep well last night?"

"No, Mr. Bingham."

"Did you have curious dreams?"

"Yes, I did," she answered, looking straight before her.

He turned a shade paler. Then it was true!

"Beatrice," he said in a half whisper, "what do they mean?"

"As much as anything else, or as little," she answered.

"What are people to do who dream such dreams?" he said again, in the same constrained voice.

"Forget them," she whispered.

"And if they come back?"

"Forget them again."

"And if they will not be forgotten?"

She turned and looked him full in the eyes.

"Die of them," she said; "then they will be forgotten, or—"

"Or what, Beatrice?"

"Here is the station," said Beatrice, "and Betty is quarrelling with the flyman."

Five minutes more and Geoffrey was gone.

CHAPTER XVI

THE FLAT NEAR THE EDGWARE ROAD

Geoffrey's journey to town was not altogether a cheerful one. To begin with, Effie wept copiously at parting with her beloved "auntie," as she called Beatrice, and would not be comforted. The prospect of rejoining her mother and the voluble Anne had no charms for Effie. They all three got on best apart. Geoffrey himself had also much to think about, and found little satisfaction in the thinking. He threw his mind back over the events of the past few weeks. He remembered how he had first seen Beatrice's face through the thick mist on the Red Rocks, and how her beauty had struck him as no beauty ever had before. Then he thought of the adventure of their shipwreck, and of the desperate courage with which she had saved his life, almost at the cost of her own. He thought, too, of that scene when on the following day he had entered the room where she was asleep, when the wandering ray of light had wavered from her breast to his own, when that strange presentiment of the ultimate intermingling of their lives had flashed upon him, and when she had awakened with an unearthly greeting on her lips. While Effie slowly sobbed herself to silence in the corner opposite to him, one by one, he recalled every phase and scene of their ever-growing intimacy, till the review culminated in his mysterious experience of the past night, and the memory of Beatrice's parting words.

Of all men Geoffrey was among those least inclined to any sort of superstition; from boyhood he had been noted for common sense, and a somewhat disbelieving turn of mind. But he had intellect, and imagination which is simply intellect etherealised. Without these, with his peculiar mental constitution, he would, for instance, probably have been a religious sceptic; having them, he was nothing of the sort. So in this matter of his experience of the previous night, and generally of the strange and almost unnatural sympathy in which he found himself with this lady, common sense and the results of his observation and experience pointed to the whole thing being nonsense—the result of "propinquity, Sir, propinquity," and a pretty face—and nothing more.

But here his intellect and his imagination stepped in, telling him plainly that it was not nonsense, that he had not merely made a donkey of himself over an hysterical, or possibly a love-sick girl. They told him that because a thing is a mystery it is not necessarily a folly, though mysteries are for the most part dealt in by fools. They suggested that there may be many things and forces above us and around us, invisible as an electric current, intangible as light, yet existent and capable of manifestation under certain rare and favourable conditions.

And was it not possible that such conditions should unite in a woman like Beatrice, who combined in herself a beauty of body which was only outpassed by the beauty of her mind? It was no answer to say that most women could never inspire the unearthly passion with which he had been shaken some ten hours past, or that most men could never become aware of the inspiration. Has not humanity powers and perceptions denied to the cattle of the fields, and may there not be men and women as far removed from their fellows in this respect as these are from the cattle?

But the weak point of mysterious occurrences is that they lead nowhere, and do not materially alter the facts of life. One cannot, for instance, plead a mystery in a court of law; so, dropping the imaginative side of the question as one beyond him, Geoffrey came to its practical aspect, only to find it equally thorny.

Odd as it may seem, Geoffrey did not to this moment know the exact position which he occupied in the mind of Beatrice, or that she occupied in his. He was not in love with her, at least not in a way in which he had ever experienced the influence of that, on the whole, inconvenient and disagreeable passion. At any rate he argued from the hypothesis that he was not in love with her. This he refused to admit now in the light of day, though he had admitted it fully in the watches of the night. It would not do to admit it.

But he was forced to acknowledge that she had crept into his life and possessed it so completely that then and for months afterwards, except in deep sleep or in hours of severe mental strain, not a single half hour would pass without bringing its thought of Beatrice. Everything that was beautiful, or grand, or elevating, reminded him of her—and what higher compliment could a mistress have? If he listened to glorious music, the voice of Beatrice spoke to him through the notes; if he watched the clouds rolling in heavy pomp across a broken sky he thought of Beatrice; if some chance poem or novel moved him, why Beatrice was in his mind to share the pleasure. All of which was very interesting, and in some ways delightful, but under our current system not otherwise than inconvenient to a married man.

And now Beatrice was gone, and he must come back to his daily toil, sweetened by Honoria's bitter complaints of their poverty, and see her no more. The thought made Geoffrey's heart ache with a physical pain, but his reason told him that it was best so. After all, there were no bones broken; there had been no love scenes, no kiss, no words that cannot be recalled; whatever there was lay beneath the surface, and while appearances were kept up all was well. No doubt it was an hypocrisy, but then hypocrisy is one of the great pillars of civilization, and how does it matter what the heart says while the lips are silent? The Recording Angel can alone read hearts, and he must often find them singularly contradictory and untrustworthy writings.

Die of them, die of her dreams! No, Beatrice would not die of them, and certainly he should not. Probably in the end she would marry that pious earthly lump, Owen Davies. It was not pleasant to think of, it was even dreadful, but really if she were to ask him his opinion, "as a friend," he should tell her it was the best thing that she could do. Of course it would be hypocrisy again, the lips would give his heart the lie; but when the heart rises in rebellion against the intelligence it must be suppressed. Unfortunately, however, though a small member, it is very strong.

They reached London at last, and as had been arranged, Anne, the French bonne, met them at the station to take Effie home. Geoffrey noticed that she looked smarter and less to his taste than ever. However, she embraced Effie with an enthusiasm which the child scarcely responded to, and at the same time carried on an ocular flirtation with a ticket collector. Although early in the year for yellow fogs, London was plunged in a dense gloom. It had been misty that morning at Bryngelly, and become more and more so as the day advanced; but, though it was not yet four o'clock, London was dark as night. Luckily, however, it is not far from Paddington to the flat near the Edgware Road, where Geoffrey lived, so having personally instructed the cabman, he left Anne to convoy Effie and the luggage, and went on to the Temple by Underground Railway with an easy mind.

Shortly after Geoffrey reached his chambers in Pump Court the solicitor arrived as had been arranged, not his uncle—who was, he learned, very unwell—but a partner. To his delight he then found that Beatrice's ghost theory was perfectly accurate; the boy with the missing toe-joint had been discovered who saw the whole horrible tragedy through a crack in the blind; moreover the truth had been wrung from him and he would be produced at the trial—indeed a proof of his evidence was already forthcoming. Also some specimens of the ex-lawyer's clerk's handwriting had been obtained, and were declared by two experts to be identical with the writing on the will. One thing, however, disturbed him: neither the Attorney-General nor Mr. Candleton was yet in town, so no conference was possible that evening. However, both were expected that night—the Attorney-General from Devonshire and Mr. Candleton from the Continent; so the case being first on the list, it was arranged that the conference should take place at ten o'clock on the following morning.

On arriving home Geoffrey was informed that Lady Honoria was dressing, and had left a message saying he must be quick and do likewise as a gentleman was coming to dinner. Accordingly he went to his own room—which was at the other end of the flat—and put on his dress clothes. Before going to the dining-room, however, he said good-night to Effie—who was in bed, but not asleep—and asked her what time she had reached home.

"At twenty minutes past five, daddy," Effie said promptly.

"Twenty minutes past five! Why, you don't mean to say that you were an hour coming that little way! Did you get blocked in the fog?"

"No, daddy, but—"

"But what, dear?"

"Anne did tell me not to say!"

"But I tell you to say, dear—never mind Anne!"

"Anne stopped and talked to the ticket-man for a long, long time."

"Oh, did she?" he said.

At that moment the parlourmaid came to say that Lady Honoria and the "gentleman" were waiting for dinner. Geoffrey asked her casually what time Miss Effie had reached home.

"About half-past five, sir. Anne said the cab was blocked in the fog."

"Very well. Tell her ladyship that I shall be down in a minute."

"Daddy," said the child, "I haven't said my prayers. Mother did not come, and Anne said it was all nonsense about prayers. Auntie did always hear me my prayers."

"Yes, dear, and so will I. There, kneel upon my lap and say them."

In the middle of the prayers—which Effie did not remember as well as she might have done—the parlourmaid arrived again.

"Please, sir, her ladyship—"

"Tell her ladyship I am coming, and that if she is in a hurry she can go to dinner! Go on, love."

Then he kissed her and put her to bed again.

"Daddy," said Effie, as he was going, "shall I see auntie Beatrice any more?"

"I hope so, dear."

"And shall you see her any more? You want to see her, don't you, daddy? She did love you very much!"

Geoffrey could bear it no longer. The truth is always sharper when it comes from the mouth of babes and sucklings. With a hurried good-night he fled.

In the little drawing-room he found Lady Honoria, very well dressed, and also her friend, whose name was Mr. Dunstan. Geoffrey knew him at once for an exceedingly wealthy man of small birth, and less breeding, but a burning and a shining light in the Garsington set. Mr. Dunstan was anxious to raise himself in society, and he thought that notwithstanding her poverty, Lady Honoria might be useful to him in this respect. Hence his presence there to-night.

"How do you do, Geoffrey?" said his wife, advancing to greet him with a kiss of peace. "You look very well. But what an immense time you have been dressing. Poor Mr. Dunstan is starving. Let me see. You know Mr. Dunstan, I think. Dinner, Mary."

Geoffrey apologised for being late, and shook hands politely with Mr. Dunstan—Saint Dunstan he was generally called on account of his rather clerical appearance and in sarcastic allusion to his somewhat shady reputation. Then they went in to dinner.

"Sorry there is no lady for you, Geoffrey; but you must have had plenty of ladies' society lately. By the way, how is Miss—Miss Granger? Would you believe it, Mr. Dunstan? that shocking husband of mine has been passing the last month in the company of one of the loveliest girls I ever saw, who knows Latin and law and everything else under the sun. She began by saving his life, they were upset together out of a canoe, you know. Isn't it romantic?"

Saint Dunstan made some appropriate—or, rather inappropriate—remark to the effect that he hoped Mr. Bingham had made the most of such unrivalled opportunities, adding, with a deep sigh, that no lovely young lady had ever saved his life that he might live for her, &c., &c.

Here Geoffrey broke in without much ceremony. To him it seemed a desecration to listen while this person was making his feeble jokes about Beatrice.

"Well, dear," he said, addressing his wife, "and what have you been doing with yourself all this time?"

"Mourning for you, Geoffrey, and enjoying myself exceedingly in the intervals. We have had a delightful time, have we not, Mr. Dunstan? Mr. Dunstan has also been staying at the Hall, you know."

"How could it be otherwise when you were there, Lady Honoria?" answered the Saint in that strain of compliment affected by such men, and which, to tell the truth, jarred on its object, who was after all a lady.

"You know, Geoffrey," she went on, "the Garsingtons have re-furnished the large hall and their drawing-room. It cost eighteen hundred pounds, but the result is lovely. The drawing-room is done in hand-painted white satin, walls and all, and the hall in old oak."

"Indeed!" he answered, reflecting the while that Lord Garsington might as well have paid some of his debts before he spent eighteen hundred pounds on his drawing-room furniture.

Then the Saint and Lady Honoria drifted into a long and animated conversation about their fellow guests, which Geoffrey scarcely tried to follow. Indeed, the dinner was a dull one for him, and he added little or nothing to the stock of talk.

When his wife left the room, however, he had to say something, so they spoke of shooting. The Saint had a redeeming feature—he was somewhat of a sportsman, though a poor one, and he described to Geoffrey a new pair of hammerless guns, which he had bought for a trifling sum of a hundred and forty guineas, recommending the pattern to his notice.

"Yes," answered Geoffrey, "I daresay that they are very nice; but, you see, they are beyond me. A poor man cannot afford so much for a pair of guns."

"Oh, if that is all," answered his guest, "I will sell you these; they are a little long in the stock for me, and you can pay me when you like. Or, hang it all, I have plenty of guns. I'll be generous and give them to you. If I cannot afford to be generous, I don't know who can!"

"Thank you very much, Mr. Dunstan," answered Geoffrey coldly, "but I am not in the habit of accepting such presents from my—acquaintances. Will you have a glass of sherry?—no. Then shall we join Lady Honoria?"

This speech quite crushed the vulgar but not ill-meaning Saint, and Geoffrey was sorry for it a moment after he had made it. But he was weary and out of temper. Why did his wife bring such people to the house? Very shortly afterwards their guest took his leave, reflecting that Bingham was a conceited ass, and altogether too much for him. "And I don't believe that he has got a thousand a year," he reflected to himself, "and the title is his wife's. I suppose that is what he married her for. She's a much better sort than he is, any way, though I don't quite make her out either—one can't go very far with her. But she is the daughter of a peer and worth cultivating, but not when Bingham is at home—not if I know it."

"What have you said to Mr. Dunstan to make him go away so soon, Geoffrey?" asked his wife.

"Said to him? oh, I don't know. He offered to give me a pair of guns, and I told him that I did not accept presents from my acquaintances. Really, Honoria, I don't want to interfere with your way of life, but I do not understand how you can associate with such people as this Mr. Dunstan."

"Associate with him!" answered Lady Honoria. "Do you suppose I want to associate with him? Do you suppose that I don't know what the man is? But beggars cannot be choosers; he may be a cad, but he has thirty thousand a year, and we simply cannot afford to throw away an acquaintance with thirty thousand a year. It is too bad of you, Geoffrey," she went on with rising temper, "when you know all that I must put up with in our miserable poverty-stricken life, to take every opportunity of making yourself disagreeable to the people I think it wise to ask to come and see us. Here I return from comfort to this wretched place, and the first thing that you do is make a fuss. Mr. Dunstan has got boxes at several of the best theaters, and he offered to let me have one whenever I liked—and now of course there is an end of it. It is too bad, I say!"

"It is really curious, Honoria," said her husband, "to see what obligations you are ready to put yourself under in search of pleasure. It is not dignified of you to accept boxes at theatres from this gentleman."

"Nonsense. There is no obligation about it. If he gave us a box, of course he would make a point of looking in during the evening, and then telling his friends that it was Lady Honoria Bingham he was speaking to—that is the exchange. I want to go to the theatre; he wants to get into good society—there you have the thing in a nutshell. It is done every day. The fact of the matter is, Geoffrey," she went on, looking very much as though she were about to burst into a flood of angry tears, "as I said just now, beggars cannot be choosers—I cannot live like the wife of a banker's clerk. I must have some amusement, and some comfort, before I become an old woman. If you don't like it, why did you entrap me into this wretched marriage, before I was old enough to know better, or why do you not make enough money to keep me in a way suitable to my position?"

"We have argued that question before, Honoria," said Geoffrey, keeping his temper with difficulty, "and now there is another thing I wish to say to you. Do you know that detestable woman Anne stopped for more than half an hour at Paddington Station this evening, flirting with a ticket collector, instead of bringing Effie home at once, as I told her to do. I am very angry about it. She is not to be relied on; we shall have some accident with the child before we have done. Cannot you discharge her and get another nurse?"

"No, I cannot. She is the one comfort I have. Where am I going to find another woman who can make dresses like Anne—she saves me a hundred a year—I don't care if she flirted with fifty ticket collectors. I suppose you got this story from Effie; the child ought to be whipped for tale-bearing, and I daresay that it is not true."

"Effie will certainly not be whipped," answered Geoffrey sternly. "I warn you that it will go very badly with anybody who lays a finger on her."

"Oh, very well, ruin the child. Go your own way, Geoffrey! At any rate I am not going to stop here to listen to any more abuse. Good-night," and she went.

Geoffrey sat down, and lit a cigarette. "A pleasant home-coming," he thought to himself. "Honoria shall have money as much as she can spend—if I kill myself to get it, she shall have it. What a life, what a life! I wonder if Beatrice would treat her husband like this—if she had one."

He laughed aloud at the absurdity of the idea, and then with a gesture of impatience threw his cigarette into the fire and went to his room to try and get some sleep, for he was thoroughly wearied.

CHAPTER XVII

GEOFFREY WINS HIS CASE

Before ten o'clock on the following morning, having already spent two hours over his brief, that he had now thoroughly mastered, Geoffrey was at his chambers, which he had some difficulty in reaching owing to the thick fog that still hung over London, and indeed all England.

To his surprise nothing had been heard either of the Attorney-General or of Mr. Candleton. The solicitors were in despair; but he consoled them by saying that one or the other was sure to turn up in time, and that a few words would suffice to explain the additional light which had been thrown on the case. He occupied his half hour, however, in making a few rough notes to guide him in the altogether improbable event of his being called on to open, and then went into court. The case was first on the list, and there were a good many counsel engaged on the other side. Just as the judge took his seat, the solicitor, with an expression of dismay, handed Geoffrey a telegram which had that moment arrived from Mr. Candleton. It was dated from Calais on the previous night, and ran, "Am unable to cross on account of thick fog. You had better get somebody else in Parsons and Douse."

"And we haven't got another brief prepared," said the agonised solicitor. "What is more, I can hear nothing of the Attorney-General, and his clerk does not seem to know where he is. You must ask for an adjournment, Mr. Bingham; you can't manage the case alone."

"Very well," said Geoffrey, and on the case being called he rose and stated the circumstances to the court. But the Court was crusty. It had got the fog down its throat, and altogether It didn't seem to see it. Moreover the other side, marking its advantage, objected strongly. The witnesses, brought at great expense, were there; his Lordship was there, the jury was there; if this case was not taken there was no other with which they could go on, &c., &c.

The court took the same view, and lectured Geoffrey severely. Every counsel in a case, the Court remembered, when It was at the Bar, used to be able to open that case at a moment's notice, and though things had, It implied, no doubt deteriorated to a considerable extent since those palmy days, every counsel ought still to be prepared to do so on emergency.

Of course, however, if he, Geoffrey, told the court that he was absolutely unprepared to go on with the case, It would have no option but to grant an adjournment.

"I am perfectly prepared to go on with it, my lord," Geoffrey interposed calmly.

"Very well," said the Court in a mollified tone, "then go on! I have no doubt that the learned Attorney-General will arrive presently."

Then, as is not unusual in a probate suit, followed an argument as to who should open it, the plaintiff or the defendant. Geoffrey claimed that this right clearly lay with him, and the opposing counsel raised no great objection, thinking that they would do well to leave the opening in the hands of a rather inexperienced man, who would very likely work his side more harm than good. So, somewhat to the horror of the solicitors, who thought with longing of the eloquence of the Attorney-General, and the unrivalled experience and finesse of Mr. Candleton, Geoffrey was called upon to open the case for the defendants, propounding the first will.

He rose without fear or hesitation, and with but one prayer in his heart, that no untimely Attorney-General would put in an appearance. He had got his chance, the chance for which many able men have to wait long years, and he knew it, and meant to make the most of it. Naturally a brilliant speaker, Geoffrey was not, as so many good speakers are, subject to fits of nervousness, and he was, moreover, thoroughly master of his case. In five minutes judge, jury and counsel were all listening to him with attention; in ten they were absorbed in the lucid and succinct statement of the facts which he was unfolding to them. His ghost theory was at first received with a smile, but presently counsel on the other side ceased to smile, and began to look uneasy. If he could prove what he said, there was an end of their case. When he had been speaking for about forty minutes one of the opposing counsel interrupted him with some remark, and at that moment he noticed that the Attorney-General's clerk was talking to the solicitor beneath him.

"Bother it, he is coming," thought Geoffrey.

But no, the solicitor bending forward informed him that the Attorney-General had been unavoidably detained by some important Government matter, and had returned his brief.

"Well, we must get on as we can," Geoffrey said.

"If you continue like that we shall get on very well," whispered the solicitors, and then Geoffrey knew that he was doing well.

"Yes, Mr. Bingham!" said his Lordship.

Then Geoffrey went on with his statement.

At lunch time it was a question whether another leader should be briefed. Geoffrey said that so far as he was concerned he could get on alone. He knew every point of the case, and he had got a friend to "take a note" for him while he was speaking.

After some hesitation the solicitors decided not to brief fresh counsel at this stage of the case, but to leave it entirely in his hands.

It would be useless to follow the details of this remarkable will suit, which lasted two days, and attracted much attention. Geoffrey won it and won it triumphantly. His address to the jury on the whole case was long remembered in the courts, rising as it did to a very high level of forensic eloquence. Few who saw it ever forgot the sight of his handsome face and commanding presence as he crushed the case of his opponents like an eggshell, and then with calm and overwhelming force denounced the woman who with her lover had concocted the cruel plot that robbed her uncle of life and her cousins of their property, till at the last, pointing towards her with outstretched hand, he branded her to the jury as a murderess.

Few in that crowded court have forgotten the tragic scene that followed, when the trembling woman, worn out by the long anxiety of the trial, and utterly unnerved by her accuser's brilliant invective, rose from her seat and cried:

"We did it—it is true that we did it to get the money, but we did not mean to frighten him to death," and then fell fainting to the ground—or Geoffrey Bingham's quiet words as he sat down:

"My lord and gentlemen of the jury, I do not think it necessary to carry my case any further."

There was no applause, the occasion was too dramatically solemn, but the impression made both upon the court and the outside public, to whom such a scene is peculiarly fitted to appeal, was deep and lasting.

Geoffrey himself was under little delusion about the matter. He had no conceit in his composition, but neither had he any false modesty. He merely accepted the situation as really powerful men do accept such events—with thankfulness, but without surprise. He had got his chance at last, and like any other able man, whatever his walk of life, he had risen to it. That was all. Most men get such chances in some shape or form, and are unable to avail themselves of them. Geoffrey was one of the exceptions; as Beatrice had said, he was born to succeed. As he sat down, he knew that he was a made man.

And yet while he walked home that night, his ears still full of the congratulations which had rained in on him from every quarter, he was conscious of a certain pride. He will have felt as Geoffrey felt that night, whose lot it has been to fight long and strenuously against circumstances so adverse as to be almost overwhelming, knowing in his heart that he was born to lead and not to follow; and who at last, by one mental effort, with no friendly hand to help, and no friendly voice to guide, has succeeded in bursting a road through the difficulties which hemmed him in, and has suddenly found himself, not above competition indeed, but still able to meet it. He will not have been too proud of that endeavour; it will have seemed but a little thing to him—a thing full of faults and imperfections, and falling far short of his ideal. He will not even have attached a great importance to his success, because, if he is a person of this calibre, he must remember how small it is, when all is said and done; that even in his day there are those who can beat him on his own ground; and also that all worldly success, like the most perfect flower, yet bears in it the elements of decay. But he will have reflected with humble satisfaction on those long years of patient striving which have at length lifted him to an eminence whence he can climb on and on, scarcely encumbered by the jostling crowd; till at length, worn out, the time comes for him to fall.

So Geoffrey thought and felt. The thing was to be done, and he had done it. Honoria should have money now; she should no longer be able to twit him with their poverty. Yes, and a better thought still, Beatrice would be glad to hear of his little triumph.

He reached home rather late. Honoria was going out to dinner with a distinguished cousin, and was already dressing. Geoffrey had declined the invitation, which was a short one, because he had not expected to be back from chambers. In this enthusiasm, however, he went to his wife's room to tell her of the event.

"Well," she said, "what have you been doing? I think that you might have arranged to come out with me. My going out so much by myself does not look well. Oh, I forgot; of course you are in that case."

"Yes—that is, I was. I have won the case. Here is a very fair report of it in the St. James's Gazette if you care to read it."

"Good heavens, Geoffrey! How can you expect me to read all that stuff when I am dressing?"

"I don't expect you to, Honoria; only, as I say, I have won the case, and I shall get plenty of work now."

"Will you? I am glad to hear it; perhaps we shall be able to escape from this horrid flat if you do. There, Anne! Je vous l'ai toujours dit, cette robe ne me va pas bien."

"Mais, milady, la robe va parfaitement—"

"That is your opinion," grumbled Lady Honoria. "Well, it isn't mine. But it will have to do. Good-night, Geoffrey; I daresay that you will have gone to bed when I get back," and she was gone.

Geoffrey picked up his St. James's Gazette with a sigh. He felt hurt, and knew that he was a fool for his pains. Lady Honoria was not a sympathetic person; it was not fair to expect it from her. Still he felt hurt. He went upstairs and heard Effie her prayers.

"Where has you beed, daddy?—to the Smoky Town?" The Temple was euphemistically known to Effie as the Smoky Town.

"Yes, dear."

"You go to the Smoky Town to make bread and butter, don't you, daddy?"

"Yes, dear, to make bread and butter."

"And did you make any, daddy?"

"Yes, Effie, a good deal to-day."

"Then where is it? In your pocket?"

"No, love, not exactly. I won a big lawsuit to-day, and I shall get a great many pennies for it."

"Oh," answered Effie meditatively, "I am glad that you did win. You do like to win, doesn't you, daddy, dear."

"Yes, love."

"Then I will give you a kiss, daddy, because you did win," and she suited the action to the word.

Geoffrey went from the little room with a softened heart. He dressed and ate some dinner.

Then he sat down and wrote a long letter to Beatrice, telling her all about the trial, and not sparing her his reasons for adopting each particular tactic and line of argument which conduced to the great result.

And though his letter was four sheets in length, he knew that Beatrice would not be bored at having to read it.

CHAPTER XVIII

THE RISING STAR

As might be expected, the memorable case of Parsons and Douse proved to be the turning point in Geoffrey's career, which was thenceforward one of brilliant and startling success. On the very next morning when he reached his chambers it was to find three heavy briefs awaiting him, and they proved to be but the heralds of an uninterrupted flow of lucrative business. Of course, he was not a Queen's Counsel, but now that his great natural powers of advocacy had become generally known, solicitors frequently employed him alone, or gave him another junior, so that he might bring those powers to bear upon juries. Now it was, too, that Geoffrey reaped the fruits of the arduous legal studies which he had followed without cessation from the time when he found himself thrown upon his own resources, and which had made a sound lawyer of him as well as a brilliant and effective advocate. Soon, even with his great capacity for work, he had as much business as he could attend to. When fortune gives good gifts, she generally does so with a lavish hand.

Thus it came to pass that, about three weeks after the trial of Parsons and Douse, Geoffrey's uncle the solicitor died, and to his surprise left him twenty thousand pounds, "believing," he said in his will, which was dated three days before the testator's death, "that this sum will assist him to rise to the head of his profession."

Now that it had dawned upon her that her husband really was a success, Honoria's manner towards him modified very considerably. She even became amiable, and once or twice almost affectionate. When Geoffrey told her of the twenty thousand pounds she was radiant.

"Why, we shall be able to go back to Bolton Street now," she said, "and as luck will have it, our old house is to let. I saw a bill in the window yesterday."

"Yes," he said, "you can go back as soon as you like."

"And can we keep a carriage?"

"No, not yet; I am doing well, but not well enough for that. Next year, if I live, you will be able to have a carriage. Don't begin to grumble, Honoria. I have got £150 to spare, and if you care to come round to a jeweller's you can spend it on what you like."

"Oh, you delightful person!" said his wife.

So they went to the jeweller's, and Lady Honoria bought ornaments to the value of £150, and carried them home and hung over them, as another class of woman might hang over her first-born child, admiring them with a tender ecstasy. Whenever he had a sum of money that he could afford to part with, Geoffrey would take her thus to a jeweller's or a dressmaker's, and stand by coldly while she bought things to its value. Lady Honoria was delighted. It never entered into her mind that in a sense he was taking a revenge upon her, and that every fresh exhibition of her rejoicings over the good things thus provided added to his contempt for her.

Those were happy days for Lady Honoria! She rejoiced in this return of wealth like a school-boy at the coming of the holidays, or a half-frozen wanderer at the rising of the sun. She had been miserable during all this night of poverty, as miserable as her nature admitted of, now she was happy again, as she understood happiness. For bred, educated, civilized—what you will—out of the more human passions, Lady Honoria had replaced them by this idol-worship of wealth, or rather of what wealth brings. It gave her a positive physical satisfaction; her beauty, which had begun to fade, came back to her; she looked five years younger. And all the while Geoffrey watched her with an ever-growing scorn.

Once it broke out. The Bolton Street house had been furnished; he gave her fifteen hundred pounds to do it, and with what things they owned she managed very well on that. They moved into it, and Honoria had set herself up with a sufficient supply of grand dresses and jewellery, suitable to her recovered position. One day however, it occurred to her that Effie was a child of remarkable beauty, who, if properly dressed, would look very nice in the drawing-room at tea-time. So she ordered a lovely costume for her—this deponent is not able to describe it, but it consisted largely of velvet and lace. Geoffrey heard nothing of this dress, but coming home rather early one afternoon—it was on a Saturday, he found the child being shown off to a room full of visitors, and dressed in a strange and wonderful attire with which, not unnaturally, she was vastly pleased. He said nothing at the time, but when at length the dropping fire of callers had ceased, he asked who put Effie into that dress.

"I did," said Lady Honoria, "and a pretty penny it has cost, I can tell you. But I can't have the child come down so poorly clothed, it does not look well."

"Then she can stay upstairs," said Geoffrey frowning.

"What do you mean?" asked his wife.

"I mean that I will not have her decked out in those fine clothes. They are quite unsuitable to her age. There is plenty of time for her to take to vanity."

"I really don't understand you, Geoffrey. Why should not the child be handsomely dressed?"

"Why not! Great heaven, Honoria, do you suppose that I want to see Effie grow up like you, to lead a life of empty pleasure-seeking idleness, and make a god of luxury. I had rather see her"—he was going to add, "dead first," but checked himself and said—"have to work for her living. Dress yourself up as much as you like, but leave the child alone."

Lady Honoria was furious, but she was also a little frightened. She had never heard her husband speak quite like this before, and there was something underneath his words that she did not quite understand. Still less did she understand when on the Monday Geoffrey suddenly told her that he had fifty pounds for her to spend as she liked; then accompanied her to a mantle shop, and stood patiently by, smiling coldly while she invested it in lace and embroideries. Honoria thought that he was making reparation for his sharp words, and so he was, but to himself, and in another sense. Every time he gave her money in this fashion, Geoffrey felt like a man who has paid off a debt of honour. She had taunted him again and again with her poverty—the poverty she said that he had brought her; for every taunt he would heap upon her all those things in which her soul delighted. He would glut her with wealth as, in her hour of victory, Queen Tomyris glutted dead Cyrus with the blood of men.

It was an odd way of taking a revenge, and one that suited Lady Honoria admirably; but though its victim felt no sting, it gave Geoffrey much secret relief. Also he was curious; he wished to see if there was any bottom to such a woman's desire for luxury, if it would not bring satiety with it. But Lady Honoria was a very bad subject for such an experiment. She never showed the least sign of being satiated, either with fine things, with pleasures, or with social delights. They were her natural element, and he might as soon have expected a fish to weary of the water, or an eagle of the rushing air.

The winter wore away and the spring came. One day, it was in April, Geoffrey, who was a moderate Liberal by persuasion, casually announced at dinner that he was going to stand for Parliament in the Unionist interest. The representation of one of the few Metropolitan divisions which had then returned a Home Ruler had fallen vacant. As it chanced he knew the head Unionist whip very well. They had been friends since they were lads at school together, and this gentleman, having heard Geoffrey make a brilliant speech in court, was suddenly struck with the idea that he was the very man to lead a forlorn hope.

The upshot of it was that Geoffrey was asked if he would stand, and replied that he must have two days to think it over. What he really wanted the two days for was to enable him to write to Beatrice and receive an answer from her. He had an almost superstitious faith in her judgment, and did not like to act without it. After carefully weighing the pros and cons, his own view was that he should do well to stand. Probably he would be defeated, and it might cost him five hundred pounds. On the other hand it would certainly make his name known as a politician, and he was now in a fair way to earn so large an income that he could well afford to risk the money. The only great objection which he saw, was that if he happened to get in, it must mean that he would have to work all day and all night too. Well, he was strong and the more work he did the better—it kept him from thinking.

In due course Beatrice's answer came. Her view coincided with his own; she recommended him to take the opportunity, and pointed out that with his growing legal reputation there was no office in the State to which he might not aspire, when he had once proved himself a capable member of Parliament. Geoffrey read the letter through; then immediately sat down and wrote to his friend the whip, accepting the suggestion of the Government.

The next fortnight was a hard one for him, but Geoffrey was as good a man on the platform as in court, and he had, moreover, the very valuable knack of suiting himself to his audience. As his canvass went on it was generally recognised that the seat which had been considered hopeless was now doubtful. A great amount of public interest was concentrated on the election, both upon the Unionist and the Separatist side, each claiming that the result of the poll would show to their advantage. The Home Rule party strained every nerve against him, being most anxious to show that the free and independent electors of this single division, and therefore of the country at large, held the Government policy in particular horror. Letters were obtained from great authorities and freely printed. Irish members, fresh from gaol, were brought down to detail their grievances. It was even suggested that one of them should appear on the platform in prison garb—in short, every electioneering engine known to political science was brought to bear to forward the fortunes of either side.

As time went on Lady Honoria, who had been somewhat indifferent at first, grew quite excited about the result. For one thing she found that the contest attached an importance to herself in the eyes of the truly great, which was not without its charm. On the day of the poll she drove about all day in an open carriage under a bright blue parasol, having Effie (who had become very bored) by her side, and two noble lords on the front seat. As a consequence the result was universally declared by a certain section of the press to be entirely due to the efforts of an unprincipled but titled and lovely woman. It was even said that, like another lady of rank in a past generation, she kissed a butcher in order to win his vote. But those who made the remark did not know Lady Honoria; she was incapable of kissing a butcher, or indeed anybody else. Her inclinations did not lie in that direction.

In the end Geoffrey was returned by a magnificent majority of ten votes, reduced on a scrutiny to seven. He took his seat in the House on the following night amidst loud Unionist cheering. In the course of the evening's debate a prominent member of the Government made allusion to his return as a proof of the triumph of Unionist principles. Thereon a very leading member of the Separatist opposition retorted that it was nothing of the sort, "that it was a matter of common notoriety that the honourable member's return was owing to the unusual and most uncommon ability displayed by him in the course of his canvass, aided as it was, by artfully applied and aristocratic feminine influence." This was a delicate allusion to Honoria and her blue parasol.

As Geoffrey and his wife were driving back to Bolton Street, after the declaration of the poll, a little incident occurred. Geoffrey told the coachman to stop at the first telegraph office and, getting out of the carriage, wired to Beatrice, "In by ten votes."

"Who have you been telegraphing to, Geoffrey?" asked Lady Honoria.

"I telegraphed to Miss Granger," he answered.

"Ah! So you still keep up a correspondence with that pupil teacher girl."

"Yes, I do. I wish that I had a few more such correspondents."

"Indeed. You are easy to please. I thought her one of the most disagreeable young women whom I ever met."

"Then it does not say much for your taste, Honoria."

His wife made no further remark, but she had her thoughts. Honoria possessed good points: among others she was not a jealous person; she was too cold and too indifferent to be jealous. But she did not like the idea of another woman obtaining an influence over her husband, who, as she now began to recognise, was one of the most brilliant men of his day, and who might well become one of the most wealthy and powerful. Clearly he existed for her benefit, not for that of any other woman. She was no fool, and she saw that a considerable intimacy must exist between the two. Otherwise Geoffrey would not have thought of telegraphing to Beatrice at such a moment.

Within a week of his election Geoffrey made a speech. It was not a long speech, nor was it upon any very important issue; but it was exceedingly good of its kind, good enough to be reported verbatim indeed, and those listening to it recognised that they had to deal with a new man who would one day be a very big man. There is no place where an able person finds his level quicker than in the House of Commons, composed as it is for the most part, of more or less wealthy or frantic mediocrities. But Geoffrey was not a mediocrity, he was an exceedingly able and powerful man, and this fact the House quickly recognised.

For the next few months Geoffrey worked as men rarely work. All day he was at his chambers or in court, and at night he sat in the House, getting up his briefs when he could. But he always did get them up; no solicitors had to complain that the interests of their client were neglected by him; also he still found time to write to Beatrice. For the rest he went out but little, and except in the way of business associated with very few. Indeed he grew more and more silent and reserved, till at last he won the reputation of being cold and hard. Not that he was really so. He threw himself head and soul into his work with a fixed determination to reach the top of the tree. He knew that he should not care very much about it when he got there, but he enjoyed the struggle.

Geoffrey was not a truly ambitious man; he was no mere self-seeker. He knew the folly of ambition too well, and its end was always clearly before his eyes. He often thought to himself that if he could have chosen his lot, he would have asked for a cottage with a good garden, five hundred a year, and somebody to care for. But perhaps he would soon have wearied of his cottage. He worked to stifle thought, and to some extent he succeeded. But he was at bottom an affectionate-natured man, and he could not stifle the longing for sympathy which was his secret weakness, though his pride would never allow him to show it. What did he care for his triumphs when he had nobody with whom to share them? All he could share were their fruits, and these he gave away freely enough. It was but little that Geoffrey spent upon his own gratification. A certain share of his gains he put by, the rest went in expenses. The house in Bolton Street was a very gay place in those days, but its master took but little part in its gaieties.

And what was the fact? The longer he remained separated from Beatrice the more intensely did he long for her society. It was of no use; try as he would, he could not put that sweet face from his mind; it drew him as a magnet draws a needle. Success did not bring him happiness, except in the sense that it relieved him from money cares.

People of coarse temperament only can find real satisfaction in worldly triumphs, and eat, drink, and be merry, for to-morrow they die! Men like Geoffrey soon learn that this also is vanity. On the contrary, as his mind grew more and more wearied with the strain of work, melancholy took an ever stronger hold of it. Had he gone to a doctor, he might have been told that his liver was out of order, which was very likely true. But this would not mend matters. "What a world," he might have cried, "what a world to live in when all the man's happiness depends upon his liver!" He contracted an accursed habit of looking on the black side of things; trouble always caught his eye.

It was no wonderful case. Men of large mind are very rarely happy men. It is your little animal-minded individual who can be happy. Thus women, who reflect less, are as a class much happier and more contented than men. But the large-minded man sees too far, and guesses too much of what he cannot see. He looks forward, and notes the dusty end of his laborious days; he looks around and shudders at the unceasing misery of a coarse struggling world; the sight of the pitiful beggar babe craving bread on tottering feet, pierces his heart. He cannot console himself with a reflection that the child had no business to be born, or that if he denuded himself of his last pound he would not materially help the class which bred it.

And above the garish lights of earthly joys and the dim reek of earthly wretchedness, he sees the solemn firmament that veils his race's destiny. For such a man, in such a mood, even religion has terrors as well as hopes, and while the gloom gathers about his mind these are with him more and more. What lies beyond that arching mystery to whose horizon he daily draws more close—whose doors may even now be opening for him? A hundred hands point out a hundred roads to knowledge—they are lost half way. Only the cold spiritual firmament, unlit by any guiding stars, unbrightened by the flood of human day, and unshadowed by the veils of human night, still bends above his head in awful changelessness, and still his weary feet draw closer to the portals of the West.

It is very sad and wrong, but it is not altogether his fault; it is rather a fault of the age, of over-education, of over-striving to be wise. Cultivate the searching spirit and it will grow and rend you. The spirit would soar, it would see, but the flesh weighs it down, and in all flesh there is little light. Yet, at times, brooding on some unnatural height of Thought, its eyes seem to be opened, and it catches gleams of terrifying days to come, or perchance, discerns the hopeless gates of an immeasurable night.

Oh, for that simpler faith which ever recedes farther from the ken of the cultivated, questioning mind! There alone can peace be found, and for the foolish who discard it, setting up man's wisdom at a sign, soon the human lot will be one long fear. Grown scientific and weary with the weight of knowledge, they will reject their ancient Gods, and no smug-faced Positivism will bring them consolation. Science, here and there illumining the gloom of destiny with its poor electric lights, cries out that they are guiding stars. But they are no stars, and they will flare away. Let us pray for darkness, more darkness, lest, to our bewildered sight, they do but serve to show that which shall murder Hope.

So think Geoffrey and his kin, and in their unexpressed dismay, turn, seeking refuge from their physical and spiritual loneliness, but for the most part finding none. Nature, still strong in them, points to the dear fellowship of woman, and they make the venture to find a mate, not a companion. But as it chanced in Geoffrey's case he did find such a companion in Beatrice, after he had, by marriage, built up an impassable wall between them.

And yet he longed for her society with an intensity that alarmed him. He had her letters indeed, but what are letters! One touch of a beloved hand is worth a thousand letters. In the midst of his great success Geoffrey was wretched at heart, yet it seemed to him that if he once more could have Beatrice at his side, though only as a friend, he would find rest and happiness.

When a man's heart is thus set upon an object, his reason is soon convinced of its innocence, even of its desirability, and a kindly fate will generally contrive to give him the opportunity of ruin which he so ardently desires.

CHAPTER XIX

GEOFFREY HAS A VISITOR

And Beatrice—had she fared better during these long months? Alas, not at all. She had gone away from the Bryngelly Station on that autumn morning of farewell sick at heart, and sick at heart she had remained. Through all the long winter months sorrow and bitterness had been her portion, and now in the happiness of spring, sorrow and bitterness were with her still. She loved him, she longed for his presence, and it was denied to her. She could not console herself as can some women, nor did her deep passion wear away; on the contrary, it seemed to grow and gather with every passing week. Neither did she wish to lose it, she loved too well for that. It was better to be thus tormented by conscience and by hopelessness than to lose her cause of pain.

One consolation Beatrice had and one only: she knew that Geoffrey did not forget her. His letters told her this. These letters indeed were everything to her—a woman can get so much more comfort out of a letter than a man. Next to receiving them she loved to answer them. She was a good and even a brilliant letter writer, but often and often she would tear up what she had written and begin again. There was not much news in Bryngelly; it was difficult to make her letters amusing. Also the farcical nature of the whole proceeding seemed to paralyse her. It was ridiculous, having so much to say, to be able to say nothing. Not that Beatrice wished to indite love-letters—such an idea had never crossed her mind, but rather to write as they had talked. Yet when she tried to do so the results were not satisfactory to her, the words looked strange on paper—she could not send them.

In Geoffrey's meteor-like advance to fame and fortune she took the keenest joy and interest, far more than he did indeed. Though, like that of most other intelligent creatures, her soul turned with loathing from the dreary fustian of politics, she would religiously search the parliamentary column from beginning to end on the chance of finding his name or the notice of a speech by him. The law reports also furnished her with a happy hunting-ground in which she often found her game.

But they were miserable months. To rise in the morning, to go through the round of daily duty—thinking of Geoffrey; to come home wearied, and finally to seek refuge in sleep and dreams of him—this was the sum of them. Then there were other troubles. To begin with, things had gone from bad to worse at the Vicarage. The tithes scarcely came in at all, and every day their poverty pinched them closer. Had it not been for Beatrice's salary it was difficult to see how the family could have continued to exist. She gave it almost all to her father now, only keeping back a very small sum for her necessary clothing and such sundries as stamps and writing paper. Even then, Elizabeth grumbled bitterly at her extravagance in continuing to buy a daily paper, asking what business she had to spend sixpence a week on such a needless luxury. But Beatrice would not make up her mind to dock the paper with its occasional mention of Geoffrey.

Again, Owen Davies was a perpetual anxiety to her. His infatuation for herself was becoming notorious; everybody saw it except her father. Mr. Granger's mind was so occupied with questions connected with tithe that fortunately for Beatrice little else could find an entry. Owen dogged her about; he would wait whole hours outside the school or by the Vicarage gate merely to speak a few words to her. Sometimes when at length she appeared he seemed to be struck dumb, he could say nothing, but would gaze at her with his dull eyes in a fashion that filled her with vague alarm. He never ventured to speak to her of his love indeed, but he looked it, which was almost as bad. Another thing was that he had grown jealous. The seed which Elizabeth had planted in his mind had brought forth abundantly, though of course Beatrice did not know that this was her sister's doing.

On the very morning that Geoffrey went away Mr. Davies had met her as she was walking back from the station and asked her if Mr. Bingham had gone. When she replied that this was so, she had distinctly heard him murmur, "Thank God! thank God!" Subsequently she discovered also that he bribed the old postman to keep count of the letters which she sent and received from Geoffrey.

These things filled Beatrice with alarm, but there was worse behind. Mr. Davies began to send her presents, first such things as prize pigeons and fowls, then jewellery. The pigeons and fowls she could not well return without exciting remark, but the jewellery she sent back by one of the school children. First came a bracelet, then a locket with his photograph inside, and lastly, a case that, when she opened it, which her curiosity led her to do, nearly blinded her with light. It was a diamond necklace, and she had never seen such diamonds before, but from their size and lustre she knew that each stone must be worth hundreds of pounds. Beatrice put it in her pocket and carried it until she met him, which she did in the course of that afternoon.

"Mr. Davies," she said before he could speak, and handing him the package, "this has been sent to me by mistake. Will you kindly take it back?"

He took it, abashed.

"Mr. Davies," she went on, looking him full in the eyes, "I hope that there will be no more such mistakes. Please understand that I cannot accept presents from you."

"If Mr. Bingham had sent it, you would have accepted it," he muttered sulkily.

Beatrice turned and flashed such a look on him that he fell back and left her. But it was true, and she knew that it was true. If Geoffrey had given her a sixpence with a hole in it, she would have valued it more than all the diamonds on earth. Oh! what a position was hers. And it was wrong, too. She had no right to love the husband of another woman. But right or wrong the fact remained: she did love him.

And the worst of it was that, as she well knew, sooner or later all this about Mr. Davies must come to the ears of her father, and then what would happen? One thing was certain. In his present poverty-stricken condition he would move heaven and earth to bring about her marriage to this rich man. Her father never had been very scrupulous where money was concerned, and the pinch of want was not likely to make him more so.

Nor, we may be sure, did all this escape the jealous eye of Elizabeth. Things looked black for her, but she did not intend to throw up the cards on that account. Only it was time to lead trumps. In other words, Beatrice must be fatally compromised in the eyes of Owen Davies, if by any means this could be brought about. So far things had gone well for her schemes. Beatrice and Geoffrey loved each other, of that Elizabeth was certain. But the existence of this secret, underhand affection would avail her naught unless it could be ripened into acts. Everybody is free to indulge in secret predilections, but if once they are given way to, if once a woman's character is compromised, then the world avails itself of its opportunities and destroys her. What man, thought Elizabeth, would marry a compromised woman? If Beatrice could be compromised, Owen Davies would not take her to wife—therefore this must be brought about.

It sounds wicked and unnatural. "Impossible that sister should so treat sister," the reader of this history may say, thinking of her own, and of her affectionate and respectable surroundings. But it is not impossible. If you, who doubt, will study the law reports, and no worse occupation can be wished to you, you will find that such things are possible. Human nature can rise to strange heights, and it can also fall to depths beyond your fathoming. Because a thing is without parallel in your own small experience it in no way follows that it cannot be.

Elizabeth was a very remorseless person; she was more—she was a woman actuated by passion and by greed: the two strongest motives known to the human heart. But with her recklessness she united a considerable degree of intelligence, or rather of intellect. Had she been a savage she might have removed her sister from her path by a more expeditious way; being what she was, she merely strove to effect the same end by a method not punishable by law, in short, by murdering her reputation. Would she be responsible if her sister went wrong, and was thus utterly discredited in the eyes of this man who wished to marry her, and whom Elizabeth wished to marry? Of course not; that was Beatrice's affair. But she could give her every chance of falling into temptation, and this it was her fixed design to do.

Circumstances soon gave her an opportunity. The need of money became very pressing at the Vicarage. They had literally no longer the wherewithal to live. The tithe payers absolutely refused to fulfil their obligations. As it happened, Jones, the man who had murdered the auctioneer, was never brought to trial. He died shortly after his arrest in a fit of delirium tremens and nervous prostration brought on by the sudden cessation of a supply of stimulants, and an example was lost, that, had he been duly hanged, might have been made of the results of defying the law. Mr. Granger was now too poor to institute any further proceedings, which, in the state of public feeling in Wales, might or might not succeed; he could only submit, and submission meant beggary. Indeed he was already a beggar. In this state of affairs he took counsel with Elizabeth, pointing out that they must either get money or starve. Now the only possible way to get money was by borrowing it, and Mr. Granger's suggestion was that he should apply to Owen Davies, who had plenty. Indeed he would have done so long ago, but that the squire had the reputation of being an exceedingly close-fisted man.

But this proposition did not at all suit Elizabeth's book. Her great object had been to conceal Mr. Davies's desires as regards Beatrice from her father, and her daily dread was that he might become acquainted with them from some outside source. She knew very well that if her father went up to the Castle to borrow money it would be lent, or rather given, freely enough; but she also knew that the lender would almost certainly take the opportunity, the very favourable opportunity, to unfold his wishes as regards the borrower's daughter. The one thing would naturally lead to the other—the promise of her father's support of Owen's suit would be the consideration for the money received. How gladly that support would be given was also obvious to her, and with her father pushing Beatrice on the one side and Owen Davies pushing her on the other, how could Elizabeth be sure that she would not yield? Beatrice would be the very person to be carried away by an idea of duty. Their father would tell her that he had got the money on this undertaking, and it was quite possible that her pride might bring her to fulfil a bond thus given, however distasteful the deed might be to her personally. No, her father must at all hazards be prevented from seeking assistance from Owen Davies. And yet the money must be had from somewhere, or they would be ruined.

Ah, she had it—Geoffrey Bingham should lend the money! He could well afford it now, and she shrewdly guessed that he would not grudge the coat off his back if he thought that by giving it he might directly or indirectly help Beatrice. Her father must go up to town to see him, she would have no letter-writing; one never knows how a letter may be read. He must see Mr. Bingham, and if possible bring him down to Bryngelly. In a moment every detail of the plot became clear to Elizabeth's mind, and then she spoke.

"You must not go to Mr. Davies, father," she said; "he is a hard man, and would only refuse and put you in a false position; you must go to Mr. Bingham. Listen: he is rich now, and he is very fond of you and of Beatrice. He will lend you a hundred pounds at once. You must go to London by the early train to-morrow, and drive straight to his chambers and see him. It will cost two pounds to get there and back, but that cannot be helped; it is safer than writing, and I am sure that you will not go for nothing. And see here, father, bring Mr. Bingham back with you for a few days if you can. It will be a little return for his kindness, and I know that he is not well. Beatrice had a letter from him in which he said that he was so overworked that he thought he must take a little rest soon. Bring him back for Whit-Sunday."

Mr. Granger hesitated, demurred, and finally yielded. The weak, querulous old farmer clergyman, worn out with many daily cares and quite unsupported by mental resources, was but a tool in Elizabeth's able hands. He did not indeed feel any humiliation at the idea of trying to borrow the cash, for his nature was not finely strung, and money troubles had made him callous to the verge of unscrupulousness; but he did not like the idea of a journey to London, where he had not been for more than twenty years, and the expenditure that it entailed. Still he acted as Elizabeth bade him, even to keeping the expedition secret from Beatrice. Beatrice, as her sister explained to him, was proud as Lucifer, and might raise objections if she knew that he was going to London to borrow money of Mr. Bingham. This indeed she would certainly have done.

On the following afternoon—it was the Friday before Whit-Sunday, and the last day of the Easter sittings—Geoffrey sat in his chambers, in the worst possible spirits, thoroughly stale and worn out with work. There was a consultation going on, and his client, a pig-headed Norfolk farmer, who was bent upon proceeding to trial with some extraordinary action for trespass against his own landlord, was present with his solicitor. Geoffrey in a few short, clear words had explained the absurdity of the whole thing, and strongly advised him to settle, for the client had insisted on seeing him, refusing to be put off with a written opinion. But the farmer was not satisfied, and the solicitor was now endeavouring to let the pure light of law into the darkness of his injured soul.

Geoffrey threw himself back in his chair, pushed the dark hair from his brow, and pretended to listen. But in a minute his mind was far away. Heavens, how tired he was! Well, there would be rest for a few days—till Tuesday, when he had a matter that must be attended to—the House had risen and so had the courts. What should he do with himself? Honoria wished to go and stay with her brother, Lord Garsington, and, for a wonder, to take Effie with her. He did not like it, but he supposed that he should have to consent. One thing was, he would not go. He could not endure Garsington, Dunstan, and all their set. Should he run down to Bryngelly? The temptation was very great; that would be happiness indeed, but his common sense prevailed against it. No, it was better that he should not go there. He would leave Bryngelly alone. If Beatrice wished him to come she would have said so, and she had never even hinted at such a thing, and if she had he did not think that he would have gone. But he lacked the heart to go anywhere else. He would stop in town, rest, and read a novel, for Geoffrey, when he found time, was not above this frivolous occupation. Possibly, under certain circumstances, he might even have been capable of writing one. At that moment his clerk entered, and handed him a slip of paper with something written on it. He opened it idly and read:

"Revd. Mr. Granger to see you. Told him you were engaged, but he said he would wait."

Geoffrey started violently, so violently that both the solicitor and the obstinate farmer looked up.

"Tell the gentleman that I will see him in a minute," he said to the retreating clerk, and then, addressing the farmer, "Well, sir, I have said all that I have to say. I cannot advise you to continue this action. Indeed, if you wish to do so, you must really direct your solicitor to retain some other counsel, as I will not be a party to what can only mean a waste of money. Good afternoon," and he rose.

The farmer was convoyed out grumbling. In another moment Mr. Granger entered, dressed in a somewhat threadbare suit of black, and his thin white hair hanging, as usual, over his eyes. Geoffrey glanced at him with apprehension, and as he did so noticed that he had aged greatly during the last seven months. Had he come to tell him some ill news of Beatrice—that she was ill, or dead, or going to be married?

"How do you do, Mr. Granger?" he said, as he stretched out his hand, and controlling his voice as well as he could. "How are you? This is a most unexpected pleasure."

"How do you do, Mr. Bingham?" answered the old man, while he seated himself nervously in a chair, placing his hat with a trembling hand upon the floor beside him. "Yes, thank you, I am pretty well, not very grand—worn out with trouble as the sparks fly upwards," he added, with a vague automatic recollection of the scriptural quotation.

"I hope that Miss Elizabeth and Be—that your daughters are well also," said Geoffrey, unable to restrain his anxiety.

"Yes, yes, thank you, Mr. Bingham. Elizabeth isn't very grand either, complains of a pain in her chest, a little bilious perhaps—she always is bilious in the spring."

"And Miss Beatrice?"

"Oh, I think she's well—very quiet, you know, and a little pale, perhaps; but she is always quiet—a strange woman Beatrice, Mr. Bingham, a very strange woman, quite beyond me! I do not understand her, and don't try to. Not like other women at all, takes no pleasure in things seemingly; curious, with her good looks—very curious. But nobody understands Beatrice."

Geoffrey breathed a sigh of relief. "And how are tithes being paid, Mr. Granger? not very grandly, I fear. I saw that scoundrel Jones died in prison."

Mr. Granger woke up at once. Before he had been talking almost at random; the subject of his daughters did not greatly interest him. What did interest him was this money question. Nor was it very wonderful; the poor narrow-minded old man had thought about money till he could scarcely find room for anything else, indeed nothing else really touched him closely. He broke into a long story of his wrongs, and, drawing a paper from his breast pocket, with shaking finger pointed out to Geoffrey how that his clerical income for the last six months had been at the rate of only forty pounds a year, upon which sum even a Welsh clergyman could not consider himself passing rich. Geoffrey listened and sympathised; then came a pause.

"That's how we've been getting on at Bryngelly, Mr. Bingham," Mr. Granger said presently, "starving, pretty well starving. It's only you who have been making money; we've been sitting on the same dock-leaf while you have become a great man. If it had not been for Beatrice's salary—she's behaved very well about the salary, has Beatrice—I am sure I don't understand how the poor girl clothes herself on what she keeps; I know that she had to go without a warm cloak this winter, because she got a cough from it—we should have been in the workhouse, and that's where we shall be yet," and he rubbed the back of his withered hand across his eyes.

Geoffrey gasped. Beatrice with scarcely enough means to clothe herself—Beatrice shivering and becoming ill from the want of a cloak while he lived in luxury! It made him sick to think of it. For a moment he could say nothing.

"I have come here—I've come," went on the old man in a broken voice, broken not so much by shame at having to make the request as from fear lest it should be refused, "to ask you if you could lend me a little money. I don't know where to turn, I don't indeed, or I would not do it, Mr. Bingham. I have spent my last pound to get here. If you could lend me a hundred pounds I'd give you note of hand for it and try to pay it back little by little; we might take twenty pounds a year from Beatrice's salary—"

"Don't, please—do not talk of such a thing!" ejaculated the horrified Geoffrey. "Where the devil is my cheque-book? Oh, I know, I left it in Bolton Street. Here, this will do as well," and he took up a draft note made out to his order, and, rapidly signing his name on the back of it, handed it to Mr. Granger. It was in payment of the fees in the great case of Parsons and Douse and some other matters. Mr. Granger took the draft, and, holding it close to his eyes, glanced at the amount; it was £200.

"But this is double what I asked for," he said doubtfully. "Am I to return you £100?"

"No, no," answered Geoffrey, "I daresay that you have some debts to pay. Thank Heaven, I can get on very well and earn more money than I want. Not enough clothing—it is shocking to think of!" he added, more to himself than to his listener.

The old man rose, his eyes full of tears. "God bless you," he said, "God bless you. I do not know how to thank you—I don't indeed," and he caught Geoffrey's hand between his trembling palms and pressed it.

"Please do not say any more, Mr. Granger; it really is only a matter of mutual obligation. No, no, I don't want any note of hand. If I were to die it might be used against you. You can pay me whenever it is convenient."

"You are too good, Mr. Bingham," said the old clergyman. "Where could another man be found who would lend me £200 without security?" (where indeed!) "By the way," he added, "I forgot; my mind is in such a whirl. Will you come back with me for a few days to Bryngelly? We shall all be so pleased if you can. Do come, Mr. Bingham; you look as though you want a change, you do indeed."

Geoffrey dropped his hand heavily on the desk. But half an hour before he had made up his mind not to go to Bryngelly. And now—The vision of Beatrice rose before his eyes. Beatrice who had gone cold all winter and never told him one word of their biting poverty—the longing for the sight of Beatrice came into his heart, and like a hurricane swept the defences of his reason to the level ground. Temptation overwhelmed him; he no longer struggled against it. He must see her, if it was only to say good-bye.

"Thank you," he said quietly, lifting his bowed head. "Yes, I have nothing particular to do for the next day or two. I think that I will come. When do you go back?"

"Well, I thought of taking the night mail, but I feel so tired. I really don't know. I think I shall go by the nine o'clock train to-morrow."

"That will suit me very well," said Geoffrey; "and now what are you going to do to-night? You had better come and dine and sleep at my house. No dress clothes? Oh, never mind; there are some people coming but they won't care; a clergyman is always dressed. Come along and I will get that draft cashed. The bank is shut, but I can manage it."

CHAPTER XX

BACK AT BRYNGELLY

Geoffrey and Mr. Granger reached Bolton Street about six o'clock. The drawing-room was still full of callers. Lady Honoria's young men mustered in great force in those days. They were very inoffensive young men and Geoffrey had no particular objection to them. Only he found it difficult to remember all their names. When Geoffrey entered the drawing-room there were no fewer than five of them, to say nothing of two stray ladies, all superbly dressed and sitting metaphorically at Honoria's very pretty feet. Otherwise their contributions to the general store of amusement did not amount to much, for her ladyship did most of the talking.

Geoffrey introduced Mr. Granger, whom Honoria could not at first remember. Nor did she receive the announcement that he was going to dine and stay the night with any particular enthusiasm. The young men melted away at Geoffrey's advent like mists before a rising sun. He greeted them civilly enough, but with him they had nothing in common. To tell the truth they were a little afraid of him. This man with his dark handsome face sealed with the stamp of intellect, his powerful-looking form (ill dressed, according to their standard) and his great and growing reputation, was a person with whom they had no sympathy, and who, they felt, had no sympathy with them. We talk as though there is one heaven and one hell for all of us, but here must be some mistake. An impassable gulf yawns between the different classes of mankind. What has such a man as Geoffrey to do with the feeble male and female butterflies of a London drawing-room? There is only one link between them: they live on the same planet.

When the fine young men and the two stray ladies had melted away, Geoffrey took Mr. Granger up to his room. Coming downstairs again he found Lady Honoria waiting for him in the study.

"Is that individual really going to dine and sleep here?" she asked.

"Certainly, Honoria, and he has brought no dress clothes," he answered.

"Really, Geoffrey, it is too bad of you," said the lady with some pardonable irritation. "Why do you bring people to dinner in this promiscuous way? It will quite upset the table. Just fancy asking an old Welsh clergyman to dine, who has not the slightest pretensions to being a gentleman, when one has the Prime Minister and a Bishop coming—and a clergyman without dress clothes too. What has he come for?"

"He came to see me on business, and as to the people coming to dinner, if they don't like it they can grumble when they go home. By the way, Honoria, I am going down to Wales for a day or two to-morrow. I want a change."

"Indeed! Going to see the lovely Beatrice, I suppose. You had better be careful, Geoffrey. That girl will get you into a mess, and if she does there are plenty of people who are ready to make an example of you. You have enemies enough, I can tell you. I am not jealous, it is not in my line, but you are too intimate with that girl, and you will be sorry for it one day."

"Nonsense," said Geoffrey angrily, but nevertheless he felt that Lady Honoria's words were words of truth. It struck him, moreover, that she must feel this strongly, or she would not have spoken in that tone. Honoria did not pose as a household philosopher. Still he would not draw back now. His heart was set on seeing Beatrice.

"Am I to understand," went on his wife, "that you still object to my staying with the Garsingtons? I think it is a little hard if I do not make a fuss about your going to see your village paragon, that you should refuse to allow me to visit my own brother."

Geoffrey felt that he was being bargained with. It was degrading, but in the extremity of his folly he yielded.

"Go if you like," he said shortly, "but if you take Effie, mind she is properly looked after, that is all," and he abruptly left the room.

Lady Honoria looked after him, slowly nodding her handsome head. "Ah," she said to herself, "I have found out how to manage you now. You have your weak point like other people, Master Geoffrey—and it spells Beatrice. Only you must not go too far. I am not jealous, but I am not going to have a scandal for fifty Beatrices. I will not allow you to lose your reputation and position. Just imagine a man like that pining for a village girl—she is nothing more! And they talk about his being so clever. Well, he always liked ladies' society; that is his failing, and now he has burnt his fingers. They all do sooner or later, especially these clever men. The women flatter them, that's it. Of course the girl is trying to get hold of him, and she might do worse, but so surely as my name is Honoria Bingham I will put a spoke in her wheel before she has done. Bah! and they laugh at the power of women when a man like Geoffrey, with all the world to lose, grows love-sick for a pretty face; it is a very pretty face by the way. I do believe that if I were out of the way he would marry her. But I am in the way, and mean to stay there. Well, it is time to dress for dinner. I only hope that old clown of a clergyman won't do something ridiculous. I shall have to apologise for him."

Dinner-time had come; it was a quarter past eight, and the room was filled with highly bred people all more or less distinguished. Mr. Granger had duly appeared, arrayed in his threadbare black coat, relieved, however, by a pair of Geoffrey's dress shoes. As might have been expected, the great folk did not seem surprised at his presence, or to take any particular notice of his attire, the fact being that such people never are surprised. A Zulu chief in full war dress would only excite a friendly interest in their breasts. On the contrary they recognised vaguely that the old gentleman was something out of the common run, and as such worth cultivating. Indeed the Prime Minister, hearing casually that he was a clergyman from Wales, asked to be introduced to him, and at once fell into conversation about tithes, a subject of which Mr. Granger was thoroughly master.

Presently they went down to dinner, Mr. Granger escorting the wife of the Bishop, a fat and somewhat apoplectic lady, blessed with an excellent appetite. On his other side was the Prime Minister, and between the two he got on very well, especially after a few glasses of wine. Indeed, both the apoplectic wife of the Bishop and the head of Her Majesty's Government were subsequently heard to declare that Mr. Granger was a very entertaining person. To the former he related with much detail how his daughter had saved their host's life, and to the latter he discoursed upon the subject of tithes, favouring him with his ideas of what legislation was necessary to meet the question. Somewhat to his own surprise, he found that his views were received with attention and even with respect. In the main, too, they received the support of the Bishop, who likewise felt keenly on the subject of tithes. Never before had Mr. Granger had such a good dinner nor mingled with company so distinguished. He remembered both till his dying day.

Next morning Geoffrey and Mr. Granger started before Lady Honoria was up. Into the details of their long journey to Wales (in a crowded third-class carriage) we need not enter. Geoffrey had plenty to think of, but his fears had vanished, as fears sometimes do when we draw near to the object of them, and had been replaced by a curious expectancy. He saw now, or thought he saw, that he had been making a mountain out of a molehill. Probably it meant nothing at all. There was no real danger. Beatrice liked him, no doubt; possibly she had even experienced a fit of tenderness towards him. Such things come and such things go. Time is a wonderful healer of moral distempers, and few young ladies endure the chains of an undesirable attachment for a period of seven whole months. It made him almost blush to think that this might be so, and that the gratuitous extension of his misfortune to Beatrice might be nothing more than the working of his own unconscious vanity—a vanity which, did she know of it, would move her to angry laughter.

He remembered how once, when he was quite a young fellow, he had been somewhat smitten with a certain lady, who certainly, if he might judge from her words and acts, reciprocated the sentiment. And he remembered also, how when he met that lady some months afterwards she treated him with a cold indifference, indeed almost with an insolence, that quite bewildered him, making him wonder how the same person could show in such different lights, till at length, mortified and ashamed by his mistake, he had gone away in a rage and seen her face no more. Of course he had set it down to female infidelity; he had served her turn, she had made a fool of him, and that was all she wanted. Now he might enjoy his humiliation. It did not occur to him that it might be simple "cussedness," to borrow an energetic American term, or that she had not really changed, but was angry with him for some reason which she did not choose to show. It is difficult to weigh the motives of women in the scales of male experience, and many other men besides Geoffrey have been forced to give up the attempt and to console themselves with the reflection that the inexplicable is generally not worth understanding.

Yes, probably it would be the same case over again. And yet, and yet—was Beatrice of that class? Had she not too much of a man's straightforwardness of aim to permit her to play such tricks? In the bottom of his soul he thought that she had, but he would not admit it to himself. The fact of the matter was that, half unknowingly, he was trying to drug his conscience. He knew that in his longing to see her dear face once more he had undertaken a dangerous thing. He was about to walk with her over an abyss on a bridge which might bear them, or—might break. So long as he walked there alone it would be well, but would it bear them both? Alas for the frailty of human nature, this was the truth; but he would not and did not acknowledge it. He was not going to make love to Beatrice, he was going to enjoy the pleasure of her society. In friendship there could be no harm.

It is not difficult thus to still the qualms of an uneasy mind, more especially when the thing in question at its worst is rather an offence against local custom than against natural law. In many countries of the world—in nearly all countries, indeed, at different epochs of their history—it would have been no wrong that Geoffrey and Beatrice should love each other, and human nature in strong temptation is very apt to override artificial barriers erected to suit the convenience or promote the prosperity of particular sections of mankind. But, as we have heard, even though all things may be lawful, yet all things are not expedient. To commit or even to condone an act because the principle that stamps it as wrong will admit of argument on its merits is mere sophistry, by the aid of which we might prove ourselves entitled to defy the majority of laws of all calibres. Laws vary to suit the generations, but each generation must obey its own, or confusion will ensue. A deed should be judged by its fruits; it may even be innocent in itself, yet if its fruits are evil the doer in a sense is guilty.

Thus in some countries to mention the name of your mother-in-law entails the most unpleasant consequences on that intimate relation. Nobody can say that to name the lady is a thing wicked in itself; yet the man who, knowing the penalties which will ensue, allows himself, even in a fit of passion against that relative, to violate the custom and mention her by name is doubtless an offender. Thus, too, the result of an entanglement between a woman and a man already married generally means unhappiness and hurt to all concerned, more especially to the women, whose prospects are perhaps irretrievably injured thereby. It is useless to point to the example of the patriarchs, some foreign royal families, and many respectable Turks; it is useless to plead that the love is deep and holy love, for which a man or woman might well live and die, or to show extenuating circumstances in the fact of loneliness, need of sympathy, and that the existing marriage is a hollow sham. The rule is clear. A man may do most things except cheat at cards or run away in action; a woman may break half-a-dozen hearts, or try to break them, and finally put herself up at auction and take no harm at all—but neither of them may in any event do this.

Not that Geoffrey, to do him justice, had any such intentions. Most men are incapable of plots of that nature. If they fall, it is when the voice of conscience is lost in the whirlwind of passion, and counsel is darkened by the tumultuous pleadings of the heart. Their sin is that they will, most of them, allow themselves to be put in positions favourable to the development of these disagreeable influences. It is not safe to light cigarettes in a powder factory. If Geoffrey had done what he ought to have done, he would never have gone to Bryngelly, and there would have been no story to tell, or no more than there usually is.

At length Mr. Granger and his guest reached Bryngelly; there was nobody to meet them, for nobody knew that they were coming, so they walked up to the Vicarage. It was strange to Geoffrey once more to pass by the little church through those well-remembered, wind-torn pines and see that low long house. It seemed wonderful that all should still be just as it was, that there should be no change at all, when he himself had seen so much. There was Beatrice's home; where was Beatrice?

He passed into the house like a man in a dream. In another moment he was in the long parlour where he had spent so many happy hours, and Elizabeth was greeting him. He shook hands with her, and as he did so, noticed vaguely that she too was utterly unchanged. Her straw-coloured hair was pushed back from the temples in the same way, the mouth wore the same hard smile, her light eyes shone with the same cold look; she even wore the same brown dress. But she appeared to be very pleased to see him, as indeed she was, for the game looked well for Elizabeth. Her father kissed her hurriedly, and bustled from the room to lock up his borrowed cash, leaving them together.

Somehow Geoffrey's conversational powers failed him. Where was Beatrice? she ought to be back from school. It was holiday time indeed. Could she be away?

He made an effort, and remarked absently that things seemed very unchanged at Bryngelly.

"You are looking for Beatrice," said Elizabeth, answering his thought and not his words. "She has gone out walking, but I think she will be back soon. Excuse me, but I must go and see about your room."

Geoffrey hung about a little, then he lit his pipe and strolled down to the beach, with a vague unexpressed idea of meeting Beatrice. He did not meet Beatrice, but he met old Edward, who knew him at once.

"Lord, sir," he said, "it's queer to see you here again, specially when I thinks as how I saw you first, and you a dead 'un to all purposes, with your mouth open, and Miss Beatrice a-hanging on to your hair fit to pull your scalp off. You never was nearer old Davy than you was that night, sir, nor won't be. And now you've been spared to become a Parliament man, I hears, and much good may you do there—it will take all your time, sir—and I think, sir, that I should like to drink your health."

Geoffrey put his hand in his pocket and gave the old man a sovereign. He could afford to do so now.

"Does Miss Beatrice go out canoeing now?" he asked while Edward mumbled his astonished thanks.

"At times, sir—thanking you kindly; it ain't many suvrings as comes my way—though I hate the sight on it, I do. I'd like to stave a hole in the bottom of that there cranky concern; it ain't safe, and that's the fact. There'll be another accent out of it one of these fine days and no coming to next time. But, Lord bless you, it's her way of pleasuring herself. She's a queer un is Miss Beatrice, and she gets queerer and queerer, what with their being so tight screwed up at the Vicarage, no tithes and that, and one thing and another. Not but what I'm thinking, sir," he added in a portentous whisper, "as the squire has got summut to do with it. He's a courting of her, he is; he's as hard after her as a dog fish after a stray herring, and why she can't just say yes and marry him I'm sure I don't know."

"Perhaps she doesn't like him," said Geoffrey coldly.

"May be, sir, may be; maids all have their fancies, in whatsoever walk o' life it has pleased God to stick 'em, but it's a wonderful pity, it is. He ain't no great shakes, he ain't, but he's a sound man—no girl can't want a sounder—lived quiet all his days you see, sir, and what's more he's got the money, and money's tight up at the Vicarage, sir. Gals must give up their fancies sometimes, sir. Lord! a brace of brats and she'd forget all about 'em. I'm seventy years old and I've seen their ways, sir, though in a humble calling. You should say a word to her, sir; she'd thank you kindly five years after. You'd do her a good turn, sir, you would, and not a bad un as the saying goes, and give it the lie—no, beg your pardon, that is the other way round—she's bound to do you the bad turn having saved your life, though I don't see how she could do that unless, begging your pardon, she made you fall in love with her, being married, which though strange wouldn't be wunnerful seeing what she is and seeing how I has been in love with her myself since she was seven, old missus and all, who died eight years gone and well rid of the rheumatics."

Beatrice was one of the few subjects that could unlock old Edward's breast, and Geoffrey retired before his confusing but suggestive eloquence. Hurriedly bidding the old man good-night he returned to the house, and leaning on the gate watched the twilight dying on the bosom of the west.

Suddenly, a bunch of wild roses in her girdle, Beatrice emerged from the gathering gloom and stood before him face to face.

CHAPTER XXI

THE THIRD APPEAL

Face to face they stood, while at the vision of her sweetness his heart grew still. Face to face, and the faint light fell upon her tender loveliness and died in her deep eyes, and the faint breeze fragrant with the breath of pines gently stirred her hair. Oh, it was worth living to see her thus!

"I beg your pardon," she said in a puzzled tone, stepping forward to pass the gate.

"Beatrice!"

She gave a little cry, and clutched the railing, else she would have fallen. One moment she stayed so, looking up towards his face that was hid in the deepening shadow—looking with wild eyes of hope and fear and love.

"Is it you," she said at length, "or another dream?"

"It is I, Beatrice!" he answered, amazed.

She recovered herself with an effort.

"Then why did you frighten me so?" she asked. "It was unkind—oh, I did not mean to say anything cross. What did I say? I forget. I am so glad that you have come!" and she put her hand to her forehead and looked at him again as one might gaze at a ghost from the grave.

"Did you not expect me?" Geoffrey asked.

"Expect you? no. No more than I expected—" and she stopped suddenly.

"It is very odd," he said; "I thought you knew that your father was going to ask me down. I returned from London with him."

"From London," she murmured. "I did not know; Elizabeth did not tell me anything about it. I suppose that she forgot."

"Here I am at any rate, and how are you?"

"Oh, well now, quite well. There, I am all right again. It is very wrong to frighten people in that way, Mr. Bingham," she added in her usual voice. "Let me pass through the gate and I will shake hands with you— if," she added, in a tone of gentle mockery, "one may shake hands with so great a man. But I told you how it would be, did I not, just before we were drowned together, you know? How is Effie?"

"Effie flourishes," he answered. "Do you know, you do not look very grand. Your father told me that you had a cold in the winter," and Geoffrey shivered as he thought of the cause.

"Oh, thank you, I have nothing to complain of. I am strong and well. How long do you stay here?"

"Not long. Perhaps till Tuesday morning, perhaps till Monday."

Beatrice sighed. Happiness is short. She had not brought him here, she would not have lifted a finger to bring him here, but since he had come she wished that he was going to stay longer.

"It is supper time," she said; "let us go in."

So they went in and ate their supper. It was a happy meal. Mr. Granger was in almost boisterous spirits. It is wonderful what a difference the possession of that two hundred pounds made in his demeanour; he seemed another man. It was true that a hundred of it must go in paying debts, but a hundred would be left, which meant at least a year's respite for him. Elizabeth, too, relaxed her habitual grimness; the two hundred pounds had its influence on her also, and there were other genial influences at work in her dark secret heart. Beatrice knew nothing of the money and sat somewhat silent, but she too was happy with the wild unreal happiness that sometimes visits us in dreams.

As for Geoffrey, if Lady Honoria could have seen him she would have stared in astonishment. Of late he had been a very silent man, many people indeed had found him a dull companion. But under the influence of Beatrice's presence he talked and talked brilliantly. Perhaps he was unconsciously striving to show at his very best before her, as a man naturally does in the presence of a woman whom he loves. So brilliantly did he talk that at last they all sat still and listened to him, and they might have been worse employed.

At length supper was done, and Elizabeth retired to her room. Presently, too, Mr. Granger was called out to christen a sick baby and went grumbling, and they were left alone. They sat in the window-place and looked out at the quiet night.

"Tell me about yourself," said Beatrice.

So he told her. He narrated all the steps by which he had reached his present position, and showed her how from it he might rise to the topmost heights of all. She did not look at him, and did not answer him, but once when he paused, thinking that he had talked enough about himself, she said, "Go on; tell me some more."

At last he had told her all.

"Yes," she said, "you have the power and the opportunity, and you will one day be among the foremost men of your generation."

"I doubt it," he said with a sigh. "I am not ambitious. I only work for the sake of work, not for what it will bring. One day I daresay that I shall weary of it all and leave it. But while I do work, I like to be among the first in my degree."

"Oh, no," she answered, "you must not give it up; you must go on and on. Promise me," she continued, looking at him for the first time—"promise me that while you have health and strength you will persevere till you stand alone and quite pre-eminent. Then you can give it up."

"Why should I promise you this, Beatrice?"

"Because I ask it of you. Once I saved your life, Mr. Bingham, and it gives me some little right to direct its course. I wish that the man whom I saved to the world should be among the first men in the world, not in wealth, which is an accident, but in intellect and force. Promise me this and I shall be happy."

"I promise you," he said, "I promise that I will try to rise because you ask it, not because the prospect attracts me; but as he spoke his heart was wrung. It was bitter to hear her speak thus of a future in which she would have no share, which, as her words implied, would be a thing utterly apart from her, as much apart as though she were dead.

"Yes," he said again, "you gave me my life, and it makes me very unhappy to think that I can give you nothing in return. Oh, Beatrice, I will tell you what I have never told to any one. I am lonely and wretched. With the exception of yourself, I do not think that there is anybody who really cares for—I mean who really sympathises with me in the world. I daresay that it is my own fault and it sounds a humiliating thing to say, and, in a fashion, a selfish thing. I never should have said it to any living soul but you. What is the use of being great when there is nobody to work for? Things might have been different, but the world is a hard place. If you—if you—"

At this moment his hand touched hers; it was accidental, but in the tenderness of his heart he yielded to the temptation and took it. Then there was a moment's pause, and very gently she drew her hand away and thrust it in her bosom.

"You have your wife to share your fortune," she said; "you have Effie to inherit it, and you can leave your name to your country."

Then came a heavy pause.

"And you," he said, breaking it, "what future is there for you?"

She laughed softly. "Women have no future and they ask none. At least I do not now, though once I did. It is enough for them if they can ever so little help the lives of others. That is their happiness, and their reward is—rest."

Just then Mr. Granger came back from his christening, and Beatrice rose and went to bed.

"Looks a little pale, doesn't she, Mr. Bingham?" said her father. "I think she must be troubled in her mind. The fact is—well, there is no reason why I should not tell you; she thinks so much of you, and you might say a word to brighten her up—well, it's about Mr. Davies. I fancy, you know, that she likes him and is vexed because he does not come forward. Well, you see—of course I may be mistaken, but I have sometimes thought that he may. I have seen him look as if he was thinking of it, though of course it is more than Beatrice has got any right to expect. She's only got herself and her good looks to give him, and he's a rich man. Think of it, Mr. Bingham," and the old gentleman turned up his eyes piously, "just think what a thing it would be for her, and indeed for all of us, if it should please God to send a chance like that in her way; she would be rich for life, and such a position! But it is possible; one never knows; he might take a fancy to her. At any rate, Mr. Bingham, I think you could cheer her up a little; there is no need for her to give up hope yet."

Geoffrey burst into a short grim laugh. The idea of Beatrice languishing for Owen Davies, indeed the irony of the whole position, was too much for his sense of humour.

"Yes," he said, "I daresay that it might be a good match for her, but I do not know how she would get on with Mr. Davies."

"Get on! why, well enough, of course. Women are soft, and can squeeze into most holes, especially if they are well lined. Besides, he may be a bit heavy, but I think she is pining for him, and it's a pity that she should waste her life like that. What, are you going to bed? Well, good-night—good-night."

Geoffrey did go to bed, but not to sleep. For a long while he lay awake, thinking. He thought of the last night which he had spent in this little room, of its strange experiences, of all that had happened since, and of the meeting of to-day. Could he, after that meeting, any longer doubt what were the feelings with which Beatrice regarded him? It was difficult to so, and yet there was still room for error. Then he thought of what old Edward had said to him, and of what Mr. Granger had said with reference to Beatrice and Owen Davies. The views of both were crudely and even vulgarly expressed, but they coincided, and, what was more, there was truth in them, and he knew it. The idea of Beatrice marrying Mr. Davies, to put it mildly, was repulsive to him; but had he any claim to stand between her and so desirable a settlement in life? Clearly, he had not, his conscience told him so.

Could it be right, moreover, that this kind of tie which existed between them should be knitted more closely? What would it mean? Trouble, and nothing but trouble, more especially to Beatrice, who would fret her days away to no end. He had done wrong in coming here at all, he had done wrong in taking her hand. He would make the only reparation in his power (as though in such a case as that of Beatrice reparation were now possible)! He would efface himself from her life and see her no more. Then she might learn to forget him, or, at the worst, to remember him with but a vague regret. Yes, cost what it might, he would force himself to do it before any actual mischief ensued. The only question was, should he not go further? Should he not tell her that she would do well to marry Mr. Davies?

Pondering over this most painful question, at last he went to sleep.

When men in Geoffrey's unhappy position turn penitent and see the error of their ways, the prudent resolves that ensue are apt to overshoot the mark and to partake of an aggressive nature. Not satisfied with leaving things alone, they must needs hasten to proclaim their new-found virtue to the partner of their fault, and advertise their infallible specific (to be taken by the partner) for restoring the status quo ante. Sometimes as a consequence of this pious zeal they find themselves misunderstood, or even succeed in precipitating the catastrophe which they laudably desire to prevent.

The morrow was Whit-Sunday, and a day that Geoffrey had occasion to remember for the rest of his life. They all met at breakfast and shortly afterwards went to church, the service being at half-past ten. By way of putting into effect the good resolutions with which he was so busy paving an inferno of his own, Geoffrey did not sit by Beatrice, but took a seat at the end of the little church, close to the door, and tried to console himself by looking at her.

It was a curious sullen-natured day, and although there was not very much sun the air was as hot as though they were in midsummer. Had they been in a volcanic region, Geoffrey would have thought that such weather preceded a shock of earthquake. As it was he knew that the English climate was simply indulging itself at the expense of the population. But as up to the present, the season had been cold, this knowledge did not console him. Indeed he felt so choked in the stuffy little church that just before the sermon (which he happened to be aware was not written by Beatrice) he took an opportunity to slip out unobserved. Not knowing where to go, he strolled down to the beach, on which there was nobody to be seen, for, as has been observed, Bryngelly slept on Sundays. Presently, however, a man approached walking rapidly, and to all appearance aimlessly, in whom he recognised Owen Davies. He was talking to himself while he walked, and swinging his arms. Geoffrey stepped aside to let him pass, and as he did so was surprised and even shocked to see the change in the man. His plump healthy-looking face had grown thin, and wore a half sullen, half pitiful expression; there were dark circles round his blue eyes, once so placid, and his hair would have been the better for cutting. Geoffrey wondered if he had had an illness. At that moment Owen chanced to look round and saw him.

"How do you do, Mr. Bingham?" he said. "I heard that you were here. They told me at the station last night. You see this is a small place and one likes to know who comes and goes," he added as though in excuse.

He walked on and Geoffrey walked with him.

"You do not look well, Mr. Davies," he said. "Have you been laid up?"

"No, no," he answered, "I am quite right; it is only my mind that is ill."

"Indeed," said Geoffrey, thinking that he certainly did look strange. "Perhaps you live too much alone and it depresses you."

"Yes, I live alone, because I can't help myself. What is a man to do, Mr. Bingham, when the woman he loves will not marry him, won't look at him, treats him like dirt?"

"Marry somebody else," suggested Geoffrey.

"Oh, it is easy for you to say that—you have never loved anybody, and you don't understand. I cannot marry anybody else, I want her only."

"Her? Whom?"

"Who! why, Beatrice—whom else could a man want to marry, if once he had seen her. But she will not have me; she hates me."

"Really," said Geoffrey.

"Yes, really, and do you know why? Shall I tell you why? I will tell you," and he grasped him by the arm and whispered hoarsely in his ear: "Because she loves you, Mr. Bingham."

"I tell you what it is, Mr. Davies," said Geoffrey shaking his arm free, "I am not going to stand this kind of thing. You must be off your head."

"Don't be angry with me," he answered. "It is true. I have watched her and I know that it is true. Why does she write to you every week, why does she always start and listen when anybody mentions your name? Oh, Mr. Bingham," Owen went on piteously, "be merciful—you have your wife and lots of women to make love to if you wish—leave me Beatrice. If you don't I think that I shall go crazed. I have always loved her, ever since she was a child, and now my love travels faster and grows stronger every day, and carries me away with it like a rock rolling down a hill. You can only bring Beatrice to shame, but I can give her everything, as much money as she wants, all that she wants, and I will make her a good husband; I will never leave her side."

"I have no doubt that would be delightful for her," answered Geoffrey; "but does it not strike you that all this is just a little undignified? These remarks, interesting as they are, should be made to Miss Granger, not to me, Mr. Davies."

"I know," he said, "but I don't care; it is my only chance, and what do I mind about being undignified? Oh, Mr. Bingham, I have never loved any other woman, I have been lonely all my days. Do not stand in my path now. If you only knew what I have suffered, how I have prayed God night after night to give me Beatrice, you would help me. Say that you will help me! You are one of those men who can do anything; she will listen to you. If you tell her to marry me she will do so, and I shall bless you my whole life."

Geoffrey looked upon this abject suppliant with the most unmitigated scorn. There is always something contemptible in the sight of one man pleading to another for assistance in his love affairs—that is a business which he should do for himself. How much greater, then, is the humiliation involved when the amorous person asks the aid of one whom he believes to be his rival—his successful rival—in the lady's affection?

"Do you know, Mr. Davies," Geoffrey said, "I think that I have had enough of this. I am not in a position to force Miss Granger to accept advances which appear to be unwelcome according to your account. But if I get an opportunity I will do this: I will tell her what you say. You really must manage the rest for yourself. Good morning to you, Mr. Davies."

He turned sharply and went while Owen watched him go.

"I don't believe him," he groaned to himself. "He will try to make her his lover. Oh, God help me—I cannot bear to think of it. But if he does, and I find him out, let him be careful. I will ruin him, yes, I will ruin him! I have the money and I can do it. Ah, he thinks me a fool, they all think me a fool, but I haven't been quiet all these years for nothing. I can make a noise if necessary. And if he is a villain, God will help me to destroy him. I have prayed to God, and God will help me."

Then he went back to the Castle. Owen Davies was a type of the class of religious men who believe that they can enlist the Almighty on the side of their desires, provided only that those desires receive the sanction of human law or custom.

Thus within twenty-four hours Geoffrey received no less than three appeals to help the woman whom he loved to the arms of a distasteful husband. No wonder then that he grew almost superstitious about the matter.

CHAPTER XXII

A NIGHT OF STORM

That afternoon the whole Vicarage party walked up to the farm to inspect another litter of young pigs. It struck Geoffrey, remembering former editions, that the reproductive powers of Mr. Granger's old sow were something little short of marvellous, and he dreamily worked out a calculation of how long it would take her and her progeny to produce a pig to every square yard of the area of plucky little Wales. It seemed that the thing could be done in six years, which was absurd, so he gave up calculating.

He had no words alone with Beatrice that afternoon. Indeed, a certain coldness seemed to have sprung up between them. With the almost supernatural quickness of a loving woman's intuition, she had divined that something was passing in his mind, inimical to her most vital interests, so she shunned his company, and received his conventional advances with a politeness which was as cold as it was crushing. This did not please Geoffrey; it is one thing (in her own interests, of course) to make up your mind heroically to abandon a lady whom you do not wish to compromise, and quite another to be snubbed by that lady before the moment of final separation. Though he never put the idea into words or even defined it in his mind—for Geoffrey was far too anxious and unhappy to be flippant, at any rate in thought—he would at heart have wished her to remain the same, indeed to wax ever tenderer, till the fatal time of parting arrived, and even to show appreciation of his virtuous conduct.

But to the utter destruction of most such hands as Geoffrey held, loving women never will play according to the book. Their conduct imperils everything, for it is obvious that it takes two to bring an affair of this nature to a dignified conclusion, even when the stakes are highest, and the matter is one of life and death. Beatrice after all was very much of a woman, and she did not behave much better than any other woman would have done. She was angry and suspicious, and she showed it, with the result that Geoffrey grew angry also. It was cruel of her, he thought, considering all things. He forgot that she could know nothing of what was in his mind, however much she might guess; also as yet he did not know the boundless depth and might of her passion for him, and all that it meant to her. Had he realised this he would have acted very differently.

They came home and took tea, then Mr. Granger and Elizabeth made ready to go to evening service. To Geoffrey's dismay Beatrice did the same. He had looked forward to a quiet walk with her—really this was not to be borne. Fortunately, or rather unfortunately, she was ready the first, and he got a word with her.

"I did not know that you were going to church," he said; "I thought that we might have had a walk together. Very likely I shall have to go away early to-morrow morning."

"Indeed," answered Beatrice coldly. "But of course you have your work to attend to. I told Elizabeth that I was coming to church, and I must go; it is too sultry to walk; there will be a storm soon."

At this moment Elizabeth came in.

"Well, Beatrice," she said, "are you coming to church? Father has gone on."

Beatrice pretended not to hear, and reflected a moment. He would go away and she would see him no more. Could she let slip this last hour? Oh, she could not do it!

In that moment of reflection her fate was sealed.

"No," she answered slowly, "I don't think that I am coming; it is too sultry to go to church. I daresay that Mr. Bingham will accompany you."

Geoffrey hastily disclaimed any such intention, and Elizabeth started alone. "Ah!" she said to herself, "I thought that you would not come, my dear."

"Well," said Geoffrey, when she had well gone, "shall we go out?"

"I think it is pleasanter here," answered Beatrice.

"Oh, Beatrice, don't be so unkind," he said feebly.

"As you like," she replied. "There is a fine sunset—but I think that we shall have a storm."

They went out, and turned up the lonely beach. The place was utterly deserted, and they walked a little way apart, almost without speaking. The sunset was magnificent; great flakes of golden cloud were driven continually from a home of splendour in the west towards the cold lined horizon of the land. The sea was still quiet, but it moaned like a thing in pain. The storm was gathering fast.

"What a lovely sunset," said Geoffrey at length.

"It is a fatal sort of loveliness," she answered; "it will be a bad night, and a wet morrow. The wind is rising; shall we turn?"

"No, Beatrice, never mind the wind. I want to speak to you, if you will allow me to do so."

"Yes," said Beatrice, "what about, Mr. Bingham."

To make good resolutions in a matter of this sort is comparatively easy, but the carrying of them out presents some difficulties. Geoffrey, conscience-stricken into priggishness, wished to tell her that she would do well to marry Owen Davies, and found the matter hard. Meanwhile Beatrice preserved silence.

"The fact is," he said at length, "I most sincerely hope you will forgive me, but I have been thinking a great deal about you and your future welfare."

"That is very kind of you," said Beatrice, with an ominous humility.

This was disconcerting, but Geoffrey was determined, and he went on in a somewhat flippant tone born of the most intense nervousness and hatred of his task. Never had he loved her so well as now in this moment when he was about to counsel her to marry another man. And yet he persevered in his folly. For, as so often happens, the shrewd insight and knowledge of the world which distinguished Geoffrey as a lawyer, when dealing with the affairs of others, quite deserted him in this crisis of his own life and that of the woman who worshipped him.

"Since I have been here," he said, "I have had made to me no less than three appeals on your behalf and by separate people—by your father, who fancies that you are pining for Owen Davies; by Owen Davies, who is certainly pining for you; and by old Edward, intervening as a kind of domestic amicus curiæ."

"Indeed," said Beatrice, in a voice of ice.

"All these three urged the same thing—the desirability of your marrying Owen Davies."

Beatrice's face grew quite pale, her lips twitched and her grey eyes flashed angrily.

"Really," she said, "and have you any advice to give on the subject, Mr. Bingham?"

"Yes, Beatrice, I have. I have thought it over, and I think that—forgive me again—that if you can bring yourself to it, perhaps you had better marry him. He is not such a bad sort of man, and he is well off."

They had been walking rapidly, and now they were reaching the spot known as the "Amphitheatre," that same spot where Owen Davies had proposed to Beatrice some seven months before.

Beatrice passed round the projecting edge of rock, and walked some way towards the flat slab of stone in the centre before she answered. While she did so a great and bitter anger filled her heart. She saw, or thought she saw, it all. Geoffrey wished to be rid of her. He had discerned an element of danger in their intimacy, and was anxious to make that intimacy impossible by pushing her into a hateful marriage.

Suddenly she turned and faced him—turned like a thing at bay. The last red rays of the sunset struck upon her lovely face made more lovely still by its stamp of haughty anger: they lay upon her heaving breast. Full in the eyes she looked him with those wide angry eyes of hers—never before had he seen her so imperial a mien. Her dignity and the power of her presence literally awed him, for at times Beatrice's beauty was of that royal stamp which when it hides a heart, is a compelling force, conquering and born to conquer.

"Does it not strike you, Mr. Bingham," she said quietly, "that you are taking a very great liberty? Does it not strike you that no man who is not a relation has any right to speak to a woman as you have spoken to me?—that, in short, you have been guilty of what in most people would be an impertinence? What right have you to dictate to me as to whom I should or should not marry? Surely of all things in the world that is my own affair."

Geoffrey coloured to the eyes. As would have been the case with most men of his class, he felt her accusation of having taken a liberty, of having presumed upon an intimacy, more keenly than any which she could have brought against him.

"Forgive me," he said humbly. "I can only assure you that I had no such intention. I only spoke—ill-judgedly, I fear—because—because I felt driven to it."

Beatrice took no notice of his words, but went on in the same cold voice.

"What right have you to speak of my affairs with Mr. Davies, with an old boatman, or even with my father? Had I wished you to do so I should have asked you. By what authority do you constitute yourself an intermediary for the purpose of bringing about a marriage which you are so good as to consider would be to my pecuniary interest? Do you not know that such a matter is one which the woman concerned, the woman whose happiness and self-respect are at stake, alone can judge of? I have nothing more to say except this. I said just now that you had been guilty of what would in most people be an impertinence. Well, I will add something. In this case, Mr. Bingham, there are circumstances which make it—a cruel insult!"

She stopped speaking, then suddenly, without the slightest warning, burst into passionate weeping. As she did so, the first rush of the storm passed over them, winnowing the air as with a thousand eagles' wings, and was lost on the moaning depths beyond.

The light went out of the sky. Now Geoffrey could only see the faint outlines of her weeping face. One moment he hesitated and one only; then Nature prevailed against him, for the next she was in his arms.

Beatrice scarcely resisted him. Her energies seemed to fail her, or perhaps she had spent them in her bitter words. Her head fell upon his shoulder, and there she sobbed her fill. Presently she lifted it and their lips met in a first long kiss. It was finished; this was the end of it—and thus did Geoffrey prosper Owen Davies's suit.

"Oh, you are cruel, cruel!" he whispered in her ear. "You must have known I loved you, Beatrice, that I spoke against myself because I thought it to be my duty. You must have known that, to my sin and sorrow, I have always loved you, that you have never been an hour from my mind, that I have longed to see your face like a sick man for the light. Tell me, did you not know it, Beatrice?"

"How should I know?" she answered very softly; "I could only guess, and if indeed you love me how could you wish me to marry another man? I thought that you had learned my weakness and took this way to reproach me. Oh, Geoffrey, what have we done? What is there between you and me—except our love?"

"It would have been better if we had been drowned together at the first," he said heavily.

"No, no," she answered, "for then we never should have loved one another. Better first to love, and then to die!"

"Do not speak so," he said; "let us sit here and be happy for a little while to-night, and leave trouble till to-morrow."

And, where on a bygone day Beatrice had tarried with another wooer, side by side they sat upon the great stone and talked such talk as lovers use.

Above them moaned the rising gale, though sheltered as they were by cliffs its breath scarcely stirred their hair. In front of them the long waves boomed upon the beach, while far out to sea the crescent moon, draped in angry light, seemed to ride the waters like a boat.

And were they alone with their great bliss, or did they only dream? Nay, they were alone with love and lovers' joys, and all the truth was told, and all their doubts were done. Now there was an end of hopes and fears; now reason fell and Love usurped his throne, and at that royal coming Heaven threw wide her gates. Oh, Sweetest and most dear! Oh, Dearest and most sweet! Oh, to have lived to find this happy hour—oh, in this hour to die!

See heaviness is behind us, see now we are one. Blow, you winds, blow out your stormy heart; we know the secret of your strength, you rush to your desire. Fall, deep waters of the sea, fall in thunder at the feet of earth; we hear the music of your pleading.

Earth, and Seas, and Winds, sing your great chant of love! Heaven and Space and Time, echo back the melody! For Life has called to us the answer of his riddle! Heart to heart we sit, and lips to lips, and we are more wise than Solomon, and richer than barbarian kings, for Happiness is ours.

To this end were we born, Dearest and most sweet, and from all time predestinate! To this end, Sweetest and most dear, do we live and die, in death to find completer unity. For here is that secret of the world which wise men search and cannot find, and here too is the gate of Heaven.

Look into my eyes, and let me gaze on yours, and listen how these things shall be. The world is but a mockery, and a shadow is our flesh, for where once they were there shall be naught. Only Love is real; Love shall endure till all the suns are dead, and yet be young.

Kiss me, thou Conqueror, for Destiny is overcome, Sorrow is gone by; and the flame that we have hallowed upon this earthly altar shall still burn brightly, and yet more bright, when yonder stars have lost their fire.

But alas! words cannot give a fitting form to such a song as this. Let music try! But music also folds her wings. For in so supreme an hour

"A bolt is shot back somewhere in our breast,"

and through that opened door come sights and sounds such as cannot be written.

They tell us it is madness, that this unearthly glory is but the frenzy of a passion gross in its very essence. Let those think it who will, but to dreamers let them leave their dreams. Why then, at such a time, do visions come to children of the world like Beatrice and Geoffrey? Why do their doubts vanish, and what is that breath from heaven which they seem to feel upon their brow? The intoxication of earthly love born of the meeting of youth and beauty. So be it! Slave, bring more such wine and let us drink—to Immortality and to those dear eyes that mirror forth a spirit's face!

Such loves indeed are few. For they must be real and deep, and natures thus shaped are rare, nor do they often cross each other's line of life. Yes, there are few who can be borne so high, and none can breathe that ether long. Soon the wings which Love lent them in his hour of revelation will shrink and vanish, and the borrowers will fall back to the level of this world, happy if they escape uncrushed. Perchance even in their life-days, they may find these spirit wings again, overshadowing the altar of their vows in the hour of earthly marriage, if by some happy fate, marriage should be within their reach, or like the holy pinions of the goddess Nout, folded about a coffin, in the time of earthly death. But scant are the occasions, and few there are who know them.

Thus soared Beatrice and Geoffrey while the wild night beat around them, making a fit accompaniment to their stormy loves. And thus they too fell from heaven to earth.

"We must be going, Geoffrey; it grows late," said Beatrice. "Oh, Geoffrey, Geoffrey, what have we done? What can be the end of all this? It will bring trouble on you, I know that it must. The old saying will come true. I saved your life, and I shall bring ruin on you!"

It is characteristic of Beatrice that already she was thinking of the consequences to Geoffrey, not of those to herself.

"Beatrice," said Geoffrey, "we are in a desperate position. Do you wish to face it and come away with me, far away to the other side of the world?"

"No, no," she answered vehemently, "it would be your ruin to abandon the career that is before you. What part of the world could you go to where you would not be known? Besides there is your wife to think of. Ah, God, your wife—what would she say of me? You belong to her, you have no right to desert her. And there is Effie too. No, Geoffrey, no, I have been wicked enough to learn to love you—oh, as you were never loved before, if it is wicked to do what one cannot help—but I am not bad enough for this. Walk quicker, Geoffrey; we shall be late, and they will suspect something."

Poor Beatrice, the pangs of conscience were finding her out!

"We are in a dreadful position," he said again. "Oh, dearest, I have been to blame. I should never have come back here. It is my fault; and though I never thought of this, I did my best to please you."

"And I thank you for it," she answered. "Do not deceive yourself, Geoffrey. Whatever happens, promise me never for one moment to believe that I reproached or blamed you. Why should I blame you because you won my heart? Let me sooner blame the sea on which we floated, the beach where we walked, the house in which we lived, and the Destiny that brought us together. I am proud and glad to love you, dear, but I am not so selfish as to wish to ruin you: Geoffrey—I had rather die."

"Don't talk so," he said, "I cannot bear it. What are we to do? Am I to go away and see you no more? How can we live so, Beatrice?"

"Yes, Geoffrey," she answered heavily, taking him by the hand and gazing up into his face, "you are to go away and see me no more, not for years and years. This is what we have brought upon ourselves, it is the price that we must pay for this hour which has gone. You are to go away to-morrow, that we may be put out of temptation, and you must come back no more. Sometimes I shall write to you, and sometimes perhaps you will write to me, till the thing becomes a burden, then you can stop. And whether you forget me or not—and, Geoffrey, I do not think you will—you will know that I shall never forget you, whom I saved from the sea—to love me."

There was something so sweet and infinitely tender about her words, instinct as they were with natural womanly passion, that Geoffrey bent at heart beneath their weight as a fir bends beneath the gentle, gathering snow. What was he to do, how could he leave her? And yet she was right. He must go, and go quickly, lest his strength might fail him, and hand in hand they should pass a bourne from which there is no return.

"Heaven help us, Beatrice," he said. "I will go to-morrow morning and, if I can, I will keep away."

"You must keep away. I will not see you any more. I will not bring trouble on you, Geoffrey."

"You talk of bringing trouble on me," he said; "you say nothing of yourself, and yet a man, even a man with eyes on him like myself, is better fitted to weather such a storm. If it ruined me, how much more would it ruin you?"

They were at the gate of the Vicarage now, and the wind rushed so strongly through the firs that she needed to put her lips quite close to his ear to make her words heard.

"Stop, one minute," she said, "perhaps you do not quite understand. When a woman does what I have done, it is because she loves with all her life and heart and soul, because all these are a part of her love. For myself, I no longer care anything—I have no self away from you; I have ceased to be of myself or in my own keeping. I am of you and in yours. For myself and my own fate or name I think no more; with my eyes open and of my own free will I have given everything to you, and am glad and happy to give it. But for you I still do care, and if I took any step, or allowed you to take any that could bring sorrow on you, I should never forgive myself. That is why we must part, Geoffrey. And now let us go in; there is nothing more to say, except this: if you wish to bid me good-bye, a last good-bye, dear Geoffrey, I will meet you to-morrow morning on the beach."

"I shall leave at half-past eight," he said hoarsely.

"Then we will meet at seven," Beatrice said, and led the way into the house.

Elizabeth and Mr. Granger were already seated at supper. They supped at nine on Sunday nights; it was just half-past.

"Dear me," said the old gentleman, "we began to think that you two must have been out canoeing and got yourselves drowned in good earnest this time. What have you been doing?"

"We have had a long walk," answered Geoffrey; "I did not know that it was so late."

"One wants to be pleased with one's company to walk far on such a night as this," put in Elizabeth maliciously.

"And so we were—at least I was," Geoffrey answered with perfect truth, "and the night is not so bad as you might think, at least under the lee of the cliffs. It will be worse by and by!"

Then they sat down and made a desperate show of eating supper. Elizabeth, the keen-eyed, noticed that Geoffrey's hand was shaking. Now what, she wondered, would make the hand of a strong man shake like a leaf? Deep emotion might do it, and Elizabeth thought that she detected other signs of emotion in them both, besides that of Geoffrey's shaking hand. The plot was working well, but could it be brought to a climax? Oh, if he would only throw prudence to the winds and run away with Beatrice, so that she might be rid of her, and free to fight for her own hand.

Shortly after supper both Elizabeth and Beatrice went to bed, leaving their father with Geoffrey.

"Well," said Mr. Granger, "did you get a word with Beatrice? It was very kind of you to go that long tramp on purpose. Gracious, how it blows! we shall have the house down presently. Lightning, too, I declare."

"Yes," answered Geoffrey, "I did."

"Ah, I hope you told her that there was no need for her to give up hope of him yet, of Mr. Davies, I mean?"

"Yes, I told her that—that is if the greater includes the less," he added to himself.

"And how did she take it?"

"Very badly," said Geoffrey; "she seemed to think that I had no right to interfere."

"Indeed, that is strange. But it doesn't mean anything. She's grateful enough to you at heart, depend upon it she is, only she did not like to say so. Dear me, how it blows; we shall have a night of it, a regular gale, I declare. So you are going away to-morrow morning. Well, the best of friends must part. I hope that you will often come and see us. Good-bye."

Once more a sense of the irony of the position overcame Geoffrey, and he smiled grimly as he lit his candle and went to bed. At the back of the house was a long passage, which terminated at one end in the room where he slept, and at the other in that occupied by Elizabeth and Beatrice. This passage was lit by two windows, and built out of it were two more rooms—that of Mr. Granger, and another which had been Effie's. The windows of the passage, like most of the others in the Vicarage, were innocent of shutters, and Geoffrey stood for a moment at one of them, watching the lightning illumine the broad breast of the mountain behind. Then looking towards the door of Beatrice's room, he gazed at it with the peculiar reverence that sometimes afflicts people who are very much in love, and, with a sigh, turned and sought his own.

He could not sleep, it was impossible. For nearly two hours he lay turning from side to side, and thinking till his brain seemed like to burst. To-morrow he must leave her, leave her for ever, and go back to his coarse unprofitable struggle with the world, where there would be no Beatrice to make him happy through it all. And she, what of her?

The storm had lulled a little, now it came back in strength, heralded by the lightning. He rose, threw on a dressing-gown, and sat by a window watching it. Its tumult and fury seemed to ease his heart of some little of its pain; in that dark hour a quiet night would have maddened him.

In eight hours—eight short hours—this matter would be ended so far as concerned their actual intercourse. It would be a secret locked for ever in their two breasts, a secret eating at their hearts, cruel as the worm that dieth not. Geoffrey looked up and threw out his heart's thought towards his sleeping love. Then once more, as in a bygone night, there broke upon his brain and being that mysterious spiritual sense. Stronger and more strong it grew, beating on him in heavy unnatural waves, till his reason seemed to reel and sink, and he remembered naught but Beatrice, knew naught save that her very life was with him now.

He stretched out his arms towards the place where she should be.

"Beatrice," he whispered to the empty air, "Beatrice! Oh, my love! my sweet! my soul! Hear me, Beatrice!"

There came a pause, and ever the unearthly sympathy grew and gathered in his heart, till it seemed to him as though separation had lost its power and across dividing space they were mingled in one being.

A great gust shook the house and passed away along the roaring depths.

Oh! what was this? Silently the door opened, and a white draped form passed its threshold. He rose, gasping; a terrible fear, a terrible joy, took possession of him. The lightning flared out wildly in the eastern sky. There in the fierce light she stood before him—she, Beatrice, a sight of beauty and of dread. She stood with white arms outstretched, with white uncovered feet, her bosom heaving softly beneath her night-dress, her streaming hair unbound, her lips apart, her face upturned, and a stamp of terrifying calm.

"In the wide, blind eyes uplift Thro' the darkness and the drift."

Great Heaven, she was asleep!

Hush! she spoke.

"You called me, Geoffrey," she said, in a still, unnatural voice. "You called me, my beloved, and I—have—come."

He rose aghast, trembling like an aspen with doubt and fear, trembling at the sight of the conquering glory of the woman whom he worshipped.

See! She drew on towards him, and she was asleep. Oh, what could he do?

Suddenly the draught of the great gale rushing through the house caught the opened door and crashed it to.

She awoke with a wild stare of terror.

"Oh, God, where am I?" she cried.

"Hush, for your life's sake!" he answered, his faculties returning. "Hush! or you are lost."

But there was no need to caution here to silence, for Beatrice's senses failed her at the shock, and she sank swooning in his arms.

CHAPTER XXIII

A DAWN OF RAIN

That crash of the closing door did not awake Beatrice only; it awoke both Elizabeth and Mr. Granger. Elizabeth sat up in bed straining her eyes through the gloom to see what had happened. They fell on Beatrice's bed—surely—surely—

Elizabeth slipped up, cat-like she crept across the room and felt with her hand at the bed. Beatrice was not there. She sprang to the blind and drew it, letting in such light as there was, and by it searched the room. She spoke: "Beatrice, where are you?"

No answer.

"Ah—h," said Elizabeth aloud; "I understand. At last—at last!"

What should see do? Should she go and call her father and put them to an open shame? No. Beatrice must come back some time. The knowledge was enough; she wanted the knowledge to use if necessary. She did not wish to ruin her sister unless in self-defence, or rather, for the cause of self-advancement. Still less did she wish to injure Geoffrey, against whom she had no grudge. So she peeped along the passage, then returning, crept back to her bed like a snake into a hole and watched.

Mr. Granger, hearing the crash, thought that the front door had blown open. Rising, he lit a candle and went to see.

But of all this Geoffrey knew nothing, and Beatrice naturally less than nothing.

She lay senseless in his arms, her head rested on his shoulder, her heavy hair streamed down his side almost to his knee. He lifted her, touched her on the forehead with his lips and laid her on the bed. What was to be done? Bring her back to life? No, he dared not—not here. While she lay thus her helplessness protected her; but if once more she was a living, loving woman here and so—oh, how should they escape? He dared not touch her or look towards her—till he had made up his mind. It was soon done. Here she must not bide, and since of herself she could not go, why he must take her now, this moment! However far Geoffrey fell short of virtue's stricter standard, let this always be remembered in his favour.

He opened the door, and as he did so, thought that he heard some one stirring in the house. And so he did; it was Mr. Granger in the sitting-room. Hearing no more, Geoffrey concluded that it was the wind, and turning, groped his way to the bed where Beatrice lay as still as death. For one moment a horrible fear struck him that she might be dead. He had heard of cases of somnambulists who, on being startled from their unnatural sleep, only woke to die. It might be so with her. Hurriedly he placed his hand upon her breast. Yes, her heart stirred—faintly indeed, but still it stirred. She had only swooned. Then he set his teeth, and placing his arms about her, lifted her as though she were a babe. Beatrice was no slip of a girl, but a well-grown woman of full size. He never felt her weight; it seemed nothing to him. Stealthily as one bent on midnight murder, he stepped with her to the door and through it into the passage. Then supporting her with one arm, he closed the door with his left hand. Stealthily in the gloom he passed along the corridor, his bare feet making no noise upon the boarded floor, till he reached the bisecting passage leading from the sitting-rooms.

He glanced up it apprehensively, and what he saw froze the blood in his veins, for there coming down it, not eight paces from him, was Mr. Granger, holding a candle in his hand. What could be done? To get back to his room was impossible—to reach that of Beatrice was also impossible. With an effort he collected his thoughts, and like a flash of light it passed into his mind that the empty room was not two paces from him. A stride and he had reached it. Oh, where was the handle? and oh, if the room should be locked! By a merciful chance it was not. He stepped through the door, knocking Beatrice's feet against the framework as he did so, closed it—to shut it he had no time—and stood gasping behind it.

The gleam of light drew nearer. Merciful powers! he had been seen—the old man was coming in. What could he say? Tell the truth, that was all; but who would believe such a story? why, it was one that he should scarcely care to advance in a court of law. Could he expect a father to believe it—a father finding a man crouched like a thief behind a door at the dead of night with his lovely daughter senseless in his arms? He had already thought of going straight to Mr. Granger, but had abandoned the idea as hopeless. Who would believe this tale of sleep-walking? For the first time in his life Geoffrey felt terribly afraid, both for Beatrice and himself; the hair rose on his head, his heart stood still, and a cold perspiration started on to his face.

"It's very odd," he heard the old man mutter to himself; "I could almost swear that I saw something white go into that room. Where's the handle? If I believed in ghosts—hullo! my candle has blown out! I must go and hunt for a match. Don't quite like going in there without a light."

For the moment they were saved. The fierce draught rushing through the open crack of the door from the ill-fitting window had extinguished the candle.

Geoffrey waited a few seconds to allow Mr. Granger to reach his room, and then once more started on his awful journey. He passed out of the room in safety; happily Beatrice showed no signs of recovery. A few quick steps and he was at her own door. And now a new terror seized him. What if Elizabeth was also walking the house or even awake? He thought of putting Beatrice down at the door and leaving her there, but abandoned the idea. To begin with, her father might see her, and then how could her presence be accounted for? or if he did not, she would certainly suffer ill effects from the cold. No, he must risk it, and at once, though he would rather have faced a battery of guns. The door fortunately was ajar. Geoffrey opened it with his foot, entered, and with his foot pushed it to again. Suddenly he remembered that he had never been in the room, and did not know which bed belonged to Beatrice. He walked to the nearest; a deep-drawn breath told him that it was the wrong one. Drawing some faint consolation from the fact that Elizabeth was evidently asleep, he groped his way to the second bed through the deep twilight of the room. The clothes were thrown back. He laid Beatrice down and threw them over her. Then he fled.

As he reached the door he saw Mr. Granger's light disappear into his own room and heard his door close. After that it seemed to him that he took but two steps and was in his own place.

He burst out laughing; there was as much hysteria in the laugh as a man gives way to. His nerves were shattered by struggle, love and fear, and sought relief in ghastly merriment. Somehow the whole scene reminded him of one in a comic opera. There was a ludicrous side to it. Supposing that the political opponents, who already hated him so bitterly, could have seen him slinking from door to door at midnight with an unconscious lady in his arms—what would they have said?

He ceased laughing; the fit passed—indeed it was no laughing matter. Then he thought of the first night of their strange communion, that night before he had returned to London. The seed sown in that hour had blossomed and borne fruit indeed. Who would have dreamed it possible that he should thus have drawn Beatrice to him? Well, he ought to have known. If it was possible that the words which floated through her mind could arise in his as they had done upon that night, what was not possible? And were there not other words, written by the same master-hand, which told of such things as these:

"'Now—now,' the door is heard; Hark, the stairs! and near— Nearer—and here— 'Now'! and at call the third, She enters without a word.

Like the doors of a casket shrine, See on either side, Her two arms divide Till the heart betwixt makes sign, 'Take me, for I am thine.'

First, I will pray. Do Thou That ownest the soul, Yet wilt grant control To another, nor disallow For a time, restrain me now!"

Did they not run thus? Oh, he should have known! This he could plead, and this only—that control had been granted to him.

But how would Beatrice fare? Would she come to herself safely? He thought so, it was only a fainting fit. But when she did recover, what would she do? Nothing rash, he prayed. And what could be the end of it all? Who might say? How fortunate that the sister had been so sound asleep. Somehow he did not trust Elizabeth—he feared her.

Well might Geoffrey fear her! Elizabeth's sleep was that of a weasel. She too was laughing at this very moment, laughing, not loud but long—the laugh of one who wins.

She had seen him enter, his burden in his arms; saw him come with it to her own bedside, and had breathed heavily to warn him of his mistake. She had watched him put Beatrice on her bed, and heard him sigh and turn away; nothing had escaped her. As soon as he was gone, she had risen and crept up to Beatrice, and finding that she was only in a faint had left her to recover, knowing her to be in no danger.

Elizabeth was not a nervous person. Then she had listened till at length a deep sigh told her of the return of her sister's consciousness. After this there was a pause, till presently Beatrice's long soft breaths showed that she had glided from swoon to sleep.

The slow night wore away, and at length the cold dawn crept through the window. Elizabeth still watching, for she was not willing to lose a single scene of a drama so entrancing in itself and so important to her interests, saw her sister suddenly sit up in bed and press her hands to her forehead, as though she was striving to recall a dream. Then Beatrice covered her eyes with her hands and groaned heavily. Next she looked at her watch, rose, drank a glass of water, and dressed herself, even to the putting on of an old grey waterproof with a hood to it, for it was wet outside.

"She is going to meet her lover," thought Elizabeth. "I wish I could be there to see that too, but I have seen enough."

She yawned and appeared to wake. "What, Beatrice, going out already in this pouring rain?" she said, with feigned astonishment.

"Yes, I have slept badly and I want to get some air," answered Beatrice, starting and colouring; "I suppose that it was the storm."

"Has there been a storm?" said Elizabeth, yawning again. "I heard nothing of it—but then so many things happen when one is asleep of which one knows nothing at the time," she added sleepily, like one speaking at random. "Mind that you are back to say good-bye to Mr. Bingham; he goes by the early train, you know—but perhaps you will see him out walking," and appearing to wake up thoroughly, she raised herself in bed and gave her sister one piercing look.

Beatrice made no answer; that look sent a thrill of fear through her. Oh; what had happened! Or was it all a dream? Had she dreamed that she stood face to face with Geoffrey in his room before a great darkness struck her and overwhelmed her? Or was it an awful truth, and if a truth, how came she here again? She went to the pantry, found a morsel of bread and ate it, for faintness still pursued her. Then feeling better, she left the house and set her face towards the beach.

It was a dreary morning. The great wind had passed; now it only blew in little gusts heavy with driving rain. The sea was sullen and grey and grand. It beat in thunder on the shore and flew over the sunken rocks in columns of leaden spray. The whole earth seemed one desolation, and all its grief was centred in this woman's broken heart.

Geoffrey, too, was up. How he had passed the remainder of that tragic night we need not inquire—not too happily we may be sure. He heard the front door close behind Beatrice, and followed out into the rain.

On the beach, some half of a mile away, he found her gazing at the sea, a great white gull wheeling about her head. No word of greeting passed between them; they only grasped each other's hands and looked into each other's hollow eyes.

"Come under the shelter of the cliff," he said, and she came. She stood beneath the cliff, her head bowed low, her face hidden by the hood, and spoke.

"Tell me what has happened," she said; "I have dreamed something, a worse dream than any that have gone before—tell me if it is true. Do not spare me."

And Geoffrey told her all.

When he had finished she spoke again.

"By what shall I swear," she said, "that I am not the thing which you must think me? Geoffrey, I swear by my love for you that I am innocent. If I came—oh, the shame of it! if I came—to your room last night, it was my feet which led me, not my mind that led my feet. I went to sleep, I was worn out, and then I knew no more till I heard a dreadful sound, and saw you before me in a blaze of light, after which there was darkness."

"Oh, Beatrice, do not be distressed," he answered. "I saw that you were asleep. It is a dreadful thing which has happened, but I do not think that we were seen."

"I do not know," she said. "Elizabeth looked at me very strangely this morning, and she sees everything. Geoffrey, for my part, I neither know nor care. What I do care for is, what must you think of me? You must believe, oh!—I cannot say it. And yet I am innocent. Never, never did I dream of this. To come to you—thus—oh, it is shameless!"

"Beatrice, do not talk so. I tell you I know it. Listen—I drew you. I did not mean that you should come. I did not think that you would come, but it was my doing. Listen to me, dear," and he told her that which written words can ill express.

When he had finished, she looked up, with another face; the deep shadow of her shame had left her. "I believe you, Geoffrey," she said, "because I know that you have not invented this to shield me, for I have felt it also. See by it what you are to me. You are my master and my all. I cannot withstand you if I would. I have little will apart from yours if you choose to gainsay mine. And now promise me this upon your word. Leave me uninfluenced; do not draw me to you to be your ruin. I make no pretence, I have laid my life at your feet, but while I have any strength to struggle against it, you shall never take it up unless you can do so to your own honour, and that is not possible. Oh, my dear, we might have been very happy together, happier than men and women often are, but it is denied to us. We must carry our cross, we must crucify the flesh upon it; perhaps so—who can say?—we may glorify the spirit. I owe you a great deal. I have learnt much from you, Geoffrey. I have learned to hope again for a Hereafter. Nothing is left to me now—but that—that and an hour hence—your memory.

"Oh, why should I weep? It is ungrateful, when I have your love, for which this misery is but a little price to pay. Kiss me, dear, and go—and never see me more. You will not forget me, I know now that you will never forget me all your life. Afterwards—perhaps—who can tell? If not, why then—it will indeed be best—to die."

It is not well to linger over such a scene as this. After all, too, it is nothing. Only another broken heart or so. The world breaks so many this way and the other that it can have little pleasure in gloating over such stale scenes of agony.

Besides we must not let our sympathies carry us away. Geoffrey and Beatrice deserved all they got; they had no business to put themselves into such a position. They had defied the customs of their world, and the world avenged itself upon them and their petty passions. What happens to the worm that tries to burrow on the highways? Grinding wheels and crushing feet; these are its portion. Beatrice and Geoffrey point a moral and adorn a tale. So far as we can see and judge there was no need for them to have plunged into that ever-running river of human pain. Let them struggle and drown, and let those who are on the bank learn wisdom from the sight, and hold out no hand to help them.

Geoffrey drew a ring from his finger and gave it to his love. It was a common flat-sided silver ring that had been taken from the grave of a Roman soldier: one peculiarity it had, however; on its inner surface were roughly cut the words, "ave atque vale." Greeting and farewell! It was a fitting gift to pass between people in their position. Beatrice, trembling sorely, whispered that she would wear it on her heart, upon her hand she could not put it yet awhile—it might be recognised.

Then thrice did they embrace there upon the desolate shore, once, as it were, for past joy, once for present pain, and once for future hope, and parted. There was no talk of after meetings—they felt them to be impossible, at any rate for many years. How could they meet as indifferent friends? Too much they loved for that. It was a final parting, than which death had been less dreadful—for Hope sits ever by the bed of death—and misery crushed them to the earth.

He left her, and happiness went out of his life as at nightfall the daylight goes out of the day. Well, at least he had his work to go to. But Beatrice, poor woman, what had she?

Geoffrey left her. When he had gone some thirty paces he turned again and gazed his last upon her. There she stood or rather leant, her hand resting against the wet rock, looking after him with her wide grey eyes. Even through the drizzling rain he could see the gleam of her rich hair, the marking of her lovely face, and the carmine of her lips. She motioned to him to go on. He went, and when he had traversed a hundred paces looked round once more. She was still there, but now her face was a blur, and again the great white gull hovered about her head.

Then the mist swept up and hid her.

Ah, Beatrice, with all your brains you could never learn those simple principles necessary to the happiness of woman; principles inherited through a thousand generations of savage and semi-civilized ancestresses. To accept the situation and the master that situation brings with it—this is the golden rule of well-being. Not to put out the hand of your affection further than you can draw it back, this is another, at least not until you are quite sure that its object is well within your grasp. If by misfortune, or the anger of the Fates, you are endowed with those deeper qualities, those extreme capacities of self-sacrificing affection, such as ruined your happiness, Beatrice, keep them in stock; do not expose them to the world. The world does not believe in them; they are inconvenient and undesirable; they are even immoral. What the world wants, and very rightly, in a person of your attractiveness is quiet domesticity of character, not the exhibition of attributes which though they might qualify you for the rank of heroine in a Greek drama, are nowadays only likely to qualify you for the reprobation of society.

What? you would rather keep your love, your reprehensible love which never can be satisfied, and bear its slings and arrows, and die hugging a shadow to your heart, straining your eyes into the darkness of that beyond whither you shall go—murmuring with your pale lips that there you will find reason and fulfilment? Why it is folly. What ground have you to suppose that you will find anything of the sort? Go and take the opinion of some scientific person of eminence upon this infatuation of yours and those vague visions of glory that shall be. He will explain it clearly enough, will show you that your love itself is nothing but a natural passion, acting, in your case, on a singularly sensitive and etherealised organism. Be frank with him, tell him of your secret hopes. He will smile tenderly, and show you how those also are an emanation from a craving heart, and the innate superstitions of mankind. Indeed he will laugh and illustrate the absurdity of the whole thing by a few pungent examples of what would happen if these earthly affections could be carried beyond the grave. Take what you can now will be the burden of his song, and for goodness' sake do not waste your precious hours in dreams of a To Be.

Beatrice, the world does not want your spirituality. It is not a spiritual world; it has no clear ideas upon the subject—it pays its religious premium and works off its aspirations at its weekly church going, and would think the person a fool who attempted to carry theories of celestial union into an earthly rule of life. It can sympathise with Lady Honoria; it can hardly sympathise with you.

And yet you will still choose this better part: you will still "live and love, and lose."

"With blinding tears and passionate beseeching, And outstretched arms through empty silence reaching."

Then, Beatrice, have your will, sow your seed of tears, and take your chance. You may find that you were right and the worldlings wrong, and you may reap a harvest beyond the grasp of their poor imaginations. And if you find that they are right and you are wrong, what will it matter to you who sleep? For of this at least you are sure. If there is no future for such earthly love as yours, then indeed there is none for the children of this world and all their troubling.

CHAPTER XXIV

LADY HONORIA TAKES THE FIELD

Geoffrey hurried to the Vicarage to fetch his baggage and say good-bye. He had no time for breakfast, and he was glad of it, for he could not have eaten a morsel to save his life. He found Elizabeth and her father in the sitting-room.

"Why, where have you been this wet morning, Mr. Bingham?" said Mr. Granger.

"I have been for a walk with Miss Beatrice; she is coming home by the village," he answered. "I don't mind rain, and I wanted to get as much fresh air as I could before I go back to the mill. Thank you—only a cup of tea—I will get something to eat as I go."

"How kind of him," reflected Mr. Granger; "no doubt he has been speaking to Beatrice again about Owen Davies."

"Oh, by the way," he added aloud, "did you happen to hear anybody moving in the house last night, Mr. Bingham, just when the storm was at its height? First of all a door slammed so violently that I got up to see what it was, and as I came down the passage I could almost have sworn that I saw something white go into the spare room. But my candle went out and by the time that I had found a light there was nothing to be seen."

"A clear case of ghosts," said Geoffrey indifferently. It was indeed a "case of ghosts," and they would, he reflected, haunt him for many a day.

"How very odd," put in Elizabeth vivaciously, her keen eyes fixed intently on his face. "Do you know I thought that I twice saw the door of our room open and shut in the most mysterious fashion. I think that Beatrice must have something to do with it; she is so uncanny in her ways."

Geoffrey never moved a muscle, he was trained to keep his countenance. Only he wondered how much this woman knew. She must be silenced somehow.

"Excuse me for changing the subject," he said, "but my time is short, and I have none to spare to hunt the 'Vicarage Ghost.' By the way, there's a good title for somebody. Mr. Granger, I believe that I may speak of business matters before Miss Elizabeth?"

"Certainly, Mr. Bingham," said the clergyman; "Elizabeth is my right hand, and has the best business head in Bryngelly."

Geoffrey thought that this was very evident, and went on. "I only want to say this. If you get into any further difficulties with your rascally tithe-payers, mind and let me know. I shall always be glad to help you while I can. And now I must be going."

He spoke thus for two reasons. First, naturally enough, he meant to make it his business to protect Beatrice from the pressure of poverty, and well knew that it would be useless to offer her direct assistance. Secondly, he wished to show Elizabeth that it would not be to the advantage of her family to quarrel with him. If she had seen a ghost, perhaps this fact would make her reticent on the subject. He did not know that she was playing a much bigger game for her own hand, a game of which the stakes were thousands a year, and that she was moreover mad with jealousy and what, in such a woman, must pass for love.

Elizabeth made no comment on his offer, and before Mr. Granger's profuse thanks were nearly finished, Geoffrey was gone.

Three weeks passed at Bryngelly, and Elizabeth still held her hand. Beatrice, pale and spiritless, went about her duties as usual. Elizabeth never spoke to her in any sense that could awaken her suspicions, and the ghost story was, or appeared to be, pretty well forgotten. But at last an event occurred that caused Elizabeth to take the field. One day she met Owen Davies walking along the beach in the semi-insane way which he now affected. He stopped, and, without further ado, plunged into conversation.

"I can't bear it any longer," he said wildly, throwing up his arms. "I saw her yesterday, and she cut me short before I could speak a word. I have prayed for patience and it will not come, only a Voice seemed to say to me that I must wait ten days more, ten short days, and then Beatrice, my beautiful Beatrice, would be my wife at last."

"If you go on in this way, Mr. Davies," said Elizabeth sharply, her heart filled with jealous anger, "you will soon be off your head. Are you not ashamed of yourself for making such a fuss about a girl's pretty face? If you want to get married, marry somebody else."

"Marry somebody else," he said dreamily; "I don't know anybody else whom I could marry except you, and you are not Beatrice."

"No," answered Elizabeth angrily, "I should hope that I have more sense, and if you wanted to marry me you would have to set about it in a different way from this. I am not Beatrice, thank Heaven, but I am her sister, and I warn you that I know more about her than you do. As a friend I warn you to be careful. Supposing that Beatrice were not worthy of you, you would not wish to marry her, would you?"

Now Owen Davies was at heart somewhat afraid of Elizabeth, like most other people who had the privilege of her acquaintance. Also, apart from matters connected with his insane passion, he was very fairly shrewd. He suspected Elizabeth of something, he did not know of what.

"No, no, of course not," he said. "Of course I would not marry her if she was not fit to be my wife—but I must know that first, before I talk of marrying anybody else. Good afternoon, Miss Elizabeth. It will soon be settled now; it cannot go on much longer now. My prayers will be answered, I know they will."

"You are right there, Owen Davies," thought Elizabeth, as she looked after him with ineffable bitterness, not to say contempt. "Your prayers shall be answered in a way that will astonish you. You shall not marry Beatrice, and you shall marry me. The fish has been on the line long enough, now I must begin to pull in."

Curiously enough it never really occurred to Elizabeth that Beatrice herself might prove to be the true obstacle to the marriage she plotted to prevent. She knew that her sister was fond of Geoffrey Bingham, but, when it came to the point that she would absolutely allow her affection to interfere with so glorious a success in life, she never believed for one moment. Of course she thought it was possible that if Beatrice could get possession of Geoffrey she might prefer to do so, but failing him, judging from her own low and vulgar standard, Elizabeth was convinced that she would take Owen. It did not seem possible that what was so precious in her own eyes might be valueless and even hateful to those of her sister. As for that little midnight incident, well, it was one thing and marriage was another. People forget such events when they marry; sometimes even they marry in order to forget them.

Yes, she must strike, but how? Elizabeth had feelings like other people. She did not mind ruining her sister and rival, but she would very much prefer it should not be known that hers was the hand to cut her down. Of course, if the worst came to the worst, she must do it. Meanwhile, might not a substitute be found—somebody in whom the act would seem not one of vengeance, but of virtue? Ah! she had it: Lady Honoria! Who could be better for such a purpose than the cruelly injured wife? But then how should she communicate the facts to her ladyship without involving herself? Again she hit upon a device much favoured by such people—"un vieux truc mais toujours bon"—the pristine one of an anonymous letter, which has the startling merit of not committing anybody to anything. An anonymous letter, to all appearance written by a servant: it was the very thing! Most likely it would result in a searching inquiry by Lady Honoria, in which event Elizabeth, of course against her will, would be forced to say what she knew; almost certainly it would result in a quarrel between husband and wife, which might induce the former to show his hand, or even to take some open step as regards Beatrice. She was sorry for Geoffrey, against whom she had no ill feeling, but it could not be helped; he must be sacrificed.

That very evening she wrote her letter and sent it to be posted by an old servant living in London. It was a master-piece in its way, especially phonetically. This precious epistle, which was most exceedingly ill writ in a large coarse hand, ran thus:

"My Ladi,—My consence druvs me to it, much again my will. I've tried hard, my ladi, not to speek, first acorse of miss B. as i heve knowed good and peur and also for the sakes of your evil usband that wulf in scheeps cloathin. But when i think on you my ladi a lorful legel wife gud and virtus and peur and of the things as i hev seen which is enuf to bring a blush to the face of a stater, I knows it is my holy dooty to rite your ladishipp as follers. Your ladishipp forgif me but on the nite of whittsundey last Miss B. Grainger wint after midnite inter the room of your bad usband—as I was to mi sham ther to se. Afterward more nor an hour, she cum out ain being carred in his harmes. And if your ladishipp dont believ me, let your ladishipp rite to miss elizbeth, as had this same misfortune to see as your tru frend,

"The Riter."

In due course this charming communication reached Lady Honoria, bearing a London post-mark. She read and re-read it, and soon mastered its meaning. Then, after a night's thought, she took the "Riter's" advice and wrote to Elizabeth, sending her a copy of the letter (her own), vehemently repudiating all belief in it, and asking for a reply that should dissipate this foul slander from her mind for ever.

The answer came by return. It was short and artful.

"Dear Lady Honoria Bingham," it ran, "you must forgive me if I decline to answer the questions in your letter. You will easily understand that between a desire to preserve a sister's reputation and an incapacity (to be appreciated by every Christian) to speak other than the truth—it is possible for a person to be placed in the most cruel of positions—a position which I am sure will command even your sympathy, though under such circumstances I have little right to expect any from a wife believing herself to have been cruelly wronged. Let me add that nothing short of the compulsion of a court of law will suffice to unseal my lips as to the details of the circumstances (which are, I trust, misunderstood) alluded to in the malicious anonymous letter of which you inclose a copy."

That very evening, as the Fates would have it, Lady Honoria and her husband had a quarrel. As usual, it was about Effie, for on most other subjects they preserved an armed neutrality. Its details need not be entered into, but at last Geoffrey, who was in a sadly irritable condition of mind, fairly lost his temper.

"The fact is," he said, "that you are not fit to look after the child. You only think of yourself, Honoria."

She turned on him with a dangerous look upon her cold and handsome face.

"Be careful what you say, Geoffrey. It is you who are not fit to have charge of Effie. Be careful lest I take her away from you altogether, as I can if I like."

"What do you mean by that threat?" he asked.

"Do you want to know? Then I will tell you. I understand enough law to be aware that a wife can get a separation from an unfaithful husband, and what is more, can take away his children."

"Again I ask what you mean," said Geoffrey, turning cold with anger.

"I mean this, Geoffrey. That Welsh girl is your mistress. She passed the night of Whit-Sunday in your room, and was carried from it in your arms."

"It is a lie," he said; "she is nothing of the sort. I do not know who gave you this information, but it is a slanderous lie, and somebody shall suffer for it."

"Nobody will suffer for it, Geoffrey, because you will not dare to stir the matter up—for the girl's sake if not for your own. Can you deny that you were seen carrying her in your arms from your room on Whit-Sunday night? Can you deny that you are in love with her?"

"And supposing that I am in love with her, is it to be wondered at, seeing how you treat me and have treated me for years?" he answered furiously. "It is utterly false to say that she is my mistress."

"You have not answered my question," said Lady Honoria with a smile of triumph. "Were you seen carrying that woman in your arms and from your room at the dead of night? Of course it meant nothing, nothing at all. Who would dare to asperse the character of this perfect, lovely, and intellectual schoolmistress? I am not jealous, Geoffrey—"

"I should think not, Honoria, seeing how things are."

"I am not jealous, I repeat, but please understand that I will not have this go on, in your own interests and mine. Why, what a fool you must be. Don't you know that a man who has risen, as you have, has a hundred enemies ready to spring on him like a pack of wolves and tear him to pieces? Why many even of those who fawn upon you and flatter you to your face, hate you bitterly in secret, because you have succeeded where they have failed. Don't you know also that there are papers here in London which would give hundreds of pounds for the chance of publishing such a scandal as this, especially against a powerful political opponent. Let it once come out that this obscure girl is your mistress—"

"Honoria, I tell you she is nothing of the sort. It is true I carried her from my room in a fainting fit, but she came there in her sleep."

Lady Honoria laughed. "Really, Geoffrey, I wonder that you think it worth while to tell me such nonsense. Keep it for the divorce court, if ever we get there, and see what a jury says to it. Look here; be sensible. I am not a moralist, and I am not going to play the outraged wife unless you force me to it. I do not mean to take any further notice of this interesting little tale as against you. But if you go on with it, beware! I will not be made to look a fool. If you are going to be ruined you can be ruined by yourself. I warn you frankly, that at the first sign of it, I shall put myself in the right by commencing proceedings against you. Now, of course, I know this, that in the event of a smash, you would be glad enough to be rid of me in order that you might welcome your dear Beatrice in my place. But there are two things to remember: first, that you could not marry her, supposing you to be idiot enough to wish to do so, because I should only get a judicial separation, and you would still have to support me. Secondly, if I go, Effie goes with me, for I have a right to claim her at law; and that fact, my dear Geoffrey, makes me mistress of the situation, because I do not suppose that you would part with Effie even for the sake of Miss Beatrice. And now I will leave you to think it over."

And with a little nod she sailed out of the room, completely victorious. She was indeed, reflected Geoffrey, "mistress of the situation." Supposing that she brought a suit against him where would he be? She must have evidence, or she would not have known the story. The whole drama had clearly been witnessed by someone, probably either by Elizabeth or the servant girl, and that some one had betrayed it to Honoria and possibly to others. The thought made him sick. He was a man of the world, and a practical lawyer, and though, indeed, they were innocent, he knew that under the circumstances few would be found to believe it. At the very best there must be a terrible and shocking scandal, and Beatrice would lose her good name. He placed himself in the position of counsel for the petitioner in a like case, and thought how he would crush and crumple such a defence in his address to the jury. A probable tale forsooth!

Undoubtedly, too, Honoria would be acting wisely from her point of view. Public sympathy would be with her throughout. He knew that, as it was, he was believed generally to owe much of his success to his handsome and high-born wife. Now it would be said that he had used her as a ladder and then thrown her over. With all this, however, he might cope; he could even bear with the vulgar attacks of a vulgar press, and the gibes and jeers of his political and personal enemies, but to lose Effie he could not bear. And if such a case were brought against him it was almost certain that he would lose her, for, if he was worsted, custody of the child would be given to the injured wife.

Then there was Beatrice to be considered. The same malicious tongue that had revealed this matter to Honoria would probably reveal it to the rest of the world, and even if he escaped the worst penalties of outraged morality, they would certainly be wreaked upon her. Beatrice's reputation would be blasted, her employment lost, and her life made a burden to her. Yes, decidedly, Honoria had the best of the position; decidedly, also, she spoke words of weight and common sense.

What was to be done? Was there no way out of it? All that night as Geoffrey sat in the House, his arms folded on his breast, and to appearance intently listening to the long harangues of the Opposition, this question haunted him. He argued the situation out this way and that way, till at the last he came to a conclusion. Either he must wait for the scandal to leak out, let Beatrice be ruined, and direct his efforts to the softening of Honoria, and generally to self-preservation, or he must take the bull by the horns, must abandon his great career and his country and seek refuge in another land, say America, taking Beatrice and Effie with him. Once the child was out of the jurisdiction, of course no court could force her from him.

Of the two courses, even in so far as he himself was concerned, what between the urgency of the matter and the unceasing pressure of his passion, Geoffrey inclined to the latter. The relations between himself and Honoria had for years been so strained, so totally different from those which should exist between man and wife, that they greatly mitigated in his mind the apparent iniquity of such a step. Nor would he feel much compunction at removing the child from her mother, for there was no love lost between the two, and as time went on he guessed shrewdly there would be less and less. For the rest, he had some seventeen thousand pounds in hand; he would take half and leave Honoria half. He knew that he could always earn a living wherever he went, and probably much more than a living, and of whatever he earned a strict moiety should be paid to Honoria. But first and above everything, there was Beatrice to be considered. She must be saved, even if he ruined himself to save her.

Lady Honoria, it is scarcely necessary to say, had little idea that she was driving her husband to such dangerous and determined councils. She wanted to frighten Geoffrey, not to lose him and all he meant to her; this was the last thing that she would wish to do. She did not greatly care about the Beatrice incident, but her shrewd common sense told her that it might well be used as an engine to ruin them all. Therefore she spoke as she did speak, though in reality matters would have to be bad indeed before she sought the aid of a court of law, where many things concerning herself might come to the light of day which she would prefer to leave in darkness.

Nor did she stop here; she determined to attack Geoffrey's position in another way, namely, through Beatrice herself. For a long time Honoria hesitated as to the method of this attack. She had some knowledge of the world and of character, and from what she knew of Beatrice she came to the sound conclusion that she was not a woman to be threatened, but rather one to be appealed to. So after much thought she wrote to her thus:—

"A story, which I still hesitate to believe, has come to me by means of anonymous letters, as to your conduct with my husband. I do not wish to repeat it now, further than to say that, if true, it establishes circumstances which leave no doubt as to the existence of relations so intimate between you as to amount to guilt. It may not be true or it may, in which latter event I wish to say this: With your morality I have nothing to do; it is your affair. Nor do I wish to plead to you as an injured wife or to reproach you, for there are things too wicked for mere reproach. But I will say this: if the story is true, I must presume that you have some affection for the partner of your shame. I put myself out of the question, and in the name of that affection, however guilty it may be, I ask you to push matters no further. To do so will be to bring its object to utter ruin. If you care for him, sever all connection with him utterly and for ever. Otherwise he will live to curse and hate you. Should you neglect this advice, and should the facts that I have heard become public property, I warn you, as I have already warned him, that in self-preservation and for the sake of self-respect, I shall be forced to appeal to the law for my remedy. Remember that his career is at stake, and that in losing it and me he will lose also his child. Remember that if this comes about it will be through you. Do not answer this, it will do no good, for I shall naturally put no faith in your protestations, but if you are in any way or measure guilty of this offence, appealing to you as one woman to another, and for the sake of the man who is dear to both, I say do your best to redeem the evil, by making all further communication between yourself and him an impossibility. H.B."

It was a clever letter; Lady Honoria could not have devised one more powerful to work on a woman like Beatrice. The same post that took it to her took another from Geoffrey himself. It was long, though guarded, and need not be quoted in its entirety, but it put the whole position before her in somewhat veiled language, and ended by saying, "Marriage I cannot give you, only life-long love. In other circumstances to offer this would be an insult, but if things should be as I fear, it is worth your consideration. I do not say to you come, I say come if you wish. No, Beatrice, I will not put this cruel burden of decision upon you. I say come! I do not command you to come, because I promised to leave you uninfluenced. But I pray you to do so. Let us put an end to this wretchedness, and count the world well lost as our price of love. Come, dearest Beatrice—to leave me no more till death. I put my life in your hands; if you take it up, whatever trouble you may have to face, you will never lose my affection or esteem. Do not think of me, think of yourself. You have given me your love as you once gave me my life. I owe something in return; I cannot see you shamed and make no offer of reparation. Indeed, so far as I am concerned, I shall think all I lose as nothing compared to what I gain in gaining you. Will you come? If so, we will leave this country and begin afresh elsewhere. After all, it matters little, and will matter less when everything is said and done. My life has for years been but as an unwholesome dream. The one real thing, the one happy thing that I have found in it has been our love. Do not let us throw it away, Beatrice."

By return of post he received this answer written in pencil.

"No, dear Geoffrey. Things must take their course.—B."

That was all.

CHAPTER XXV

ELIZABETH SHOWS HER TEETH

Hard had been Beatrice's hours since that grey morning of separation. She must bear all the inner wretchedness of her lot; she must conceal her grief, must suffer the slings and arrows of Elizabeth's sharp tongue, and strive to keep Owen Davies at a distance. Indeed, as the days went on, this last task grew more and more portentous. The man was quite unmanageable; his passion, which was humiliating and hateful to Beatrice, became the talk of the place. Everybody knew of it, except her father, and even his eyes began to be opened.

One night—it was the same upon which Geoffrey and Honoria respectively had posted their letters to Beatrice—anybody looking into the little room at Bryngelly Castle, which served its owner for all purposes except that of sleeping, would have witnessed a very strange sight. Owen Davies was walking to and fro—walking rapidly with wild eyes and dishevelled hair. At the turn of each length of the apartment he would halt, and throwing his arms into the air ejaculate:

"Oh, God, hear me, and give me my desire! Oh, God, answer me!"

For two long hours thus he walked and thus cried aloud, till at length he sank panting and exhausted into a chair. Suddenly he raised his head, and appeared to listen intently.

"The Voice," he said aloud; "the Voice again. What does it say? To-morrow, to-morrow I must speak; and I shall win her."

He sprang up with a shout, and once more began his wild march. "Oh, Beatrice!" he said, "to-morrow you will promise to marry me; the Voice says so, and soon, soon, perhaps in one short month, you will be my own—mine only! Geoffrey Bingham shall not come between us then, for I will watch you day and night. You shall be my very, very own—my own beautiful Beatrice," and he stretched out his arms and clasped at the empty air—a crazy and unpleasant sight to see.

And so he walked and spoke till the dawn was grey in the east. This occurred on the Friday night. It was on the following morning that Beatrice, the unfortunate and innocent object of these amorous invocations, received the two letters. She had gone to the post-office on her way to the school, on the chance of there being a note from Geoffrey. Poor woman, his letters were the one bright thing in her life. From motives of prudence they were written in the usual semi-formal style, but she was quick to read between the lines, and, moreover, they came from his dear hand.

There was the letter sure enough, and another in a woman's writing. She recognised the hand as that of Lady Honoria, which she had often seen on envelopes directed to Geoffrey, and a thrill of fear shot through her. She took the letters, and walking as quickly as she could to the school, locked herself in her own little room, for it was not yet nine o'clock, and looked at them with a gathering terror. What was in them? Why did Lady Honoria write to her? Which should she read first? In a moment Beatrice had made up her mind. She would face the worst at once. With a set face she opened Lady Honoria's letter, unfolded it, and read. We already know its contents. As her mind grasped them her lips grew ashy white, and by the time that the horrible thing was done she was nigh to fainting.

Anonymous letters! oh, who could have done this cruel thing? Elizabeth, it must be Elizabeth, who saw everything, and thus stabbed her in the back. Was it possible that her own sister could treat her so? She knew that Elizabeth disliked her; she could never fathom the cause, still she knew the fact. But if this were her doing, then she must hate her, and most bitterly; and what had she done to earn such hate? And now Geoffrey was in danger on her account, danger of ruin, and how could she prevent it? This was her first idea. Most people might have turned to their own position and been content to leave their lover to fight his own battle. But Beatrice thought little of herself. He was in danger, and how could she protect him? Why here in the letter was the answer! "If you care for him sever all connection with him utterly, and for ever. Otherwise, he will live to curse and hate you." No, no! Geoffrey would never do that. But Lady Honoria was quite right; in his interest, for his sake, she must sever all connection with him—sever it utterly and for ever. But how—how?

She thrust the letter into her dress—a viper would have been a more welcome guest—and opened Geoffrey's.

It told the same tale, but offered a different solution. The tears started to her eyes as she read his offer to take her to him for good and all, and go away with her to begin life afresh. It seemed a wonderful thing to Beatrice that he should be willing to sacrifice so much upon such a worthless altar as her love— a wonderful and most generous thing. She pressed the senseless paper to her heart, then kissed it again and again. But she never thought of yielding to this great temptation, never for one second. He prayed her to come, but that she would not do while her will remained. What, she bring Geoffrey to ruin? No, she had rather starve in the streets or perish by slow torture. How could he ever think that she would consent to such a scheme? Indeed she never would; she had brought enough trouble on him already. But oh, she blessed him for that letter. How deeply must he love her when he could offer to do this for her sake!

Hark! the children were waiting; she must go and teach. The letter, Geoffrey's dear letter, could be answered in the afternoon. So she thrust it in her breast with the other, but closer to her heart, and went.

That afternoon as Mr. Granger, in a happy frame of mind—for were not his debts paid, and had he not found a most convenient way of providing against future embarrassment?—was engaged peaceably in contemplating his stock over the gate of his little farm buildings, he was much astonished suddenly to discover Owen Davies at his elbow.

"How do you do, Mr. Davies?" he said; "how quietly you must have come."

"Yes," answered Owen absently. "The fact is, I have followed you because I want to speak to you alone— quite alone."

"Indeed, Mr. Davies—well, I am at your service. What is wrong? You don't look very well."

"Oh, I am quite well, thank you. I never was better; and there's nothing wrong, nothing at all. Everything is going to be bright now, I know that full surely."

"Indeed," said Mr. Granger, again looking at him with a puzzled air, "and what may you want to see me about? Not but what I am always at your service, as you know," he added apologetically.

"This," he answered, suddenly seizing the clergyman by the coat in a way that made him start.

"What—my coat, do you mean?"

"Don't be so foolish, Mr. Granger. No, about Beatrice."

"Oh. indeed, Mr. Davies. Nothing wrong at the school, I hope? I think that she does her duties to the satisfaction of the committee, though I admit that the arithmetic—"

"No! no, no! It is not about the school. I don't wish her to go to the school any more. I love her, Mr. Granger, I love her dearly, and I want to marry her."

The old man flushed with pleasure. Was it possible? Did he hear aright? Owen Davies, the richest man in that part of Wales, wanted to marry his daughter, who had nothing but her beauty. It must be too good to be true!

"I am indeed flattered," he said. "It is more than she could expect—not but what Beatrice is very good-looking and very clever," he added hastily, fearing lest he was detracting from his daughter's market value.

"Good-looking—clever; she is an angel," murmured Owen.

"Oh, yes, of course she is," said her father, "that is, if a woman—yes, of course—and what is more, I think she's very fond of you. I think she is pining for you. I've though so for a long time."

"Is she?" said Owen anxiously. "Then all I have to say is that she takes a very curious way of showing it. She won't say a word to me; she puts me off on every occasion. But it will be all right now—all right now."

"Oh, there, there, Mr. Davies, maids will be maids until they are wives. We know about all that," said Mr. Granger sententiously.

His would-be son-in-law looked as though he knew very little about it indeed, although the inference was sufficiently obvious.

"Mr. Granger," he said, seizing his hand, "I want to make Beatrice my wife—I do indeed."

"Well, I did not suppose otherwise, Mr. Davies."

"If you help me in this I will do whatever you like as to money matters and that sort of thing, you know. She shall have as fine a settlement as any woman in Wales. I know that goes a long way with a father, and I shall raise no difficulties."

"Very right and proper, I am sure," said Mr. Granger, adopting a loftier tone as he discovered the advantages of his position. "But of course on such matters I shall take the advice of a lawyer. I daresay that Mr. Bingham would advise me," he added, "as a friend of the family, you know. He is a very clever lawyer, and, besides, he wouldn't charge anything."

"Oh, no, not Mr. Bingham," answered Owen anxiously. "I will do anything you like, or if you wish to have a lawyer I'll pay the bill myself. But never mind about that now. Let us settle it with Beatrice first. Come along at once."

"Eh, but hadn't you better arrange that part of the business privately?"

"No, no. She always snubs me when I try to speak to her alone. You had better be there, and Miss Elizabeth too, if she likes. I won't speak to her again alone. I will speak to her in the face of God and man, as God directed me to do, and then it will be all right—I know it will."

Mr. Granger stared at him. He was a clergyman of a very practical sort, and did not quite see what the Power above had to do with Owen Davies's matrimonial intentions.

"Ah, well," he said, "I see what you mean; marriages are made in heaven; yes, of course. Well, if you want to get on with the matter, I daresay that we shall find Beatrice in."

So they walked back to the Vicarage, Mr. Granger exultant and yet perplexed, for it struck him that there was something a little odd about the proceeding, and Owen Davies in silence or muttering occasionally to himself.

In the sitting-room they found Elizabeth.

"Where is Beatrice?" asked her father.

"I don't know," she answered, and at that moment Beatrice, pale and troubled, walked into the room, like a lamb to the slaughter.

"Ah, Beatrice," said her father, "we were just asking for you."

She glanced round, and with the quick wit of a human animal, instantly perceived that some new danger threatened her.

"Indeed," she said, sinking into a chair in an access of feebleness born of fear. "What is it, father?"

Mr. Granger looked at Owen Davies and then took a step towards the door. It struck him forcibly that this scene should be private to the two persons principally concerned.

"Don't go," said Owen Davies excitedly, "don't go, either of you; what I have to say had better be said before you both. I should like to say it before the whole world; to cry it from the mountain tops."

Elizabeth glared at him fiercely—glared first at him and then at the innocent Beatrice. Could he be going to propose to her, then? Ah, why had she hesitated? Why had she not told him the whole truth before? But the heart of Beatrice, who sat momentarily expecting to be publicly denounced, grew ever fainter. The waters of desolation were closing in over her soul.

Mr. Granger sat down firmly and worked himself into the seat of his chair, as though to secure an additional fixedness of tenure. Elizabeth set her teeth, and leaned her elbow on the table, holding her hand so as to shade her face. Beatrice drooped upon her seat like a fading lily, or a prisoner in the dock. She was opposite to them, and Owen Davies, his face alight with wild enthusiasm, stood up and addressed them all like the counsel for the prosecution.

"Last autumn," he began, speaking to Mr. Granger, who might have been a judge uncertain as to the merits of the case, "I asked your daughter Beatrice to marry me."

Beatrice gave a sigh, and collected her scattered energies. The storm had burst at last, and she must face it.

"I asked her to marry me, and she told me to wait a year. I have waited as long as I could, but I could not wait the whole year. I have prayed a great deal, and I am bidden to speak."

Elizabeth made a gesture of impatience. She was a person of strong common sense, and this mixture of religion and eroticism disgusted her. She also know that the storm had burst, and that she must face it.

"So I come to tell you that I love your daughter Beatrice, and want to make her my wife. I have never loved anybody else, but I have loved her for years; and I ask your consent."

"Very flattering, very flattering, I am sure, especially in these hard times," said Mr. Granger apologetically, shaking his thin hair down over his forehead, and then rumpling it up again. "But you see, Mr. Davies, you don't want to marry me" (here Beatrice smiled faintly)—"you want to marry my daughter, so you had better ask her direct—at least I suppose so."

Elizabeth made a movement as though to speak, then changed her mind and listened.

"Beatrice," said Owen Davies, "you hear. I ask you to marry me."

There was a pause. Beatrice, who had sat quite silent, was gathering up her strength to answer. Elizabeth, watching her from beneath her hand, thought that she read upon her face irresolution, softening into consent. What she really saw was but doubt as to the fittest and most certain manner of refusal. Like lightning it flashed into Elizabeth's mind that she must strike now, or hold her hand for ever. If once Beatrice spoke that fatal "yes," her revelations might be of no avail. And Beatrice would speak it; she was sure she would. It was a golden road out of her troubles.

"Stop!" said Elizabeth in a shrill, hard voice. "Stop! I must speak; it is my duty as a Christian. I must tell the truth. I cannot allow an honest man to be deceived."

There was an awful pause. Beatrice broke it. Now she saw all the truth, and knew what was at hand. She placed her hand upon her heart to still its beating.

"Oh, Elizabeth," she said, "in our dead mother's name—" and she stopped.

"Yes," answered her sister, "in our dead mother's name, which you have dishonoured, I will do it. Listen, Owen Davies, and father: Beatrice, who sits there"—and she pointed at her with her thin hand—"Beatrice is a scarlet woman!"

"I really don't understand," gasped Mr. Granger, while Owen looked round wildly, and Beatrice sunk her head upon her breast.

"Then I will explain," said Elizabeth, still pointing at her sister. "She is Geoffrey Bingham's mistress. On the night of Whit-Sunday last she rose from bed and went into his room at one in the morning. I saw her with my own eyes. Afterwards she was brought back to her bed in his arms—I saw it with my own eyes, and I heard him kiss her." (This was a piece of embroidery on Elizabeth's part.) "She is his lover, and has been in love with him for months. I tell you this, Owen Davies, because, though I cannot bear to bring disgrace upon our name and to defile my lips with such a tale, neither can I bear that you should marry a girl, believing her to be good, when she is what Beatrice is."

"Then I wish to God that you had held your wicked tongue," said Mr. Granger fiercely.

"No, father. I have a duty to perform, and I will perform it at any cost, and however much it pains me. You know that what I say is true. You heard the noise on the night of Whit-Sunday, and got up to see what it was. You saw the white figure in the passage—it was Geoffrey Bingham with Beatrice in his arms. Ah! well may she hang her head. Let her deny if it she can. Let her deny that she loves him to her shame, and that she was alone in his room on that night."

Then Beatrice rose and spoke. She was pale as death and more beautiful in her shame and her despair than ever she had been before; her glorious eyes shone, and there were deep black lines beneath them.

"My heart is my own," she said, "and I will make no answer to you about it. Think what you will. For the rest, it is not true. I am not what Elizabeth tells you that I am. I am not Geoffrey Bingham's mistress. It is true that I was in his room that night, and it is true that he carried me back to my own. But it was in my sleep that I went there, not of my own free will. I awoke there, and fainted when I woke, and then at once he bore me back."

Elizabeth laughed shrill and loud—it sounded like the cackle of a fiend.

"In her sleep," she said; "oh, she went there in her sleep!"

"Yes, Elizabeth, in my sleep. You do not believe me, but it is true. You do not wish to believe me. You wish to bring the sister whom you should love, who has never offended against you by act or word, to utter disgrace and ruin. In your cowardly spite you have written anonymous letters to Lady Honoria Bingham, to prevail upon her to strike the blow that should destroy her husband and myself, and when you fear that this has failed, you come forward and openly accuse us. You do this in the name of Christian duty; in the name of love and charity, you believe the worst, and seek to ruin us. Shame on you, Elizabeth! shame on you! and may the same measure that you have meted out to me never be paid back to you. We are no longer sisters. Whatever happens, I have done with you. Go your ways."

Elizabeth shrank and quailed beneath her sister's scorn. Even her venomous hatred could not bear up against the flash of those royal eyes, and the majesty of that outraged innocence. She gasped and bit her lip till the blood started, but she said nothing.

Then Beatrice turned to her father, and spoke in another and a pleading voice, stretching out her arms towards him.

"Oh, father," she said, "at least tell me that you believe me. Though you may think that I might love to all extremes, surely, having known me so many years, you cannot think that I would lie even for my love's sake."

The old man looked wildly round, and shook his head.

"In his room and in his arms," he said. "I saw it, it seems. You, too, who have never been known to walk in your sleep from a child; and you will not say that you do not love him—the scoundrel. It is wicked of Elizabeth—jealousy bitter as the grave. It is wicked of her to tell the tale; but as it is told, how can I say that I do not believe it?"

Then Beatrice, her cup being full, once more dropped her head, and turned to go.

"Stop," said Owen Davies in a hoarse voice, and speaking for the first time. "Hear what I have to say."

She lifted her eyes. "With you, Mr. Davies, I have nothing to do; I am not answerable to you. Go and help your accomplice," and she pointed to Elizabeth, "to cry this scandal over the whole world."

"Stop," he said again. "I will speak. I believe that it is true. I believe that you are Geoffrey Bingham's mistress, curse him! but I do not care. I am still willing to marry you."

Elizabeth gasped. Was this to be the end of her scheming? Would the blind passion of this madman prevail over her revelations, and Beatrice still become his rich and honoured wife, while she was left poor and disgraced? Oh, it was monstrous! Oh, she had never dreamed of this!

"Noble, noble!" murmured Mr. Granger; "noble! God bless you!"

So the position was not altogether beyond recovery. His erring daughter might still be splendidly married; he might still look forward to peace and wealth in his old age.

Only Beatrice smiled faintly.

"I thank you," she said. "I am much honoured, but I could never have married you because I do not love you. You must understand me very little if you think that I should be the more ready to do so on account of the danger in which I stand," and she ceased.

"Listen, Beatrice," Owen went on, an evil light shining on his heavy face, while Elizabeth sat astounded, scarcely able to believe her ears. "I want you, and I mean to marry you; you are more to me than all the world. I can give you everything, and you had better yield to me, and you shall hear no more of this. But if you won't, then this is what I will do. I will be revenged upon you—terribly revenged."

Beatrice shook her head and smiled again, as though to bid him do his worst.

"And look, Beatrice," he went on, waxing almost eloquent in his jealous despair, "I have another argument to urge on you. I will not only be revenged on you, I will be revenged upon your lover—on this Geoffrey Bingham."

"Oh!" said Beatrice sharply, like one in pain. He had found the way to move her now, and with the cunning of semi-madness he drove the point home.

"Yes, you may start—I will. I tell you that I will never rest till I have ruined him, and I am rich and can do it. I have a hundred thousand pounds, that I will spend on doing it. I have nothing to fear, except an action for libel. Oh, I am not a fool, though you think I am, I know. Well, I can pay for a dozen actions. There are papers in London that will be glad to publish all this—yes, the whole story—with plans and pictures too. Just think, Beatrice, what it will be when all England—yes, and all the world—is gloating over your shame, and half-a-dozen prints are using the thing for party purposes, clamouring for the disgrace of the man who ruined you, and whom you will ruin. He has a fine career; it shall be utterly destroyed. By God! I will hunt him to his grave, unless you promise to marry me, Beatrice. Do that, and not a word of this shall be said. Now answer."

Mr. Granger sank back in his chair; this savage play of human passions was altogether beyond his experience—it overwhelmed him. As for Elizabeth, she bit her thin fingers, and glared from one to the other. "He reckons without me," she thought. "He reckons without me—I will marry him yet."

But Beatrice leant for a moment against the wall and shut her eyes to think. Oh, she saw it all—the great posters with her name and Geoffrey's on them, the shameless pictures of her in his arms, the sickening details, the letters of the outraged matrons, the "Mothers of ten," and the moral-minded colonels—all, all! She heard the prurient scream of every male Elizabeth in England; the allusions in the House—the jeers, the bitter attacks of enemies and rivals. Then Lady Honoria would begin her suit, and it would all be dragged up afresh, and Geoffrey's fault would be on every lip, till he was ruined. For herself she did not care; but could she bring this on one whose only crime was that she had learned to love him? No, no; but neither could she marry this hateful man. And yet what escape was there? She flung herself upon her woman's wit, and it did not fail her. In a few seconds she had thought it all out and made up her mind.

"How can I answer you at a moment's notice, Mr. Davies?" she said. "I must have time to think it over. To threaten such revenge upon me is not manly, but I know that you love me, and therefore I excuse it. Still, I must have time. I am confused."

"What, another year? No, no," he said. "You must answer."

"I do not ask a year or a month. I only ask for one week. If you will not give me that, then I will defy you, and you may do your worst. I cannot answer now."

This was a bold stroke, but it told. Mr. Davies hesitated.

"Give the girl a week," said her father to him. "She is not herself."

"Very well; one week, no more," said he.

"I have another stipulation to make," said Beatrice, "You are all to swear to me that for that week no word of this will pass your mouths; that for that week I shall not be annoyed or interfered with, or spoken to on the subject, not by one of you. If at the end of it I still refuse to accept your terms, you can do your worst, but till then you must hold your hand."

Owen Davies hesitated; he was suspicious.

"Remember," Beatrice went on, raising her voice, "I am a desperate woman. I may turn at bay, and do something which you do not expect, and that will be very little to the advantage of any of you. Do you swear?"

"Yes," said Owen Davies.

Then Beatrice looked at Elizabeth, and Elizabeth looked at her. She saw that the matter had taken a new form. She saw what her jealous folly had hitherto hidden from her—that Beatrice did not mean to marry Owen Davies, that she was merely gaining time to execute some purpose of her own. What this might be Elizabeth cared little so that it did not utterly extinguish chances that at the moment seemed faint enough. She did not want to push matters against her sister, or her lover Geoffrey, beyond the boundary of her own interests. Beatrice should have her week, and be free from all interference so far as she was concerned. She realised now that it was too late how great had been her error. Oh, if only she had sought Beatrice's confidence at first! But it had seemed to her impossible that she would really throw away such an opportunity in life.

"Certainly I promise, Beatrice," she said mildly. "I do not swear, for 'swear not at all,' you know. I only did what I thought my duty in warning Mr. Davies. If he chooses to go on with the matter, it is no affair of mine. I had no wish to hurt you, or Mr. Bingham. I acted solely from my religious convictions."

"Oh, stop talking religion, Elizabeth, and practise it a little more!" said her father, for once in his life stirred out of his feeble selfishness. "We have all undertaken to keep our mouths sealed for this week."

Then Beatrice left the room, and after her went Owen Davies without another word.

"Elizabeth," said her father, rising, "you are a wicked woman! What did you do this for?"

"Do you want to know, father?" she said coolly; "then I will tell you. Because I mean to marry Owen Davies myself. We must all look after ourselves in this world, you know; and that is a maxim which you never forget, for one. I mean to marry him; and though I seem to have failed, marry him I will, yet! And now you know all about it; and if you are not a fool, you will hold your tongue and let me be!" and she went also, leaving him alone.

Mr. Granger held up his hands in astonishment. He was a selfish, money-seeking old man, but he felt that he did not deserve to have such a daughter as this.

CHAPTER XXVI

WHAT BEATRICE SWORE

Beatrice went to her room, but the atmosphere of the place seemed to stifle her. Her brain was reeling, she must go out into the air—away from her tormentors. She had not yet answered Geoffrey's letter, and it must be answered by this post, for there was none on Sunday. It was half-past four—the post went out at five; if she was going to write, she should do so at once, but she could not do so here.

Besides, she must find time for thought. Ah, she had it; she would take her canoe and paddle across the bay to the little town of Coed and write her letter there. The post did not leave Coed till half-past six. She put on her hat and jacket, and taking a stamp, a sheet of paper, and an envelope with her, slipped quietly from the house down to old Edward's boat-house where the canoe was kept. Old Edward was not there himself, but his son was, a boy of fourteen, and by his help Beatrice was soon safely launched. The sea glittered like glass, and turning southwards, presently she was paddling round the shore of the island on which the Castle stood towards the open bay.

As she paddled her mind cleared, and she was able to consider the position. It was bad enough. She saw no light, darkness hemmed her in. But at least she had a week before her, and meanwhile what should she write to Geoffrey?

Then, as she thought, a great temptation assailed Beatrice, and for the first time her resolution wavered. Why should she not accept Geoffrey's offer and go away with him—far away from all this misery? Gladly would she give her life to spend one short year at his dear side. She had but to say the word, and he would take her to him, and in a month from now they would be together in some foreign land, counting the world well lost, as he had said. Doubtless in time Lady Honoria would get a divorce, and they might be married. A day might even come when all this would seem like a forgotten night of storm and fear; when, surrounded by the children of their love, they would wend peaceably, happily, through the evening of their days towards a bourne robbed of half its terrors by the fact that they would cross it hand-in-hand.

Oh, that would be well for her; but would it be well for him? When the first months of passion had passed by, would he not begin to think of all that he had thrown away for the sake of a woman's love? Would not the burst of shame and obloquy which would follow him to the remotest corners of the earth wear away his affection, till at last, as Lady Honoria said, he learned to curse and hate her. And if it did not—if he still loved her through it all—as, being what he was, he well might do—could she be the one to bring this ruin on him? Oh, it would have been more kind to let him drown on that night of the storm, when fate first brought them together to their undoing.

No, no; once and for all, once and for ever, she would not do it. Cruel as was her strait, heavy as was her burden, not one feather's weight of it should he carry, if by any means in her poor power she could hold it from his back. She would not even tell him of what had happened—at any rate, not now. It would distress him; he might take some desperate step; it was almost certain that he would do so. Her answer must be very short.

She was quite close to Coed now, and the water lay calm as a pond. So calm was it that she drew the sheet of paper and the envelope from her pocket, and leaning forward, rested them on the arched covering of the canoe, and pencilled those words which we have already read.

"No, dear Geoffrey. Things must take their course.—B."

Thus she wrote. Then she paddled to the shore. A fisherman standing on the beach caught her canoe and pulled it up. Leaving it in his charge, she went into the quaint little town, directed and posted her letter, and bought some wool. It was an excuse for having been there should any one ask questions. After that she returned to her canoe. The fisherman was standing by it. She offered him sixpence for his trouble, but he would not take it.

"No, miss," he said, "thanking you kindly—but we don't often get a peep at such sweet looks. It's worth sixpence to see you, it is. But, miss, if I may make so bold as to say so, it isn't safe for you to cruise about in that craft, any ways not alone."

Beatrice thanked him and blushed a little. Vaguely it occurred to her that she must have more than a common share of beauty, when a rough man could be so impressed with it. That was what men loved women for, their beauty, as Owen Davies loved and desired her for this same cause and this only.

Perhaps it was the same with Geoffrey—no, she did not believe it. He loved her for other things besides her looks. Only if she had not been beautiful, perhaps he would not have begun to love her, so she was thankful for her eyes and hair, and form.

Could folly and infatuation go further? This woman in the darkest hour of her bottomless and unhorizoned despair, with conscience gnawing at her heart, with present misery pressing on her breast, and shame to come hanging over her like a thunder cloud, could yet feel thankful that she had won this barren love, the spring of all her woe. Or was her folly deep wisdom in disguise?—is there something divine in a passion that can so override and defy the worst agonies of life?

She was at sea again now, and evening was falling on the waters softly as a dream. Well, the letter was posted. Would it be the last, she wondered? It seemed as though she must write no more letters. And what was to be done? She would not marry Owen Davies—never would she do it. She could not so shamelessly violate her feelings, for Beatrice was a woman to whom death would be preferable to dishonour, however legal. No, for her own sake she would not be soiled with that disgrace. Did she do this, she would hold herself the vilest of the vile. And still less would she do it for Geoffrey's sake. Her instinct told her what he would feel at such a thing, though he might never say a word. Surely he would loathe and despise her. No, that idea was done with—utterly done with.

Then what remained to her? She would not fly with Geoffrey, since to do so would be to ruin him. She would not marry Owen, and not to do so would still be to ruin Geoffrey. She was no fool, she was innocent in act, but she knew that her innocence would indeed be hard to prove—even her own father did not believe in it, and her sister would openly accuse her to the world. What then should she do? Should she hide herself in some remote half-civilised place, or in London? It was impossible; she had no money, and no means of getting any. Besides, they would hunt her out, both Owen Davies and Geoffrey would track her to the furthest limits of the earth. And would not the former think that Geoffrey had spirited her away, and at once put his threats into execution? Obviously he would. There was no hope in that direction. Some other plan must be found or her lover would still be ruined.

So argued Beatrice, still thinking not of herself, but of Geoffrey, of that beloved one who was more to her than all the world, more, a thousand times, than her own safety or well-being. Perhaps she overrated the matter. Owen Davies, Lady Honoria, and even Elizabeth might have done all they threatened; the first of them, perhaps the first two of them, certainly would have done so. But still Geoffrey might have escaped destruction. Public opinion, or the sounder part of it, is sensibly enough hard to move in such a matter, especially when the person said to have been wronged is heart and soul on the side of him who is said to have wronged her.

Moreover there might have been ways out of it, of which she knew nothing. But surrounded as she was by threatening powers—by Lady Honoria threatening actions in the Courts on one side, by Owen Davies threatening exposure on another, by Elizabeth ready and willing to give the most damning evidence on the third, to Beatrice the worst consequences seemed an absolutely necessary sequence. Then there was her own conscience arrayed against her. This particular charge was a lie, but it was not a lie that she loved Geoffrey, and to her the two things seemed very much the same thing. Hers was not a mind to draw fine distinctions in such matters. Se posuit ut culpabilem: she "placed herself as guilty," as the old Court rolls put it in miserable Latin, and this sense of guilt disarmed her. She did not realise the enormous difference recognised by the whole civilised world between thought and act, between disposing mind and inculpating deed. Beatrice looked at the question more from the scriptural point of view, remembering that in the Bible such fine divisions are expressly stated to be distinctions without a difference.

Had she gone to Geoffrey and told him her whole story it is probable that he would have defied the conspiracy, faced it out, and possibly come off victorious. But, with that deadly reticence of which women alone are capable, this she did not and would not do. Sweet loving woman that she was, she would not burden him with her sorrows, she would bear them alone—little reckoning that thereby she was laying up a far, far heavier load for him to carry through all his days.

So Beatrice accepted the statements of the plaintiff's attorney for gospel truth, and from that false standpoint she drew her auguries.

Oh, she was weary! How lovely was the falling night, see how it brooded on the seas! and how clear were the waters—there a fish passed by her paddle—and there the first start sprang into the sky! If only Geoffrey were here to see it with her. Geoffrey! she had lost him; she was alone in the world now—alone with the sea and the stars. Well, they were better than men—better than all men except one. Theirs was a divine companionship, and it soothed her. Ah, how hateful had been Elizabeth's face, more hateful even than the half-crazed cunning of Owen Davies, when she stretched her hand towards her and called her "a scarlet woman." It was so like Elizabeth, this mixing up of Bible terms with her accusation. And after all perhaps it was true.—What was it, "Though thy sins be as scarlet, yet shall they be white as snow." But that was only if one repented. She did not repent, not in the least. Conscience, it is true, reproached her with a breach of temporal and human law, but her heart cried that such love as she had given was immortal and divine, and therefore set beyond the little bounds of time and man. At any rate, she loved Geoffrey and was proud and glad to love him. The circumstances were unfortunate, but she did not make the world or its social arrangements any more than she had made herself, and she could not help that. The fact remained, right or wrong—she loved him, loved him!

How clear were the waters! What was that wild dream which she had dreamt about herself sitting at the bottom of the sea, and waiting for him—till at last he came. Sitting at the bottom of the sea—why did it strike her so strangely—what unfamiliar thought did it waken in her mind? Well, and why not? It would be pleasant there, better at any rate than on the earth. But things cannot be ended so; one is burdened with the flesh, and one must wear it till it fails. Why must she wear it? Was not the sea large enough to hide her bones? Look now, she had but to slip over the edge of the canoe, slip without a struggle into those mighty arms, and in a few short minutes it would all be done and gone!

She gasped as the thought struck home. Here was the answer to her questionings, the same answer that is given to every human troubling, to all earthly hopes and fears and strivings. One stroke of that black knife and everything would be lost or found. Would it be so great a thing to give her life for Geoffrey?—why she had well nigh done as much when she had known him but an hour, and now that he was all in all, oh, would it be so great a thing? If she died—died secretly, swiftly, surely—Geoffrey would be saved; they would not trouble him then, there would be no one to trouble about: Owen Davies could not marry her then, Geoffrey could not ruin himself over her, Elizabeth could pursue her no further. It would be well to do this thing for Geoffrey, and he would always love her, and beyond that black curtain there might be something better.

They said that it was sin. Yes, it might be sin to act thus for oneself alone. But to do it for another—how of that! Was not the Saviour whom they preached a Man of Sacrifice? Would it be a sin in her to die for Geoffrey, to sacrifice herself that Geoffrey might go free?

Oh, it would be no great merit. Her life was not so easy that she should fear this pure embrace. It would be better, far better, than to marry Owen Davies, than to desecrate their love and teach Geoffrey to despise her. And how else could she ward this trouble from him except by her death, or by a marriage that in her eyes was more dreadful than any death?

She could not do it yet. She could not die until she had once more seen his face, even though he did not see hers. No, not to-night would she seek this swift solution. She had words to say—or words to write—before the end. Already they rushed in upon her mind!

But if no better plan presented itself she would do it, she was sure that she would. It was a sin—well, let it be a sin; what did she care if she sinned for Geoffrey? He would not think the worse of her for it. And she had hope, yes, Geoffrey had taught her to hope. If there was a Hell, why it was here. And yet not all a Hell, for in it she had found her love!

It grew dark; she could hear the whisper of the waves upon Bryngelly beach. It grew dark; the night was closing round. She paddled to within a few fathoms of the shore, and called in her clear voice.

"Ay, ay, miss," answered old Edward from the beach. "Come in on the next wave."

She came in accordingly and her canoe was caught and dragged high and dry.

"What, Miss Beatrice," said the old man shaking his head and grumbling, "at it again! Out all alone in that thing," and he gave the canoe a contemptuous kick, "and in the dark, too. You want a husband to look after you, you do. You'll never rest till you're drowned."

"No, Edward," she answered with a little laugh. "I don't suppose that I shall. There is no peace for the wicked above seas, you know. Now do not scold. The canoe is as safe as church in this weather and in the bay."

"Oh, yes, it's safe enough in the calm and the bay," he answered, "but supposing it should come on to blow and supposing you should drift beyond the shelter of Rumball Point there, and get the rollers down on you—why you would be drowned in five minutes. It's wicked, miss, that's what it is."

Beatrice laughed again and went.

"She's a funny one she is," said the old man scratching his head as he looked after her, "of all the woman folk as ever I knowed she is the rummest. I sometimes thinks she wants to get drowned. Dash me if I haven't half a mind to stave a hole in the bottom of that there damned canoe, and finish it."

Beatrice reached home a little before supper time. Her first act was to call Betty the servant and with her assistance to shift her bed and things into the spare room. With Elizabeth she would have nothing more to do. They had slept together since they were children, now she had done with her. Then she went in to supper, and sat through it like a statue, speaking no word. Her father and Elizabeth kept up a strained conversation, but they did not speak to her, nor she to them. Elizabeth did not even ask where she had been, nor take any notice of her change of room.

One thing, however, Beatrice learnt. Her father was going on the Monday to Hereford by an early train to attend a meeting of clergymen collected to discuss the tithe question. He was to return by the last train on the Tuesday night, that is, about midnight. Beatrice now discovered that Elizabeth proposed to accompany him. Evidently she wished to see as little as possible of her sister during this week of truce—possibly she was a little afraid of her. Even Elizabeth might have a conscience.

So she should be left alone from Monday morning till Tuesday night. One can do a good deal in forty hours.

After supper Beatrice rose and left the room, without a word, and they were glad when she went. She frightened them with her set face and great calm eyes. But neither spoke to the other on the subject. They had entered into a conspiracy of silence.

Beatrice locked her door and then sat at the window lost in thought. When once the idea of suicide has entered the mind it is apt to grow with startling rapidity. She reviewed the whole position; she went over all the arguments and searched the moral horizon for some feasible avenue of escape. But she could find none that would save Geoffrey, except this. Yes, she would do it, as many another wretched woman had done before her, not from cowardice indeed, for had she alone been concerned she would have faced the thing out, fighting to the bitter end—but for this reason only, it would cut off the dangers which threatened Geoffrey at their very root and source. Of course there must be no scandal; it must never be known that she had killed herself, or she might defeat her own object, for the story would be raked up. But she well knew how to avoid such a possibility; in her extremity Beatrice grew cunning as a fox. Yes, and there might be an inquest at which awkward questions would be asked. But, as she well knew also, before an inquest can be held there must be something to hold it on, and that something would not be there.

And so in the utter silence of the night and in the loneliness of her chamber did Beatrice dedicate herself to sacrifice upon the altar of her immeasurable love. She would face the last agonies of death when the bloom of her youthful strength and beauty was but opening as a rose in June. She would do more, she would brave the threatened vengeance of the most High, coming before Him a self murderess, and with but one plea for pity—that she loved so well: quia multum amavit. Yes, she would do all this, would leave the warm world in the dawning summer of her days, and alone go out into the dark—alone would face those visions which might come—those Shapes of terror, and those Things of fear, that perchance may wait for sinful human kind. Alone she would go—oh, hand in hand with him it had been easy, but this must not be. The door of utter darkness would swing to behind her, and who could say if in time to come it should open to Geoffrey's following feet, or if he might ever find the path that she had trod. It must be done, it should be done! Beatrice rose from her seat with bright eyes and quick-coming breath, and swore before God, if God there were, that she would do it, trusting to Him for pardon and for pity, or failing these—for sleep.

Yes, but first she must once more look upon Geoffrey's dear face—and then farewell!

Pity her! poor mistaken woman, making of her will a Providence, rushing to doom. Pity her, but do not blame her overmuch, or if you do, then blame Judith and Jephtha's daughter and Charlotte Corday, and all the glorious women who from time to time have risen on this sordid world of self, and given themselves as an offering upon the altars of their love, their religion, their honour or their country!

It was finished. Now let her rest while she could, seeing what was to come. With a sigh for all that was, and all that might have been, Beatrice lay down and soon slept sweetly as a child.

CHAPTER XXVII

THE HOUSE OF COMMONS

Next day was Sunday. Beatrice did not go to church. For one thing, she feared to see Owen Davies there. But she took her Sunday school class as usual, and long did the children remember how kind and patient she was with them that day, and how beautifully she told them the story of the Jewish girl of long ago, who went forth to die for the sake of her father's oath.

Nearly all the rest of the day and evening she spent in writing that which we shall read in time—only in the late afternoon she went out for a little while in her canoe. Another thing Beatrice did also: she called at the lodging of her assistant, the head school teacher, and told her it was possible that she would not be in her place on the Tuesday (Monday was, as it chanced, a holiday). If anybody inquired as to her absence, perhaps she would kindly tell them that Miss Granger had an appointment to keep, and had taken a morning's holiday in order to do so. She should, however, be back that afternoon. The teacher assented without suspicion, remarking that if Beatrice could not take a morning's holiday, she was sure she did not know who could.

Next morning they breakfasted very early, because Mr. Granger and Elizabeth had to catch the train. Beatrice sat through the meal in silence, her calm eyes looking straight before her, and the others, gazing on them, and at the lovely inscrutable face, felt an indefinable fear creep into their hearts. What did this woman mean to do? That was the question they asked of themselves, though not of each other. That she meant to do something they were sure, for there was purpose written on every line of her cold face.

Suddenly, as they sat thinking, and making pretence to eat, a thought flashed like an arrow into Beatrice's heart, and pierced it. This was the last meal that they could ever take together, this was the last time that she could ever see her father's and her sister's faces. For her sister, well, it might pass—for there are some things which even a woman like Beatrice can never quite forgive—but she loved her father. She loved his very faults, even his simple avarice and self-seeking had become endeared to her by long and wondering contemplation. Besides, he was her father; he gave her the life she was about to cast away. And she should never see him more. Not on that account did she hesitate in her purpose, which was now set in her mind, like Bryngelly Castle on its rock, but at the thought tears rushed unbidden to her eyes.

Just then breakfast came to an end, and Elizabeth hurried from the room to fetch her bonnet.

"Father," said Beatrice, "if you can before you go, I should like to hear you say that you do not believe that I told you what was false—about that story."

"Eh, eh!" answered the old man nervously, "I thought that we had agreed to say nothing about the matter at present."

"Yes, but I should like to hear you say it, father. It cuts me that you should think that I would lie to you, for in my life I have never wilfully told you what was not true;" and she clasped her hands about his arms, and looked into his face.

He gazed at her doubtfully. Was it possible after all she was speaking the truth? No; it was not possible.

"I can't, Beatrice," he said—"not that I blame you overmuch for trying to defend yourself; a cornered rat will show fight."

"May you never regret those words," she said; "and now good-bye," and she kissed him on the forehead.

At this moment Elizabeth entered, saying that it was time to start, and he did not return the kiss.

"Good-bye, Elizabeth," said Beatrice, stretching out her hand. But Elizabeth affected not to see it, and in another moment they were gone. She followed them to the gate and watched them till they vanished down the road. Then she returned, her heart strained almost to bursting. But she wept no tear.

Thus did Beatrice bid a last farewell to her father and her sister.

"Elizabeth," said Mr. Granger, as they drew near to the station, "I am not easy in my thoughts about Beatrice. There was such a strange look in her eyes; it—in short, it frightens me. I have half a mind to give up Hereford, and go back," and he stopped upon the road, hesitating.

"As you like," said Elizabeth with a sneer, "but I should think that Beatrice is big enough and bad enough to look after herself."

"Before the God who made us," said the old man furiously, and striking the ground with his stick, "she may be bad, but she is not so bad as you who betrayed her. If Beatrice is a Magdalene, you are a woman Judas; and I believe that you hate her, and would be glad to see her dead."

Elizabeth made no answer. They were nearing the station, for her father had started on again, and there were people about. But she looked at him, and he never forgot the look. It was quite enough to chill him into silence, nor did he allude to the matter any more.

When they were gone, Beatrice set about her own preparations. Her wild purpose was to travel to London, and catch a glimpse of Geoffrey's face in the House of Commons, if possible, and then return. She put on her bonnet and best dress; the latter was very plainly made of simple grey cloth, but on her it looked well enough, and in the breast of it she thrust the letter which she had written on the previous day. A small hand-bag, with some sandwiches and a brush and comb in it, and a cloak, made up the total of her baggage.

The train, which did not stop at Bryngelly, left Coed at ten, and Coed was an hour and a half's walk. She must be starting. Of course, she would have to be absent for the night, and she was sorely puzzled how to account for her absence to Betty, the servant girl; the others being gone there was no need to do so to anybody else. But here fortune befriended her. While she was thinking the matter over, who should come in but Betty herself, crying. She had just heard, she said, that her little sister, who lived with their mother at a village about ten miles away, had been knocked down by a cart and badly hurt. Might she go home for the night? She could come back on the morrow, and Miss Beatrice could get somebody in to sleep if she was lonesome.

Beatrice sympathised, demurred, and consented, and Betty started at once. As soon as she was gone, Beatrice locked up the house, put the key in her pocket, and started on her five miles' tramp. Nobody saw her leave the house, and she passed by a path at the back of the village, so that nobody saw her on the road. Reaching Coed Station quite unobserved, and just before the train was due, she let down her veil, and took a third-class ticket to London. This she was obliged to do, for her stock of money was very small; it amounted, altogether, to thirty-six shillings, of which the fare to London and back would cost her twenty-eight and fourpence.

In another minute she had entered an empty carriage, and the train had steamed away.

She reached Paddington about eight that night, and going to the refreshment room, dined on some tea and bread and butter. Then she washed her hands, brushed her hair, and started.

Beatrice had never been in London before, and as soon as she left the station the rush and roar of the huge city took hold of her, and confused her. Her idea was to walk to the Houses of Parliament at Westminster. She would, she thought, be sure to see Geoffrey there, because she had bought a daily paper in which she had read that he was to be one of the speakers in a great debate on the Irish Question, which was to be brought to a close that night. She had been told by a friendly porter to follow Praed Street till she reached the Edgware Road, then to walk on to the Marble Arch, and ask again. Beatrice followed the first part of this programme—that is, she walked as far as the Edgware Road. Then it was that confusion seized her and she stood hesitating. At this juncture, a coarse brute of a man came up and made some remark to her. It was impossible for a woman like Beatrice to walk alone in the streets of London at night, without running the risk of such attentions. She turned from him, and as she did so, heard him say something about her beauty to a fellow Arcadian. Close to where she was stood two hansom cabs. She went to the first and asked the driver for how much he would take her to the House of Commons.

"Two bob, miss," he answered.

Beatrice shook her head, and turned to go again. She was afraid to spend so much on cabs, for she must get back to Bryngelly.

"I'll take yer for eighteenpence, miss," called out the other driver. This offer she was about to accept when the first man interposed.

"You leave my fare alone, will yer? Tell yer what, miss, I'm a gentleman, I am, and I'll take yer for a bob."

She smiled and entered the cab. Then came a whirl of great gas-lit thoroughfares, and in a quarter of an hour they pulled up at the entrance to the House. Beatrice paid the cabman his shilling, thanked him, and entered, only once more to find herself confused with a vision of white statues, marble floors, high arching roofs, and hurrying people. An automatic policeman asked her what she wanted. Beatrice answered that she wished to get into the House.

"Pass this way, then, miss—pass this way," said the automatic officer in a voice of brass. She passed, and passed, and finally found herself in a lobby, among a crowd of people of all sorts—seedy political touts, Irish priests and hurrying press-men. At one side of the lobby were more policemen and messengers, who were continually taking cards into the House, then returning and calling out names. Insensibly she drifted towards these policemen.

"Ladies' Gallery, miss?" said a voice; "your order, please, though I think it's full."

Here was a fresh complication. Beatrice had no order. She had no idea that one was necessary.

"I haven't got an order," she said faintly. "I did not know that I must have one. Can I not get in without?"

"Most certainly not, miss," answered the voice, while its owner, suspecting dynamite, surveyed her with a cold official eye. "Now make way, make way, please."

Beatrice's grey eyes filled with tears, as she turned to go in bitterness of heart. So all her labour was in vain, and that which would be done must be done without the mute farewell she sought. Well, when sorrow was so much, what mattered a little more? She turned to go, but not unobserved. A certain rather youthful Member of Parliament, with an eye for beauty in distress, had been standing close to her, talking to a constituent. The constituent had departed to wherever constituents go—and many representatives, if asked, would cheerfully point out a locality suitable to the genus, at least in their judgment—and the member had overheard the conversation and seen Beatrice's eyes fill with tears. "What a lovely woman!" he had said to himself, and then did what he should have done, namely, lifted his hat and inquired if, as a member of the House, he could be of any service to her. Beatrice listened, and explained that she was particularly anxious to get into the Ladies' Gallery.

"I think that I can help you, then," he said. "As it happens a lady, for whom I got an order, has telegraphed to say that she cannot come. Will you follow me? Might I ask you to give me your name?"

"Mrs. Everston," answered Beatrice, taking the first that came into her head. The member looked a little disappointed. He had vaguely hoped that this lovely creature was unappropriated. Surely her marriage could not be satisfactory, or she would not look so sad.

Then came more stairs and passages, and formalities, till presently Beatrice found herself in a kind of bird-cage, crowded to suffocation with every sort of lady.

"I'm afraid—I am very much afraid—" began her new-found friend, surveying the mass with dismay.

But at that moment, a stout lady in front feeling faint with the heat, was forced to leave the Gallery, and almost before she knew where she was, Beatrice was installed in her place. Her friend had bowed and vanished, and she was left to all purposes alone, for she never heeded those about her, though some of them looked at her hard enough, wondering at her form and beauty, and who she might be.

She cast her eye down over the crowded House, and saw a vision of hats, collars, and legs, and heard a tumult of sounds: the sharp voice of a speaker who was rapidly losing his temper, the plaudits of the Government benches, the interruptions from the Opposition—yes, even yells, and hoots, and noises, that reminded her remotely of the crowing of cocks. Possibly had she thought of it, Beatrice would not have been greatly impressed with the dignity of an assembly, at the doors of which so many of its members seemed to leave their manners, with their overcoats and sticks; it might even have suggested the idea of a bear garden to her mind. But she simply did not think about it. She searched the House keenly enough, but it was to find one face, and one only—Ah! there he was.

And now the House of Commons might vanish into the bottomless abyss, and take with it the House of Lords, and what remained of the British Constitution, and she would never miss them. For, at the best of times, Beatrice—in common with most of her sex—in all gratitude be it said, was not an ardent politician.

There Geoffrey sat, his arms folded—the hat pushed slightly from his forehead, so that she could see his face. There was her own beloved, whom she had come so far to see, and whom to-morrow she would dare so much to save. How sad he looked—he did not seem to be paying much attention to what was going on. She knew well enough that he was thinking of her; she could feel it in her head as she had often felt it before. But she dared not let her mind go out to him in answer, for, if once she did so, she knew also that he would discover her. So she sat, and fed her eyes upon his face, taking her farewell of it, while round her, and beneath her, the hum of the House went on, as ever present and as unnoticed as the hum of bees upon a summer noon.

Presently the gentleman who had been so kind to her, sat down in the next seat to Geoffrey, and began to whisper to him, as he did so glancing once or twice towards the grating behind which she was. She guessed that he was telling him the story of the lady who was so unaccountably anxious to hear the debate, and how pretty she was. But it did not seem to interest Geoffrey much, and Beatrice was feminine enough to notice it, and to be glad of it. In her gentle jealousy, she did not like to think of Geoffrey as being interested in accounts of mysterious ladies, however pretty.

At length a speaker rose—she understood from the murmur of those around her that he was one of the leaders of the Opposition, and commenced a powerful and bitter speech. She noticed that Geoffrey roused himself at this point, and began to listen with attention.

"Look," said one of the ladies near her, "Mr. Bingham is taking notes. He is going to speak next—he speaks wonderfully, you know. They say that he is as good as anybody in the House, except Gladstone, and Lord Randolph."

"Oh!" answered another lady. "Lady Honoria is not here, is she? I don't see her."

"No," replied the first; "she is a dear creature, and so handsome too—just the wife for a rising man—but I don't think that she takes much interest in politics. Are not her dinners charming?"

At this moment, a volley of applause from the Opposition benches drowned the murmured conversation.

This speaker spoke for about three-quarters of an hour, and then at last Geoffrey stood up. One or two other members rose at the same time, but ultimately they gave way.

He began slowly—and somewhat tamely, as it seemed to Beatrice, whose heart was in her mouth—but when he had been speaking for about five minutes, he warmed up. And then began one of the most remarkable oratorical displays of that Parliament. Geoffrey had spoken well before, and would speak well again, but perhaps he never spoke so well as he did upon that night. For nearly an hour and a half he held the House in chains, even the hoots and interruptions died away towards the end of his oration. His powerful presence seemed to tower in the place, like that of a giant among pigmies, and his dark, handsome face, lit with the fires of eloquence, shone like a lamp. He leaned forward with a slight stoop of his broad shoulders, and addressed himself, nominally to the Speaker, but really to the Opposition. He took their facts one by one, and with convincing logic showed that they were no facts; amid a hiss of anger he pulverised their arguments and demonstrated their motives. Then suddenly he dropped them altogether, and addressing himself to the House at large, and the country beyond the House, he struck another note, and broke out into that storm of patriotic eloquence which confirmed his growing reputation, both in Parliament and in the constituencies.

Beatrice shut her eyes and listened to the deep, rich voice as it rose from height to height and power to power, till the whole place seemed full of it, and every contending sound was hushed.

Suddenly, after an invocation that would have been passionate had it not been so restrained and strong, he stopped. She opened her eyes and looked. Geoffrey was seated as before, with his hat on. He had been speaking for an hour and a half, and yet, to her, it seemed but a few minutes since he rose. Then broke out a volley of cheers, in the midst of which a leader of the Opposition rose to reply, not in the very best of tempers, for Geoffrey's speech had hit them hard.

He began, however, by complimenting the honourable member on his speech, "as fine a speech as he had listened to for many years, though, unfortunately, made from a mistaken standpoint and the wrong side of the House." Then he twitted the Government with not having secured the services of a man so infinitely abler than the majority of their "items," and excited a good deal of amusement by stating, with some sarcastic humour, that, should it ever be his lot to occupy the front Treasury bench, he should certainly make a certain proposal to the honourable member. After this good-natured badinage, he drifted off into the consideration of the question under discussion, and Beatrice paid no further attention to him, but occupied herself in watching Geoffrey drop back into the same apparent state of cold indifference, from which the necessity of action had aroused him.

Presently the gentleman who had found her the seat came up and spoke to her, asking her how she was getting on. Very soon he began to speak of Geoffrey's speech, saying that it was one of the most brilliant of the session, if not the most brilliant.

"Then Mr. Bingham is a rising man, I suppose?" Beatrice said.

"Rising? I should think so," he answered. "They will get him into the Government on the first opportunity after this; he's too good to neglect. Very few men can come to the fore like Mr. Bingham. We call him the comet, and if only he does not make a mess of his chances by doing something foolish, there is no reason why he should not be Attorney-General in a few years."

"Why should he do anything foolish?" she asked.

"Oh, for no reason on earth, that I know of; only, as I daresay you have noticed, men of this sort are very apt to do ridiculous things, throw up their career, get into a public scandal, run away with somebody or something. Not that there should be any fear of such a thing where Mr. Bingham is concerned, for he has a charming wife, and they say that she is a great help to him. Why, there is the division bell. Good-bye, Mrs. Everston, I will come back to see you out."

"Good-bye," Beatrice answered, "and in case I should miss you, I wish to say something—to thank you for your kindness in helping me to get in here to-night. You have done me a great service, a very great service, and I am most grateful to you."

"It is nothing—nothing," he answered. "It has been a pleasure to help you. If," he added with some confusion, "you would allow me to call some day, the pleasure will be all the greater. I will bring Mr. Bingham with me, if you would like to know him—that is, if I can."

Beatrice shook her head. "I cannot," she answered, smiling sadly. "I am going on a long journey to-morrow, and I shall not return here. Good-bye."

In another second he was gone, more piqued and interested about this fair unknown than he had been about any woman for years. Who could she be? and why was she so anxious to hear the debate? There was a mystery in it somewhere, and he determined to solve it if he could.

Meanwhile the division took place, and presently the members flocked back, and amidst ringing Ministerial cheers, and counter Opposition cheers, the victory of the Government was announced. Then came the usual formalities, and the members began to melt away. Beatrice saw the leader of the House and several members of the Government go up to Geoffrey, shake his hand, and congratulate him. Then, with one long look, she turned and went, leaving him in the moment of his triumph, that seemed to interest him so little, but which made Beatrice more proud at heart than if she had been declared empress of the world.

Oh, it was well to love a man like that, a man born to tower over his fellow men—and well to die for him! Could she let her miserable existence interfere with such a life as his should be? Never, never! There should be no "public scandal" on her account.

She drew her veil over her face, and inquired the way from the House. Presently she was outside. By one of the gateways, and in the shadow of its pillars, she stopped, watching the members of the House stream past her. Many of them were talking together, and once or twice she caught the sound of Geoffrey's name, coupled with such words as "splendid speech," and other terms of admiration.

"Move on, move on," said a policeman to her. Lifting her veil, Beatrice turned and looked at him, and muttering something he moved on himself, leaving her in peace. Presently she saw Geoffrey and the gentleman who had been so kind to her walking along together. They came through the gateway; the lappet of his coat brushed her arm, and he never saw her. Closer she crouched against the pillar, hiding herself in its shadow. Within six feet of her Geoffrey stopped and lit a cigar. The light of the match flared upon his face, that dark, strong face she loved so well. How tired he looked. A great longing took possession of her to step forward and speak to him, but she restrained herself almost by force.

Her friend was speaking to him, and about her.

"Such a lovely woman," he was saying, "with the clearest and most beautiful grey eyes that I ever saw. But she has gone like a dream. I can't find her anywhere. It is a most mysterious business."

"You are falling in love, Tom," answered Geoffrey absently, as he threw away the match and walked on. "Don't do that; it is an unhappy thing to do," and he sighed.

He was going! Oh, heaven! she would never, never see him more! A cold horror seized upon Beatrice, her blood seemed to stagnate. She trembled so much that she could scarcely stand. Leaning forward, she looked after him, with such a face of woe that even the policeman, who had repented him of his forbearance, and was returning to send her away, stood astonished. The two men had gone about ten yards, when something induced Beatrice's friend to look back. His eye fell upon the white, agony-stricken face, now in the full glare of the gas lamp.

Beatrice saw him turn, and understood her danger. "Oh, good-bye, Geoffrey!" she murmured, for a second allowing her heart to go forth towards him. Then realising what she had done, she dropped her veil, and went swiftly. The gentleman called "Tom"—she never learnt his name—stood for a moment dumbfounded, and at that instant Geoffrey staggered, as though he had been struck by a shot, turned quite white, and halted.

"Why," said his companion, "there is that lady again; we must have passed quite close to her. She was looking after us, I saw her face in the gaslight—and I never want to see such another."

Geoffrey seized him by the arm. "Where is she?" he asked, "and what was she like?"

"She was there a second ago," he said, pointing to the pillar, "but I've lost her now—I fancy she went towards the railway station, but I could not see. Stop, is that she?" and he pointed to a tall person walking towards the Abbey.

Quickly they moved to intercept her, but the result was not satisfactory, and they retreated hastily from the object of their attentions.

Meanwhile Beatrice found herself opposite the entrance to the Westminster Bridge Station. A hansom was standing there; she got into it and told the man to drive to Paddington.

Before the pair had retraced their steps she was gone. "She has vanished again," said "Tom," and went on to give a description of her to Geoffrey. Of her dress he had unfortunately taken little note. It might be one of Beatrice's, or it might not. It seemed almost inconceivable to Geoffrey that she should be masquerading about London, under the name of Mrs. Everston. And yet—and yet—he could have sworn—but it was folly!

Suddenly he bade his friend good-night, and took a hansom. "The mystery thickens," said the astonished "Tom," as he watched him drive away. "I would give a hundred pounds to find out what it all means. Oh! that woman's face—it haunts me. It looked like the face of an angel bidding farewell to Heaven."

But he never did find out any more about it, though the despairing eyes of Beatrice, as she bade her mute farewell, still sometimes haunt his sleep.

Geoffrey reflected rapidly. The thing was ridiculous, and yet it was possible. Beyond that brief line in answer to his letter, he had heard nothing from Beatrice. Indeed he was waiting to hear from her before taking any further step. But even supposing she were in London, where was he to look for her? He knew that she had no money, he could not stay there long. It occurred to him there was a train leaving Euston for Wales about four in the morning. It was just possible that she might be in town, and returning by this train. He told the cabman to drive to Euston Station, and on arrival, closely questioned a sleepy porter, but without satisfactory results.

Then he searched the station; there were no traces of Beatrice. He did more; he sat down, weary as he was, and waited for an hour and a half, till it was time for the train to start. There were but three passengers, and none of them in the least resembled Beatrice.

"It is very strange," Geoffrey said to himself, as he walked away. "I could have sworn that I felt her presence just for one second. It must have been nonsense. This is what comes of occult influences, and that kind of thing. The occult is a nuisance."

If he had only gone to Paddington!

CHAPTER XXVIII

I WILL WAIT FOR YOU

Beatrice drove back to Paddington, and as she drove, though her face did not change from its marble cast of woe the great tears rolled down it, one by one.

They reached the deserted-looking station, and she paid the man out of her few remaining shillings—seeing that she was a stranger, he insisted upon receiving half-a-crown. Then, disregarding the astonished stare of a night porter, she found her way to the waiting room, and sat down. First she took the letter from her breast, and added some lines to it in pencil, but she did not post it yet; she knew that if she did so it would reach its destination too soon. Then she laid her head back against the wall, and utterly outworn, dropped to sleep—her last sleep upon this earth, before the longest sleep of all.

And thus Beatrice waited and slept at Paddington, while her lover waited and watched at Euston.

At five she woke, and the heavy cloud of sorrow, past, present, and to come, rushed in upon her heart. Taking her bag, she made herself as tidy as she could. Then she stepped outside the station into the deserted street, and finding a space between the houses, watched the sun rise over the waking world. It was her last sunrise, Beatrice remembered.

She came back filled with such thoughts as might well strike the heart of a woman about to do the thing she had decreed. The refreshment bar was open now, and she went to it, and bought a cup of coffee and some bread and butter. Then she took her ticket, not to Bryngelly or to Coed, but to the station on this side of Bryngelly, and three miles from it. She would run less risk of being noticed there. The train was shunted up; she took her seat in it. Just as it was starting, an early newspaper boy came along, yawning. Beatrice bought a copy of the Standard, out of the one and threepence that was left of her money, and opened it at the sheet containing the leading articles. The first one began, "The most powerful, closely reasoned, and eloquent speech made last night by Mr. Bingham, the Member for Pillham, will, we feel certain, produce as great an effect on the country as it did in the House of Commons. We welcome it, not only on account of its value as a contribution to the polemics of the Irish Question, but as a positive proof of what has already been suspected, that the Unionist party has in Mr. Bingham a young statesman of a very high order indeed, and one whom remarkable and rapid success at the Bar has not hampered, as is too often the case, in the larger and less technical field of politics."

And so on. Beatrice put the paper down with a smile of triumph. Geoffrey's success was splendid and unquestioned. Nothing could stop him now. During all the long journey she pleased her imagination by conjuring up picture after picture of that great future of his, in which she would have no share. And yet he would not forget her; she was sure of this. Her shadow would go with him from year to year, even to the end, and at times he might think how proud she would have been could she be present to record his triumphs. Alas! she did not remember that when all is lost which can make life beautiful, when the sun has set, and the spirit gone out of the day, the poor garish lights of our little victories can but ill atone for the glories that have been. Happiness and content are frail plants which can only flourish under fair conditions if at all. Certainly they will not thrive beneath the gloom and shadow of a pall, and when the heart is dead no triumphs, however splendid, and no rewards, however great, can compensate for an utter and irredeemable loss. She never guessed, poor girl, that time upon time, in the decades to be, Geoffrey would gladly have laid his honours down in payment for one year of her dear and unforgotten presence. She was too unselfish; she did not think that a man could thus prize a woman's love, and took it for an axiom that to succeed in life was his one real object—a thing to which so divine a gift as she had given Geoffrey is as nothing. It was therefore this Juggernaut of her lover's career that Beatrice would cast down her life, little knowing that thereby she must turn the worldly and temporal success, which he already held so cheap, to bitterness and ashes.

At Chester Beatrice got out of the train and posted her letter to Geoffrey. She would not do so till then because it might have reached him too soon—before all was finished! Now it would be delivered to him in the House after everything had been accomplished in its order. She looked at the letter; it was, she thought, the last token that could ever pass between them on this earth. Once she pressed it to her heart, once she touched it with her lips, and then put it from her beyond recall. It was done; there was no going back now. And even as she stood the postman came up, whistling, and opening the box carelessly swept its contents into his canvas bag. Could he have known what lay among them he would have whistled no more that day.

Beatrice continued her journey, and by three o'clock arrived safely at the little station next to Bryngelly. There was a fair at Coed that day, and many people of the peasant class got in here. Amidst the confusion she gave up her ticket to a small boy, who was looking the other way at the time, and escaped without being noticed by a soul. Indeed, things happened so that nobody in the neighbourhood of Bryngelly ever knew that Beatrice had been to London and back upon those dreadful days.

Beatrice walked along the cliff, and in an hour was at the door of the Vicarage, from which she seemed to have been away for years. She unlocked it and entered. In the letter-box was a post-card from her father stating that he and Elizabeth had changed their plans and would not be back till the train which arrived at half-past eight on the following morning. So much the better, she thought. Then she disarranged the clothes upon her bed to make it seem as though it had been slept it, lit the kitchen fire, and put the kettle on to boil, and as soon as it was ready she took some food. She wanted all her nerve, and that could not be kept up without food.

Shortly after this the girl Betty returned, and went about her duties in the house quite unconscious that Beatrice had been away from it for the whole night. Her sister was much better, she said, in answer to Beatrice's inquiries.

When she had eaten what she could—it was not much—Beatrice went to her room, undressed herself, bathed, and put on clean, fresh things. Then she unbound her lovely hair, and did it up in a coronet upon her head. It was a fashion that she did not often adopt, because it took too much time, but on this day, of all days, she had a strange fancy to look her best. Also her hair had been done like this on the afternoon when Geoffrey first met her. Next she put on the grey dress once more which she had worn on her journey to London, and taking the silver Roman ring that Geoffrey had given her from the string by which she wore it about her neck, placed it on the third finger of her left hand.

All this being done, Beatrice visited the kitchen and ordered the supper. She went further in her innocent cunning. Betty asked her what she would like for breakfast on the following morning, and she told her to cook some bacon, and to be careful how she cut it, as she did not like thick bacon. Then, after one long last look at the Vicarage, she started for the lodging of the head teacher of the school, and, having found her, inquired as to the day's work.

Further, Beatrice told her assistant that she had determined to alter the course of certain lessons in the school. The Wednesday arithmetic class had hitherto been taken before the grammar class. On the morrow she had determined to change this; she would take the grammar class at ten and the arithmetic class at eleven, and gave her reasons for so doing. The teacher assented, and Beatrice shook hands with her and bade her good-night. She would have wished to say how much she felt indebted to her for her help in the school, but did not like to do so, fearing lest, in the light of pending events, the remark might be viewed with suspicion.

Poor Beatrice, these were the only lies she ever told!

She left the teacher's lodgings, and was about to go down to the beach and sit there till it was time, when she was met by the father of the crazed child, Jane Llewellyn.

"Oh, Miss Beatrice," he said, "I have been looking for you everywhere. We are in sad trouble, miss. Poor Jane is in a raving fit, and talking about hell and that, and the doctor says she's dying. Can you come, miss, and see if you can do anything to quiet her? It's a matter of life and death, the doctor says, miss."

Beatrice smiled sadly; matters of life and death were in the air. "I will come," she said, "but I shall not be able to stay long."

How could she better spend her last hour?

She accompanied the man to his cottage. The child, dressed only in a night-shirt, was raving furiously, and evidently in the last stage of exhaustion, nor could the doctor or her mother do anything to quiet her.

"Don't you see," she screamed, pointing to the wall, "there's the Devil waiting for me? And, oh, there's the mouth of hell where the minister said I should go! Oh, hold me, hold me, hold me!"

Beatrice walked up to her, took the thin little hands in hers, and looked her fixedly in the eyes.

"Jane," she said. "Jane, don't you know me?"

"Yes, Miss Granger," she said, "I know the lesson; I will say it presently."

Beatrice took her in her arms, and sat down on the bed. Quieter and quieter grew the child till suddenly an awful change passed over her face.

"She is dying," whispered the doctor.

"Hold me close, hold me close!" said the child, whose senses returned before the last eclipse. "Oh, Miss Granger, I shan't go to hell, shall I? I am afraid of hell."

"No, love, no; you will go to heaven."

Jane lay still awhile. Then seeing the pale lips move, Beatrice put her ear to the child's mouth.

"Will you come with me?" she murmured; "I am afraid to go alone."

And Beatrice, her great grey eyes fixed steadily on the closing eyes beneath, whispered back so that no other soul could hear except the dying child:

"Yes, I will come presently." But Jane heard and understood.

"Promise," said the child.

"Yes, I promise," answered Beatrice in the same inaudible whisper. "Sleep, dear, sleep; I will join you very soon."

And the child looked up, shivered, smiled—and slept.

Beatrice gave it back to the weeping parents and went her way. "What a splendid creature," said the doctor to himself as he looked after her. "She has eyes like Fate, and the face of Motherhood Incarnate. A great woman, if ever I saw one, but different from other women."

Meanwhile Beatrice made her way to old Edward's boat-shed. As she expected, there was nobody there, and nobody on the beach. Old Edward and his son were at tea, with the rest of Bryngelly. They would come back after dark and lock up the boat-house.

She looked at the sea. There were no waves, but the breeze freshened every minute, and there was a long slow swell upon the water. The rollers would be running beyond the shelter of Rumball Point, five miles away.

The tide was high; it mounted to within ten yards of the end of the boat-house. She opened the door, and dragged out her canoe, closing the door again after her. The craft was light, and she was strong for a woman. Close to the boat-house one of the timber breakwaters, which are common at sea-side places, ran down into the water. She dragged the canoe to its side, and then pushed it down the beach till its bow was afloat. Next, mounting on the breakwater, she caught hold of the little chain in the bow, and walking along the timber baulks, pulled with all her force till the canoe was quite afloat. On she went, dragging it after her, till the waves washing over the breakwater wetted her shoes.

Then she brought the canoe quite close, and, watching her opportunity, stepped into it, nearly falling into the water as she did so. But she recovered her balance, and sat down. In another minute she was paddling out to sea with all her strength.

For twenty minutes or more she paddled unceasingly. Then she rested awhile, only keeping the canoe head on to the sea, which, without being rough, was running more and more freshly. There, some miles away, was the dark mass of Rumball Point. She must be off it before the night closed in. There would be sea enough there; no such craft as hers could live in it for five minutes, and the tide was on the turn. Anything sinking in those waters would be carried far away, and never come back to the shore of Wales.

She turned her head and looked at Bryngelly, and the long familiar stretch of cliff. How fair it seemed, bathed in the quiet lights of summer afternoon. Oh! was there any afternoon where the child had gone, and where she was following fast?—or was it all night, black, eternal night, unbroken by the dram of dear remembered things?

There were the Dog Rocks, where she had stood on that misty autumn day, and seen the vision of her coffined mother's face. Surely it was a presage of her fate. There beyond was the Bell Rock, where in that same hour Geoffrey and she had met, and behind it was the Amphitheatre, where they had told their love. Hark! what was that sound pealing faintly at intervals across the deep? It was the great ship's bell that, stirred from time to time by the wash of the high tide, solemnly tolled her passing soul.

She paddled on; the sound of that death-knell shook her nerves, and made her feel faint and weak. Oh, it would have been easier had she been as she was a year ago, before she learned to love, and hand in hand had seen faith and hope re-arise from the depths of her stirred soul. Then being but a heathen, she could have met her end with all a heathen's strength, knowing what she lost, and believing, too, that she would find but sleep. And now it was otherwise, for in her heart she did not believe that she was about utterly to perish. What, could the body live on in a thousand forms, changed indeed but indestructible and immortal, while the spiritual part, with all its hopes and loves and fears, melted into nothingness? It could not be; surely on some new shore she should once again greet her love. And if it was not, how would they meet her in that under world, coming self-murdered, her life-blood on her hands? Would her mother turn away from her? and the little brother, whom she had loved, would he reject her? And what Voice of Doom might strike her into everlasting hopelessness?

But, be the sin what it might, yet would she sin it for the sake of Geoffrey; ay, even if she must reap a harvest of eternal woe. She bent her head and prayed. "Oh, Power, that art above, from whom I come, to whom I go, have mercy on me! Oh, Spirit, if indeed thy name is Love, weigh my love in thy balance, and let it lift the scale of sin. Oh, God of Sacrifice, be not wroth at my deed of sacrifice and give me pardon, give me life and peace, that in a time to come I may win the sight of him for whom I die."

A somewhat heathenish prayer indeed, and far too full of human passion for one about to leave the human shores. But, then—well, it was Beatrice who prayed—Beatrice, who could realise no heaven beyond the limits of her passion, who still thought more of her love than of saving her own soul alive. Perhaps it found a home—perhaps, like her who prayed it, it was lost upon the pitiless deep.

Then Beatrice prayed no more. Short was her time. See, there sank the sun in glory; and there the great rollers swept along past the sullen headland, where the undertow met wind and tide. She would think no more of self; it was, it seemed to her, so small, this mendicant calling on the Unseen, not for others, but for self: aid for self, well-being for self, salvation for self—this doing of good that good might come to self. She had made her prayer, and if she prayed again it should be for Geoffrey, that he might prosper and be happy—that he might forgive the trouble her love had brought into his life. That he might forget her she could not pray. She had prayed her prayer and said her say, and it was done with. Let her be judged as it seemed good to Those who judge! Now she would fix her thoughts upon her love, and by its strength would she triumph over the bitterness of death. Her eyes flashed and her breast heaved: further out to sea, further yet—she would meet those rollers a knot or more from the point of the headland, that no record might remain.

Was it her wrong if she loved him? She could not help it, and she was proud to love him. Even now, she would not undo the past. What were the lines that Geoffrey had read to her. They haunted her mind with a strange persistence—they took time to the beat of her falling paddle, and would not leave her:

"Of once sown seed, who knoweth what the crop is? Alas, my love, Love's eyes are very blind! What would they have us do? Sunflowers and poppies Stoop to the wind—"[*]

[*] Oliver Madox Brown.

Yes, yes, Love's eyes are very blind, but in their blindness there was more light than in all other earthly things. Oh, she could not live for him, and with him—it was denied to her—but she still could die for him, her darling, her darling!

"Geoffrey, hear me—I die for you; accept my sacrifice, and forget me not." So!—she is in the rollers—how solemn they are with their hoary heads of foam, as one by one they move down upon her.

The first! it towers high, but the canoe rides it like a cork. Look! the day is dying on the distant land, but still his glory shines across the sea. Presently all will be finished. Here the breeze is strong; it tears the bonnet from her head, it unwinds the coronet of braided locks, and her bright hair streams out behind her. Feel how the spray stings, striking like a whip. No, not this wave, she rides that also; she will die as she has lived—fighting to the last; and once more, never faltering, she sets her face towards the rollers and consigns her soul to doom.

Ah! that struck her full. Oh, see! Geoffrey's ring has slipped from her wet hand, falling into the bottom of the boat. Can she regain it? she would die with that ring upon her finger—it is her marriage-ring, wedding her through death to Geoffrey, upon the altar of the sea. She stoops! oh, what a shock of water at her breast! What was it—what was it?—Of once sown seed, who knoweth what the crop is? She must soon learn now!

"Geoffrey! hear me, Geoffrey!—I die, I die for you! I will wait for you at the foundations of the sea, on the topmost heights of heaven, in the lowest deeps of hell—wherever I am I will always wait for you!"

It sinks—it has sunk—she is alone with God, and the cruel waters. The sun goes out! Look on that great white wave seething through the deepening gloom; hear it rushing towards her, big with fate.

"Geoffrey, my darling—I will wait—"

Farewell to Beatrice! The light went out of the sky and darkness gathered on the weltering sea. Farewell to Beatrice, and all her love and all her sin.

CHAPTER XXIX

A WOMAN'S LAST WORD

Geoffrey came down to breakfast about eleven o'clock on the morning of that day the first hours of which he had spent at Euston Station. Not seeing Effie, he asked Lady Honoria where she was, and was informed that Anne, the French bonne, said the child was not well and that she had kept her in bed to breakfast.

"Do you mean to say that you have not been up to see what is the matter with her?" asked Geoffrey.

"No, not yet," answered his wife. "I have had the dressmaker here with my new dress for the duchess's ball to-morrow; it's lovely, but I think that there is a little too much of that creamy lace about it."

With an exclamation of impatience, Geoffrey rose and went upstairs. He found Effie tossing about in bed, her face flushed, her eyes wide open, and her little hands quite hot.

"Send for the doctor at once," he said.

The doctor came and examined the child, asking her if she had wet her feet lately.

"Yes, I did, two days ago. I wet my feet in a puddle in the street," she answered. "But Anne did say that they would soon get dry, if I held them to the fire, because my other boots was not clean. Oh, my head does ache, daddie."

"Ah," said the doctor, and then covering the child up, took Geoffrey aside and told him that his daughter had a mild attack of inflammation of the lungs. There was no cause for anxiety, only she must be looked after and guarded from chills.

Geoffrey asked if he should send for a trained nurse.

"Oh, no," said the doctor. "I do not think it is necessary, at any rate at present. I will tell the nurse what to do, and doubtless your wife will keep an eye on her."

So Anne was called up, and vowed that she would guard the cherished child like the apple of her eye. Indeed, no, the boots were not wet—there was a little, a very little mud on them, that was all.

"Well, don't talk so much, but see that you attend to her properly," said Geoffrey, feeling rather doubtful, for he did not trust Anne. However, he thought he would see himself that there was no neglect. When she heard what was the matter, Lady Honoria was much put out.

"Really," she said, "children are the most vexatious creatures in the world. The idea of her getting inflammation of the lungs in this unprovoked fashion. The end of it will be that I shall not be able to go to the duchess's ball to-morrow night, and she was so kind about it, she made quite a point of my coming. Besides I have bought that lovely new dress on purpose. I should never have dreamed of going to so much expense for anything else."

"Don't trouble yourself," said Geoffrey. "The House does not sit to-morrow; I will look after her. Unless Effie dies in the interval, you will certainly be able to go to the ball."

"Dies—what nonsense! The doctor says that it is a very slight attack. Why should she die?"

"I am sure I hope that there is no fear of anything of the sort, Honoria. Only she must be properly looked after. I do not trust this woman Anne. I have half a mind to get in a trained nurse after all."

"Well, if you do, she will have to sleep out of the house, that's all. Amelia (Lady Garsington) is coming up to-night, and I must have somewhere to put her maid, and there is no room for another bed in Effie's room."

"Oh, very well, very well," said Geoffrey, "I daresay that it will be all right, but if Effie gets any worse, you will please understand that room must be made."

But Effie did not get worse. She remained much about the same. Geoffrey sat at home all day and employed himself in reading briefs; fortunately he had not to go to court. About six o'clock he went down to the House, and having dined very simply and quietly, took his seat and listened to some dreary talk, which was being carried on for the benefit of the reporters, about the adoption of the Welsh language in the law courts of Wales.

Suddenly he became aware of a most extraordinary sense of oppression. An indefinite dread took hold of him, his very soul was filled with terrible apprehensions and alarm. Something dreadful seemed to knock at the portals of his sense, a horror which he could not grasp. His mind was confused, but little by little it grew clearer, and he began to understand that a danger threatened Beatrice, that she was in great peril. He was sure of it. Her agonised dying cries reached him where he was, though in no form which he could understand; once more her thought beat on his thought—once more and for the last time her spirit spoke to his.

Then suddenly a cold wind seemed to breathe upon his face and lift his hair, and everything was gone. His mind was as it had been; again he heard the dreary orator and saw the members slipping away to dinner. The conditions that disturbed him had passed, things were as they had been. Nor was this strange! For the link was broken. Beatrice was dead. She had passed into the domains of impenetrable silence.

Geoffrey sat up with a gasp, and as he did so a letter was placed in his hand. It was addressed in Beatrice's handwriting and bore the Chester postmark. A chill fear seized him. What did it contain? He hurried with it into a private room and opened it. It was dated from Bryngelly on the previous Sunday and had several inclosures.

"My dearest Geoffrey," it began, "I have never before addressed you thus on paper, nor should I do so now, knowing to what risks such written words might put you, were it not that occasions may arise (as in this case) which seem to justify the risk. For when all things are ended between a man and a woman who are to each other what we have been, then it is well that the one who goes should speak plainly before speech becomes impossible, if only that the one who is left should not misunderstand that which has been done.

"Geoffrey, it is probable—it is almost certain—that before your eyes read these words I shall be where in the body they can never see me more. I write to you from the brink of the grave; when you read it, it will have closed over me.

"Geoffrey, I shall be dead.

"I received your dear letter (it is destroyed now) in which you expressed a wish that I should come away with you to some other country, and I answered it in eight brief words. I dared not trust myself to write more, nor had I any time. How could you think that I should ever accept such an offer for my own sake, when to do so would have been to ruin you? But first I will tell you all that has happened here." (Here followed a long and exact description of those events with which we are already acquainted, including the denunciation of Beatrice by her sister, the threats of Owen Davies as regards Geoffrey himself, and the measures which she had adopted to gain time.)

"Further," the letter continued, "I inclose you your wife's letter to me. And here I wish to state that I have not one word to say against Lady Honoria or her letter. I think that she was perfectly justified in writing as she did, for after all, dear Geoffrey, you are her husband, and in loving each other we have offended against her. She tells me truly that it is my duty to make all further communications between us impossible. There is only one way to do this, and I take it.

"And now I have spoken enough about myself, nor do I wish to enter into details that could only give you pain. There will be no scandal, dear, and if any word should be raised against you after I am gone, I have provided an answer in the second letter which I have inclosed. You can print it if necessary; it will be a sufficient reply to any talk. Nobody after reading it can believe that you were in any way connected with the accident which will happen. Dear, one word more—still about myself, you see! Do not blame yourself in this matter, for you are not to blame; of my own free will I do it, because in the extremity of the circumstances I think it best that one should go and the other be saved, rather than that both should be involved in a common ruin.

"Dear, do you remember how in that strange vision of mine, I dreamed that you came and touched me on the breast and showed me light? So it has come to pass, for you have given me love—that is light; and now in death I shall seek for wisdom. And this being fulfilled, shall not the rest be fulfilled in its season? Shall I not sit in those cloudy halls till I see you come to seek me, the word of wisdom on your lips? And since I cannot have you to myself, and be all in all to you, why I am glad to go. For here on the world is neither rest nor happiness; as in my dream, too often does 'Hope seem to rend her starry robes.'

"I am glad to go from such a world, in which but one happy thing has found me—the blessing of your love. I am worn out with the weariness and struggle, and now that I have lost you I long for rest. I do not know if I sin in what I do; if so, may I be forgiven. If forgiveness is impossible, so be it! You will forgive me, Geoffrey, and you will always love me, however wicked I may be; even if, at the last, you go where I am not, you will remember and love the erring woman to whom, being so little, you still were all in all. We are not married, Geoffrey, according to the customs of the world, but two short days hence I shall celebrate a service that is greater and more solemn than any of the earth. For Death will be the Priest and that oath which I shall take will be to all eternity. Who can prophesy of that whereof man has no sure knowledge? Yet I do believe that in a time to come we shall look again into each other's eyes, and kiss each other's lips, and be one for evermore. If this is so, it is worth while to have lived and died; if not, then, Geoffrey, farewell!

"If I may I will always be near you. Listen to the night wind and you shall hear my voice; look on the stars, you will see my eyes; and my love shall be as the air you breathe. And when at last the end comes, remember me, for if I live at all I shall be about you then. What have I more to say? So much, my dear, that words cannot convey it. Let it be untold; but whenever you hear or read that which is beautiful or tender, think 'this is what Beatrice would have said to me and could not!'

"You will be a great man, dear, the foremost or one of the foremost of your age. You have already promised me to persevere to this end: I will not ask you to promise afresh. Do not be content to accept the world as women must. Great men do not accept the world; they reform it—and you are of their number. And when you are great, Geoffrey, you will use your power, not for self-interest, but to large and worthy ends; you will always strive to help the poor, to break down oppression from those who have to bar it, and to advance the honour of your country. You will do all this from your own heart and not because I ask it of you, but remember that your fame will be my best monument—though none shall ever know the grave it covers.

"Farewell, farewell, farewell! Oh, Geoffrey, my darling, to whom I have never been a wife, to whom I am more than any wife—do not forget me in the long years which are to come. Remember me when others forsake you. Do not forget me when others flatter you and try to win your love, for none can be to you what I have been—none can ever love you more than that lost Beatrice who writes these heavy words to-night, and who will pass away blessing you with her last breath, to await you, if she may, in the land to which your feet also draw daily on."

Then came a tear-stained postscript in pencil dated from Paddington Station on that very morning.

"I journeyed to London to see you, Geoffrey. I could not die without looking on your face once more. I was in the gallery of the House and heard your great speech. Your friend found me a place. Afterwards I touched your coat as you passed by the pillar of the gateway. Then I ran away because I saw your friend turn and look at me. I shall kiss this letter—just here before I close it—kiss it there too—it is our last cold embrace. Before the end I shall put on the ring you gave me—on my hand, I mean. I have always worn it upon my breast. When I touched you as you passed through the gateway I thought that I should have broken down and called to you—but I found strength not to do so. My heart is breaking and my eyes are blind with tears; I can write no more; I have no more to say. Now once again good-bye. Ave atque vale— oh, my love!—B."

The second letter was a dummy. That is to say it purported to be such an epistle as any young lady might have written to a gentleman friend. It began, "Dear Mr. Bingham," and ended, "Yours sincerely, Beatrice Granger," was filled with chit-chat, and expressed hopes that he would be able to come down to Bryngelly again later in the summer, when they would go canoeing.

It was obvious, thought Beatrice, that if Geoffrey was accused by Owen Davies or anybody else of being concerned with her mysterious end, the production of such a frank epistle written two days previously would demonstrate the absurdity of the idea. Poor Beatrice, she was full of precautions!

Let him who may imagine the effect produced upon Geoffrey by this heartrending and astounding epistle! Could Beatrice have seen his face when he had finished reading it she would never have committed suicide. In a minute it became like that of an old man. As the whole truth sank into his mind, such an agony of horror, of remorse, of unavailing woe and hopelessness swept across his soul, that for a moment he thought his vital forces must give way beneath it, and that he should die, as indeed in this dark hour he would have rejoiced to do. Oh, how pitiful it was—how pitiful and how awful! To think of this love, so passionately pure, wasted on his own unworthiness. To think of this divine woman going down to lonely death for him—a strong man; to picture her crouching behind that gateway pillar and touching him as he passed, while he, the thrice accursed fool, knew nothing till too late; to know that he had gone to Euston and not to Paddington; to remember the matchless strength and beauty of the love which he had lost, and that face which he should never see again! Surely his heart would break. No man could bear it!

And of those cowards who hounded her to death, if indeed she was already dead! Oh, he would kill Owen Davies—yes, and Elizabeth too, were it not that she was a woman; and as for Honoria he had done with her. Scandal, what did he care for scandal? If he had his will there should be a scandal indeed, for he would beat this Owen Davies, this reptile, who did not hesitate to use a woman's terrors to prosper the fulfilling of his lust—yes, and then drag him to the Continent and kill him there. Only vengeance was left to him!

Stop, he must not give way—perhaps she was not dead—perhaps that horrible presage of evil which had struck him like a storm was but a dream. Could he telegraph? No, it was too late; the office at Bryngelly would be closed—it was past eight now. But he could go. There was a train leaving a little after nine—he should be there by half-past six to-morrow. And Effie was ill—well, surely they could look after her for twenty-four hours; she was in no danger, and he must go—he could not bear this torturing suspense. Great God! how had she done the deed!

Geoffrey snatched a sheet of paper and tried to write. He could not, his hand shook so. With a groan he rose, and going to the refreshment room swallowed two glasses of brandy one after another. The spirit took effect on him; he could write now. Rapidly he scribbled on a sheet of paper:

"I have been called away upon important business and shall probably not be back till Thursday morning. See that Effie is properly attended to. If I am not back you must not go to the duchess's ball.—Geoffrey Bingham."

Then he addressed the letter to Lady Honoria and dispatched a commissionaire with it. This done, he called a cab and bade the cabman drive to Euston as fast as his horse could go.

CHAPTER XXX

AVE ATQUE VALE

That frightful journey—no nightmare was ever half so awful! But it came to an end at last—there was the Bryngelly Station. Geoffrey sprang from the train, and gave his ticket to the porter, glancing in his face as he did so. Surely if there had been a tragedy the man would know of it, and show signs of half-joyous emotion as is the fashion of such people when something awful and mysterious has happened to somebody else. But he showed no such symptoms, and a glimmer of hope found its way into Geoffrey's tormented breast.

He left the station and walked rapidly towards the Vicarage. Those who know what a pitch of horror suspense can reach may imagine his feelings as he did so. But it was soon to be put an end to now. As he drew near the Vicarage gate he met the fat Welsh servant girl Betty running towards him. Then hope left Geoffrey.

The girl recognised him, and in her confusion did not seem in the least astonished to see him walking there at a quarter to seven on a summer morning. Indeed, even she vaguely connected Geoffrey with Beatrice in her mind, for she at once said in her thick English:

"Oh, sir, do you know where Miss Beatrice is?"

"No," he answered, catching at a railing for support. "Why do you ask? I have not seen her for weeks."

Then the girl plunged into a long story. Mr. Granger and Miss Granger were away from home, and would not be back for another two hours. Miss Beatrice had gone out yesterday afternoon, and had not come back to tea. She, Betty, had not thought much of it, believing that she had stopped to spend the evening somewhere, and, being very tired, had gone to bed about eight, leaving the door unlocked. This morning, when she woke, it was to find that Miss Beatrice had not slept in the house that night, and she came out to see if she could find her.

"Where was she going when she went out?" Geoffrey asked.

She did not know, but she thought that Miss Beatrice was going out in the canoe. Leastways she had put on her tennis shoes, which she always wore when she went out boating.

Geoffrey understood it all now. "Come to the boat-house," he said.

They went down to the beach, where as yet none were about except a few working people. Near the boat-house Geoffrey met old Edward walking along with a key in his hand.

"Lord, sir!" he said. "You here, sir! and in that there queer hat, too. What is it, sir?"

"Did Miss Beatrice go out in her canoe yesterday evening, Edward?" Geoffrey asked hoarsely.

"No, sir; not as I know on. My boy locked up the boat-house last night, and I suppose he looked in it first. What! You don't mean to say—Stop; we'll soon know. Oh, Goad! the canoe's gone!"

There was a silence, an awful silence. Old Edward broke it.

"She's drowned, sir—that's what she is—drowned at last; and she the finest woman in Wales. I knewed she would be one day, poor dear! and she the beauty that she was; and all along of that damned unlucky little craft. Goad help her! She's drowned, I say—"

Betty burst out into loud weeping at his words.

"Stop that noise, girl," said Geoffrey, turning his pale face towards her. "Go back to the Vicarage, and if Mr. Granger comes home before I get back, tell him what we fear. Edward, send some men to search the shore towards Coed, and some more in a sailing boat. I will walk towards the Bell Rock—you can follow me."

He started and swiftly tramped along the sands, searching the sea with his eye. On he walked sullenly, desperately striving to hope against hope. On, past the Dog Rocks, round the long curve of beach till he came to the Amphitheatre. The tide was high again; he could barely pass the projecting point. He was round it, and his heart stood still. For there, bottom upwards, and gently swaying to and fro as the spent waves rocked it, was Beatrice's canoe.

Sadly, hopelessly, heavily, Geoffrey waded knee deep into the water, and catching the bow of the canoe, dragged it ashore. There was, or appeared to be, nothing in it; of course he could not expect anything else. Its occupant had sunk and been carried out to sea by the ebb, whereas the canoe had drifted back to shore with the morning tide.

He reared it upon its end to let the water drain out of it, and from the hollow of the bow arch something came rolling down, something bright and heavy, followed by a brown object. Hastily he lowered the canoe again, and picked up the bright trinket. It was his own ring come back to him—the Roman ring he had given Beatrice, and which she told him in the letter she would wear in her hour of death. He touched it with his lips and placed it back upon his hand, this token from the beloved dead, vowing that it should never leave his hand in life, and that after death it should be buried on him. And so it will be, perhaps to be dug up again thousands of years hence, and once more to play a part in the romance of unborn ages.

Ave atque vale—that was the inscription rudely cut within its round. Greeting and farewell—her own last words to him. Oh, Beatrice, Beatrice! to you also ave atque vale. You could not have sent a fitter message. Greeting and farewell! Did it not sum it all? Within the circle of this little ring was writ the epitome of human life: here were the beginning and the end of Love and Hate, of Hope and fear, of Joy and Sorrow.

Beatrice, hail! Beatrice, farewell! till perchance a Spirit rushing earthward shall cry "Greeting," in another tongue, and Death, descending to his own place, shaking from his wings the dew of tears, shall answer "Farewell to me and Night, ye Children of Eternal Day!"

And what was this other relic? He lifted it—it was Beatrice's tennis shoe, washed from her foot— Geoffrey knew it, for once he had tied it.

Then Geoffrey broke down—it was too much. He threw himself upon the great rock and sobbed—that rock where he had sat with her and Heaven had opened to their sight. But men are not given to such exhibitions of emotion, and fortunately for him the paroxysm did not last. He could not have borne it for long.

He rose and went again to the edge of the sea. At this moment old Edward and his son arrived. Geoffrey pointed to the boat, then held up the little shoe.

"Ah," said the old man, "as I thought. Goad help her! She's gone; she'll never come ashore no more, she won't. She's twenty miles away by now, she is, breast up, with the gulls a-screaming over her. It's that there damned canoe, that's what it is. I wish to Goad I had broke it up long ago. I'd rather have built her a boat for nothing, I would. Damn the unlucky craft!" screamed the old man at the top of his voice, and turning his head to hide the tears that were streaming down his rugged face. "And her that I nursed and pulled out of the waters once all but dead. Damn it, I say! There, take that, you Sea Witch, you!" and he picked up a great boulder and crashed it through the bottom of the canoe with all his strength. "You shan't never drown no more. But it has brought you good luck, it has, sir; you'll be a fortunit man all your life now. It has brought you the Drowned One's shoe."

"Don't break it any more," said Geoffrey. "She used to value it. You had better bring it along between you—it may be wanted. I am going to the Vicarage."

He walked back. Mr. Granger and Elizabeth had not yet arrived, but they were expected every minute. He went into the sitting-room. It was full of memories and tokens of Beatrice. There lay a novel which he had given her, and there was yesterday's paper that she had brought from town, the Standard, with his speech in it.

Geoffrey covered his eyes with his hand, and thought. None knew that she had committed suicide except himself. If he revealed it things might be said of her; he did not care what was said of him, but he was jealous of her dead name. It might be said, for instance, that the whole tale was true, and that Beatrice died because she could no longer face life without being put to an open shame. Yes, he had better hold his tongue as to how and why she died. She was dead—nothing could bring her back. But how then should he account for his presence there? Easily enough. He would say frankly that he came because Beatrice had written to him of the charges made against her and the threats against himself—came to find her dead. And on that point he would still have a word with Owen Davies and Elizabeth.

Scarcely had he made up his mind when Elizabeth and her father entered. Clearly from their faces they had as yet heard nothing.

Geoffrey rose, and Elizabeth caught sight of him standing with glowing eyes and a face like that of Death himself. She recoiled in alarm.

"What brings you here, Mr. Bingham?" she said, in her hard voice.

"Cannot you guess, Miss Granger?" he said sternly. "A few days back you made certain charges against your sister and myself in the presence of your father and Mr. Owen Davies. These charges have been communicated to me, and I have come to answer them and to demand satisfaction for them."

Mr. Granger fidgeted nervously and looked as though he would like to escape, but Elizabeth, with characteristic courage, shut the door and faced the storm.

"Yes, I did make those charges, Mr. Bingham," she said, "and they are true charges. But stop, we had better send for Beatrice first."

"You may send, but you will not find her."

"What do you mean?—what do you mean?" asked her father apprehensively.

"It means that he has hidden her away, I suppose," said Elizabeth with a sneer.

"I mean, Mr. Granger, that your daughter Beatrice is dead."

For once startled out of her self-command, Elizabeth gave a little cry, while her father staggered back against the wall.

"Dead! dead! What do you mean? How did she die?" he asked.

"That is known to God and her alone," answered Geoffrey. "She went out last evening in her canoe. When I arrived here this morning she was missed for the first time. I walked along the beach and found the canoe and this inside of it," and he placed the sodden shoe upon the table.

There was a silence. In the midst of it, Owen Davies burst into the room with wild eyes and dishevelled hair.

"Is it true?" he cried, "tell me—it cannot be true that Beatrice is drowned. She cannot have been taken from me just when I was going to marry her. Say that it is not true!"

A great fury filled Geoffrey's heart. He walked down the room and shut the door, a red light swimming before his eyes. Then he turned and gripped Owen Davies's shoulder like a vice.

"You accursed blackguard—you unmanly cur!" he said; "you and that wicked woman," and he shook his hand at Elizabeth, "conspired together to bring a slur upon Beatrice. You did more: you threatened to attack me, to try and ruin me if she would not give herself up to you. You loathsome hypocrite, you tortured her and frightened her; now I am here to frighten you. You said that you would make the country ring with your tales. I tell you this—are you listening to me? If you dare to mention her name in such a sense, or if that woman dares, I will break every bone in your wretched body—by Heaven I will kill you!" and he cast Davies from him, and as he did so, struck him heavily across the face with the back of his hand.

The man took no notice either of his words or of the deadly insult of the blow.

"Is it true?" he screamed, "is it true that she is dead?"

"Yes," said Geoffrey, following him, and bending his tall square frame over him, for Davies had fallen against the wall, "yes, it is true—she is dead—and beyond your reach for ever. Pray to God that you may not one day be called her murderers, all of you—you shameless cowards."

Owen Davies gave one shrill cry and sank in a huddled heap upon the ground.

"There is no God," he moaned; "God promised her to me, to be my own—you have killed her; you—you seduced her first and then you killed her. I believe you killed her. Oh, I shall go mad!"

"Mad or sane," said Geoffrey, "say those words once more and I will stamp the life out of you where you are. You say that God promised her to you—promised that woman to a hound like you. Ah, be careful!"

Owen Davies made no answer. Crouched there upon the ground he rocked himself to and fro, and moaned in the madness of his baulked desire.

"This man," said Geoffrey, turning towards and pointing to Elizabeth, who was glaring at him like a wild cat from the corner of the room, "said that there is no God. I say that there is a God, and that one day, soon or late, vengeance will find you out—you murderess, you writer of anonymous letters; you who, to advance your own wicked ends whatever they may be, were not ashamed to try to drag your innocent sister's name into the dirt. I never believed in a hell till now, but there must be a hell for such as you, Elizabeth Granger. Go your ways; live out your time; but live every hour of it in terror of the vengeance that shall come so surely as you shall die.

"Now for you, sir," he went on, addressing the trembling father. "I do not blame you so much, because I believe that this viper poisoned your mind. You might have thought that the tale was true. It is not true; it was a lie. Beatrice, who now is dead, came into my room in her sleep, and was carried from it as she came. And you, her father, allowed this villain and your daughter to use her distress against her; you allowed him to make a lever of it, with which to force her into a marriage that she loathed. Yes, cover up your face—you may well do so. Do your worst, one and all of you, but remember that this time you have to deal with a man who can and will strike back, not a poor friendless girl."

"Before Heaven, it was not my fault, Mr. Bingham," gasped the old man. "I am innocent of it. That Judas-woman Elizabeth betrayed her sister because she wanted to marry him herself," and he pointed to the Heap upon the floor. "She thought that it would prejudice him against Beatrice, and he—he believed that she was attached to you, and tried to work upon her attachment."

"So," said Geoffrey, "now we have it all. And you, sir, stood by and saw this done. You stood by thinking that you would make a profit of her agony. Now I will tell you what I meant to hide from you. I did love her. I do love her—as she loved me. I believe that between you, you drove her to her grave. Her blood be on your heads for ever and for ever!"

"Oh, take me home," groaned the Heap upon the floor—"take me home, Elizabeth! I daren't go alone. Beatrice will haunt me. My brain goes round and round. Take me away, Elizabeth, and stop with me. You are not afraid of her, you are afraid of nothing."

Elizabeth sidled up to him, keeping her fierce eyes on Geoffrey all the time. She was utterly cowed and terrified, but she could still look fierce. She took the Heap by the hand and drew him thence still moaning and quite crazed. She led him away to his castle and his wealth. Six months afterwards she came forth with him to marry him, half-witted as he was. A year and eight months afterwards she came out again to bury him, and found herself the richest widow in Wales.

They went forth, leaving Geoffrey and Mr. Granger alone. The old man rested his head upon the table and wept bitterly.

"Be merciful," he said, "do not say such words to me. I loved her, indeed I did, but Elizabeth was too much for me, and I am so poor. Oh, if you loved her also, be merciful! I do not reproach you because you loved her, although you had no right to love her. If you had not loved her, and made her love you, all this would never have happened. Why do you say such dreadful things to me, Mr. Bingham?"

"I loved her, sir," answered Geoffrey, humbly enough now that his fury had passed, "because being what she was all who looked on her must love her. There is no woman left like her in the world. But who am I that I should blame you? God forgive us all! I only live henceforth in the hope that I may one day rejoin her where she has gone."

There was a pause.

"Mr. Granger," said Geoffrey presently, "never trouble yourself about money. You were her father; anything you want and what I have is yours. Let us shake hands and say good-bye, and let us never meet again. As I said, God forgive us all!"

"Thank you—thank you," said the old man, looking up through the white hair that fell about his eyes. "It is a strange world and we are all miserable sinners. I hope there is a better somewhere. I'm well-nigh tired of this, especially now that Beatrice has gone. Poor girl, she was a good daughter and a fine woman. Good-bye. Good-bye!"

Then Geoffrey went.

CHAPTER XXXI

THE DUCHESS'S BALL

Geoffrey reached Town a little before eleven o'clock that night—a haunted man—haunted for life by a vision of that face still lovely in death, floating alone upon the deep, and companioned only by the screaming mews—or perchance now sinking or sunk to an unfathomable grave. Well might such a vision haunt a man, the man whom alone of all men those cold lips had kissed, and for whose dear sake this dreadful thing was done.

He took a cab directing the driver to go to Bolton Street and to stop at his club as he passed. There might be letters for him there, he thought—something which would distract his mind a little. As it chanced there was a letter, marked "private," and a telegram; both had been delivered that evening, the porter said, the former about an hour ago by hand.

Idly he opened the telegram—it was from his lawyers: "Your cousin, the child George Bingham, is, as we have just heard, dead. Please call on us early to-morrow morning."

He started a little, for this meant a good deal to Geoffrey. It meant a baronetcy and eight thousand a year, more or less. How delighted Honoria would be, he thought with a sad smile; the loss of that large income had always been a bitter pill to her, and one which she had made him swallow again and again. Well, there it was. Poor boy, he had always been ailing—an old man's child!

He put the telegram in his pocket and got into the hansom again. There was a lamp in it and by its light he read the letter. It was from the Prime Minister and ran thus:

"My dear Bingham,—I have not seen you since Monday to thank you for the magnificent speech you made on that night. Allow me to add my congratulations to those of everybody else. As you know, the Under Secretaryship of the Home Office is vacant. On behalf of my colleagues and myself I write to ask if you will consent to fill it for a time, for we do not in any way consider that the post is one commensurate with your abilities. It will, however, serve to give you practical experience of administration, and us the advantage of your great talents to an even larger extent than we now enjoy. For the future, it must of course take care of itself; but, as you know, Sir—'s health is not all that could be desired, and the other day he told me that it was doubtful if he would be able to carry on the duties of the Attorney-Generalship for very much longer. In view of this contingency I venture to suggest that you would do well to apply for silk as soon as possible. I have spoken to the Lord Chancellor about it, and he says that there will be no difficulty, as although you have only been in active practice for so short a while, you have a good many years' standing as a barrister. Or if this prospect does not please doubtless some other opening to the Cabinet can be found in time. The fact is, that we cannot in our own interest overlook you for long."

Geoffrey smiled again as he finished this letter. Who could have believed a year ago that he would have been to-day in a position to receive such an epistle from the Prime Minister of England? Ah, here was the luck of the Drowned One's shoe with a vengeance. And what was it all worth to him now?

He put the letter in his pocket with the telegram and looked out. They were turning into Bolton Street. How was little Effie, he wondered? The child seemed all that was left him to care for. If anything happened to her—bah, he would not think of it!

He was there now. "How is Miss Effie?" he asked of the servant who opened the door. At that moment his attention was attracted by the dim forms of two people, a man and a woman, who were standing not far from the area gate, the man with his arm round the woman's waist. Suddenly the woman appeared to catch sight of the cab and retired swiftly down the area. It crossed his mind that her figure was very like that of Anne, the French nurse.

"Miss Effie is doing nicely, sir, I'm told," answered the man.

Geoffrey breathed more freely. "Where is her ladyship?" he asked. "In Effie's room?"

"No, sir," answered the man, "her ladyship has gone to a ball. She left this note for you in case you should come in."

He took the note from the hall table and opened it.

"Dear Geoffrey," it ran, "Effie is so much better that I have made up my mind to go to the duchess's ball after all. She would be so disappointed if I did not come, and my dress is quite lovely. Had your mysterious business anything to do with Bryngelly?—

"Yours, Honoria."

"She would go on to a ball from her mother's funeral," said Geoffrey to himself, as he walked up to Effie's room; "well, it is her nature and there's an end of it."

He knocked at the door of Effie's room. There was no answer, so he walked in. The room was lit but empty—no, not quite! On the floor, clothed only in her white night-shirt, lay his little daughter, to all appearance dead.

With something like an oath he sprang to her and lifted her. The face was pale and the small hands were cold, but the breast was still hot and fevered, and the heart beat. A glance showed him what had happened. The child being left alone, and feeling thirsty, had got out of bed and gone to the water bottle—there was the tumbler on the floor. Then weakness had overcome her and she had fainted—fainted upon the cold floor with the inflammation still on her.

At that moment Anne entered the room sweetly murmuring, "Ça va bien, chérie?"

"Help me to put the child into bed," said Geoffrey sternly. "Now ring the bell—ring it again.

"And now, woman—go. Leave this house at once, this very night. Do you hear me? No, don't stop to argue. Look here! If that child dies I will prosecute you for manslaughter; yes, I saw you in the street," and he took a step towards her. Then Anne fled, and her face was seen no more in Bolton Street or indeed in this country.

"James," said Geoffrey to the servant, "send the cook up here—she is a sensible woman; and do you take a hansom and drive to the doctor, and tell him to come here at once, and if you cannot find him go for another doctor. Then go to the Nurses' Home, near St. James' Station, and get a trained nurse—tell them one must be had from somewhere instantly."

"Yes, sir. And shall I call for her ladyship at the duchess's, sir?"

"No," he answered, frowning heavily, "do not disturb her ladyship. Go now."

"That settles it," said Geoffrey, as the man went. "Whatever happens, Honoria and I must part. I have done with her."

He had indeed, though not in the way he meant. It would have been well for Honoria if her husband's contempt had not prevented him from summoning her from her pleasure.

The cook came up, and between them they brought the child back to life.

She opened her eyes and smiled. "Is that you, daddy," she whispered, "or do I dreams?"

"Yes, dear, it is I."

"Where has you been, daddy—to see Auntie Beatrice?"

"Yes, love," he said, with a gasp.

"Oh, daddy, my head do feel funny; but I don't mind now you is come back. You won't go away no more, will you, daddy?"

"No, dear, no more."

After that she began to wander a little, and finally dropped into a troubled sleep.

Within half an hour both the doctor and the nurse arrived. The former listened to Geoffrey's tale and examined the child.

"She may pull through it," he said, "she has got a capital constitution; but I'll tell you what it is—if she had lain another five minutes in that draught there would have been an end of her. You came in the nick of time. And now if I were you I should go to bed. You can do no good here, and you look dreadfully ill yourself."

But Geoffrey shook his head. He said he would go downstairs and smoke a pipe. He did not want to go to bed at present; he was too tired.

Meanwhile the ball went merrily. Lady Honoria never enjoyed herself more in her life. She revelled in the luxurious gaiety around her like a butterfly in the sunshine. How good it all was—the flash of diamonds, the odour of costly flowers, the homage of well-bred men, the envy of other women. Oh! it was a delightful world after all—that is when one did not have to exist in a flat near the Edgware Road. But Heaven be praised! thanks to Geoffrey's talents, there was an end of flats and misery. After all, he was not a bad sort of husband, though in many ways a perfect mystery to her. As for his little weakness for the Welsh girl, really, provided that there was no scandal, she did not care twopence about it.

"Yes, I am so glad you admire it. I think it is rather a nice dress, but then I always say that nobody in London can make a dress like Madame Jules. Oh, no, Geoffrey did not choose it; he thinks of other things."

"Well, I'm sure you ought to be proud of him, Lady Honoria," said the handsome Guardsman to whom she was talking; "they say at mess that he is one of the cleverest men in England. I only wish I had a fiftieth part of his brains."

"Oh, please do not become clever, Lord Atleigh; please don't, or I shall really give you up. Cleverness is all very well, but it isn't everything, you know. Yes, I will dance if you like, but you must go slowly; to be quite honest, I am afraid of tearing my lace in this crush. Why, I declare there is Garsington, my brother, you know," and she pointed to a small red-haired man who was elbowing his way towards them. "I wonder what he wants; it is not at all in his line to come to balls. You know him, don't you? he is always racing horses, like you."

But the Guardsman had vanished. For reasons of his own he did not wish to meet Garsington. Perhaps he too had been a member of a certain club.

"Oh, there you are, Honoria," said her brother, "I thought that I should be sure to find you somewhere in this beastly squash. Look here, I have something to tell you."

"Good news or bad?" said Lady Honoria, playing with her fan. "If it is bad, keep it, for I am enjoying myself very much, and I don't want my evening spoilt."

"Trust you for that, Honoria; but look here, it's jolly good, about as good as can be for that prig of a husband of yours. What do you think? that brat of a boy, the son of old Sir Robert Bingham and the cook or some one, you know, is—"

"Not dead, not dead?" said Honoria in deep agitation.

"Dead as ditch-water," replied his lordship. "I heard it at the club. There was a lawyer fellow there dining with somebody there, and they got talking about Bingham, when the lawyer said, 'Oh, he's Sir Geoffrey Bingham now. Old Sir Robert's heir is dead. I saw the telegram myself.'"

"Oh, this is almost too good to be true," said Honoria. "Why, it means eight thousand a year to us."

"I told you it was pretty good," said her brother. "You ought to stand me a commission out of the swag. At any rate, let's go and drink to the news. Come on, it is time for supper and I am awfully done. I must screw myself up."

Lady Honoria took his arm. As they walked down the wide flower-hung stair they met a very great Person indeed, coming up.

"Ah, Lady Honoria," said the great Person, "I have something to say that will please you, I think," and he bent towards her, and spoke very low, then, with a little bow, passed on.

"What is the old boy talking about?" asked her brother.

"Why, what do you think? We are in luck's way to-night. He says that they are offering Geoffrey the Under Secretaryship of the Home Office."

"He'll be a bigger prig than ever now," growled Lord Garsington. "Yes, it is luck though; let us hope it won't turn."

They sat down to supper, and Lord Garsington, who had already been dining, helped himself pretty freely to champagne. Before them was a silver candelabra and on each of the candles was fixed a little painted paper shade. One of them got wrong, and a footman tried to reach over Lord Garsington's head to put it straight.

"I'll do it," said he.

"No, no; let the man," said Lady Honoria. "Look! it is going to catch fire!"

"Nonsense," he answered, rising solemnly and reaching his arm towards the shade. As he touched it, it caught fire; indeed, by touching it he caused it to catch fire. He seized hold of it, and made an effort to put it out, but it burnt his fingers.

"Curse the thing!" he said aloud, and threw it from him. It fell flaming in his sister's dress among the thickest of the filmy laces; they caught, and instantly two wreathing snakes of fire shot up her. She sprang from her seat and rushed screaming down the room, an awful mass of flame!

In ten more minutes Lady Honoria had left this world and its pleasures to those who still lived to taste them.

An hour passed. Geoffrey still sat brooding heavily over his pipe in the study in Bolton Street and waiting for Honoria, when a knock came to his door. The servants had all gone to bed, all except the sick nurse. He rose and opened it himself. A little red-haired, pale-faced man staggered in.

"Why, Garsington, is it you? What do you want at this hour?"

"Screw yourself up, Bingham, I've something to tell you," he answered in a thick voice.

"What is it? another disaster, I suppose. Is somebody else dead?"

"Yes; somebody is. Honoria's dead. Burnt to death at the ball."

"Great God! Honoria burnt to death. I had better go—"

"I advise you not, Bingham. I wouldn't go to the hospital if I were you. Screw yourself up, and if you can, give me something to drink—I'm about done—I must screw myself up."

And here we may leave this most fortunate and gifted man. Farewell to Geoffrey Bingham.

.

ENVOI

Thus, then, did these human atoms work out their destinies, these little grains of animated dust, blown hither and thither by a breath which came they knew not whence.

If there be any malicious Principle among the Powers around us that deigns to find amusement in the futile vagaries of man, well might it laugh, and laugh again, at the great results of all this scheming, of all these desires, loves and hates; and if there be any pitiful Principle, well might it sigh over the infinite pathos of human helplessness. Owen Davies lost in his own passion; Geoffrey crowned with prosperity and haunted by undying sorrow; Honoria perishing wretchedly in her hour of satisfied ambition; Beatrice sacrificing herself in love and blindness, and thereby casting out her joy.

Oh, if she had been content to humbly trust in the Providence above her; if she had but left that deed undared for one short week!

But Geoffrey still lived, and the child recovered, after hanging for a while between life and death, and was left to comfort him. May she survive to be a happy wife and mother, living under conditions more favourable to her well-being than those which trampled out the life of that mistaken woman, the ill-starred, great-souled Beatrice, and broke her father's heart.

Say—what are we? We are but arrows winged with fears and shot from darkness into darkness; we are blind leaders of the blind, aimless beaters of this wintry air; lost travellers by many stony paths ending in one end. Tell us, you, who have outworn the common tragedy and passed the narrow way, what lies beyond its gate? You are dumb, or we cannot hear you speak.

But Beatrice knows to-day!

H. Rider Haggard – A Short Biography

Sir Henry Rider Haggard, KBE was born on June 22nd, 1856 at Bradenham in Norfolk, England.

More familiarly known as H. Rider Haggard, he was the eighth of ten children born to Sir William Meybohm Rider Haggard, a barrister (born, incidentally, in St Petersburg, Russia), and Ella Doveton, an author, poet and daughter of a merchant in the East India Trading Company.

Haggard was initially schooled at Garsington Rectory in Oxfordshire where he studied under the tutelage of Reverend H. J. Graham. His elder brothers, who seemed to find more favour with their father, graduated from various private schools whilst Haggard was sent to Ipswich Grammar School, saving his father a considerable sum in fees.

He failed his army entrance exam, and was therefore sent to a private crammer in London in preparation for the entrance exam to the British Foreign Office, which he appears never to have sat. However, it was during his two years in London that Haggard came into contact with a circle of people interested in the study of psychical phenomena and for which he too now developed a life-long interest together with a series of enduring friendships.

In 1875, Haggard's father used his family's connections to send him to Southern Africa to take up an unpaid position as assistant to the secretary to Sir Henry Bulwer, Lieutenant-Governor of the Colony of Natal. In 1876 he was transferred to the staff of Sir Theophilus Shepstone, Special Commissioner for the Transvaal. It was in this role that Haggard was present in Pretoria in April 1877 for the official announcement of the British annexation of the Boer Republic of the Transvaal. The official who had been nominated to read out the Proclamation lost his voice and Haggard was his replacement. It was a moment in history.

Haggard was to remain in the country for six years, during which time he served as Master of the High Court of the Transvaal and an adjutant of the Pretoria Horse.

It was here that he fell in love with Mary Elizabeth "Lilly" Jackson. He hoped to marry her once he obtained more certainty in his career path.

In 1878 he became Registrar of the High Court in the Transvaal and now the time seemed opportune to write to his father to tell him of his hope to marry. The reply from his father was uncompromising. He forbade it until his son had made a proper career for himself.

The following year, 1879, Lily married Frank Archer, a well-to-do banker.

Haggard returned briefly to England to marry a friend of his sister's, Marianna Louisa Margitson, a 21 year old, in 1880, and the couple travelled to Africa together. Haggard's years in Africa had proved, at least on a writing level, rich and inspirational for him, and while still in Natal he wrote two articles for The Gentleman's Magazine describing his experiences.

Moving back to England in (and accounts here differ as to whether it was 1881 or 1882) the couple settled in Ditchingham, Norfolk, Louisa's ancestral home. Later they moved to Kessingland and established connections with the church in Bungay, Suffolk. The marriage produced four children. A son named Jack (who tragically died at age 10 of measles) and three daughters, Angela, Dorothy and Lilias. (Lilias grew to become an author and her father's biographer.)

In England Law was to be the fulcrum of his career. However, although he studied, writing was growing in its appeal to him. His first book, Cetywayo and His White Neighbours, was an account and study of Britain's policies in South Africa.

From this point his career as a writer began to take substantial hold and with it a dramatic shift to fiction. Two years later he published his first fiction, Dawn followed in 1885 by arguably his most popular novel, King Solomon's Mines—detailing the life of the adventurer Allan Quatermain. This was followed the following year, 1886, by She: A History of Adventure, which introduced the female character Ayesha. Both characters, Quatermain and Ayesha, developed a series of books about their adventures.

The study of Law now fell away entirely. He appeared also to have a keen sense of his commercial appreciation. Rather than sell the copyright of his first best-seller, King Solomon's Mines, for a £100 fee he, instead, accepted a 10% royalty. This book is also generally accepted as the first of the Lost World writing genre.

Haggard obviously thought there were many further adventures to tell and it would be hard to find a publisher who would disagree given the start he had made. Sequels soon followed. Allan Quatermain continued his epic and swash-buckling adventures in Africa whilst the sequel to She entitled Ayesha played out her adventures in Tibet. Interestingly Haggard would later extend his characters adventures around the world with Eric Brighteyes, being the basis for an epic Viking romance.

The Haggard family lived at 69 Gunterstone Road in Hammersmith, London, from mid-1885 to mid-1888. It was here that he wrote his most famous works. His time in Africa had given him the experience and atmosphere as well as several observations and friendships of the people who would so influence his fictional characters. Chief among them were the larger-than-life adventurers Frederick Selous and Frederick Russell Burnham. Both were men of Empire and huge ambition as they helped uncover the great mineral wealth of Africa, as well as the ruins of ancient lost civilisations of the continent, such as Great Zimbabwe.

Three of Haggard's books, The Wizard (1896), Black Heart and White Heart; a Zulu Idyll (1896), and Elissa; the Doom of Zimbabwe (1898), are dedicated to Burnham's daughter Nada, the first white child born in Bulawayo; she had been named after Haggard's 1892 book Nada the Lily.

As is typical of the writing of the time his novels contain many of the stereotypes associated with colonialism, yet they also sympathise, to a degree, with the native populations. Africans often play heroic roles in the novels, although the protagonists are more often than not European. The time around the turn of the century was, after all, the great sprint to Empire by many European countries intent on gaining possessions of land, people and resources.

Three of Haggard's novels were written in collaboration with his friend Andrew Lang who shared his interest in the spiritual realm and paranormal phenomena and who was also a greatly admired editor.

Haggard's stories are still widely read today. Ayesha, the female protagonist of She, has been cited as a prototype by psychoanalysts such as Sigmund Freud (in The Interpretation of Dreams) and Carl Jung. Her epithet is, of course, "She Who Must Be Obeyed" and has for decades been used tongue-in-cheek to describe the presumed balance of influence between the sexes.

As a legacy it is easy to establish Haggard, and his pioneering work, as the author of the Lost World branch of writing and its influence of such other writers as Edgar Rice Burroughs, Robert E. Howard and Talbot Mundy. The Allan Quatermain character influenced many 'serials' in Hollywood during the 30s & 40s and can readily be seen as a template for Indiana Jones, the American archaeologist and explorer and huge box office film character.

Years later, when Haggard was a successful novelist, he was contacted by his former love, Lilly Archer, née Jackson. Lily had been deserted by her husband, who had embezzled funds and fled bankrupt to Africa. Haggard installed her and her sons in a house and saw to the children's education. Lilly eventually followed her husband to Africa, where he infected her with syphilis before dying of it himself. Lilly returned to England in late 1907, where Haggard again supported her until her death on April 22nd, 1909.

Haggard also wrote about agricultural and social reform, in part inspired by his experiences in Africa, but also based on what he saw in Europe. By the end of his life, he was adamantly opposed to Bolshevism, a position that he shared with his life-long friend Rudyard Kipling. The two had found friendship upon Kipling's arrival at London in 1889 largely on the strength of their shared opinions.

Haggard was extremely interested in the social affairs of the Country and eager to play a more active part in attempting reform. In 1895 he stood unsuccessfully for Parliament as a Conservative candidate for the Eastern division of Norfolk losing by 198 votes.

Also in 1895 he served on a government commission to examine Salvation Army labour colonies. This, and his heavy involvement in agriculture reform, led to him being a member of several further commissions on land use and related affairs, work that involved several trips to the Colonies and Dominions. This work, in part, helped lead to the passage of the 1909 Development Bill.

In 1911 he served on the Royal Commission examining coastal erosion.

He was an absorbed and dedicated writer of letters to The Times, nearly one hundred were published by them and the bibliography attached below reveals much in the range of subjects he wished to bring attention to.

He was made a Knight Bachelor in 1912 and a Knight Commander of the Order of the British Empire in 1919. Haggard was a member of several clubs including the Athenaeum, Savile, and Authors' clubs.

The district of Rider in British Columbia, Canada, was named in his honour.

Henry Rider Haggard died on May 14th, 1925 at the age of 68. His ashes were buried at Ditchingham Church. His papers are held at the Norfolk Record Office.

The first chapter of his book People of the Mist (1894) is credited with inspiring the 1912 motto of the Royal Air Force (formerly the Royal Flying Corps), Per ardua ad astra. "Through adversity to the stars" (or alternately "Through struggle to the stars") it is also used by other Commonwealth air forces such as the RAAF, RCAF, RNZAF, and the SAAF.

H. Rider Haggard – A Concise Bibliography

Novels
Dawn (1884) Published in three volumes
The Witch's Head (1884) Published in three volumes
King Solomon's Mines (1885) Allan Quatermain series
She: A History of Adventure (1886) Ayesha series
Allan Quatermain (1887) Allan Quatermain series
Jess (1887)
A Tale of Three Lions (1887) Allan Quatermain series
Maiwa's Revenge, or the War of the Little Hand (1888) Allan Quatermain series
Colonel Quaritch, VC (1889) Published in three volumes
Cleopatra (1889)
Beatrice (1890)
The World's Desire (1890) Co-written with Andrew Lang
Eric Brighteyes (1891)
Nada the Lily (1892)
An Heroic Effort (1893)
Montezuma's Daughter (1893)
The People of the Mist (1894)
Heart of the World (1895)
Joan Haste (1895)
The Wizard (1896)
Doctor Therne (1898)
Swallow: A Tale of the Great Trek (1899)
Lysbeth (1901)
Pearl Maiden (1903)
Stella Fregelius: A Tale of Three Destinies (1903)
The Brethren (1904)
Ayesha: The Return of She (1905) Ayesha series
The Way of the Spirit (1906)
Benita (1906)
Fair Margaret (1907)
The Ghost Kings(1908)
The Yellow God (1908)
The Lady of Blossholme (1909)
Morning Star (1910)

Queen Sheba's Ring (1910)
Red Eve (1911)
The Mahatma and the Hare (1911)
Marie (1912) Allan Quatermain series
Child of Storm (1913) Allan Quatermain series
The Wanderer's Necklace (1914)
The Holy Flower (1915) Allan Quatermain series
The Ivory Child (1916) Allan Quatermain series
Finished (1917) Allan Quatermain series]
Love Eternal (1918)
Moon of Israel (1918)
When the World Shook (1919)
The Ancient Allan (1920) Allan Quatermain series
She and Allan (1921) Allan Quatermain series / Ayesha series
The Virgin of the Sun (1922)
Wisdom's Daughter (1923) Ayesha series
Heu-Heu (1924) Allan Quatermain series]
Queen of the Dawn (1925)
The Treasure of the Lake (1926) Allan Quatermain series
Allan and the Ice-Gods (1927) Allan Quatermain series
Mary of Marion Isle (1929)
Belshazzar (1930)

Short Story Collections
Allan's Wife and Other Tales (1889)
Black Heart and White Heart: A Zulu Idyll (1900)
Smith and the Pharaohs (1920)

Publications in Periodicals and Newspapers
A Zulu War-Dance (July 1877) The Gentleman's Magazine
A Visit to the Chief (September 1877) The Gentleman's Magazine
Hydrophobia (letter) (3 November 1885) The Times
The Land Question (letter) (28 April 1886) The Times
About Fiction (February 1887) The Contemporary Review
Mr Rider Haggard and His Critics (letter) (27 April 1887) The Times
Our Position in Cyprus (July 1887) The Contemporary Review
American Copyright (letter) (11 October 1887) The Times
On Going Back (November 1887) Longman's Magazine
Delagoa Bay (letter) (17 December 1887) The Times
South African Policy (letter) (27 December 1887) The Times
Suggested Prologue to a Dramatised Version of She (March 1888) Longman's Magazine
Mr. Meeson's Will (18 June 1888) The Illustrated London News
The Wreck of the Copeland (18 August 1888) The Illustrated London News
Cleopatra (3 December 1888) The Illustrated London News
Hydrophobia and Muzzling (letter) (25 October 1889) The Times
The Annals of Natal (23 November 1889) The Saturday Review

Mummy at St Mary/Woolnoth's (letter) (25 December 1889) The Times
Mummies (letter) (27 December 1889) The Times
The Fate of Swaziland (January 1890) The New Review
In Memoriam (17 May 1890) Thompson's Seasons
American Copyright (letter) (5 June 1890) The Times
Mr Herbert Ward and Mr Stanley (10 November 1890) The Times
Nada the Lily (2 January 1892) The Illustrated London News
A New Argument Against Creation (19 December 1892) The Times
My First Book. Dawn. By H. Rider Haggard (April 1893) The Idler
The Tale of Isandlwana and Rorke's Drift (4 October 1893) The True Story Book
Lobengula (letter) (19 October 1893) The Times
The New Sentiment (letter) (6 November 1893) The Times
Wanted—Imagination   (25 December 1893) The Times
The Fate of Captain Patterson's Party (28 December 1893) The Times
The Three Volume Novel (letter) (27 July 1894) The Times
The Adventures of John Gladwyn Jebb (letter) (30 October 1894) The Times
Agriculture in Norfolk (letter) (30 October 1894) The Times
The Nelson Bazaar (letter) (16 February 1895) The Times
Everything is Peaceful (letter) (20 March 1895) The Times
Lord Kimberley in Norfolk (letter) (17 April 1895) The Times
The East Norfolk Election (letter) (23 July 1895) The Times
The East Norfolk Election (letter) (29 July 1895) The Times
Wilson's Last Fight (7 October 1895) The True Story Book
The Crisis in the Transvaal (letter) (2 January 1896) The Times
The Transvaal Crisis (letter) (13 January 1896) The Times
Jameson's Surrender (letter) (14 March 1896) The Times
The Rinderpest in South Africa (letter) (5 November 1896) The Times
Mr Rider Haggard and Dr Neufeld (letter) (9 January 1899) The Times
Shrinkage of Population in Agricultural Districts (letter) (9 May 1899) The Times
The South African Crisis—An Appeal (letter) (1 July 1899) The Times
Commandant-General Joubert and Mr H Rider Haggard (letter) (8 September 1899) The Times
Anglo-African Writers' Club (17 October 1899) The Times
The War (letter) (25 October 1899) The Times
Farming in 1899 (letter) (22 December 1899) The Times
Farming in 1899 (letter) (1 January 1900) The Times
Settlement of Soldiers in South Africa (letter) (5 May 1900) The Times
1881 and 1900 (letter) (2 October 1900) The Times
Farming in 1900 (letter) (1 January 1901) The Times
Central and Associated Chambers of Agriculture (letter) (6 November 1901) The Times
Small Holdings (letter) (8 November 1901) The Times
Rural England (letter) (4 February 1903) The Times
Mr Rider Haggard on Rural Depopulation (3 May 1903) The Times
Agricultural Distress (letter) (11 June 1903) The Times
The Motor Problem (letter) (24 June 1903) The Times
Fiscal Policy and Agriculture (letter) (16 December 1903) The Times
Telepathy Between a Human Being and a Dog (letter) (21 July 1904) The Times
Telepathy Between a Human Being and a Dog (letter) (9 August 1904) The Times
Mr Rider Haggard on Small Holdings (12 September 1904) The Times

Case L.1139 Dream (October 1904) Journal of the Society for Psychical Research
Mr Rider Haggard on Agriculture (22 October 1904) The Times
Mr Rider Haggard on Rural Housing (27 October 1904) The Times
The Deserted Village (letter) (25 August 1905) The Times
Decrease of Population and the Land (letter) (6 January 1906) The Times
Prevention of Cruelty to Children (3 February 1906) The Times
The New Land and Tenure Bill (letter) (12 March 1906) The Times
Garden City Association (17 March 1906) The Times
Mr H. Rider Haggard on the Zulus (19 May 1906) The Illustrated London News
To Be Proof against British Bullets: A Zulu Incantation (19 May 1906) The Illustrated London News
Housing of the Working Classes (26 June 1906) The Times
Mr Rider Haggard on Small Holdings (4 July 1906) The Times
The Unemployed and Waste City Lands (letter) (19 July 1906) The Times
Mr Rider Haggard on the Transvaal Constitution (7 August 1906) The Times
Vanishing East Anglia (1 September 1906) The Saturday Review
The Land Grabbing at Plaistow (5 September 1906) The Times
The Land Tenure Bill (22 November 1906) The Times
Publishers and the Public (letter) (19 February 1907) The Times
The Careless Children (2 March 1907) The Saturday Review
The Government and the Land (letter) (29 April 1907) The Times
Chambers of Agriculture (2 May 1907) The Times
The Government and the Land (letter) (8 May 1907) The Times
Miss Jebb on Small Holdings (15 June 1907) Country Life
Rural Housing and Sanitation Association (27 June 1907) The Times
St Thomas Hospital Medical School (28 June 1907) The Times
The Land Question (4 July 1907) The Times
A Plea for the Sitting Tennant (letter) (12 August 1907) The Times
A Literary Coincidence (letter) (19 October 1907) The Spectator
Town Planning Conference (26 October 1907) The Times
Dr Barnardo's Homes (16 November 1907) The Times
The Proposed Agricultural Party (5 December 1907) The Times
Mr Rider Haggard and Small Holdings (10 January 1908) The Times
Mr Haggard and Children's Legislation (13 March 1908) The Times
The Drink Trade and Common Sense (letter) (2 April 1908) The Times
The Zulus: The Finest Savage Race in the World (June 1908) The Pall Mall Magazine
Sparrows (letter) (18 August 1908) The Times
Sparrows, Rats and Humanity (letter) (5 September 1908) The Times
The Letters of Queen Victoria (letter) (26 November 1908) The Times
The Romance of the World's Greatest Rivers (December 1908) Travel Magazine
Afforestation. Mr Rider Haggard's View (1 March 1909) The Times
The Late Sir Marshal Clarke (letter) (13 April 1909) The Times
Mr Rider Haggard on Agriculture (27 November 1909) The Times
Mr Rider Haggard on South Africa (11 March 1910) The Times
Why? (letter) (25 April 1910) The Times
Mr Rider Haggard on Irish Agriculture (23 May 1910) The Times
Why Not? (letter) (12 July 1910) The Times
Mr Rider Haggard on Agriculture (16 September 1910) The Times
Mr Rider Haggard on Vermin (8 November 1910) The Times

Danish High Schools (21 December 1910) The Times
Sugar Beet Growing in Norfolk (6 March 1911) The Times
Rural Denmark (letter) (22 March 1911) The Times
Rural Denmark (letter) (3 April 1911) The Times
The Copyright Bill (letter) (6 June 1911) The Times
Mr Rider Haggard on Poverty. The Burden of Civilization (15 July 1911) The Times
Mr Rider Haggard and the Public Records (28 July 1911) The Times
The Farmers' Burden (1 December 1911) The Times
Egyptian Date Farm. The Financial Aspect (11 October 1912) The Times
Umslopogaas and Makokel. Sir H. Rider Haggard on Zulu Types (letter) (16 August 1913) The Times
The Death of Mark Haggard (letter) (10 October 1914) The Times
On the Land. Old Problems and New Ways. The War—and After. (15 March 1915) The Times
Soldiers as Settlers. After-War Problem for the Empire (20 August 1915) The Times
Raids by Air. Zeppelins and Zeppelins (letter) (22 October 1915) The Times
Women's Work on the Land. A Palliative in Hard Times (letter) (29 November 1915) The Times
Women on the Land. Town Girls' Unfitness for Farm Work (letter) (9 December 1915) The Times
Soldiers as Settlers. Sir Rider Haggard's Oversea Mission (2 February 1916) The Times
Soldiers as Settlers (letter) (7 February 1916) The Times
Soldier Settlers. The Future of Rural England (letter) (10 February 1916) The Times
Farewell Luncheon to Sir Rider Haggard (March 1916) United Empire
Soldier Settlers for the Empire. Offer from Victoria (18 April 1916) The Times
Sir R Haggard's Tour. Land for Ex-Service Men (22 July 1916) The Times
Sir H. Rider Haggard's Mission. Land for Ex-Soldiers (1 August 1916) The Times
Land for Ex-Soldiers. Outline of Sir R. Haggard's Report   (12 August 1916) The Times
Empire Land Settlement Deputation to the Secretary of State for the Colonies and the President of the
Board of Agriculture (September 1916) United Empire
Empire Land Settlement by Sir Rider Haggard (December 1916) United Empire
A Journey through Zululand by Sir H Rider Haggard (December 1916) The Windsor Magazine
Mr Wilson's Note. British Publicity (28 December 1916) The Times
Home Produce (letter) (22 February 1917) The Times
The Milk Supply (letter) (11 April 1917) The Times
Corn Production Bill. A National Measure (letter) (13 June 1917) The Times
A Protest and a Plea. Farmers and Meat (letter) (9 October 1917) The Times
Pig-Breeding. A Subject for Municipal Enterprise (letter) (22 February 1918) The Times
The German Colonies. Interests of the Dominions (letter) (5 November 1918) The Times
Light—More Light! (letter) (19 November 1918) The Times
A Great American. Tributes to the Late Mr Roosevelt (letter) (8 January 1919) The Times
Shut the Door (letter) (10 March 1919) The Times
Population and Housing. Emigration v Birth Control (25 March 1919) The Times
The Ex-Kaiser (letter) (11 April 1919) The Times
Empire Birth-Rate. Sir Rider Haggard on Emigration (17 April 1919) The Times
Ex-Service Men Abroad. Warnings from California (letter) (10 May 1919) The Times
Edith Cavell (letter) (16 May 1919) The Times
The Ex-Kaiser. Uncertainties of Trial (letter) (8 July 1919) The Times
Race Suicide Peril. Western Civilization Threatened (11 October 1919) The Times
The British Cinema. Production of Reputable Films (letter) (5 November 1919) The Times
Horrors on the Film. Limits of Publicity (letter) (19 November 1919) The Times
The British Museum (letter) (24 January 1920) The Times

Air Exploration and Empire (letter) (7 February 1920) The Times
The Liberty League. A Campaign Against Bolshevism (letter) (3 March 1920) The Times
Bolshevist Peril. Counter-Propaganda (4 March 1920) The Times
The Empire's Vacant Lands. Settlers and the Food Supply (14 April 1920) The Times
Films and Happy Endings. The Tyranny of a Convention (letter)   (21 April 1921) The Times
Land and its Burdens. Evil of Grinding Taxation (letter) (8 August 1921) The Times
Boy Emigrants (letter) (31 March 1922) The Times
Migration and Morals. Declining Birther Rate (7 April 1922) The Times
Labour Party's Programme. Confiscation and Class Hatred (letter) (28 October 1922) The Times
Efficient Denmark. Keeping the People on the Land (7 December 1922) The Times
The Egyptian Find. Tombs of Eighteenth Dynasty Queens (letter) (19 December 1922) The Times
King Tutankhamen. Reburial in Great Pyramid (letter) (13 February 1923) The Times
The Norfolk Dispute. A Truce while There is Time (letter) (3 April 1923) The Times
Rural Post and Telephone. Minister's Reply to Deputation (19 April 1923) The Times
Liberalism and Land Reform (letter) (1 May 1923) The Times
Small Holdings. Influence of Heredity (letter) (4 July 1923) The Times
Agricultural Parcel Post (26 July 1923) The Times
Country Houses for Sale. Empty East Anglian Mansions (letter) (14 June 1924) The Times
Plight of Agriculture (24 July 1924) The Times
Loans From the British Museum (letter) (30 July 1924) The Times
Zinovieff Letter. Mr MacDonald and a Political Plot (letter) (29 October 1924) The Times
Two Centuries of Publishing. Tributes to Messrs. Longmans (6 November 1924) The Times
Imagination and War (26 November 1924) The Times

Non-Fiction
Cetywayo and His White Neighbours (1882)
A Farmer's Year (1899)
The Last Boer War (1899)
A Winter Pilgrimage (1901)
Rural England (1902)
A Gardener's Year (1905)
The Poor and the Land (1905)
Regeneration (1910)
Rural Denmark (1911)
The Days of My Life (1926)

Film Adaptations

King Solomon's Mines
This novel has been adapted at least six times. The first version, King Solomon's Mines, directed by
Robert Stevenson, premiered in 1937. The best known version premiered in 1950: King Solomon's
Mines, directed by Compton Bennett and Andrew Marton, was followed in 1959 by a sequel, Watusi. In
1979 a low-budget version directed by Alvin Rakoff, King Solomon's Treasure, combined both King
Solomon's Mines and Allan Quatermain in one story. The 1985 film King Solomon's Mines was a tongue-
in-cheek parody of the story, with a 1987 sequel in the same vein, Allan Quatermain and the Lost City of

Gold. Around the same time an Australian animated TV film came out, King Solomon's Mines. In 2008 a direct-to-video adaptation, Allan Quatermain and the Temple of Skulls, was released.

She
She has been adapted for the cinema at least ten times, and was one of the earliest films to be made, in 1899 as La Colonne de feu (The Pillar of Fire), by Georges Méliès. A 1911 version starred Marguerite Snow, a British-produced version appeared in 1916, and in 1917 Valeska Suratt appeared in a production for Fox which is lost. In 1925 a silent film of She, starring Betty Blythe, was produced with the active participation of Rider Haggard, who wrote the intertitles. This film combines elements from all the books in the series.

A decade later another cinematic version of the novels was released, featuring Helen Gahagan, Randolph Scott and Nigel Bruce. Unlike the book and the other films, this 1935 version was set in the Arctic, rather than Africa, and depicts the ancient civilisation of the story in an Art Deco style, with music by Max Steiner.

The 1965 film She was produced by Hammer Film Productions; it starred Ursula Andress as Ayesha and John Richardson as her reincarnated love, with Peter Cushing and Bernard Cribbins as other members of the expedition.

In 2001 another adaption was released direct-to-video with Ian Duncan as Leo Vincey, Ophélie Winter as Ayesha and Marie Bäumer as Roxane.

Dawn
The film Dawn was released in 1917, starring Hubert Carter and Annie Esmond.

Jess
This book was filmed in 1912, featuring Marguerite Snow, Florence La Badie and James Cruze, in 1914 with Constance Crawley and Arthur Maude, and in 1917 as Heart and Soul, starring Theda Bara in the title role.

Beatrice
The book was adapted into a 1921 Italian silent drama film called The Stronger Passion, directed by Herbert Brenon and starring Marie Doro and Sandro Salvini.

Swallow
The novel was adapted into a 1922 South African film.

Stella Fregelius
The book was adapted into a 1921 British film, Stella.

Moon of Israel
This novel was the basis of a script by Ladislaus Vajda, for film-director Michael Curtiz in his 1924 Austrian epic known as Die Sklavenkönigin (Queen of the Slaves).

www.ingramcontent.com/pod-product-compliance
Lightning Source LLC
Chambersburg PA
CBHW071311200626
46813CB00015B/1492